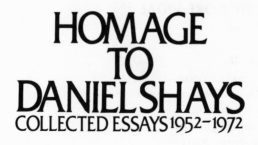

HOMAGE
TO
DANIEL SHAYS
COLLECTED ESSAYS 1952–1972

BOOKS BY GORE VIDAL

Novels
Williwaw
In a Yellow Wood
The City and the Pillar
The Season of Comfort
A Search for the King
Dark Green, Bright Red
The Judgment of Paris
Messiah
Julian
Washington, D. C.
Myra Breckinridge
Two Sisters

Short Stories
A Thirsty Evil

Plays
An Evening with Richard Nixon
Weekend
Romulus
The Best Man
Visit to a Small Planet

Essays
Rocking the Boat
Reflections upon a Sinking Ship

HOMAGE
TO
DANIEL SHAYS
COLLECTED ESSAYS 1952–1972
GORE VIDAL

RANDOM HOUSE   NEW YORK

Library of Congress Cataloging in Publication Data

Vidal, Gore, 1925–
    Homage to Daniel Shays; Collected essays, 1952–1972.

    I.   Title.
PS3543.I26A16   1972   814'.5'4   72–6082
ISBN 0–394–48210–7

First Edition

CONTENTS

NOTE

These essays are arranged in chronological order. The first
was written twenty years ago, in another world; the latest was
written a few months ago. Reading them from first to last, I
had the sense of reliving month to month two decades not only
of my life but of our most unserene republic turned empire,
now turning something else again. As themes come and go, are
developed or abandoned, as politics replaces literature replaces politics again, there is a logical (and sometimes illogical)
progression. There are also ironies. As the mandarin author of
the first essay surveyed the state of American letters in the
forties, he had no idea that he was about to give up the novel
for a decade of television, theater, movies, criticism and politics, while the engaged polemicist of 1962 would have been
appalled to know that he was soon to abandon actual politics
in order to become again (what he had been all along?) a novelist.

Since the essays are printed pretty much as they were written, footnotes have been added whenever the text appears to be unusually wrong-headed by today's standard. Also—no, no more explaining. Herewith, one writer's response to his time and place, and, oh, what a time, place!

G.V.

HOMAGE
TO
DANIEL SHAYS
COLLECTED ESSAYS 1952–1972

NOVELISTS AND CRITICS OF THE 1940's

It is a rare and lucky physician who can predict accurately at birth whether a child is to become a dwarf or a giant or an ordinary adult, since most babies look alike and the curious arrangements of chromosomes which govern stature are inscrutable and do not yield their secret order even to the shrewdest eye. Time alone gives definition. Nevertheless, interested readers and writers, like anxious parents and midwives, forever speculate upon the direction and meaning of current literary trends, and professional commentators with grave authority make analyses which the briefest interval often declares invalid. But despite their long historic record of bad guesses, bookish men continue to make judgments, and the recorded derelictions of taste and the erratic judgments of earlier times tend only to confirm in them a sense of complacency: *they* are not we, and did not know; *we* know. To disturb this complacency is occasionally worthwhile, and one way of doing it is to exhume significant critical texts from the recent past. Those of the last century, in particular, provide us with fine warnings.

For instance: "We do not believe any good end is to be effected by fictions which fill the mind with details of imaginary vice and distress and crime, or which teach it instead of endeavoring after the fulfillment of simple and ordinary duty to aim at the assurance of superiority by creating for itself fanciful and incomprehensible perplexities. Rather we believe that the effect of such fictions tends to render those who fall under their influence unfit for practical exertion by intruding on minds which ought to be guarded from impurity the unnecessary knowledge of evil." This was the *Quarterly Review* on George Eliot's *The Mill on the Floss*, and it is really quite well said: the perennial complaint of the professional reviewers and the governors of lending libraries ("enough unpleasant things in the world without reading about them in books").

Or the following attack on preciosity and obscurantism (*Blackwood's Magazine*, 1817): "Mr. Coleridge conceives himself to be a far greater man than the public is likely to admit; and we wish to waken him from what seems to us a most ludicrous delusion. He seems to believe that every tongue is wagging in his praise. . . . The truth is that Mr. Coleridge is but an obscure name in English literature" [Coleridge was forty-five years old at this time and his major work was long since done.] "In London he is well known in literary society for his extraordinary loquacity . . ." And there follows a prolix attack upon the *Biographia Literaria*.

Or this excerpt from an 1848 *Quarterly Review*, deploring the pagan, the sexual, and the vicious:

At all events there can be no interest attached to the writer of *Wuthering Heights*—a novel succeeding *Jane Eyre* and purporting to be written by Ellis Bell—unless it were for the sake of more individual reprobation. For though there is a decided resemblance between the two, yet the aspect of the Jane and Rochester animals in their native state, as Catherine and Heatfield [*sic*], is too odiously and abominably pagan to be palatable even to the most vitiated class of English readers. With all the unscrupulousness of the French school of novels it combines that repulsive vulgarity in the choice of its vice which supplies its own antidote.

Differently worded, these complaints still sound in our press. The Luce editors who cry for an "affirmative" literature echo voices once raised against George Eliot. When middle-brow reviewers deplore "morbidity" in our best writers, they only paraphrase the outrage of those who found the Brontës repellent. And the twitterings of an Orville Prescott when he has discovered a nice and busy book echo the same homely song of those long-dead reviewers who found in the three-volume novels of forgotten lady writers so much warm comfort.

As the essential problems of life remain the same from generation to generation, despite altered conditions, so the problems of literary recognition remain, for contemporaries, peculiarly difficult. Despite the warnings of other times, the impetuous and the confident continue their indiscriminate cultivation of weeds at the expense of occasional flowers.

To consider the writing of any period, including the present, it is perhaps of some importance to examine the climate in which the work is done, to chart if possible the prevailing winds, the weather of the day.

Today there is a significant distinction between the reviewers for popular newspapers and magazines, whom no one interested in literature reads, and the serious critics of the Academy, who write for one another in the quarterlies and, occasionally, for the public in the Sunday supplements. The reviewers are not sufficiently relevant or important to be considered in any but a social sense: they reflect the commonest prejudices and aspirations of the middle class for whom they write, and they need not concern us here.

The critics, however, are significant. They are dedicated men; they are serious; their learning is often respectable. They have turned to the analysis of literature with the same intensity that, born in an earlier time, they might have brought to formal philosophy, to the law, to the ministry. They tend, generically and inevitably, to be absolutists. They believe that by a close examination of "the text," the laws and the crafty "strategies" of its composition will be made clear and the findings will provide "touchstones" for a comparative criticism of other works. So far so good. They have constructed some ingenious and perhaps valuable analyses of metaphysical verse whose order is often precise and whose most disparate images proceed with a calculable wit and logic.

Unfortunately, the novel is not so easily explicated. It is a loose form, and although there is an inherent logic in those books we are accustomed to call great, the deducible "laws" which governed the execution of *Emma* are not going to be of much use in defining *The Idiot*. The best that a serious analyst can hope to do is comment intelligently from his vantage point in time on the way a work appears to him in a contemporary, a comparative, or a historic light; in which case, his opinion is no more valuable than his own subtlety and knowledge. He must be, as T. S. Eliot put it so demurely, "very intelligent." The point, finally, is that he is not an empiricist dealing with measurable quantities and calculable powers. Rather, he is a man dealing with the private vision of another, with a substance as elusive and amorphous as life itself. To *pretend* that there are absolutes is necessary in making relative judgments (Faulkner writes better than Taylor Caldwell), but to *believe* that there are absolutes and to order one's judgments accordingly is folly and disastrous. One is reminded of Matthew Arnold and his touchstones; it was his conviction that certain lines from a poet by all conceded great might be compared to those of lesser poets to determine their value. Arnold selected Dante as his great poet, an irreproachable choice, but then he misread the Italian, which naturally caused some confusion. Arnold's heirs also demand order, tidiness, labels, ultimate assurance that this work is "good" and that work is "bad," but sooner or later someone misreads the Italian and the system breaks down. In our time there are nearly as many critical systems as there are major critics, which is a pleasing anarchy. The "new critics," as they have been termed (*they* at least dislike being labeled and few will now answer when called), are fundamentally mechanics. They go about dismantling the text with the same rapture that their simpler brothers experience while taking apart combustion engines: inveterate tinkerers both, solemnly playing with what has been invented by others for use, not analysis.

Today's quarterlies are largely house organs for the academic world. They seldom publish imaginative work and one of their most distinguished editors has declared himself more interested in commentaries on writing than in the writing itself. Their quarrels and schisms and heresies do not in the least resemble the Alexandrians whom they occasionally mention, with involuted pride, as spiritual ancestors. Rather, one is reminded of the semantic and doctrinal quarrels of the church fathers in the fourth century, when a diphthong was able to break the civilized world in half and spin civilization into nearly a millennium of darkness. One could invent a most agreeable game of drawing analogies between the fourth century and today. F. R. Leavis and Saint Jerome are perfectly matched, while John Chrysostom and John Crowe Ransom suggest a possibility. The analogy works amusingly on all levels save one: the church fathers had a Christ to provide them with a primary source of revelation, while our own dogmatists must depend either upon private systems or else upon those proposed by such slender reeds as Matthew Arnold and T. S. Eliot, each, despite his genius, a ritual victim as well as a hero of literary fashion.

But the critics are indefatigable and their game is in earnest, for it is deeply involved not only with literature but with such concrete things as careers in the Academy, where frequent and prestigious publication is important. Yet for all their busyness they are by no means eclectic. In a Henry James year not one will write an analysis of George Meredith. They tend to ignore the contemporary writers, not advancing much later than F. Scott Fitzgerald, whose chief attraction is that he ex-

7

ploded before he could be great, providing a grim lesson in failure that, in its completeness, must be awfully heartening when contemplated on the safe green campus of some secluded school.

Of the critics today, Edmund Wilson, the most interesting and the most important, has shown virtually no interest in the writing of the last fifteen years, his talents engaged elsewhere in the construction of heroic sepulchers for old friends like Fitzgerald and Millay, a likable loyalty but a not entirely useful one. He can of course still make a fine point during a Peacock flurry and he has been startlingly brilliant in recent essays on Grant and Lincoln, but one can search the pages of that book of his which he calls a "Literary Chronicle of the Forties" without coming upon any but the most cursory mention of the decade's chief talents.

Malcolm Cowley, a good professional literary man, had some sharp things to say recently about the young writers. Although he made almost no reference to the better writing of the day, he did say some accurate things about the university-trained writers, whose work, he feels, is done with too reverent an eye upon their old teachers, the new critics. Cowley speaks out for a hearty freedom from university influence, citing his own generation (the men of the 1920's are loyal to their time if not to one another: *everyone* was a genius then, and liquor was cheap abroad) as being singularly independent of formal instruction. Yet McCullers, Bowles, Capote, etc. (like Hemingway, Faulkner, O'Neill, etc.) are not graduates of universities, and many of the other young lions have had enough war to wash them clean of academicism. Mr. Cowley, like most commentators, tends to bend whatever he finds to his premise. To him there is no single genius who can set the tone for a generation but one wonders if he would recognize that great writer any more than Lord Jeffrey, a century ago, was able to recognize *his* time's greatness? For the Cowleys, the novel stopped at *Gatsby*. That Carson McCullers (whom he does not mention) has influenced many works, that Tennessee Williams has influenced the theater of the world, that Paul

Bowles, among others, has reshaped the short story—none of these things impinges on him.

Mr. Cowley's gloom is supported by the young John W. Aldridge, Jr. In his amusing novel *After the Lost Generation* he got onto the subject of "values" (by way of Lionel Trilling and perhaps V. S. Pritchett). After discussing a number of fictitious characters who were writing books (using real, if unlikely, names like Truman Capote and Gore Vidal), he "proved," by the evidence of their works, that they had all failed of greatness because, except for "a pocket or two of manners" (the Army; the South; here and there in New England), there was really nothing left to write about, none of that social conflict out of which comes art, like sparks from a stone grinding metal. His coda indicated that a young writer of singular genius is at this moment hovering in the wings awaiting his cue. It will be interesting to read Mr. Aldridge's next novel.

Yet Mr. Aldridge does have a case: the old authority of church, of settled Puritan morality, *has* broken down, and if one's vision is historically limited to only a few generations in time it might seem that today's novelists are not having the fun their predecessors in the 1920's had, breaking cultural furniture. But to take a longer view, one must recall that the great times for literature and life were those of transition: from the Middle Ages to modern times by way of the Renaissance, from dying paganism to militant Christianity by way of the Antonines, and so on back to Aristophanes. The opportunity for the novelist when Mr. Aldridge's "values" are in the discard is fabulous: to create without wasting one's substance in political or social opposition. What could be more marvelous! Neither Vergil nor Shakespeare had to attack their day's morality or those in authority. They were morally free to write of life, of Henry James's "the main thing." There were certainly inequities and barbarities in sixteenth-century England and first-century Rome, but the writers, affected partly by convention (not to mention the Star Chamber), did not address themselves to attacks upon the government or the time's morality, which, apparently, did not obsess them. Writers, after all, are valuable in spite of their neuroses, obsessions, and rebellions, not because of them. It is a poor period indeed which must assess its men of letters in terms of their opposition to their society. Opposition to life's essential conditions perhaps, or to death's implacable tyranny, is something else again, and universal; but novels, no matter how clever, which attempt to change statutes or moral attitudes are, though useful at the moment, not literature at all. In fact, if Mr. Aldridge were right in his proposition we would have *not* a barren, "subjectless" world for literature but the exact opposite: a time of flowering, of creation without waste and irrelevancy. Unhappily, American society has not changed that much in the last thirty years. There is as much to satirize, as much to protest as ever before, and it will always be the task of the secondary figures to create those useful public books whose momentary effect is as stunning as their literary value is not.

There is no doubt but that the West has come to Malraux's "twilight of the absolute." One awaits with hope the period between when, unencumbered by the junk of dogma, writers can turn to the great things with confidence and delight. Loss of authority by removing targets does not destroy the true novelist, though it eliminates the doctrinaire and those busy critics who use the peculiar yardstick of social usefulness to determine merit. (It is no accident that the few works admired by Mr. Aldridge are those compositions which sturdily and loudly discuss the social scene, or some "pocket" of it—interesting books, certainly, whose public effect is often admirable; though the noise they create seldom persists long enough to enjoy even a first echo.) Actually, one might say that it is only the critic who suffers unduly from the lack of authority. A critic, to criticize, must, very simply, have standards. To have standards he must pretend there is some optimum against which like creations can be measured. By the nature of his own process he is eventually forced, often inadvertently, to accept as absolute those conditions for analysis which he has only tentatively proposed. To be himself significant he needs law and revealed order; without them he is only a civilized man commenting for others upon given works which, temperamentally, he may or may not like without altering the value, if any, of the work examined. With a law, with authority, with faith he becomes something more grand and meaningful; the pythoness through whom passes Apollo's word.

Much of the despondency and apparent confusion in the world of peripheral letters today derives partly from the nervous, bloody age in which we live and partly from that hunger for the absolute which, in our own immediate experience, delivered two great nations into the hands of tyrants, while in our own country the terror of being man alone, unsupported by a general religious belief and undirected by central authority, has reduced many intellectuals either to a bleak nihilism or, worse, to the acceptance of some external authority (Rome, Marx, Freud). One is reminded of Flaubert's comment nearly a century ago: "The melancholy of the ancients seems to me deeper than that of the moderns, who all more or less assume an immortality on the far side of the black pit. For the ancients the black pit was infinity itself; their dreams take shape and pass against a background of unchanging ebony. No cries, no struggles, only the fixity of the pensive gaze. The gods being dead and Christ not yet born [sic], there was between Cicero and Marcus Aurelius one unique moment in which there was man."

Our own age is one of man alone, but there are still cries, still struggles against our condition, against the knowledge that our works and days have value only in the human scale; and those who most clearly remember the secure authority of other times, the ordered universe, the immutable moral hierarchies, are the ones who most protest the black pit. While it is perfectly true that any instant in human history is one of transition, ours more than most seems to be marked by a startling variety of conflicting absolutes, none sufficiently great at this moment to impose itself upon the majority whose lives are acted out within an unhuman universe which some still prefer to fill with a vast manlike shadow containing stars, while others behold only a luminous dust which *is* stars, and us as well. This division between those who recognize the unhumanity of creation and those who protest the unchanging ebony sets the tone of our literature, with the imaginative writers inclining (each in his own way) to the first view and their critics to the second. The sense of man not being king of creation (nor even the work of a king of creation) is the burden, directly and indirectly, of modern literature. For the writers there is no reality for man except in his relations with his own kind. Much of the stuff of earlier centuries—like fate, high tragedy, the interventions of *dei ex machina*—have been discarded as brave but outworn devices, not applicable in a world where kings and commoners occupy the same sinking boat.

Those of our writers who might yet enjoy the adjective "affirmative" are the ones who tend to devote themselves to the dramas within the boat, the encompassing cold sea ignored in the passions of the human moment. Most of the worst and a number of the best writers belong to this category. The key words here are "love" and "compassion." And though, like most such devices, they have grown indistinct with use, one can still see them at work and marvelously so, in the novels of Carson McCullers and certain (though not all) of the plays of Tennessee Williams. Christopher Isherwood once said that to his mind the finest single line in modern letters was: "I have always depended upon the kindness of strangers," from *A Streetcar Named Desire*. At such moments, in such works, the human drama becomes so unbearably intense that time and the sea are blotted out and only the human beings are illuminated as they cease, through the high magic of art, to be mere residents in a time which stops and become, instead, archetypes—elemental figures like those wild gods our ancestors peopled heaven with.

Then there are the writers to whom neither sea nor boat exists. They have accepted some huge fantasy wherein they need never drown, where death is life, and the doings of hu-

man beings on a social and ethical level are of much consequence to some brooding source of creation who dispenses his
justice along strictly party lines at the end of a gloomy day. To
this category belong such talented writers as Graham Greene
and Evelyn Waugh. In theory at least, speculation has ended
for them; dogma supports them in all things. Yet it is odd to
find that the tone of their works differs very little from that
of the other mariners adrift. They are, if anything, perhaps a
bit more lugubrious, since for them is not the principality of
this world.

Finally, there are those who see human lives as the lunatic
workings of compulsive animals no sooner born than dead, no
sooner dead than replaced by similar creatures born of that
proliferating seed which too will die. Paul Bowles is a striking
example of this sort of writer as he coolly creates nightmare
visions in which his specimens struggle and drown in fantasy,
in madness, in death. His short stories with their plain lines
of monochromatic prose exploit extreme situations with a
chilling resourcefulness; he says, in short, "Let it sink; let us
drown."

Carson McCullers, Paul Bowles, Tennessee Williams are, at
this moment at least, the three most interesting writers in the
United States.* Each is engaged in the task of truth-saying (as
opposed to saying the truth, which is not possible this side of
revelation). Each has gone further into the rich interior of the
human drama than any of our immediate predecessors with
the possible exception of William Faulkner, whose recent
work has unfortunately resembled bad translations from Pin-

---

*This was written in 1952. McCullers was a good and fashionable novelist of
the day (I cannot say I have any great desire to read her again). Paul Bowles
was as little known then as he is now. His short stories are among the best
ever written by an American. Tennessee Williams was famous but beleaguered (*Time* magazine regularly denounced him as a decadent and "fetid
swamp," while Mary McCarthy publicly resented his success). I have not
changed my mind about Williams's early plays. Other forties writers whose
books I might have mentioned had I liked them as well then as I do now are
Saul Bellow and John Hawkes. John Horne Burns I deal with on page 181.

dar. On a social level, the hostility shown these essential artists is more significant than their occasional worldly successes, for it is traditional that he who attempts to define man's condition demoralizes the majority, whether relativist or absolutist. We do not want ever to hear that we will die but that first we must live; and those ways of living which are the fullest, the most intense, are the very ones which social man traditionally dreads, summoning all his superstition and malice to combat strangers and lovers, the eternal victims.

The obsessive concern with sexuality which informs most contemporary writing is not entirely the result of a wish *épater le bourgeois* but, more, the reflection of a serious battle between the society man has constructed so illogically and confusedly and the nature of the human being, which needs a considerably fuller expression sexually and emotionally than either the economics or morality of this time will permit. The sea is close. Two may find the interval between awareness and death more meaningful than one alone. Yet while ours is a society where mass murder and violence are perfectly ordinary and their expression in the most popular novels and comic books is accepted with aplomb, any love between two people which does not conform is attacked.

Malcolm Cowley has complained that writers no longer handle some of the more interesting social relationships of man, that there is no good stock-market novel, no Balzacian concern among the better writers with economic motive. His point is valid. The public range of the novel has been narrowed. It would be good to have well-written accounts of the way we live now, yet our important writers eschew, almost deliberately it would seem, the kind of book which provided not only Trollope but Tolstoi with so much power. Mr. Cowley catches quite well the tone of the second-rate good writers (a phenomenon peculiar to this moment; it seems as if a whole generation writes well, though not often to any point); they are concerned with the small scale, and goodness as exemplified by characters resembling the actress Shirley Booth holding out valiantly against villainous forces, usually represented by someone in business. But Mr. Cowley does not mention the novelist from whom these apotheosis-in-the-kitchen writers derive. Carson McCullers, using the small scale, the relations of human beings at their most ordinary, transcends her milieu and shows, in bright glimpses, the potentiality which exists in even the most banal of human relationships, the "we" as opposed to the meager "I."

Or again, in Tennessee Williams's remarkable play *Camino Real*, though the world is shown in a nightmare glass, a vision of those already drowned, there are still moments of private triumphs . . . in Kilroy's love with (not for) the gypsy's daughter and in Lord Byron's proud departure through the gate to *terra incognita*, his last words a reproach and an exhortation: "Make voyages! Make voyages!"

And, finally, most starkly, we have a deliberate act of murder, Gide's *l'acte gratuite*, which occurs at the end of Paul Bowles's *Let It Come Down*. Here the faceless, directionless protagonist, in a sudden storm of rage against his life, all life, commits a murder without reason or passion, and in this one terrible moment (similar perhaps to that of a nation gone to war) he at last finds "a place in the world, a definite status, a precise relationship with the rest of men. Even if it had to be one of open hostility, it was his, created by him." In each of these three writers man acts, through love, through hate, through despair. Though the act in each is different, the common emotion is sufficiently intense to dispel, for a time at least, the knowledge of that cold drowning which awaits us all.

The malady of civilized man is his knowledge of death. The good artist, like the wise man, addresses himself to life and invests with his private vision the deeds and thoughts of men. The creation of a work of art, like an act of love, is our one small "yes" at the center of a vast "no."

The lesser writers whose works do not impress Mr. Cowley despite their correctness possess the same vision as those of the major writers, but their power of illusion is not so great and their magic is only fitful: too often their creatures are only automatons acted upon. Though they may shed light on interesting aspects of ordinary life they do not, in the best sense, illuminate, flood with brilliance, our strange estate.

Among the distinguished second rank of younger writers there is much virtuosity and potentiality. The coolly observant short stories of Louis Auchincloss provide wise social comment of the sort which the Cowleys would probably admire but never seem to read in their haste to generalize. Eudora Welty fashions a subtle line and Jean Stafford, though currently obsessed with literary interior decoration, has in such stories as "The Echo and the Nemesis" displayed a talent which makes all the more irritating her recent catalogues of bric-a-brac, actual and symbolic. John Kelly, whose two novels have been neglected, has created a perverse, operatic world like nothing else in our literature, while the late John Horne Burns, out of fashion for some years, was a brilliant satirist in a time when satire is necessary but difficult to write since to attack successfully one must have a complacent, massive enemy—and though there are numerous villains today, none is entirely complacent.

The serious writers have been attacked by the reviewers for their contempt of narrative and their neglect to fashion "real live characters" (which means familiar stereotypes from Victorian fiction masquerading in contemporary clothes). The reviewers have recognized that a good deal of writing now being done doesn't resemble anything they are used to (although in almost a century there has been a royal line of which they are ignorant . . . from *The Temptation of Saint Anthony* to *The Golden Bowl* to *Mrs. Dalloway*); they still feel most at home with *The Newcomes*, or, if they came to maturity in the 1920's, with *The Sun Also Rises*. When the technique of a play like *Camino Real* seems bizarre and difficult to follow for those accustomed to the imitators of Ibsen, there must be a genuine reason for the change in technique, other than the author's presumed perversity. The change from the exterior to the interior world which has been taking place in literature for at least a century is due not only to a general dissatisfaction with the limitations of naturalism but also to the rise of a new medium, the movies, which, properly used, are infinitely superior to the old novel and to the naturalistic play, especially in the rendering of plain narrative.

The Quiet One, a movie, was far superior as a social document (as "art," too, for that matter) to any book published so far in this country dealing with Negro problems. Instinctively, the writers have reacted to the camera. If another medium can handle narrative and social comment so skillfully, even on their lowest aesthetic levels, then the novelist must go deeper, must turn into the maze of consciousness where the camera cannot follow. He must also become wise, and wisdom even in its relative sense was never a notable characteristic of novelists in our language. One can anticipate the direction of the novel by studying that of the painters who, about the time of the still camera's invention, began instinctively to withdraw into a less literal world where they might do work which a machine could not imitate. It is a possibility, perhaps even a probability, that as the novel moves toward a purer, more private expression it will cease altogether to be a popular medium, becoming, like poetry, a cloistered avocation—in which case those who in earlier times might have written great public novels will be engaged to write good public movies, redressing the balance. In our language the novel is but three centuries old and its absorption by the movies, at least the vulgar line of it, is not necessarily a bad thing. In any event, it is already happening.

For the present, however, the tone of the contemporary novel, though not cheerful, is precise. Man is on his own. In certain human actions, in love, in violence, he can communicate with others, touch and be touched, act and in the act forget his fate. The scale is often small. Kings are neglected because, to relativists, all men are the same within eternity. Or rather their crisis is the same. The concern in modern letters is with that crisis which defines the prospect.

In general, the novelists have rejected authority, parting company with their cousins-german the serious critics. To the creative man, religious dogma and political doctrine, when stated in ultimate terms, represent the last enemy, the protean Lucifer in our race's bloody progress. The artist speaks from that awareness of life, that secret knowledge of life in death the absolutists are driven to obscure and to distort, to shape, if possible, to tidy ends.

The interior drama at its most bitterly human comes into sharp focus in the writings of Williams and McCullers, and there are signs that other writers, undismayed by the hostility of the absolutists, may soon provide us with some strength in these last days before the sure if temporary victory of that authoritarian society which, thanks to science, now has every weapon with which to make even the most inspired lover of freedom conform to the official madness.

The thought of heaven, a perennial state of mind, a cheerful conception of what might be in life, in art (if not in death), may yet save our suicidally inclined race—if only because heaven is as various as there are men in the world who dream of it, and writers to evoke that dream. One recalls Constantine (to refer again to the image of the early church) when he teased a dissenting bishop at one of the synods: "Acesius, take a ladder and get up to heaven by yourself." We are fortunate in our time to have so many ladders going up. Each ladder is raised in hope, which is heaven enough.

New World Writing #4, 1953

A NOTE
ON THE NOVEL

Any discussion of the novel nowadays soon strikes the pessimistic note. It is agreed, for instance, that there are among us no novelists of sufficient importance to act as touchstones for useful judgment. There is Faulkner, but . . . and there is Hemingway, but . . . And that completes the list of near-misses, the others, poor lost legions, all drowned in the culture's soft buzz and murmur. We have embarked upon empire (Rome born again our heavy fate) without a Vergil in the crew, only tarnished silver writers in a bright uranium age, perfunctorily divided by editorialists between the "affirmative" (and good) and the "negative" (and bad). Only cultural researchers (wandering lonely as a crowd) and high critics merit serious attention. From the little red schoolhouse to the library at Alexandria in one generation is the heartening success story of American letters.

Apologists (secret lovers of the novel, few but tender) surveying the seasonal flood of first novels of promise, the smaller

wave of second novels of no promise, and, finally, most poignant of all, those minuscule ripples which continue so perversely to assault an indifferent shore—these apologists have
noted a spiritual ergot in our country's air which causes good
writers to abort young while, tributary to this new myth,
lingers the old conviction that American life, even now, lacks
the class tensions, the subtle play of manners (Hialeah but no
Ascot), the requisite amount of history to make even a small
literature. That from Levittown no art may come is still an
important critical thesis.

One senses, too, in academic dialogues and explications the
unstated burden of the discussion that, at last, all the novels
are in. The term is over, the canon assembled if not ordered,
the door to the library firmly shut to the irrelevance of new
attempts. More ominous, however, than the loss of the higher
criticism has been the gradual defection of the public itself.
After some three hundred years the novel in English has lost
the general reader (or rather the general reader has lost the
novel), and I propose that he will not again recover his old
enthusiasm.

The fault, if it be a fault, is not the novelist's (I doubt if there
ever have been so many interesting and excellent writers as
there are now working) but of the audience, an unpleasant
accusation to make in a democracy where, ultimately, the taste
of the majority is the measure of all things. Nevertheless,
appalling education combined with clever new toys has distracted that large public which found pleasure in prose
fictions. In an odd way, our civilization has now come full
circle: from the Greek mysteries and plays to the printing
press and the novel to television and plays again, the audience
has returned to the play, and it is now clear that the novel,
despite its glories, was only surrogate for the drama, which,
confined till this era to theaters, was not generally accessible.

With television (ten new "live" plays a week; from such an
awful abundance, a dramatic renaissance *must* come) the great
audience now has the immediacy it has always craved, the
picture which moves and talks, the story experienced, not

reported.* In refutation, it may indeed be argued that the large sales of paperback books, both good and bad, are proof that there are millions out there in the dark, hungering for literature. But though it is true that all those books must go *somewhere*, I suggest that their public is not a serious one, that it is simply pursuing secret vices from one bright cover picture to another—consuming, not reading.

Yet all in all, this state of affairs, though disheartening, is by no means tragic. For one thing, those novelists whose interests are in polemic or mere narrative will doubtless join the new Establishment and write plays. Adventure stories, exotic voyages, superficial histories, all the familiar accouterments of the popular novel are now the scenarists' by right of conquest. The novel is left only the best things: that exploration of the inner world's divisions and distinctions where no camera may follow, the private, the necessary pursuit of the whole which makes the novel, at its highest, the humane art that Lawrence called "The one bright book of life."

To strike an optimistic note, if faintly, it may well be that, with unpopularity, the meretricious and the ordinary will desert entirely, leaving only the devoted lashed to the mast. But now the tide is in. The course is set. The charts are explicit, for we are not the first to make the voyage out: the poets long ago preceded us into exile, and one can observe them up ahead, arms outstretched to greet the old enemy, their new companions at the edge of the known world.

The New York Times Book Review, August 5, 1956

*I certainly got that all wrong. Commercial American television abandoned the drama. Yet English and German television rather prove my point. Incidentally, this is the piece that is remembered as the one where I am supposed to have announced the novel's death. I did no such thing. I made the point that the *audience* for the novel is vanishing—a fact not to be denied. But in the pseudodemocracy one must never criticize the majority, and so what I actually wrote about the dereliction of the audience was transformed into a supposed attack on a very healthy art form. Recently a British reviewer commented that, having proclaimed the death of the novel, I was cruel enough to send Myra Breckinridge to the funeral.

BOOK REPORT

Can you hear me? Oh, good. Then I won't have to use this thing. It scares me to death! My husband always tells me, "Marian, you and your mother may not be very good but you're certainly loud enough when you give a book report." That's what he always says. Now then: the book I'm going to talk to you about today is by an American writer named Robert Penn Warren. Robert Penn Warren. He has written some poems, and of course most of us read his book a few years ago called *All the King's Men*, which they later made a movie out of and ruined, the way they always do. Mr. Warren's new book is a historical—*an* historical—novel *with a difference.* It begins with a beautiful quotation from a poem by A. E. Housman, the poet: "When shall I be dead and rid of the wrong my father did?"

And that's just what it's about. About Amantha Starr, a beautiful girl of sixteen, raised in Ohio, where she'd been sent to be educated by her father—sent by her father to be educated

—a wealthy Kentucky plantation owner. Whe
dies, she comes home for his funeral, where she
only did he die bankrupt, but that she is really
daughter of one of his slaves, and she has to be
these debts he left. Well, this is how the story st
awful situation for a girl to be in. One day she h
money and refinement could bring, and the nex
slave. The very first sentence of the book is filled
ism: "Oh, who am I? For so long that was, you m
cry of my heart." And then there follows a descri
wonderful house she lived in in Kentucky, south o
near Danville: a two-story brick house with a chim
end and a portico with pillars. The most beautifu
could imagine! All of which she lost when she fou
colored and sold to a dealer who took her to Ne
where she was put up for sale in the slave market

Fortunately, she was bought by the most interest
in the book, a fascinating older man with a lame
always walked with a heavy blackthorn stick wit
silver knob. His name was Hamish Bond, and he be
protector. Not until much later does she find out
really not named Bond but Hinks, that he was raise
timore where he was a slave trader, going to Africa
and bringing back Negroes. He had some awful exp
in Africa. One in particular, a description of a mas
really gruesome where these Amazon women go thr
entire village, slaughtering all the men, women and c
because they're so enormous and bloodthirsty, much s
than men. When Hamish, whose real name is Hinks,
keep one of the Amazons from killing a baby, this i
happens: "I just shoved her a little. It's very peculiar th
you have a habit. I just shoved her gentle because she v
a way of speaking, a lady, and I had learned manners b
Baltimore. Here she was a crocodile-hided, blood-drinkir
frau, who had been in her line of business for twenty
and I caught myself making allowance for a lady." We
wished he hadn't, because right after he pushed her she sla

23

is leg with a big razor, making a long jagged cut which is what made him lame and why he had to always walk with that blackthorn cane with the silver knob.

Anyway, Hamish was kind in his brooding way to Amantha, and he treated her like she was really a lady which made her feel a bit better about being a slave. As somebody in the book says, the trouble with Hamish is he has "kindness like a disease." Another fascinating character Amantha meets is Hamish's *k'la* (meaning Negro best friend) Rau-ru, "whose eyes were wide, large and deepset, his nose wide but not flattened, the underlip full if not to the comic fullness favored in the minstrel shows of our day, and the corners of the mouth were drawn back so that the effect of that mouth was one of arrogant reserve and not blubbering docility."

Hamish was a very unusual man, especially after the Civil War started. One night there is a storm at Hamish's house—and Hamish takes Amantha in his arms while the rain blows in the window and she knows for the first time what love is. "With the hand of Hamish Bond laid to my side, and the spreading creep and prickle of sensation across the softness of my belly from the focus of Hamish Bond's sandpaper thumb, and the unplaiting and deliquescence of the deep muscles of thighs were as much History as any death-cry at the trenchlip or in the tangle of the abatis."

Can you still hear me? Well, that's how she feels as she discovers what love is and this maybe is the only serious fault in the book. I mean *would* a young girl like Amantha, even though she was well educated in Oberlin, Ohio, think thoughts quite like *that?* I mean, older more experienced women would, but would she? However, Mr. Warren writes poetic English and we can certainly excuse an occasional symbolic sentence like that. Well, there are many beautiful passages like this in the book, but the story never gets bogged down and the parts about the Civil War are really fascinating. Especially in New Orleans where she meets, completely by accident, Seth Parton, her girlhood sweetheart, who is now an officer in the Union Army, and also Tobias Sears, "the New

England idealist to whom the butcheries of war must be justified by 'truth.' " I don't think it will spoil the book any if I tell you that everything ends all right with Tobias and Amantha . . . Miss Manty, as everybody calls her . . . together in quite a beautiful and touching ending.

I'd like to say something, by the way, if I may make a digression, about the much-maligned historical novel . . . the "bosom books" as they are disdainfully called by some critics, who think they know everything and can't keep from tearing apart books like Mr. Warren's. Now, I know and you know that maybe these books aren't *exactly* history, but they're awfully close, some of them, especially this one, and I can't help but think of Mrs. Gregg Henderson's fascinating report some meetings ago about the boys in Korea who were captured and tortured and brainwashed by the Chinese Communists who found that American boys were easy to break down BECAUSE THEY DID NOT KNOW ENOUGH ABOUT AMERICAN HISTORY AND WHY THEY WERE FIGHTING. Most of us here are mothers and we all know the trouble we have getting boys to read about history and all the things which don't seem important to them until they're caught by the enemy, when it's too late. So I don't think it's fair to make fun of novels that may be a little romantic but are still very useful ways of teaching what America is to people who are never going to read history or really deep things. I think Mr. Warren has done a wonderful job of bringing to life the Civil War and certain problems of that time—and frankly, I don't care a penny what the critics say about the book. After all, if people didn't want books like this, writers wouldn't write them and publishers wouldn't publish them. You can't argue with facts!

This book has been high on the best-seller list, and the movies have bought it, though they'll probably ruin it like they always do. A lot of people are going to be hearing about Amantha Starr and the Civil War. And they'll learn something. I firmly believe that these characters will stay with you for many a long day. Rau-ru, Miss Manty, the Amazons who go into that village killing all the men, Hamish Bond with his heavy blackthorn stick with the great silver knob—all these wonderful characters come alive for you in the pages of *Band of Angels* by Robert Penn Warren, published by Random House, three hundred and seventy-five pages long. Long? I wanted it to go on forever, and so will you!

Zero, Spring 1956

WRITING PLAYS FOR TELEVISION

Until I began to write plays for television, I entertained an amiable contempt for my stagestruck playwright friends who so meekly (masochistically, I thought) submitted their talents to the irrelevant strictures of directors and stars, of newspapermen in Wilmington and of sudden, brief acquaintances in hotel rooms. I had taken to heart the failure of the prose writer in the theater. From Smollett's irritable attempts to get his tragedy produced to Henry James as he was jeered from the stage on his first night, the novelist has cut a ponderous, sad figure beneath the proscenium arch. As a novelist, I was wary, preferring to suffer my reverses and petty triumphs on the familiar ground of prose and *not* in the theater, strewn already with the corpses of illustrious confrères.

The reason for our party's failure in what should have been a natural arena is caught in Flaubert's phrase: "The theater is not an art but a secret." And the secret is deceptively simple: dialogue is not prose. It is another language, and a talent for the novel does not necessarily mean a talent for the theater. The novel is the more private and (to me) the more satisfying art. A novel is all one's own, a world fashioned by a single intelligence, its reality in no way dependent upon the collective excellence of others. Also the mountebankery, the plain showmanship which is necessary to playwriting, strikes the novelist as disagreeably broad. One must show *every* collision on the stage, while in the novel it is often a virtue to avoid the obvious scene, to come at the great moments obliquely. Even dialogue is not the same in a novel as it is on the stage. Seldom can dialogue be taken from a book and played by actors. The reason is one of pace rather than of verisimilitude. Certainly, in our country, most novelists have an accurate ear for speech; it is a gift liberally bestowed upon the good and the bad alike, the gray badge of naturalism. Yet in the novel, *duration* differs from the stage. The novelist's arrangement of dialogue is seldom as concentrated as the playwright's, whose line must finally be achieved by people talking, unassisted by an author's stage management.

Aware of the essential difference between the novel and the play, I kept happily to my own country until the black winter of 1953, when I realized in a moment of revelation that the novel as a popular art form had come to a full halt. There were many reasons. Television had stunned it. The new critics had laid it out all neat in a blue suit, a flower in its waxy hands (HERE LIES THE NOVEL, EXPLICATED), and their funeral orations were already under way in the literary quarterlies. The newspaper reviewers, lagging in their serene way some twenty years behind the fact, wanted more Kipling and less art, while the public, its attention distracted by television and the movies, firmly refused to pay five dollars for anyone's novel, aware that if a book contained enough healthy American sadism they could eventually buy it in a cheap paperback edition. By 1953, unpopular novelists like myself were living precariously on the bounty of reprint publishers; a bounty which ended when those jolly opportunists flooded the newsstands, sinking many, both good and bad. Needless to say, none of this happened quickly. Disaster approached with stealthy tread, and not until my revelation did I awaken to the harshness of the situation: that I was on the verge of providing future thesis writers with a poignant page or two of metropolitan suffering, before I went off to Africa to run rifles.

But happily, when faced with ruin, all one's cunning and resourcefulness rush to the surface, and if one's career is conducted beneath a beneficent star, crisis is healthy. I looked about me. I had been a novelist for a decade. I had been hailed as the peer of Voltaire, Henry James, Jack London, Ronald Firbank and James T. Farrell. My early, least satisfactory works had been best-sellers. Though not yet thirty years old, I was referred to in the past tense, as one of those novelists of the 1940's from whom so much had been expected.

I turned to my peers to see what they were doing. I discovered that the most colorful was writing unsuccessful musical comedies and the most talented had virtuously contrived to die. The others had dropped from view, most of them finding dim employment either in anonymous journalism or in the academy. The cleverest ones had married rich wives and traveled a lot. The prospect was not flooded with light.

But one must live, as they say, and since I do not write popular short stories or journalism, or teach, and since I was spoiled by ten years of receiving money for the work I would have done whether I had been paid or not (the happiest of lives and the luckiest), it looked very much as if I should have to turn to the fantasy world of business and get a job. At that crucial moment, I discovered television.

I had not watched television until the winter I decided to write for it. At the time, its great advantage for me was proximity. I live on the bank of the Hudson, and there to the south, in New York City, was this fine source of revenue. I was intrigued. I was soon enthralled. Right off, there is the immediacy of playwriting. There they are, one's own creations, fleshed out by living people, the symbolic detail isolated by the camera as millions of strangers in their homes watch one's private vision made public. The day after my debut in February of 1954, I was committed seriously to writing for the camera. I discovered that although the restrictions imposed by a popular medium are not always agreeable, they do at least make creative demands upon one's ingenuity. More often than not, the tension between what one is not allowed to say and what one must say creates ingenious effects which, given total freedom, might never have been forced from the imagination. The only analogy I can think of is the nineteenth-century novel. Nearly all the productions of that extraordinary age were published first in magazines edited for gentlewomen and supervised by Mrs. Grundy, her fist full of asterisks. There was so much the harried novelist could *not* say that he was impelled to freight heavily what he *could* say with other meanings, accomplishing the great things by indirection, through association and logical echo.

The same is true now in television. With patience and ingenuity there is nothing that the imaginative writer cannot say to the innocent millions. Of course the naturalistic writer has a more difficult time. He is used to making his point directly and bluntly: *You are a slut.* And he is morose when he cannot bluntly hammer out the obvious, the way he could on the stage or in the lower novel. But for my kind of second-story work, television is less confining. Also, the dramatic art is particularly satisfying for any writer with a polemical bent; and I am at heart a propagandist, a tremendous hater, a tiresome nag, complacently positive that there is no human problem which could not be solved if people would simply do as I advise. This sort of intensity, no matter how idiotic, works well in the drama if only because there is nothing more effective than having something to say.

As for the world of television, the notable characteristics are youth and enthusiasm. The dramatists, directors and producers are all young men, and their deep pleasure in this new toy is communicable and heartening. There is none of the bored cynicism one often finds in Hollywood studios, nor any of the rapacity and bad temper endemic to the theater in New York. Most television plays are bad, but considering that television uses up hundreds of new plays a year and that there have not been a hundred fine plays written in the last two thousand years, they can be excused their failures if their intentions are honorable. And at the moment, the very real sense of honor the better television writers possess lends excitement to their work.

Another novelty for me has been working with people. I had never before worked with anyone, and the thought of belonging to a group was unnerving. But to my surprise I enjoyed it. Working on a play is not unlike being stranded on an island with a group of strangers from a foundered ship's company. For ten days, actors, director, author, technicians work together, getting to know one another almost morbidly well. Then, when the play is over, sadly, sweetly, the players and the management separate, never to meet again—until the next play together.

A play on television of the sort I write is not filmed. It is seen on the air at the exact moment it is performed. The actors build their performances as they would on the stage. The only difference is that they are being photographed by three cameras and we, the audience, are watching a play as though it were a movie.

In the last two years I have written nearly twenty plays. All but seven were either half-hour plays or adaptations. Incidentally, adapting is neither easier nor more difficult than writing an original play. There is, I think, only one basic trick to it: simply knowing how to read precisely and critically. One must get the point of the work. I make this obvious comment because just as literary men are seldom playwrights, playwrights are almost never literary men, and they are usually baffled and bored by the slower, denser order of the novel. In fact, excepting the poet-dramatists, there is a good case that the drama is not literature at all but an entirely separate art requiring collective means to achieve its moments, sharing with prose nothing beyond the general human preoccupation. A gift for playwriting is only a form of cleverness, like being adept at charades or Double-Crostics, while novel writing goes, at its best, beyond cleverness to that point where one's whole mind and experience and vision *are* the novel and the effort to translate this wholeness into prose *is* the life: a circle of creation.

Of course it can be argued that a Shaw or a Chekhov achieves a comparable wholeness in the theater, but the very exceptionalness of any play which is better than viable suggests the narrow boundaries of a literary form whose effectiveness depends as much on interpretation as on the line written, the idea proposed, the light cast. We have all been moved by plays whose productions led us to believe that truth had rent the air about us, only to find later, upon reading the script, that we were tricked, or rather *served* beautifully, in the theater by a number of talents of which the writer's was but one, and perhaps the least.

There are a number of mechanical limitations in television which time may eliminate. For instance, a play done "live" is seen only once, and that is the end. So many fine performances, so many good plays written on air, with nothing to show for all the work done but a kinescope (a filmed record of the play) that because of labor-union and technical considerations may not be shown again on television. It is a waste of many talents. Someday, perhaps on the new magnetic tape, a play which is broadcast live will be accurately recorded and reshown.

One would also like to see a repertory system in television, not only for the actors of course (television *is* a kind of repertory for actors, providing the talented with work and experience) but for the redoing of plays whose value has been established; and there are now a number of interesting plays to choose from. Finally, waiting in the wings, is something called subscription television. Certain productions will be available only to those viewers who pay to see them, a miraculous state of affairs for the writer, who will then have an audience which in a sense is *his* and not accidental. Also, he will be free of those nervous men the advertisers, who now largely control television.

All things considered, I suspect that the Golden Age for the dramatist is at hand. There is so much air to be illustrated, so many eyes watching, so much money to be spent, so many fine technicians and interpreters at one's command, that the playwright cannot but thrive.*

New World Writing #10, 1956

*See footnote to p. 21. Twenty years ago it was possible for me, on rare occasions, to make a mistake. Rest assured this no longer happens.

VISIT TO A
SMALL PLANET

I am not at heart a playwright. I am a novelist turned temporary adventurer; and I chose to write television, movies, and
plays for much the same reason that Henry Morgan selected
the Spanish Main for his peculiar—and not dissimilar—sphere
of operations. The reasons for my conversion to piracy are to
me poignant, and to students of our society perhaps significant.

If I may recall in nostalgic terms the near past, I began
writing novels at the end of the Second World War. Those
were the happy years when a new era in our letters was everywhere proclaimed. We would have, it was thought, a literature
to celebrate the new American empire. Our writers in reflecting our glory would complement the beautiful hardness of our
currency. But something went wrong. The new era did not
materialize and the work of my generation was dismissed—for
the present at least—as a false dawn. It is a fact that the novel
as a popular art form retrogressed gravely in our reign. Not

clever enough to interest the better critics or simple enough to divert the public, we lost the critics to pure criticism and the public to impure television. By the 1950's I and my once golden peers were plunged into that dim cellar of literature characterized as "serious," where, like the priests of some shattered god, we were left to tend our prose privately: so many exiles, growing mushrooms in the dark.

The passage of time has only confirmed the new order. Less and less often is that widening division between the commercially possible and the seriously meaningful bridged by the rare creator who is both. Most of the large publishing events of recent years have been the crudely recollected experiences of nonwriters. Lost is the old conception of the man of letters creating a life's work to be enjoyed by the common reader in continuity. True, that nineteenth-century phenomenon never quite took root in this country; for lovely though New England's Indian summer was, winter when it came was killing. Nowadays, our better literary men seek refuge in the universities, leaving what is left of the public novel to transient primitives and to sturdy hacks. Nor, let me say, are the serious writers themselves responsible for their unpopularity, as our more chauvinistic editorial writers would have it. The good work of the age is being done, as always. Rather it is the public which has changed. Television, movies, the ease of travel . . . so many new diversions have claimed the attention of that public which once read that I think it doubtful if the novel will ever again have the enormous prestige, the universal audience it enjoyed that fine morning when an idler on a Mississippi wharf shouted to the pilot of a passing steamer: "Is Little Nell dead?" And, alas, Mistah Kurtz, he dead, too; solemnly embalmed by the Academy.

Today, the large audience holds communion in a new, more compelling establishment. I doubt if many Americans could identify a single character in a work of modern fiction, but there are few who could not describe in exact detail the latest comedian's joke on television. Yet it is vain to deplore a cultural change. If after two pre-eminent centuries the novel no longer is useful to the public, only novelists need mourn, for it is a fact of civilization that each society creates the games it wants to play and rejects those it regards as irrelevant.

The main audience has turned back to the play (in all its various forms, both "live" and filmed). Nevertheless, it is a stoic consolation for those of us whose first allegiance is to the novel to know that there will always be some serious interest in one's work and that the keys to the kingdom of prose will continue to be passed on from hand to hand. And though I rather suspect that in a century's time the novel will be as rare and private an art form as poetry today or that delicate and laborious process by which dedicated men fire glass with color, it will always be worth the doing.

Over the years I attempted three stage plays. When I was nineteen I wrote a quasi-poetical work about, Heaven alone knows why, a man who became a were-wolf in Manhattan. I destroyed all copies of this early effort only to learn recently that a collector has somehow got hold of a copy, a ghastly prospect for some as yet unborn English major.

The next play I wrote was on an equally obscure subject, written in a frenzy in the spring of 1948 at Shepheard's Hotel in Cairo. Later that summer, I gave it to Tennessee Williams to read. He pronounced it the worst play he'd read in some time, and I solemnly abandoned playwriting for good, after first pointing out to him that a literary form which depended on the combined excellence of others for its execution could hardly be worth the attention of a serious writer, adding with deliberate cruelty that I did not envy him being stagestruck and his life taken up with such frivolous people as actors and directors. He agreed that I should not expose myself just yet to this sort of tedium.

Six years later, driven by necessity, I took the plunge into television, the very heart of darkness, and to my surprise found that I liked it. But despite television's raw youth there is a tradition already firmly established that comedies seldom work on the small screen and that satire never does. Like most traditions, this one is founded on a part truth. For one thing, the comedy timing of stage-trained actors is inevitably affected by the absence of human response during a performance, and for another several people sitting at home glumly staring at a television set are not apt to find anything very amusing unless it is heavily underscored by laughter from a studio audience. And plays on television are performed without audiences.

Satire presents a further difficulty for the mass audience. If satire is to be effective, the audience must be aware of the thing satirized. If they are not, the joke falls flat. Unfortunately for our native satirists, the American mass audience possesses very little general information on any subject. Each individual knows his own immediate world, but, as various research polls continually inform us, he holds little knowledge in common with others. Even political jokes, if they were allowed on television, would not have much relevance. Recently one national poll disclosed that almost half of those queried could not identify the Secretary of State. The size of the population has much to do with this collective ignorance. When Aristophanes made a satiric point, he could be confident that his audience would appreciate his slyest nuance because in a small community each citizen was bound to share with his fellows a certain amount of general information—literary, religious, and political. National units today are too large and, in America at least, education too bland to hope for much change. As a result, satire, unless done very broadly puzzles and irritates rather than amuses.

I have often thought that the domination of naturalism in our letters is directly attributable to the breakdown of the old homogeneous American society of the nineteenth century, caused by the influx of immigration, the discovery of exciting new machinery, the ease of travel. Before this burst of population and invention, an educated man, writing allusively, could assume that his readers would respond knowledgeably to a fairly large number of references both literary and social. Since 1900 this has been less and less possible, and it is no coincidence that naturalism should be to this day the preferred manner in the novel, if only because the naturalistic writer, by

37

definition, takes nothing for granted. He assumes that the reader knows no more than he chooses to tell. He constructs a literal world of concrete detail. His narrative is easily followed. He records the surface of life with a photographer's care, leaving the interpretation, the truth of his record, to the reader's imagination. The result is that our time's most successful *popular* writing is journalism, another dagger at the novel's heart.

The idea for *Visit to a Small Planet* (from outer space arrives a charming hobbyist named Kreton whose blithe intent it is to start a war: "I mean it's the one thing you people down here do *really* well!") was rejected by three television sponsors before Philco-Goodyear Playhouse bought it. I was told that the advertisers found the premise alarming, which was certainly disingenuous of them. Had I not spun my fragile satire about the one glittering constant in human affairs, the single pastime that never palls: war? In fact, one might say that *Visit* is the happiest of pro-war plays.

But only Philco saw the charm of this conceit, and on the night of May 8, 1955, it was telecast. With some anxiety we waited for the roof to fall in. To my surprise it did not, and most people were pleased with the result. I was then informed that a producer would like me to do a stage version for Broadway. And so it came to pass. Expansion was not difficult. As a novelist, I was accustomed to using a hundred thousand words to net my meaning. My problem theatrically has always been one of compression.

After the script was ready there were the usual trials, delays, problems of temperament; each participant convinced that the others had gone into secret league to contrive his professional ruin (and on occasion cabals did flourish, for the theater is a child's world).

On January 16, 1957, the play opened in New Haven. From that moment until the New York opening on February 7, I was more dentist than writer, extracting the sharper (and not always carious) teeth. The heart of the play's argument was a scene in the second act between Kreton and the Secretary-

General of the United Nations. At each performance the audience, charmed by the fooling that had gone before, grew deathly cold as the debate began. This was not what they had anticipated (a fault, I own, of the dramaturgy), and their confidence in the play was never entirely regained. A few days before we left Boston, I replaced the scene with a lighter one, involving the principals and giving the curtain to our subtlest player, the cat. The substitute was engaging; the play moved amiably; no one was shocked. (Earlier, some observers in New Haven had declared the entire conception unwholesomely menacing. If only they had seen the first draft of the play, in which I blew up the whole world at the end, the perfect curtain!) So by deliberate dulling of the edge of the satire, the farce flourished.

A number of reviewers described the play as a vaudeville, a very apt description and one in which I concur, recalling a letter from Bernard Shaw to Granville-Barker: "I have given you a series of first-rate music hall entertainments thinly disguised as plays, but really offering the public a unique string of turns by comics and serio-comics of every popular type." That of course is only half the truth, but it is the amiable half. In the case of *Visit*, the comedic approach to the theme tended to dictate the form. Having no real commitment to the theater, no profound convictions about the well-made or the ill-made play, I tend to write as an audience, an easily bored audience. I wrote the sort of piece I should like to go to a theater to see, one in which people say and do things that make me laugh. And though monsters lurk beneath the surface, their presence is sensed rather than dramatically revealed. My view of reality is not sanguine, and the play for all its blitheness turns resolutely toward a cold night. Fortunately for the play's success, the incisors were extracted out of town and the venture was a hit. But in that word "hit" lies the problem.

I was obliged to protect an eighty-thousand-dollar investment, and I confess freely that I obscured meanings, softened blows, and humbly turned wrath aside, emerging with a successful play which represented me only a little. It is not that what was fashioned was bad or corrupt; I rather fancy the farce we ended up with, and I think it has a good deal of wear in it. But the play that might have been, though hardly earth-shaking, was far more interesting and true. Like too many others I played the game stolidly according to rules I abhorred, realizing that the theater and its writers are seriously, perhaps fatally, hampered by economic pressure. Because it costs too much to put on a play, one works in a state of hysteria. Every-thing is geared to success. Yet art is mostly failure. It is only from a succession of daring, flawed works that the occasional masterwork comes. But in the Broadway theater to fail is death, and in an atmosphere so feverish it is difficult to work with much objectivity. Only the honest hacks have a good time of it. Cannily, they run up a banner: It's just us again, kids, trying to make a buck. And they are let off with genial con-tempt. It is the crankier, more difficult writers who must work at a disadvantage, and efforts to divert them into familiar safe channels are usually disastrous. Is there a solution? I see none; unless it be the decentralization of the theater to the smaller cities and to the universities, where the means of production will be less than good but the freedom greater, particularly the luxurious freedom to fail.

The Reporter, July 11, 1957

SATIRE IN THE 1950's

Malcolm Muggeridge has recently proposed that satire tends to flourish at those times when the Establishment is confident that its eternal truths and verities (to borrow Mr. Faulkner's most famous redundancy) are indeed eternal and therefore impervious to ill-natured wit. Mr. Muggeridge concludes that in an age like ours (other-directed, hydrogen-haunted, artificially tranquilized and doggedly togethered) satire is more apt to take than administer a beating. He is right in one thing: satire has taken a beating. It hardly exists in the more public art forms, and except for an occasional timid appearance in the novel or on a night-club floor, satire has seldom thrived in our comfortable land. But I suggest that the reasons for this are precisely opposite to those Mr. Muggeridge gives. In the first place, he underestimates the very real complacency of our culture, which despite lowering political weather (those atom bombs again) traditionally holds that boats in any weather are best left unrocked. Secondly, it would appear to me that satire, historically, has been most useful—and most used—when the moral and religious assumptions of a people about itself are in a state of serious confusion because of some dramatic change for good or ill in that people's fortunes.

As his world and city fell, Aristophanes attacked a demoralized war-minded Administration which did not long survive him. As the Roman Republic disintegrated, Cicero satirized radicals, Catullus satirized the mysteriously amiable Caesar, and Horace ticked off a number of highly placed bores; all this in a time of proscription and violent change. Later, under the Empire, Petronius and Lucan, though good courtiers, had the bad luck to find the Divine Nero irresistibly funny; and their satiric thrusts were rewarded with the optimum Roman prize, that ineluctable warm bath with open veins. Those were not, to say the least, complacent days. Nor can one argue that, fierce palace politics aside, the Roman imperium ever rested on certain common assumptions confidently held. Beyond a glum acceptance of law as necessary to commercial endeavor and the accidental discovery that government is largely a matter of filing and cross-indexing, the Roman state from Sulla to Constantine was gloriously confused in its morality, politics and religion. Confronted by so many rich absurdities and contradictions, satire became a high and useful art in the hands of such various men as Persius, Juvenal, Martial, even St. Paul; though between fatal baths and confinement upon disagreeable islands, the satirists themselves did not always have too good a time of it.

The Christian victory, though it did not bring peace on earth, did at least manage to put a severe leash on the satiric impulse. There are not many recorded attacks on the Church between the Emperor Julian's death and the Reformation, a millennium which—though marked by the usual wars of aggression as well as a number of religious wars (something new under the sun)—qualified supremely, in the West at least, as a period of firmly entrenched spiritual values and therefore a seedbed, one would think, for satire. Yet it was not. And the truth of the matter, of course, is that no well-organized central administration, temporal or spiritual, is apt to allow its beneficiaries the license of laughter at its own expense. Cardinals are no laughing matter in Ireland or in Spain today. Even in America, they must write particularly bad verse to occasion a wary joke or two. Yet in France and Italy, two nations which have been for some time in a state of moral and political confusion, cardinals are stock figures of comedy, cropping up in numerous jokes, good and bad, malicious and amiable. I worry the Roman Church only because it is an elderly institution of great significance morally and therefore an obvious target for useful satire. At present, in America, it is not.

Now I would propose that the United States in its short history has been much too preoccupied uniting and exploring, pioneering and building, inventing and consuming, to give much thought to anything not relevant to the practical and immediate. Not that we have lacked for harsh critics. In fact, most of our country's good writers have been nay-sayers, deploring the day and resolutely pessimistic about tomorrow. On the other hand, our humorists have been jolly and ubiquitous. We all know, rather wearily, about frontier humor. Mark Twain's jokes go on and on and some are funny but none is truly satiric because he was not one to rock the boat. It was his ordeal to be tamed, and the petulance and bitterness of his final book, *What is Man?*, answers as nothing else could why he did not dare question any of his society's basic assumptions.

Henry James observed that it took a great deal of history to make a little bit of literature. I suspect it takes a far more homogeneous, more settled, yet more uneasy society to produce satirists. And if one is to be met by the argument that God forbid things should be any worse simply to make matters easier for one small department of literature, I would be the first to agree that the benign incompetence of the Great Golfer and his Team is certainly preferable to a touchy Nero or to an inscrutable Caesar.

Yet there is a real need for the satirist in our affairs, especially now. Since the Second World War and its horrors there has been a remarkable change in our society. Anti-Semitism

43

seems happily to have vanished, except among the more irritable Jews, while anti-Catholics no longer smile, at least in mixed religious company, when the Vatican certifies that the sun did a dance over Portugal. Even my Southern relatives employ a certain tact in discussing the Problem. A profound tolerance is in the land, a tolerance so profound that it is not unlike terror. One dare not raise one's voice against any religion, idea or even delinquency if it is explicable by a therapist. I suspect that much of the American's hatred of Russia and Communism is simply a siphoning off of other irrational dislikes which, blocked by the stern tolerance of the day, can find expression only in Communist baiting. I do not propose that we return to the bad old days of holding people responsible for inherited characteristics. Yet I should like to have tolerance learned from within and not have it imposed from without. To put forward a recklessly unsympathetic proposition: As long as any group within the society deliberately maintains its identity, it is, or should be, a fair target for satire, both for its own good and for the society's. Laughing at someone else is an excellent way of learning how to laugh at oneself; and questioning what seem to be the absurd beliefs of another group is a good way of recognizing the potential absurdity of many of one's own cherished beliefs; witness the travels of Gulliver.

It is generally agreed and officially lamented that we are in a new age of conformity. Youth wants security, not adventure. The great questions are not asked because the realization that there are no absolute answers has at last penetrated to the bottom layer of society—and why be curious if the answers are only tentative? Now, if this time is indeed so bland, then according to Muggeridge's law, satire must flourish. Yet satire hardly exists. In perfect comfort the squares grow ever more rectilinear. And to strike the minatory note, if ever there was a people ripe for dictatorship it is the American people today. Should a homegrown Hitler appear, whose voice, amongst the public orders, would be raised against him in derision? Certainly no voice on television: "Sorry, the guy has a lot of fans. Sure, we know he's bad news, but you can't hurt people's feelings. They buy soap, too." And elsewhere there would be the tolerant reflex: "Well, he *could* be right. After all, a lot of people seem to agree with him . . ." And then the iron fist closes, and we start *our* Empire.

I have often chided my Soviet friends on the naïveté of their country's censorship. Newly literate and still awed by the printed word, the Russian governors are terrified of ideas. If only they knew what our governors know: that in a huge egalitarian society no idea which runs counter to the prevailing superstitions can successfully penetrate the national carapace. We give our solemn critics every freedom, including the one to fail to be heard. And fail they do: silence and indifference neutralize the irritant more effectively than brainwashing. Yet this age could be a marvelous one for satirists. Look at the targets: Christianity, Psychiatry, Marxism, Romantic Love, Xenophobia, Science (all capitalized and all regarded with reverence if not admiration). You need only take your pick, and not worry about bad taste. If one can make the cautious laugh by clowning, half the work is done, for laughter is the satirist's anaesthetic: he can then make his incision, darting on before the audience knows what has been done to it. But he must be swift and engaging, or the laughter will turn to indifferent silence, the ultimate censorship.

Where can the American satirist operate today? Not on television, seldom if ever in the movies, and on the stage only if he is willing to play the buffoon. But the novel remains; and it would be good to see those writers with a talent for satire (Randall Jarrell for one) strike boldly at the large targets, without that vitiating diffidence peculiar to the contemporary American novelist. We don't know very much, they seem to say; we are deep of course, often mystic, and we do know that love and compassion are the most beautiful things in the world and in our studies of loneliness we like to show the full potentiality of love (how Flaubert would have satirized these latter-day Bovarists!), but we don't know or want to know any senators, bishops, atomic scientists; as for psychiatrists—well, we

45

like ours: he is a Jungian. Shrinking each into his own skin, our novelists grow more private, and for those who lack genius (the majority) more dull. I do not suggest that everyone turns his hand to satire. It is, after all, only one of a number of ways to get the thing said. Nor do I echo those solid *Forsyte Saga* newspaper reviewers who maintain that what we need is a good novel about the wool trade or building a dam, but what I feel we do need is more engagement in the outer world. And daring. And wit. And, finally, satirists, who are needed as truth is needed—for is not satire, simply, truth grinning in a solemn canting world?*

The Nation, April 26, 1958

---

*Right on cue the "great" age of satire began. Lenny Bruce and Mort Sahl in the cellars, dozens of absurdists and black comedians in print and on the stage. Everything was labeled satire until the murderous sixties really got under way. To date we still lack a Dante to commit to hell our villains (is it because our villains are beyond satire?); we even lack a Mencken . . . or a Vidal to write a piece on the need for satire in the seventies.

LOVE LOVE LOVE

"Love love love love love love love love love"—give or take a few "loves"—was the entire lyric of a song by Charlie Chaplin and I herewith propose that it be adopted as the American theater's official anthem. Just name your problem, sit back and let love solve it: race prejudice, foreign relations—even Job reeling beneath the unkind attentions of a dubious Yale God gets off the hook at the end through Love, which has now replaced the third-act Marines of a simpler time. On those rare occasions when some other solution tries to creep into the popular theater it either fails or else survives only after whatever alien gold was in it has been transmuted to base Love by the alchemy of production. Granted, Arthur Miller worries his head about problems of the day; but as for his heart—well, scratched he bleeds Love. Even that attention we must pay his salesman is but a command to love him.

Our popular theater ponders, to the exclusion of all else, the pathos of Love withheld, of Love lost, of Love found after three acts of jittery footling while the man learns Tenderness (never the woman, since according to commercial lore, Woman *knows*). Moon-guided, triple-crowned, inscrutable, the American Woman in our theater is never so wise as when she's not thinking at all, just being, and listening with a tiny smile to the third-act speech of the man, who has had to learn Tenderness the hard way. "Gosh, Marge, I know how it was, but it won't be like that no more, honest, baby, it won't. No, sir, when I got knocked down in that fight with that two-hundred-pound woman in Salt Lake, I knew what we had was all there is and I'm gonna change, Marge, I swear, because that's all there is, what we got . . . love." And Marge, played by an actress weighing-in at ninety-seven tensely muscular pounds, opens her arms slowly as though semaphoring bad news to a foundering ship; she takes his great, empty buffalo head in her arms. "It's all right, Walter," she says in a voice meant to be tender, though aficionados will detect the approaching kill in this last veronica. "I'm *here*, Walter." And the curtain falls.

Yet in all fairness to our commercial theater, the preoccupation with Love was thrust upon it by the society it reflects or tries to reflect. By Love the theater does not mean love in Rousseau's sense (to employ him as a Romantic touchstone, pre-Agony). Nor is Love anything quite so simple as successful copulation, though that of course is of coeval (as Mr. Faulkner would say) importance. After all, one of the few goals our friendly society has set us is a more perfect union; the general failure to achieve it, of course, ensures full employment to mental therapists, causes dramatic religious conversions and, in the case of one talented theater director, has driven him to pad obsessively the crotches of the less flamboyantly hung actors (Aristophanes would have found a joke in that; we can't). No, Love in our theater is not really sex though sex is part of it. Love is a warm druggedness, a surrender of the will and the mind to inchoate feelings of Togetherness. Thought is the enemy; any exercise of mind betrays Love, and Love's vengeance in the theater is terrible, for mind must be broken and made to recant, and then to love Love. But before we score the silliness of our popular theater, we ought to recognize that it reflects, always more baldly than the novel, say, the superstitions and prejudices of the age. The flabbiness of tone in the theater differs only in its oversimplified effects from the same flabbiness in the popular (and sometimes "serious") novel, and, to get to the root, it does no more than reflect the ubiquitous flab of the Great Golfer's reign.* Whether Tocqueville's worst fears have come true or not, democracy is too much with us. It has been duly noted how often people now say "I feel" such-and-such to be true rather than "I think" such-and-such to be true. To make that shift of verb unconsciously is to eschew mind and take cover in the cozier, more democratic world of feeling. I suppose there are some who say of others pejoratively, "His feelings are not deep." But if pressed, they would admit that no one really knows what another's feelings are, though it is of course agreed that we are all pretty much alike at heart: sensitive, warm, tender, our moments of bad behavior the result of the green twig's early bending, sure to straighten and flower beneath Love's therapeutic sun. In any case, in our theater feeling is all, and the deliberate exercise of mind is thought an admission of emotional poverty. Particularly mistrusted is Bernard Shaw, whose works are dismissed as displays of debater's tricks, the plots suitable only for adaptation to musical comedy. He did not love Love; worse, he made the devil a Love-lover, and chose as hero Don Juan, a mere life-lover.

Now it is almost too easy to put down Broadway. So much of what's wrong is so obvious that most attacks on our theater lose force because of the target's size. It is impossible with a

---

*Eisenhower, the Great Golfer, is gone, yet the flab persists because the pseudodemocracy can only maintain itself by a blurring of all distinctions, a wilful ignorance of what is. But in twenty years things have changed. Where once soared on high the imperial American eagle, predatory, greedy, fierce, now in the DDT-ed greensward crouches our newest totem, the soft, fuzzy image of our present soul, the dumb bunny.

shotgun at three paces not to hit the Shubert Theater. Yet it is curious how often the serious-minded do miss the essential target. For instance, not long ago a lively young critic fired a familiar blast: no ideas in our theater, too many sensational productions *épater le box office*, too many writers revealing sexual obsessions of depressing singularity. All the usual changes were rung, but then the critic entitled his piece "The Theater Is Losing Its Minds," and confused everything. I don't know how far back his memory, both actual and learned, goes, but if there were ever any minds operative in the American theater it is news to me. Before Eugene O'Neill (whose mastery of ideas was second to none, unless it be his fellow Nobelist Pearl Buck), there was a wasteland of Owen Davises, Avery Hopwoods and Eugene Walters, stretching back to the egregious Royall Tyler, who started the American theater on its mindless way. Two centuries of junk. If anything, there are rather more signs of intelligence stirring now than in the bad old days.

A few months later, our critic was back again. This time he wondered why the better novelists did not bring "mind" to the theater. Or at least why hadn't the theater produced playwrights as good as the novelists on today's List, and he gave the List, betraying himself, I'm afraid, as an incipient Lovelover. Parenthetically, each year there is a short List of the O.K. Writers. Today's List consists of two Jews, two Negroes and a safe floating *goy* of the old American Establishment (often Wright Morris*), just to show there is no prejudice in our Loving world; only the poor old homosexuals are out. It is a list dictated not by any aesthetic but by Good Citizenship. That the writers on it happen to be admirable is irrelevant: Togetherness put them there and we all feel better seeing them belaureled. My young critic is not responsible for today's List, but he showed a certain absence of mind in trying to beat the playwrights with it, because not one of the writers named

*As of this morning John Updike.

could be thought of as an intellectual in the sense I assumed he meant (Gide, Camus, even the dervish Genet). They are all good, if fairly standard, writers, more or less in the naturalistic tradition, and, at least in their novels, betray no more mind than do the plays of Arthur Miller.

I find this sort of mistake (taking good writers of one sort and saying they are good writers of quite another sort on the grounds that to be good is good enough) yet another sign of the general corruption of aesthetic and intellectual values in this soft age. The language of criticism now tends to be as inexact as the prose of the works criticized. No one seems to know who or what anyone or anything is. Prevalent is a lazy permissiveness. Our literature as well as our theater seems at times like a terrible kindergarten. Jack is a great novelist because he *feels* he's a great novelist. Anything goes. On every side counterfeit talents flood the exchange. This was always so, but in other times and places there were certain critics whose bite authenticated coinage. They are still with us—but outside the battle, in the Academy.

I have often thought it would be a service to the audience if each writer was forced to refer to himself in a certain style and manner which would make clear what he is. Implicitly, each does, but it is confusing to all but a student of rhetoric. Arthur Miller (he is on my mind because I have just read the Preface to his collected plays) writes of himself not seriously but solemnly. With paralyzing pomp, splitting his infinitives and confusing number, he climbs the steps to the throne, with the enemy syntax crushed beneath his heavy boot: he is our prophet, our king, our guide in the dark. The only thing wrong is that he does not write awfully well. In other times, if one had made such a criticism it would have been quite enough. But Mr. Miller is ready for this stricture (and so are all the other hackers in the kindergarten). "We have had," he reminds those of us who were nodding, "more than one extraordinary dramatist who was a cripple as a writer, and this is lamentable but not ruinous." I suppose he could get out of that one by saying he meant extraordinary to mean just that:

extra-ordinary, though of course there is nothing more ordinary than writer-cripples in our theater.

Now by needling the pretensions of Mr. Miller (whom I often admire as a writer-cripple), I don't mean to scout his rightful position in the commercial theater—he is more good than bad as an influence and as a fact—but to draw attention again to the lack of any sense in our aesthetic judgments. Mr. Miller—and all the rest—can get away with just about any evaluation he wants to make of himself, and those who know differently won't bother to straighten out the matter for an audience which seems perfectly content to receive counterfeit bills for checks drawn in good faith. As a result, our commentators are so many Madame Verdurins, hopelessly confused as to true precedence. And the noncounterfeit artist must either go in to table last or make a fool of himself, much as the Baron de Charlus did that curious afternoon.

I happen to like a number of playwrights as people. For some reason they bring out my protective and pedagogic instincts. I like to reassure them, to help them, to give them reading lists. In many ways they are to be admired for stamina, since to be produced on Broadway resembles nothing so much as being shot from a cannon at a fragile net. One should not be surprised if the more sensitive dramatists tend to get a bit punchy. Most of them (I am generalizing hugely, but life is short) experience serious difficulty in reading books, which necessarily limits their fund of general information on any subject not connected with the theater or their own psychoanalysis. The literary world, to the extent they are aware of it at all, seems to them an invidious establishment where writers dislike them because they are better known and make more money than any other sort of writer. They do not realize that, having no interest in language and even less in what we like to think of as mind, they necessarily must earn the indifference of those who do bother with such things. Although in its essential preoccupations our theater cannot help but reflect the day, it has always been estranged not only from its own country's culture but, to strike that tinny gong, from Western

civilization. The result has been a curiously artificial development, resembling nothing but itself, like those amoebae which
when boxed upon a slide stop their anarchic zooming about
and make perfect right angles, as tribute to an imposed environment.

"Weariness of the theatre is the prevailing note of London
criticism. Only the ablest critics believe that the theatre is
really important; in my time, none of them would claim for
it, as I claimed for it, that it is as important as the Church was
in the Middle Ages. . . ." Ah, that crisp hopeful voice! Shaw
in 1906. "A theatre to me is a place where two or three are
'gathered together.' The apostolic succession from Eschylus to
myself is as serious and as continuously inspired as that
younger institution, the apostolic succession of the Christian
Church." Brave words and perhaps true, though there have
not been very many American gatherings-together one would
like William Morris to attend. With some justice, intellectuals
hold our popular theater in contempt, and one of the reasons
seldom explicitly stated is not so much the meretriciousness of
the exhibits—popular art is opportunist at best—as its moments of would-be seriousness. Milton Berle telling low-
comedy jokes onstage can be very beguiling; but to be lectured
to in a stern tone by a writer considerably more stupid than
much of his audience is a somber experience, and were our
collective manners not better, theater seats would be torn up
and hurled at the stage. Earnest Neanderthals implore us not
to persecute minority groups; they exhort us to tenderness;
they inform us that war is destructive; they remind us that
love is the only connection. There is nothing wrong with these
themes except the blunt obviousness with which they are handled and the self-righteous tone of writers whose aesthetic
derives partly from mental therapists and partly from those
urgent dramas that once made radio wonderful. It is not that
one does not admire Arthur Miller's real gifts for theater-
writing or his good heart. It is his stunning solemnity which
annoys. Stop telling us what we already know! And don't
write sentences like: "That he had not the intellectual fluency

53

to verbalize his situation is not the same thing as saying that he lacked awareness, even an overly intensified consciousness that the life he had made was without form and inner meaning." That is not a writer writing or a man trying to get through to others; it is the voice of the holder of a degree in Education. One sympathizes with Mr. Miller's passion to be admired, to be thought significant. All of us tend more or less consciously to arrange our personas in an attractive way. But his attempt is saddening because, though he is not taken seriously outside the popular theater and press, he is *almost* good enough to be respected in the way he wants. More to the point, he *should* be good enough: I attribute his failure to the popular theater's estrangement from the country's culture.

In the last fifteen years the French theater has been used by Gide, Sartre, Camus, de Montherlant, Genet, Anouilh, Julian Green, Giraudoux—an eclectic list which goes on and on, comprising most of the interesting French writers. And what have we had? Tennessee Williams (whom I happen to admire), Mr. Miller, one small mood play by Carson McCullers, Thornton Wilder in his later, three-cheers-for-Love manner, and, of course, the heady splendors of *J.B.* It is not a heartening record.

The cult of feeling has not only undone much of our theater writing, it has also peculiarly victimized those gentle souls, the actors. They have been taught that "truth" is everything. And what is "truth"? Feeling. And what is feeling? Their own secret core, to which the character they are to interpret must be related. To listen to actors talk about "truth" is a chilling experience. They employ a kind of baby talk compounded of analysts' jargon and the arcane prose of the late Stanislavsky. As one of them said severely of another's performance: "He's not thinking; he's only thinking he's thinking." Our actors have also been taught to condemn the better English or French actors as "technical." "Technical" here *seems* to mean—in these circles words are employed for transient emotive effects, never meaning—that a separation has been made between the ac-

tor's own feelings and those the part he is playing ca
To understand just who Iago is, the "technical" acto
deliberately make the separation. Then, having go
proper range, he will, by an effort of will, inhabit the
acter, using himself as much or as little as he please
goal being the interpretation of Shakespeare's Iago, *n*
revelation of his own inner state as he grapples with
Our actors may not be able to say a line of verse int
bly or begin to understand what Iago is all about, bu
can bet they will bring floods of irrelevant feelings t
part. It is not acting but group therapy. And the sad
is that though this kind of acting is usually disagreeal
watch, it is delightful to do. They won't change with
struggle; and since they feel rather than think, they te
be fanatics about a method whose queen, of course, i
genuinely gifted Kim Stanley. Yet the whole sad mis
thing is all there in her large bland face, the small
turned inward though they seem to be looking out
whiny voice rising and falling according to the be;
some inner metronome of "truth," her whole b
suffused in a nimbus of self-love. The final effect is on
tic.

For some years I would not read Mary McCarthy's th
criticism, after her majestically wrongheaded estimate
Streetcar Named Desire. She not only missed the point to
play but, worse, got carried away by irrelevancies: Will:
was really a slob, devoted to success, pretending to be a
artist while swinging with the Broadway set; worst of al
was guilty of "ambition." She uses this word several time
her collected pieces to tick off those writers who try, sneal
to get above their talents. Art climbers are very like so
climbers, and Miss McCarthy is a good one to put each in
place. Now I grant that there is something odd in Tenne
Williams's work which not only enrages otherwise reason;
critics but drives them to impute motives to him which
more the business of post-mortem biography than of critici
I think again of the young critic who wrote recently in *Enc*

ter that Williams's real theme was incest.* Well, his real theme is *not* incest no matter how one chooses to read the plays. One does not dare speculate on what sort of grapevine gossip led to this conclusion; thought certainly had nothing to do with it, though feeling might. But aside from Miss McCarthy's forty whacks at Williams, when I finally came to read her collected criticism I was struck by her remarkable good sense. Uncorrupted by compassion, her rather governessy severity, even cruelty, derives from the useful knowledge that the road to kitsch is paved with good ambitions, and that one must not give the "A" for ambition without also giving simultaneously the "E" for the poor thing effected. The theater needs continual reminders that there is nothing more debasing than the work of those who do well what is not worth doing at all.

A minor phenomenon of the theater today is the milieu: kitchens in Kansas, cold-water flats, Bronx apartments, the lower-middle-class venue depicted in naturalistic terms by "truthful" actors before an audience of overdressed, overfed burghers. How does that audience stand it, even when it's good? Is it that they enjoy a nostalgic *frisson* at looking back to their own origins? Or is there a desire to know about things today, to be instructed by the narcissism of a John Osborne, who tells them: "This is the way we are, young, angry, unique"? The burghers nod and belch softly, and some doze: it is the theater of the editorial and the survey. Even those who dislike Tennessee Williams must give him credit for castrating a hero here, eating one there; and with Elia Kazan racketing the actors about the stage, it is not easy to sleep. I save any further defense of Williams for another occasion, since my intention in these notes is entirely destructive.

And where do we go from here? I confess I have no very clear notion of what I should like to see the theater become. As a playwright I am a sport, whose only serious interest is the subversion of a society that bores and appalls me (no world

*The young critic was most hurt by this piece, and over the years has tried to redress the balance by writing unkindly of me. (See p. 329.)

elsewhere, alas; this is the one to fix). Yet I don't see much change for the good. Plays cost too much to put on. That means investors will be wary of new things. I also suspect that despite the enviable example of the French, our comparable good writers are not apt to be much of an improvement on the ones already in the theater. In England, the Royal Court Theatre has offered hospitality to some of the good writers, but the plays so far produced have been disappointing. In fact, it may very well be that the simplemindedness we score in our playwrights is a necessary characteristic of play-making.

In any case, there is no use in worrying about Broadway. Expect less rather than more intelligence on the stage, especially as costs increase. Revel in the graver efforts, which will more and more resemble *J.B.*—that portentous magnum of chloroform Elia Kazan so accurately broke across our collective brows, launching us upon a glum sea anodyne. In fact, the former Assistant Secretary of State may well have got our Age's number back in the 1930's, when he decided that a poem should not mean but be. Our theater certainly does not mean; it is. Yet to the extent that it is, it mirrors us. Look in it and you will see quite plain the un-Loved face of Caliban.

Partisan Review, Spring 1959

BERNARD SHAW'S
*HEARTBREAK HOUSE**

"Heartbreak House . . . rhapsodized about love; but it believed in cruelty. It was afraid of the cruel people; and it saw that cruelty was at least effective. Cruelty did things that made money, whereas Love did nothing but prove the soundness of La Rochefoucauld's saying that very few people would fall in love if they had never read about it. Heartbreak House in short did not know how to live, at which point all that was left to it was the boast that at least it knew how to die: a melancholy accomplishment which the outbreak of war presently gave it practically unlimited opportunities of displaying. Thus were the first-born of Heartbreak House smitten; and the young,

*I was briefly a drama critic for *The Reporter* magazine. At the end of my tenure I decided that the government and the foundations should subsidize not the actors, writers, theaters but the audience. We are the ones who need the money, not the actors, who should pay us for watching them, since we can never enjoy the experience as much as they do.

the innocent, the hopeful expiated the folly and worthlessness of their elders."

That is from Bernard Shaw's odd preface to his even odder play, now revived on Broadway. The preface is odd, among other things, because it is written with the wrong sort of hindsight. Shaw did not know when he began the play in 1913 that the first-born were going to be struck down. Nor is there any reference to war, actual or impending, in the first two acts. The third act, however, was completed after the first aerial bombardments in history, and Shaw, rather casually, uses this to drop a bomb and end the play. Yet it is not the residents of Heartbreak House or their first-born who get blown up; only a businessman and a burglar expiate the folly and worthless-ness of . . . what? Not Heartbreak House certainly; capitalism, perhaps.

Everything about the play is queer, even its production history. Plans to put it on during the war went awry. Shaw finally published it, with preface, in 1919. Not until 1920 was the play produced, in New York. The next year it got to the West End. The preface is unique in Shaw for its bitterness and hysteria, and the play . . . well, there are those who put it first among his work and there are those who don't know what to think of it. I'm afraid after seeing it performed for the first time the other day that I liked it a good deal less than I thought I did from having read it; parenthetically, I should put quite plainly here at the beginning that I regard Bernard Shaw as the best and most useful dramatist in English since the author of *Much Ado About Nothing* turned gentleman and let fall the feather.

What is Heartbreak House? In the context of the play it stands for the ruling class of England pre-1914: the "nice peo-ple," somewhat educated, somewhat sensitive, somewhat inde-pendent financially (their cousins the hearties lived over at Horseback Hall). They were devotees of laissez-faire; they rhapsodized about love—but I have already quoted Shaw's indictment. Heartbreak House, of course, is only another name for our new friend the Establishment, a protective association made up of public-school boys who come down from Oxbridge to take over Whitehall, the Church of England, the BBC, Fleet Street, the better-looking girls, and everything else that's fun, while (so young writers tell us) sneering at the newly articulate *Lumpenproletariat* who have gone to red-brick colleges where, if one reads the new novels accurately, the main course given is Opportunism: Don't reform, adapt. The jocose nihilism of many of the anti-Establishment novels and plays is no more than a love-hate acceptance of the Establishment; the Kingsley Amises approach it on its own terms in a way Shaw would have detested. Where he would have leveled Heartbreak House to make way for a carefully planned housing project, the new attackers of the Establishment merely want to move into some of those nice rooms at the top, an attitude ignoble to a socialist and hopelessly petty to an outsider who is aware that the rooms at the top of a diminished England are not much better than those directly under. The Establishment has only an island to tend, while Heartbreak House, with Asquith and Bonar Law and Ramsay Mac for weekend guests, governed much of the world. To put it plain, Shaw's target was important; and he knew what he wanted, which was not to adapt, or to make his own way, but to reform.

I think we know pretty much what Shaw intended to do in *Heartbreak House*, yet what actually did he do in the play itself? For one thing, it is improvised work. Shaw admitted he made it up as he went along, not knowing from day to day what his characters would do or say or become. He always tended to work this way, regarding a play essentially as an organism with a life of its own; one need only nurture it and let it assume its own shape. He even used to keep a checkerboard at hand to remind him who was onstage and who was off at any given moment in the writing. There is no doubt this method served him as well as any other; his night mind was not, to say the least, fantastic. I am sure deep in his unconscious there lurked not the usual nightmare monsters of the rest of us but yards of thesis, antithesis, and synthesis, all neatly labeled and filed. Yet in *Heartbreak House* Shaw's improvisatory genius breaks down; he keeps marching into conversational culs-de-sac.

For example, in the second act the play comes to a grinding halt after Boss Mangan, recovered from hypnotic trance, denounces and is denounced by those who happen to be onstage at the moment, and exits. Then Captain Shotover tosses a Delphic phrase or two upon the night and paddles off. (Later the Captain, while again trying for an exit, says, almost apologetically: "I must go in and out," a compulsion he shares with everyone else in this play; they all go in and out at whim.) This ill-madeness is often beguiling except on those occasions when it defeats the author, who finds himself with nobody left onstage except a couple who don't have much of anything to say to one another at the moment. It is then that Shaw invariably, shamelessly, brings on the New Character, who is very often a member of the lower classes with a colorful speech pattern usually written out phonetically in the text. This time he is the Burglar, a comic character right out of Dickens, where Shaw claimed, not entirely facetiously, to have got most of his characters, at least those who are not himself. The Burglar is one of Shaw's standbys, used in play after play; he is awful, but at least he starts the second act moving again and gives it a certain vivacity. As usual, Shaw, delighted with his own cunning, starts tying up ends; the Burglar is really the Captain's old bos'n, the nurse's husband, etc., etc. And now let's have a long chat about the poor and the exploited, the exploiters and the *rentiers*, and then end the act.

As a rule, Shaw's arbitrariness does not disturb. After all, he is conducting a seminar with enormous wit and style and we don't much mind his more casual contrivances. But in this play they don't come off. I think it has to do with a fundamental conflict between characters and settings. The characters, of course, are our old friends the Bernard Shaw Team of Fabian Debaters; we know each one of them already. But what are they doing in this peculiar Midsummer's Eve *ambiance?* They seem a bit puzzled, too. As they debate with their usual ease they tend nervously to eye the shrubbery: are there elves at the bottom of that garden? Have we been booked into an allegory?

Are we going to find out we're all dead or something? Steady, chaps, the old boy's got us into one of *those* plays. They rattle on bravely but they are clearly ill at ease, and so is the audience. I think it was one of the New York daily reviewers who observed that the mood is not Chekhov but J. M. Barrie. Which is exactly right. We are led to expect magic, fey girls upon the heath, and revelation through fantasy. But we get none of it. Instead we are offered the old Debating Team in top form but in the wrong place and mood (oh, for that dentist's office!). As a result the debaters recede as characters; we grow indifferent to them; they are too humorous in the original sense of the word. Especially Ellie, Shaw's super-girl. In this version she is more than ever iron, ready to mother not heroes but heroines. Shaw dotes on Ellie; I found her purest drip-torture. Halfway through the play I had a startling *aperçu*: Shaw regarded himself not as a man or an artist or a social meliorist but as a kind of superwoman, a chaste spinster fiercely armed with the umbrella of dialectic, asexual limbs blue-stockinged, and tongue wagging. Of all the debaters assembled, I liked only Captain Shotover, because his dottiness contrasted agreeably with the uneasy predictability of his teammates.

Finally, at the play's end, I found myself entirely confused as to what Shaw intended. Shaw is not, even when he would like to be, an impressionist, a Chekhov turning life before our eyes to no end but that life observed is sufficient. Look, we live, we are, says Chekhov. While Shaw declares briskly: Pull up your socks! Fall in line there. Come along now. Double-quick march and we'll overtake the future by morning! One loves Shaw for his optimism, but moonlight is not a time for marching, and *Heartbreak House* is a moonlight play, suitable for recapturing the past. Elegy and debate cancel one another out. Nor is the work really satiric, an attack on "folly and worthlessness." These people are splendid and unique, and Shaw knows it. He cannot blow them up at the end.

Shaw's prefaces—no matter how proudly irrelevant their content may, at first, seem to the play that follows (sometimes a bit forlornly)—usually turn out to be apposite or at least complementary. But not this preface. In fact, it is misleading. Shaw talks about Chekhov. He finds the country-house mentality Chekhov *seems* to be writing about endemic to Europe, part of the sweet sickness of the bourgeoisie. Therefore Shaw will examine the same house in the same way, only in English terms. Ever since that preface, we have all dutifully considered this play in terms of Chekhov. Does it compare? Is it as good? Why is it *un*like? It is true that both are dealing with the same dying society of "nice people," but where Chekhov's interest was the "nice people," Shaw's interest was the dying society and the birth pains of the new.

Shaw once told Sir Cedric Hardwicke that he had no idea how to end the play until the first bombs fell. I suspect he had originally planned to allow Captain Shotover to attain "the Seventh Degree of concentration," thereby detonating the dynamite he had stored in the gravel pit and blowing up the enemy Mangan. As it was, at the last minute, the bomb from the Zeppelin did the trick even better, providing Shaw quite literally with a god from the machine. Then, almost as an afterthought, Shaw comes to the point:

HECTOR: Well, I don't mean to be drowned like a rat in a trap. I still have the will to live. What am I to do?

CAPTAIN SHOTOVER: Do? Nothing simpler. Learn your business as an Englishman.

HECTOR: And what may my business as an Englishman be, pray?

CAPTAIN SHOTOVER: Navigation. Learn it and live; or leave it and be damned.

And that's it. Captain Shotover, supposed to have sold his soul to the devil, to have meddled with mysticism, to have mastered the *non sequitur*, turns out to be a good Fabian socialist after all. Obviously, Shotover was a humbug mystic, excusably deranged by the setting Shaw put him in; not until faced with his world's extinction does he throw off the mask of dottiness to reveal the bright, hard, intelligent face of Bernard

Shaw, who to this day has a good deal to tell us about the danger of a society drifting as opposed to one which has learned the virtue of setting a deliberate course by fixed stars. To navigate is to plan. Laissez-faire, though always delightful for a few, in crisis is disastrous for all. There is no alternative to a planned society; that is the burden of the Shaw debate. Almost as an afterthought he makes this familiar point as the bomb drops near Heartbreak House.

The production now on view is ambitious, and at many points successful. As usual, I found myself more attentive to the audience than to the play. As they say in physics, there is no action without reaction. I can think of no urgent reason for writing about productions in the theater unless one also writes about the audience, too. The play acts upon the audience, which is society today; the audience reacts and in its reaction one can get a sense of the superstitions and prejudices which obtain. Theater can be revelatory. In fact, I wish sociologists would spend more time in the theater and less in conducting polls and drawing graphs. Any audience at *Tea and Sympathy* or *Auntie Mame* will tell them more about the way we live now than a house-to-house canvass from Morristown to White Plains with pad and pencil.

In the case of an old play like *Heartbreak House* one may also use it as a touchstone. In the 1920's it seemed one thing, in the 1930's another, and so on. To those watching, the day I saw it, *Heartbreak House* was a delightful place, menaced by burglars, self-made men, and Zeppelins. The clothes were chic yet quaint and every woman saw herself up there pouring tea for weak enamored men who tended to burst into tears while the ladies talked a bright blue streak. Whenever the debate really got going, 1959's attention flagged: Is that a rubber plant? Can they still get egret feathers or is that an imitation? Did you leave the keys in the car? . . . Bernard Shaw, I'm afraid, was being taken for Oscar Wilde, and afflicted with un-Wildean *longueurs.* But then we are not used to debate at any level. If Bernard Shaw, who made the act of argument as pleasurable as any writer who ever lived, cannot hold his audience except by predictable paradoxes and references to adultery and all the familiar junk of the Commercialites, we the audience are in a bad way. Although in fairness it must be admitted that talking about society and the better life and planning of any sort has never been a characteristic of the Anglo-American mind.

Nevertheless, Harold Clurman has directed this production just as though we were really awake out there and knew what was going on. He is enormously helped by Diana Wynyard and Pamela Brown, who are beautifully right for this kind of thing. Maurice Evans, an actor I seem to like only as Richard II no matter what else he plays, is unexpectedly fine as Captain Shotover. I'm not sure dressing up to look like Bernard Shaw was a wise idea; I suspect Shaw would have hated it; but it does help Mr. Evans to hide beneath whiskers and putty the self-pitying face of Richard II, and I could not have liked him more. Sam Levene of course was all wrong as Boss Mangan. He is a good *farceur*, but in another style, and his scenes tended to throw everyone else off: it was not unlike casting our own beloved Marjorie Main as Lady Bracknell. The other weak link is Diane Cilento as Ellie, the supergirl. Miss Cilento plays with a grinding monotony made worse because she has gone and got herself one of those Voices. Let me explain. Right after the war, Pamela Brown's most lovely strange diction was the ambition and despair of every English girl on the stage. We got Miss Brown's Voice in every possible key. Then there was heard in the land Joan Greenwood's hoarse, intimate rasp, to our delight and her peers' despair. Now Miss Cilento has distilled herself a voice which is two-parts Brown and one-part Greenwood, and I think she ought to give it up, right now. She is a beautiful girl with some talent; yet if Ellie is to be made less than revolting she must be played with as little artifice and as much "naturalness" as possible. I daresay Mr. Clurman was aware of this, but sooner get a bird to sing Mozart than force an actress to discard a Voice she has worked on. All in all, reservations about this particular play aside, I hope it runs forever and gives heart to those who expect the theater to be something more than a business for those who, in their calculated desire to please us, only make us more than ever absent of mind.

The Reporter, November 26, 1959.

THE TWELVE CAESARS*

Tiberius, Capri. Pool of water. Small children . . . So far so good. One's laborious translation was making awful sense. Then . . . Fish. Fish? The erotic mental image became surreal. Another victory for the Loeb Library's sly translator, J. C. Rolfe, who, correctly anticipating the prurience of schoolboy readers, left Suetonius's gaudier passages in the hard original. One failed to crack those intriguing footnotes not because the syntax was so difficult (though it was not easy for students

*I don't remember why I wrote this piece. I do remember that no one would print it because what I had to say about man's sexual/power drive was shocking. Also, to be fair, Americans in general are not concerned with anything that happened before yesterday. Even in "serious" quarters, an interest in the Roman empire is regarded as a sign of deep irrelevance. To flatter me, a critic once said that of all American writers only I could have written *Julian*. I agreed, adding, "Not only am I the only American writer who could have written such a book, I am also the only American writer who would have wanted either to write or read it."

drilled in military rather than civilian Latin) but because the range of vice revealed was considerably beyond the imagination of even the most depraved schoolboy. There was a point at which one rejected one's own translation. Tiberius and the little fish, for instance.

Happily, we now have a full translation of the text, the work of Mr. Robert Graves, who, under the spell of his Triple Goddess, has lately been retranslating the classics. One of his first tributes to her was a fine rendering of *The Golden Ass*; then Lucan's *Pharsalia*; then the *Greek Myths*, a collation aimed at rearranging the hierarchy of Olympus to afford his Goddess (the female principle) a central position at the expense of the male. (Beware Apollo's wrath, Graves: the "godling" is more than front man for the "Ninefold Muse-Goddess.") Now, as a diversion, Mr. Graves has given us *The Twelve Caesars* of Suetonius in a good, dry, no-nonsense style; and, pleasantly enough, the Ancient Mother of Us All is remarkable only by her absence, perhaps a subtle criticism of an intensely masculine period in history.

Gaius Suetonius Tranquillus—lawyer and author of a dozen books, among them *Lives of Famous Whores* and *The Physical Defects of Mankind* (What was that about?)—worked for a time as private secretary to the Emperor Hadrian. Presumably it was during this period that he had access to the imperial archives, where he got the material for *The Twelve Caesars*, the only complete book of his to survive. Suetonius was born in A.D. 69, the year of the three Caesars Galba, Otho, Vitellius; and he grew up under the Flavians: Vespasian, Titus, Domitian, whom he deals with as contemporaries. He was also close enough in time to the first six Caesars to have known men who knew them intimately, at least from Tiberius on, and it is this place in time which gives such immediacy to his history.

Suetonius saw the world's history from 49 B.C. to A.D. 96 as the intimate narrative of twelve men wielding absolute power. With impressive curiosity he tracked down anecdotes, recording them dispassionately, despite a somewhat stylized reactionary bias. Like his fellow historians from Livy to the stuffy

68

but interesting Dion Cassius, Suetonius was a political reactionary to whom the old Republic was the time of virtue and the Empire, implicitly, was not. But it is not for his political convictions that we read Suetonius. Rather, it is his gift for telling us what we want to know. I am delighted to read that Augustus was under five feet seven, blond, wore lifts in his sandals to appear taller, had seven birthmarks and weak eyes; that he softened the hairs of his legs with hot walnut shells, and liked to gamble. Or to learn that the droll Vespasian's last words were: "Dear me, I must be turning into a god." ("Dear me" being Graves for *"Vae."*) The stories, true or not, are entertaining, and when they deal with sex startling, even to a post-Kinseyan.

Gibbon, in his stately way, mourned that of the twelve Caesars only Claudius was sexually "regular." From the sexual opportunism of Julius Caesar to the sadism of Nero to the doddering pederasty of Galba, the sexual lives of the Caesars encompassed every aspect of what our post-medieval time has termed "sexual abnormality." It would be wrong, however, to dismiss, as so many commentators have, the wide variety of Caesarean sensuality as simply the viciousness of twelve abnormal men. They were, after all, a fairly representative lot. They differed from us—and their contemporaries—only in the fact of power, which made it possible for each to act out his most recondite sexual fantasies. This is the psychological fascination of Suetonius. What will men so placed do? The answer, apparently, is anything and everything. Alfred Whitehead once remarked that one got the essence of a culture not by those things which were said at the time but by those things which were *not* said, the underlying assumptions of the society, too obvious to be stated. Now it is an underlying assumption of twentieth-century America that human beings are either heterosexual or, through some arresting of normal psychic growth, homosexual, with very little traffic back and forth. To us, the norm is heterosexual; the family is central; all else is deviation, pleasing or not depending on one's own tastes and moral preoccupations. Suetonius reveals a very dif-

ferent world. His underlying assumption is that man is bisexual and that given complete freedom to love—or, perhaps
more to the point in the case of the Caesars, to violate—others,
he will do so, going blithely from male to female as fancy
dictates. Nor is Suetonius alone in this assumption of man's
variousness. From Plato to the rise of Pauline Christianity,
which tried to put the lid on sex, it is explicit in classical
writing. Yet to this day Christian, Freudian and Marxian commentators have all decreed or ignored this fact of nature in the
interest each of a patented approach to the Kingdom of
Heaven. It is an odd experience for a contemporary to read of
Nero's simultaneous passion for both a man and a woman.
Something seems wrong. It must be one or the other, not both.
And yet this sexual eclecticism recurs again and again. And
though some of the Caesars quite obviously preferred women
to men (Augustus had a particular penchant for Nabokovian
nymphets), their sexual crisscrossing is extraordinary in its
lack of pattern. And one suspects that despite the stern moral
legislation of our own time human beings are no different. If
nothing else, Dr. Kinsey revealed in his dogged, arithmetical
way that we are all a good deal less predictable and bland than
anyone had suspected.

One of the few engaging aspects of the Julio-Claudians
was authorship. They all wrote; some wrote well. Julius
Caesar, in addition to his account of that famed crusade in
Gaul, wrote an *Oedipus*. Augustus wrote an *Ajax*, with
some difficulty. When asked by a friend what his *Ajax* had
been up to lately, Augustus sighed: "He has fallen not on
his sword, but wiped himself out on my sponge." Tiberius
wrote an *Elegy on the Death of Julius Caesar*. The scatter-
brained Claudius, a charmingly dim prince, was a devoted
pedant who tried to reform the alphabet. He was also
among the first to have a serious go at Etruscan history.
Nero of course is remembered as a poet. Julius Caesar and
Augustus were distinguished prose writers; each preferred
plain old-fashioned Latin. Augustus particularly disliked

what he called the "Asiatic" style, favored by, among others, his rival Marc Antony, whose speeches he found imprecise and "stinking of farfetched phrases."

Other than the fact of power, the twelve Caesars as men had little in common with one another. But that little was significant: a fear of the knife in the dark. Of the twelve, eight (perhaps nine) were murdered. As Domitian remarked not long before he himself was struck down: "Emperors are necessarily wretched men since only their assassination can convince the public that the conspiracies against their lives are real." In an understandable attempt to outguess destiny, they studied omens, cast horoscopes, and analyzed dreams (they were ingenious symbolists, anticipating Dr. Freud, himself a Roman buff). The view of life from Palatine Hill was not comforting, and though none of the Caesars was religious in our sense of the word, all inclined to the Stoic. It was Tiberius, with characteristic bleakness, who underscored their dangerous estate when he declared that it was Fate, not the gods, which ordered the lives of men.

Yet what, finally, was the effect of absolute power on twelve representative men? Suetonius makes it quite plain: disastrous. Caligula was certifiably mad. Nero, who started well, became progressively irrational. Even the stern Tiberius's character weakened. In fact, Tacitus, in covering the same period as Suetonius, observes: "Even after his enormous experience of public affairs, Tiberius was ruined and transformed by the violent influence of absolute power." Caligula gave the game away when he told a critic, "Bear in mind that I can treat anyone exactly as I please." And that cruelty which is innate in human beings, now given the opportunity to use others as toys, flowered monstrously in the Caesars. Suetonius's case history (and it is precisely that) of Domitian is particularly fascinating. An intelligent man of some charm, trained to govern, Domitian upon succeeding to the Principate at first contented himself with tearing the wings off flies, an infantile pastime which gradually palled until, inevitably, for flies he substituted men. His favorite game was to talk gently of mercy

71

to a nervous victim; then, once all fears had been allayed, execute him. Nor were the Caesars entirely unobjective about their bizarre position. There is an oddly revealing letter of Tiberius to the Senate which had offered to ensure in advance ratification of all his future deeds. Tiberius declined the offer: "So long as my wits do not fail me, you can count on the consistency of my behavior; but I should not like you to set the precedent of binding yourselves to approve a man's every action; for what if something happened to alter that man's character?" In terror of their lives, haunted by dreams and omens, giddy with dominion, it is no wonder that actual insanity was often the Caesarean refuge from a reality so intoxicating.

The unifying *Leitmotiv* in these lives is Alexander the Great. The Caesars were fascinated by him. The young Julius Caesar sighed enviously at his tomb. Augustus had the tomb opened and stared long at the conqueror's face. Caligula stole the breastplate from the corpse and wore it. Nero called his guard the "Phalanx of Alexander the Great." And the significance of this fascination? Power for the sake of power. Conquest for the sake of conquest. Earthly dominion as an end in itself: no Utopian vision, no dissembling, no hypocrisy. I knock you down; now *I* am king of the castle. Why should young Julius Caesar be envious of Alexander? It does not occur to Suetonius to explain. He assumes that *any* young man would like to conquer the world. And why did Julius Caesar, a man of first-rate mind, want the world? Simply, to have it. Even the resulting Pax Romana was not a calculated policy but a fortunate accident. Caesar and Augustus, the makers of the Principate, represent the naked will to power for its own sake. And though our own society has not much changed from the Roman (we may point with somber pride to Hitler and Stalin), we have, nevertheless, got so into the habit of dissembling motives, of denying certain dark constants of human behavior, that it is difficult to find a reputable American historian who will acknowledge the crude fact that a Franklin Roosevelt, say, wanted to be President merely to wield power, to be famed and to be feared. To learn this simple fact one must wade through a sea of evasions: history as sociology, leaders as teachers, bland benevolence as a motive force, when finally, power *is* an end to itself, and the instinctive urge to prevail the most important single human trait, the necessary force without which no city was built, no city destroyed. Yet many contemporary sociologists and religionists turned historians will propose, quite seriously: If there had not been a Julius Caesar then the *Zeitgeist* would have provided another like him, even though it is quite evident that had this particular Caesar not existed no one would have dared invent him. World events are the work of individuals whose motives are often frivolous, even casual. Had Claudius not wanted an easy conquest so that he might celebrate a triumph at Rome, Britain would not have been conquered in A.D. 44. If Britain had not been colonized in the first century . . . the chain of causality is plain.

One understands of course why the role of the individual in history is instinctively played down by a would-be egalitarian society. We are, quite naturally, afraid of being victimized by reckless adventurers. To avoid this we have created the myth of the ineluctable mass ("other-directedness") which governs all. Science, we are told, is not a matter of individual inquiry but of collective effort. Even the surface storminess of our elections disguises a fundamental indifference to human personality: if not this man, then that one; it's all the same; life will go on. Up to a point there is some virtue in this; and though none can deny that there is a prevailing grayness in our placid land, it is certainly better to be non-ruled by mediocrities than enslaved by Caesars. But to deny the dark nature of human personality is not only fatuous but dangerous. For in our insistence on the surrender of private will ("inner-directedness") to a conception of the human race as some teeming bacteria in the stream of time, unaffected by individual deeds, we have been made vulnerable not only to boredom, to that sense of meaninglessness which more than anything else is characteristic of our age, but vulnerable to the first messiah who offers the young and bored some splendid prospect, some Caesarean certainty. That is the political danger, and it is a real one.

Most of the world today is governed by Caesars. Men are more and more treated as things. Torture is ubiquitous. And, as Sartre wrote in his preface to Henri Alleg's chilling book about Algeria, "Anybody, at any time, may equally find himself victim or executioner." Suetonius, in holding up a mirror to those Caesars of diverting legend, reflects not only them but ourselves: half-tamed creatures, whose great moral task it is to hold in balance the angel and the monster within—for we are both, and to ignore this duality is to invite disaster.

NORMAN MAILER'S
SELF-ADVERTISEMENTS

I first heard of Norman Mailer in the spring of 1948, just before *The Naked and the Dead* was published. I remember thinking meanly: So somebody did it. Each previous war had had its big novel, yet so far there had been none for our war, though I knew that a dozen busy friends and acquaintances were grimly taking out tickets in the Grand War Novel Lottery. I had debated doing one myself and had (I still think) done something better: a small cool hard novel about men on the periphery of the action. *Williwaw* was written when I was nineteen and easily the cleverest young fox ever to know how to disguise his ignorance and make a virtue of his limitations. (What an attractive form the self-advertisement is: one could go on forever relighting one's image!) Not till I began *The City and the Pillar* did I begin to get bored with playing safe.

I took to the field and have often wondered since, in the course of many excursions, defeats, alarums and ambushes, what it might have been like to have been a safe shrewd custodian of one's talent, playing from strength. I did not suspect then that the ambitious, rather cold-blooded young contemporary who had set out to write the big war novel would one day be in the same fix I was. Not safe. Not wise. Not admired. A fellow victim of the Great Golfer's Age, then no more than a murmur of things to come in the Golfer's murmurous heart.

My first reaction to *The Naked and the Dead* was: it's a fake. A clever, talented, admirably executed fake. I have not changed my opinion of the book since, though I have considerably changed my opinion of Mailer, as he himself has changed. Now I confess I have never read all of *The Naked and the Dead*. I do recall a fine description of soldiers carrying a dying man down a mountain (done almost as well as the same scene in Malraux's earlier work). Yet every time I got going in the narrative I would find myself stopped cold by a set of made-up, predictable characters taken not from life, but from the same novels all of us had read, and informed by a naïveté which was at its worst when Mailer went into his Time-Machine and wrote those passages which resemble nothing so much as smudged carbons of a Dos Passos work.

Sourly, from a distance, that year I watched the fame of Mailer quite surpass John Horne Burns and myself, the heroes of the previous year. I should explain for those who have come in late or were around then but inattentive that the O.K. List of writers in 1947 and 1948 was John Horne Burns, Calder Willingham and myself. Capote and Mailer were added in 1948. Willingham was soon dropped; then Burns (my own favorite) sank, and by 1949 in the aftermath of *The City and the Pillar* I too departed the O.K. List.

"I had the freak of luck to start high on the mountain, and go down sharp while others were passing me"—so Mailer wrote, describing the time after *Barbary Shore* when he unexpectedly joined the rest of us down on the plain. Now the descent, swift or slow, is not agreeable; but on the other hand it is not as tragic as Mailer seems to find it. To be demoralized by the withdrawal of public success (a process as painful in America as the withdrawal of a drug from an addict) is to grant too easily a victory to the society one has attempted to criticize, affect, change, reform. It is clearly unreasonable to expect to be cherished by those one assaults. It is also childish, in the deepest sense of being a child, ever to expect justice. There is none beneath our moon. One can only hope not to be destroyed entirely by injustice and, to put it cynically, one can very often flourish through an injustice obtaining in one's favor. What matters finally is not the world's judgment of oneself but one's own judgment of the world. Any writer who lacks this final arrogance will not survive very long in America.

That wide graveyard of stillborn talents which contains so much of the brief ignoble history of American letters is a tribute to the power of a democracy to destroy its critics, brave fools and passionate men. If there is anything in Mailer's new book which alarms me, it is his obsession with public success. He is running for President, as he puts it. Yet though his best and most interesting works have been unjustly attacked, he should realize that in this most inequitable of worlds his one worldly success was not a very good book, that *The Naked and the Dead* is redolent of "ambition" (in the Mary McCarthy sense of the word—pejorative, needless to say) and a young man's will to be noticed. Mailer himself nearly takes this view: "I may as well confess that by December 8th or 9th of 1941 ... I was worrying darkly whether it would be more likely that a great war novel would be written about Europe or the Pacific." Ambition and the day coincided and a success was made. Yet it is much less real a book than Burns's *The Gallery*, or even some of the stories of Robert Lowry, works which had the virtue of being felt, possessed entirely by the men who made them, not created out of stern ambition and dogged competence. But, parenthetically, most war books are inadequate. War tends to be too much for any writer, especially one whose personality is already half obliterated by life in a democracy. Even the aristocrat Tolstoi, at a long remove in time, stretched his genius to the breaking point to encompass men and war and the thrust of history in a single vision.

Ernest Hemingway in *A Farewell to Arms* did a few good descriptions, but his book, too, is a work of ambition, in which can be seen the beginning of the careful, artful, immaculate idiocy of tone that since has marked both his prose and his legend as he has declined into the sort of fame which, at moments I hope are weak, Mailer seems to crave.

But it is hard for American writers not to measure themselves according to the standards of their time and place. I recall a conversation with Stephen Spender when I lapsed, unconsciously, into the national preoccupation. Some writer had unexpectedly failed, not gone on, blown up. Spender said rather pointedly, "The difference in England is that they want us to be distinguished, to be good." We order things differently; although our example is contagious, for in recent years the popular British press has discovered writers in a way ours never has. Outside the gossip column and the book page no writer except Hemingway is ever mentioned as news in the American press, but let the most obscure young English novelist attack the Establishment and there are headlines in London. Mailer can denounce Eisenhower as much as he likes in *Dissent* but the readers of the *Daily News* will never know Mailer's name, much less the quality of his anger. Publicity for the American writer is of the "personality" kind: a photograph in *Harper's Bazaar*, bland television appearances . . . the writer as minor movie star, and as unheeded.

Mailer and I finally met in 1954. I had just published my last, or perhaps I should say latest, novel, *Messiah*, which was ignored in America. (If it were not for the continuing interest of Europe, especially England, a great many of our writers would not survive as well as they do their various seasons of neglect.) I liked Mailer, though I am afraid my first impression of him was somewhat guarded. I am suspicious of people who make speeches at me, and he is a born cocktail-party orator. I have not the slightest recollection of what we talked about. I do recall telling him that I admired *Barbary Shore*, and he was shrewd enough to observe that probably I had been driven to read it to see if it was really as bad as everyone thought. Of his three novels I find it the most interesting and the least diffuse. It is hallucinatory writing of a kind Mailer attempted, as far as I know, only that one time; and though I think his talents are essentially naturalistic, he does seem again in his new novel (judging from the advance samples he displays in *Advertisements for Myself*) to be trying for that revelation through willful distortion which he achieved in *Barbary Shore*. One is curious to see the result.

I have gone into the chronology of Mailer's days and mine because they run parallel, occasionally crossing and because the book he has just published is, in effect, an autobiography covering more or less his entire career with particular attention to the days of the Golfer's dull terror. Mailer gives us his life and his work together, and therefore it is impossible to review the book without attempting to make some estimate of both his character and the corpus of his work, the tension of his present and the shape of his future. Mailer is sly to get himself all this attention, but I must point out that it is a very dangerous move for an artist to expose himself so completely. Indeed, in other times it would have been fatal for an artist not yet full grown to show us his sores and wounds, real and illusory strengths. Until very recently the artist was a magician who did his magic in public view but kept himself and his effects a matter of mystery. We know *now* of Flaubert's suffering, both emotional and aesthetic, during the days of his work, but it is hard to imagine what would have happened if the court which prosecuted *Madame Bovary* could have presented as evidence a volume of his letters. In effect, Mailer has anticipated his own posterity. He is giving us now the storms and the uncertainties, private and public, which he has undergone. He has armed the enemy and not entirely pleased his allies.

However, it may be possible to get away with this sort of thing today, for we live in the age of the confession. What Mailer has done is no different in kind from what those deranged and fallen actresses have accomplished in ghost-written memoirs where, with a shrewd eye on the comeback trail, they pathetically confess their sins to Demos, receiving for their tears the absolution of a culture obscenely interested in gossip. I suspect Mailer may create more interest in himself by having made this "clean breast of it" than he would have got by publishing a distinguished novel. The audience no longer consumes novels, but it does devour personalities. Yet what happens after one is eaten? Is one regurgitated? Or does the audience move on to its next dinner of scandal and tears, its previous meal absorbed and forgotten?

But despite a nice but small gift for self-destruction, Mailer is uncommonly adroit, with an eye to the main chance (the writer who lacks this instinct is done for in America; excellence is not nearly enough). I noted with some amusement that, despite his air of candor, he makes no new enemies in this book. He scores off those who are lost to him anyway, thus proving that essentially the work is politic. His confessions, when not too disingenuous, are often engaging and always interesting, as he tries to record his confusions. For Mailer does not begin to know what he believes or is or wants. His drive seems to be toward power of a religio-political kind. He is a messiah without real hope of paradise on earth or in heaven, and with no precise mission except that dictated by his ever-changing temperament. I am not sure, finally, that he should be a novelist at all, or even a writer, despite formidable gifts. He is too much a demagogue; he swings from one position of cant to another with an intensity that is visceral rather than intellectual. He is all fragments and pieces. He appears to be looking for an identity, and often it seems that he believes crude celebrity will give it to him again. The author of *The Naked and the Dead*, though not the real Mailer, was at least an identifiable surrogate, and duly celebrated. But Mailer was quickly bored with the war-novelist role, and as soon as possible he moved honorably to a new position: radical politics, in the hope that through Marxist action he might better identify himself to us and to himself. But politics failed him, too. Nor is the new Mailer, prophet of Hip and celebrator of sex and its connection with time, apt to interest him or us for very long.

I also noted at moments toward the end of this book that a reaction was setting in: Mailer started using military allusions. "Back in the Philippines, we . . ."—that sort of thing. And there were references to patrols, ambushes. It was startling. Most of our generation was in the war, usually ingloriously, yet I have never heard a contemporary make any reference to it in a personal way. The war to most of us was a profound irrelevance; traumatic for some, perhaps, but for most no more than an interruption. When the 1959 Mailer reminds us that he was a rifleman on Luzon, I get embarrassed for him and hope he is not going back to his first rôle to get the attention he wants.

Now for the book itself. It is a collection of stories, essays, notes, newspaper columns and part of a play. It begins with his first story at Harvard and ends with part of his new novel. I particularly liked two short stories. "The Language of Men" tells of the problems of an army cook who has an abstract passion for excellence as well as a need for the approbation of the indifferent men who eat what he cooks. His war with them and himself and his will to excel are beautifully shown and in many ways make one of the best stories of its kind I have read, certainly preferable to Hemingway's *The Old Man and the Sea*, which it resembles in theme. But where Hemingway was pretentious and external, Mailer is particular and works with gentle grace from within his characters. The other story, "The Patron Saint of Macdougal Alley," is an amusing portrait of an archetypal drifter, and I think it is of permanent value: we have had this sort of fool in every age, but I have not seen him done quite so well in our day.

By and large, excepting "The White Negro," I did not like the essays and the newspaper columns. Mailer is forever shouting at us that he is about to tell us something we must know or has just told us something revelatory and we failed to hear him or that he will, God grant his poor abused brain and body just one more chance, get through to us so that we will *know*. Actually, when he does approach a point he shifts into a swelling, throbbing rhetoric which is not easy to read but usually has something to do with love and sex and the horror of our age and the connection which must be made between time and sex (the image this bit of rhetoric suggests to me is a limitless gray sea of time with a human phallus desperately poking at a corner of it). He is at his best (who is not?) when discussing himself. He is a born defendant. The piece about getting *The Deer Park* published is especially good, and depressing for what it reveals about our society. But, finally, in every line he writes, despite the bombast, there is uncertainty: Who am I? What do I want? What am I saying? He is Thomas Wolfe but with a conscience. Wolfe's motive for writing was perfectly clear: he wanted fame; he wanted to taste the whole earth, to name all the rivers. Mailer has the same passion for fame but he has a good deal more sense of responsibility and he sees that the thing is always in danger of spinning down into meaninglessness. Nothing is quite enough: art, sex, politics, drugs, God, mind. He is sure to get tired of Hip very soon. Sex will be a dead end for him, because sex is the one purely existential act (to misuse, as he always does, a fashionable adjective of the forties). Sex is. There is nothing more to be done about it. Sex builds no roads, writes no novels, and sex certainly gives no meaning to anything in life but itself. I have often thought that much of D. H. Lawrence's self-lacerating hysteria toward the end of his life must have come out of some "blood knowledge" that the cruel priapic god was mad, bad and dangerous to know, and, finally, not even a palliative to the universal strangeness.

Perhaps what has gone wrong in Mailer, and in many of our fellow clerks, is the sense that human beings to flourish must be possessed by one idea, a central meaning to which all experience can be related. To be, in Isaiah Berlin's bright metaphor, hedgehog rather than fox. Yet the human mind is not capable of this kind of exclusivity. We are none of us hedgehogs or foxes, but both simultaneously. The human mind is in continual flux, and personality is simply a sum of those attitudes which most often repeat themselves in recognizable actions. It is naïve and dangerous to try to impose on the human mind any system of thought which lays claim to finality. Very few first-rate writers have ever subordinated their own apprehension of a most protean reality to a man-made system of thought. Tolstoi's famous attempt in *War and Peace* nearly wrecked that beautiful work. Ultimately, not Christ, not Marx, not Freud, despite their pretensions, has the final word to say about the fact of being human. And those who take solemnly the words of other men as absolute are, in the deepest sense, maiming their own sensibilities and controverting the evidence of their own senses in a fashion which may be comforting to a terrified man but disastrous for an artist.

One of the few sad results of the collapse of the Judeo-Christian ethical and religious systems has been the displacement of those who are absolutists by temperament and would in earlier times have been rabbis, priests, systematic philosophers. As the old Establishment of the West crumbles, the absolutists have turned to literature and the arts, and one by one the arts in the twentieth century have become hieratic. Serious literature has become religion, as Matthew Arnold foresaw. Those who once would have been fulfilled in Talmudic debate or suffered finely between the pull of Rome and the Church of England have turned to the writing of novels and, worse, to the criticism of novels. Now I am not sure that the novel, though it is many things, is particularly suited to didacticism. It is certainly putting an undesirable weight upon it to use it as a pretext for sermons or the resuscitation of antique religious myths. Works of fiction, at best, create not arguments but worlds, and a world by definition is an attitude toward a complex of experience, not a single argument or theme, syllogistically proposed. In the nineteenth century most of our critics (and many of our novelists) would have been writing books of sermons and quarreling over points of doctrine. With religion gone out of the intellectual world they now write solemnly and uneasily about novels; they are clearly impatient with the vulgar vitality of the art, and were it not that they had one another's books about books to analyze, I suspect many of them would despair and falter. The novelists don't seem very bright to the critics, while their commentaries seem irrelevant to the novelists. Yet each affects the other; and those writers who are unduly eager for fame and acceptance will write novels which they hope might interest "religious"-minded critics. The results range from the subliterary bleating of the Beats to Mailer's portentous cry which takes the form of: I am the way and the life ever after, crucify me, you hackers, for mine is a ritual death! Take my flesh and my blood, partake of me and *know* mysteries . . .! And the curious thing is that they *will* crucify him; they will partake of his flesh; yet no mystery will be revealed. For the priests have created the gods, and they are all of them ritual harvest gods.

I was most struck by a comment of André Gide in the posthumous *Ainsi Soit-il:* "It is affectation that makes so many of today's writings, often even the best among them, unbearable to me. The author takes on a tone that is not natural to him." Of course it is sometimes the work of a lifetime for an artist to discover who he is and it is true that a great deal of good art results from the trying on of masks, the affectation of a persona not one's own. But it seems to me that most of my contemporaries, including Mailer, are—as Gide suggests—desperately trying to convince themselves and the audience that they are something they are not. There is even a certain embarrassment about writing novels at all. Telling stories does seem a silly occupation for one fully grown; yet to be a philosopher or a religious is not easy when one is making a novel. Also, in a society such as ours, where there is no moral, political or religious center, the temptation to fill the void is irresistible. There is the empty throne, so . . . *seize* the crown! Who would not be a king or high priest in such an age? And the writers, each in his own way, are preoccupied with power. Some hope to achieve place through good deportment. Universities are filled with poets and novelists conducting demure and careful lives in imitation of Eliot and Forster and those others who (through what *seems* to have been discretion) made it. Outside the universities one finds the buccaneers who mean to seize the crown by force, blunt Bolingbrokes to the Academy's gentle Richards.

Mailer is a Bolingbroke, a born usurper. He will raise an army anywhere, live off the country as best he can, helped by a devoted underground, even assisted at brief moments by rival claimants like myself. Yet when all is said, none of this is the way to live. And it is not a way (at least it makes the way harder) to create a literature. If it helps Hemingway to think of literature as a Golden Gloves Tournament with himself pounding Maupassant to the mat or fighting Stendhal to a draw, then no doubt the fantasy has been of some use. But there is also evidence that the preoccupation with actual political power is a great waste of time. Mailer has had the honesty to confess that his own competitiveness has wasted him as he worries about reviewers and bad publicity and the seemingly spiteful successes of other novelists. Yet all the time he knows perfectly well that writers are not in competition with one another. The real enemy is the audience, which grows more and more indifferent to literature, an audience which can be reached only by phenomena, by superior pornographies or willfully meretricious accounts of the way we live now. No serious American novelist has ever had any real sense of audience. C. P. Snow made the point that he would, given a choice, prefer to be a writer in England to a writer in America because, for better or worse, the Establishment of his country would read him and know him as he knew them, as the Greek dramatists knew and were known by their city's audience. One cannot imagine the American president, any American president, reading a work by a serious contemporary American writer. This lack of response is to me at the center of Mailer's desperation. He is a public writer, not a private artist; he wants to influence those who are alive at this time, but they will not notice him even when he is good. So each time he speaks he must become more bold, more loud, put on brighter motley and shake more foolish bells. *Anything* to get their attention, and finally (and this could be his tragedy) so much energy is spent in getting the indifferent ear to listen that when the time comes for him to speak there may be not enough strength or creative imagination left him to say what he *knows*. Exhausted, he becomes like Louis Lambert in Balzac's curious novel of the visionary-artist who, having seen straight through to the heart of the mystery, dies mad, murmuring: "The angels are white."

Yet of all my contemporaries I retain the greatest affection for Mailer as a force and as an artist. He is a man whose faults, though many, add to rather than subtract from the sum of his natural achievement. There is more virtue in his failures than in most small, premeditated successes which, in Cynic's phrase, "debase currency." Mailer, in all that he does, whether he does it well or ill, is honorable, and that is the highest praise I can give any writer in this piping time.

The Nation, January 2, 1960

PRESIDENT KENNEDY

Until last month (March, 1961), I had not been at the White House since 1957, when I was asked to compose a speech for President Eisenhower.*

At that time the White House was as serene as a resort hotel out of season. The corridors were empty. In the various offices of the Executive (wings contiguous to the White House proper) quiet gray men in waistcoats talked to one another in low-pitched voices.

The only color, or choler, curiously enough, was provided by President Eisenhower himself. Apparently his temper was easily set off; he scowled when he stalked the corridors; the Smile was seldom in evidence. Fortunately, Eisenhower was not at the White House often enough to disturb that tranquillity which prevailed, no matter what storms at home, what tragedies abroad.

*Never delivered.

Last month I returned to the White House (a defeated Democratic politician, full of pluck) to find the twentieth century, for good or ill, installed. The corridors are filled with eager youthful men, while those not young are revitalized.

As Secretary of Commerce Luther Hodges (at sixty-two the oldest member of the Cabinet) remarked: "There I was a few months ago, thinking my life was over. I'd retired to a college town. Now . . . well, that fellow in there" (he indicated the President's office) "he calls me in the morning, calls me at noon, calls me at night: *Why don't we try this? Have you considered that?* Then to top it all he just now asks me: *Where do you get your suits from?* I tell you I'm a young man again."

In the White House press room reporters are permanently gathered. Photographers are on constant alert and television cameramen stand by, for news is made at all hours.

The affection of the press for Kennedy is a phenomenon, unique in presidential politics. There is of course the old saw that he was a newspaperman himself (briefly, for INS) and also that he is a bona fide intellectual (on the other hand, the working press is apt to be anti-intellectual); but, finally, and perhaps more to the point, Kennedy is candid with the press in a highly personal way. He talks to journalists easily. There is no pomp; there is little evasion in his manner; he involves them directly in what he is doing. His wit is pleasingly sardonic.

Most important, until Kennedy, it was impossible for anyone under fifty (or for an intellectual of any age) to identify himself with the President. The intellectual establishment of the country opted for "alienation," the cant word of the 1940's and 1950's, and even those who approved of this or that president's deeds invariably regarded the men set over us by the electorate as barbarians (Truman's attack on modern painting, Roosevelt's breezy philistinism, Eisenhower's inability to express himself coherently on any subject).

For twenty years the culture and the mind of the United States ignored politics. Many never voted; few engaged in active politics. Now everything has changed. From Kenneth Galbraith to Robert Frost the intellectual establishment is listened to and even, on occasion, engaged to execute policy.*

Close to, Kennedy looks older than his photographs. The outline is slender and youthful, but the face is heavily lined for his age. On the upper lip are those tiny vertical lines characteristic of a more advanced age. He is usually tanned from the sun, while his hair is what lady novelists call "chestnut," beginning to go gray. His eyes are very odd. They are, I think, a murky, opaque blue, "interested," as Gertrude Stein once said of Hemingway's eyes, "not interesting"; they give an impression of flatness, while long blond eyelashes screen expression at will. His stubby boy fingers tend to drum nervously on tables, on cups and glasses. He is immaculately dressed; although, disconcertingly, occasional white chest hairs curl over his collar.

The smile is charming even when it is simulated for the public. Franklin Roosevelt set an unhappy tradition of happy warriors, and ever since his day our politicians are obliged to beam and grin and simper no matter how grave the occasion. Recently, at a public dinner, I had a thoughtful conversation with Harry Truman. He was making a particularly solemn point when suddenly, though his tone did not change, his face jerked abruptly into a euphoric grin, all teeth showing. I thought he had gone mad, until I noticed photographers had appeared in the middle distance.

As for Kennedy's personality, he is very much what he seems. He is withdrawn, observant, icily objective in crisis, aware of the precise value of every card dealt him. Intellectually, he is dogged rather than brilliant.

*Alas. The intellectual establishment can take a great deal of credit for the attempted conquest of Asia and the subsequent collapse of America's imperial pretension. The end may be a good if serendipitous thing. Unfortunately, to achieve it, the Bundys and the Goodwins and the Rostows helped shatter those fragile balances which made the Republic, on good days, a place to take pride in. If Kennedy had devoted more time to sex and less to speed-reading the memos of the clerks, he might still be alive, a small matter, not to mention the large matter of saving the lives of those hundreds of thousands of Asiatics and Americans who died to make Harvard Yard Palatine Hill.

Over the years I've occasionally passed books on to him, which I thought would interest him (including such arcana as Byzantine economy). Not only does he read them but he will comment on what he's read when I see him next (our meetings are casual, at long intervals, and I am happy to say that I have no influence).

After his defeat for the Vice-Presidential nomination in 1956, he was amused when I suggested that he might feel more cheerful if every day he were to recite to himself while shaving the names of the vice-presidents of the United States, a curiously dim gallery of minor politicians. Also, somewhat mischievously, I suggested that he read *Coriolanus* to see if he might find Shakespeare's somewhat dark view of democracy consoling. Mrs. Kennedy and he read it aloud one foggy day at Hyannisport. Later he made the point with some charm that Shakespeare's knowledge of the democratic process was, to say the least, limited.

On another occasion, I gave him the manuscript of a play of mine (*The Best Man*) whose setting was a nominating convention for the Presidency. He read the play with interest; his comments were shrewd. I recall one in particular, because I used it.

"Whenever," he said, "a politician means to give you the knife at a convention, the last thing he'll say to you, as he leaves the room, is: 'Now look, Jack, if there's *anything* I can do for you, you just let me know!' That's the euphemism for 'You're dead.' "

Kennedy's relationships tend to be compartmentalized. There are cronies who have nothing to do with politics whom he sees for relaxation. There are advisers whom he sees politically but not socially. The only occasion where personal friendship and public policy appear to have overlapped was in his appointment of the perhaps not distinguished Earl Smith (our envoy to Cuba at the time of the Batista debacle) as ambassador to Switzerland. The Swiss, who were acting for the United States in Havana, complained loudly. To save the President embarrassment, Smith withdrew. With chilling correctness, Kennedy is reported to have called in the Swiss Ambassador to Washington and given him a lesson in international diplomacy (i.e. you do not criticize publicly an ambassadorial appointment without first apprising the Chief of State privately). The ambassador left the White House shaken and bemused. Immediately afterwards, an aide entered the President's office to find him beaming. "That was very satisfying," he said.

Kennedy is unique among recent Presidents in many ways. For one thing, he has ended (wistfully, one hopes forever) the idea that the presidency is a form of brevet rank to be given a man whose career has been distinguished in some profession other than politics or, if to a politician, one whose good years are past, the White House being merely a place to provide some old pol with a golden Indian summer.

Yet the job today is literally killing, and despite his youth, Kennedy may very well not survive. A matter, one suspects, of no great concern to him. He is fatalistic about himself. His father recalls with a certain awe that when his son nearly died during the course of a spinal operation he maintained a complete serenity: if he was meant to die at that moment he would die and complaint was useless.

Like himself, the men Kennedy has chosen to advise him have not reached any great height until now. They must prove themselves *now*. Government service will be the high point of their lives, not an agreeable reward for success achieved elsewhere. Few men have the energy or capacity to conduct successfully two separate careers in a lifetime, an obvious fact ignored by most presidents in their search, often prompted by vanity or a sense of public relations, for celebrated advisers.

Nearly half the electorate was eager to find Kennedy and his regime "intellectual," given to fiscal irresponsibility and creeping socialism. (There is, by the way, despite the cries of demagogues, no operative Left in the United States. We are divided about evenly between conservatives and reactionaries.) But now, having experienced his Administration, it is evident even to the most suspicious of the Radical Right that

Kennedy is not an adventurous reformer of the body politic, if only because this is not the time for such a reformation, and he knows it.

Essentially, he is a pragmatist with a profound sense of history, working within a generally liberal context.* Since the United States is in no immediate danger of economic collapse, and since there is no revolutionary party of Left or Right waiting to seize power, our politics are firmly of the Center. The problems of the nation are a lagging economic growth, which under an attentive Administration can be corrected, and foreign affairs, where the United States *vis-à-vis* Russia remains a perhaps insoluble problem, but one to which Kennedy is addressing himself with a commendable lack of emotion.

Perhaps Kennedy's most unusual gift is an objectivity which extends to himself. He can discuss his own motives with a precision not usual in public men, who tend to regard themselves tenderly and according to the rhetoric of the day.

Before the primaries last spring, when his main opponent for the nomination was the attractively exuberant Senator Hubert Humphrey, Kennedy remarked privately that the contest was really one of temperaments, of "images," and though he confessed he did not have the Senator's passion for liberal reform, he did not think that was what the country in its present mood wanted or needed. Kennedy admitted to being less interesting and less dramatic than Humphrey, but for this time and place he felt he himself would prove more appealing, a correct if unflattering self-estimate.

Kennedy is certainly the most accessible and least ceremonious of recent presidents. After last month's conference with the Canadian Prime Minister, the two men appeared in front of the White House for the usual television statement. Kennedy said his few words. Then he turned to the Prime

---

*This is a fairly accurate description, subtracting the word "profound." It was given me by Richard Goodwin, the Iago of the sixties. Today the same description could, of course, be used to describe Richard Nixon.

Minister and said: "Now you make your statement while I go back to the office and get your coat." And the Prime Minister made his statement and the President got his coat for him.

A few days later, when Eleanor Roosevelt came to see him at the White House, he insisted that she allow him to show her her old home. As they were about to leave his office, he motioned for her to precede him through the door.

Mrs. Roosevelt drew back. "No," she said. "You go first. You are the president."

He laughed. "I keep forgetting." With her lovely, deliberate blandness, she replied, "But you must *never* forget."

Perhaps the most distressing aspect of the last Administration was President Eisenhower's open disdain of politics and his conviction that "politician" was a dirty word. This tragic view is shared even now by the majority of the American electorate, explaining the General's continuing appeal.* Time and again during those years one used to hear: "O.K., so he is a lousy president, but thank God he's not a politician!"

Kennedy, on the other hand, regards politics as an honorable, perhaps inevitable, profession in a democracy. Not only is he a master of politics, but he also takes a real pleasure in power. He is restless; he wants to know everything; he wanders into other people's offices at odd hours; he puts in a ten-hour office day; he reads continuously, even in the bathtub.

Most interesting of all, and the greatest break with tradition, have been his visits to the houses of friends in Washington, many of them journalists. Ever since the first protocol drawn up for George Washington, the president seldom goes visiting and never returns calls. Kennedy has changed that. He goes where he pleases; he talks candidly; he tries to meet people who otherwise might never get to him through the elaborate maze of the White House, in which, even during the most enlightened Administration, unpleasant knowledge can be kept from the president.

Inevitably, a president is delivered into the hands of an

---

*Ike wasn't so wrong.

inner circle which, should he not be a man of considerable alertness and passion, tends to cut him off from reality. Eisenhower was a classic case. It was painfully evident at press conferences that he often had no knowledge of important actions taken by the government in his name; worse still, he was perhaps the only president not to read newspapers. The result was that when crises occurred, despite good intentions, he was never sufficiently aware of the nature of any problem to have a useful opinion as to its solution.

Only by constant study and getting about can a president be effective. As Harry Truman once remarked, despite the great power of the office, it is remarkably difficult to get anything done. "You tell 'em what you want and what happens? Nothing! You have to tell 'em five times."

Most presidential staffs inevitably take advantage of their president, realizing that in the rush of any day's business he will make many decisions and requests which he cannot possibly follow up. Kennedy, however, has already shown an unusual ability to recall exactly what he requested on any subject, and the impression he gives is of a man who means to be obeyed by his staff.

"He is deliberately drawing all the threads of executive power to himself," remarked one adviser. The cumbersome staff system of the Eisenhower Administration has been abandoned in favor of highly personal relationships between President and advisers. No one's function is ever clearly defined. The president moves men from project to project, testing them, extracting new points of view.

Not only is this a useful way of getting the most out of his staff, but it also ensures, rather slyly, Kennedy's own unique position at the center of the web of power: he alone can view and manipulate the entire complex of domestic and international policy. No one in his Administration may circumvent him, because none can master more than a part of the whole.

This ultimate knowledge of the whole is power, and, finally, the exercise of power is an art like any other. There is no doubt of John Kennedy's mastery of that art. He is a rare combination of intelligence, energy and opportunism. Most important, he is capable of growth. He intends to be great.

What he will accomplish depends largely upon his ability to rally the bored and cynical Western world, to fire the imagination of a generation taught never to think of "we" but only of "I." There are fragile signs (the warm response to the Peace Corps) and favorable omens (popular approbation reflected in polls) that a torpid society has at last been stirred by its youthful leader. If true, it is in the nick of time. Civilizations are seldom granted a second chance.

London *Sunday Telegraph*, April 9, 1961

I liked Kennedy personally to the end. But I did not like his presidency from the day he invaded Cuba to the last month of his life when he turned hot the cold war in Vietnam. Kennedy misplayed his cards from the beginning. Khrushchev frightened him at Vienna. Because Republicans would always suspect a Democratic president of being not only a nigger-lover but a fellow traveler, Kennedy's response was predictable. Secretly, I think he thought war was fun. He was in good American company. See p. 266.

JOHN DOS PASSOS
AT MIDCENTURY

There is a terrible garrulousness in most American writing, a
legacy no doubt of the Old Frontier. But where the inspired
tall-talesman of simpler days went on and on, never quite
certain and never much caring what the next load of breath
might contain, at his best he imparted with a new demotic
flare the sense of life living. Unfortunately, since these first
originals the main line of the American novel has reverted to
incontinent heirs, to the gabblers, maunderers, putters-in of
everything. Watch: Now the man goes into the barbershop
and sees four chairs with two people in them, one with a beard
and the other reading a comic book about Bugs Bunny, then
the man sits in the chair, he thinks of baby's first curls shorn
and (if he's been analyzed) of castration, as he lists for us the
labels on every bottle of hair tonic on the shelf, records every
word the barber has to say about the Series—all the time
wondering what happened to the stiff white brush smelling of
stale powder they used to brush the back of your neck with.

. . . To get that haircut the true gabbler will devote a dozen pages of random description and dialogue none of which finally has anything to do with his novel's theme, assuming there is one. It was included at that moment because the gabbler happened to think of a visit to a barber, the way good old Tom Wolfe once named all the rivers of America because he felt like it.

For every Scott Fitzgerald concerned with the precise word and the selection of relevant incident, there are a hundred American writers, many well regarded, who appear to believe that one word is just as good as another, and that anything which pops into the head is worth putting down. It is an attitude unique to us and deriving, I would suspect, from a corrupted idea of democracy: if everything and everyone is of equal value, then any word is as good as any other word to express a meaning, which in turn is no more valuable than any other meaning. Or to put it another way, if everyone is equally valuable, then anything the writer (who is valuable) writes must be of value, so why attempt selection? This sort of writing, which I call demotic, can be observed at its purest in the recent work of Jack Kerouac.

Thackeray said of Smollett, "I fancy he did not invent much." There it all is: the two kinds of writer, underscored by the choice of verb. To fancy. To invent. Most of our writers tend to be recorders. They tell us what happened last summer, why the marriage went wrong, how they lost custody of the children, how much they drank and whom they laid, and if they are demoticists the task of ordering that mass of words and impressions put between covers will be the reader's. Of all the recorders of what happened last summer—or last decade —John Dos Passos is the most dogged. Not since the brothers Goncourt has there been such a dedication to getting down exactly what happened, and were it not for his political passions he might indeed have been a true camera to our time. He invents little; he fancies less. He is often good when he tells you something through which he himself has lived, and noted. He is well equipped to be a good social critic, which is the role he has cast for himself: conscience to the Republic, stern reminder of good ways lost, of useful ways not taken.

With what seems defiance, the first two pages of John Dos Passos's new novel *Midcentury* are taken up with the titles of his published work, proudly spaced, seventeen titles to the first page, sixteen to the second: thirty-three books, the work of some forty years. The list is testament to Dos Passos's gallantry, to his stubbornness, and to his worldly and artistic failure. To paraphrase Hollywood's harsh wisdom, the persistent writer is only as good as his last decade. Admired extravagantly in the '20's and '30's, Dos Passos was largely ignored in the '40's and '50's, his new works passed over either in silence or else noted with that ritual sadness we reserve for those whose promise to art was not kept. He himself is aware of his own dilemma, and in a recent novel called *The Great Days* he recorded with brave if bewildered objectivity a decline similar to his own. I shall not try to ring the more obvious changes suggested by his career. Yet I should note that there is something about Dos Passos which makes a fellow writer unexpectedly protective, partly out of compassion for the man himself, and partly because the fate of Dos Passos is a chilling reminder to those condemned to write for life that this is the way it almost always is in a society which, to put it tactfully, has no great interest in the development of writers, a process too slow for the American temperament. As a result our literature is rich with sprinters but significantly short of milers.

Right off, let me say that unlike most of Dos Passos's more liberal critics, I never cared much for his early work even at its best. On the other hand, I have always enjoyed, even admired, the dottiness of his politics. His political progress from Radical Left to Radical Right seems to me very much in the American grain, and only the most humorless of doctrinaire liberals should be horrified. After all, it is not as if Dos Passos were in any way politically significant. Taken lightly, he gives pleasure. There is a good deal of inadvertent comedy in his admiration for such gorgeous Capitoline geese as Barry Goldwater, while page after page of *Midcentury* is vintage Old

Guard demagoguery. For instance there is that old Bourbon comforter "Roosevelt's war" for the Second World War, while, every now and then, a passage seems almost to parody Wisconsin's late wonder:

Hitler's invasion of the Soviet Union cut off support from the Communists. Stalin needed quick help. Warmonger Roosevelt became the Communists' god. . . . War work meant primarily help for the Soviets to many a Washington bureaucrat.

That "many" is superb. "I have here in my hand a list of MANY Washington bureaucrats who . . ." Politically, to make an atrocious pun, Dos Passos is for the Byrds.

Midcentury is about the American labor movement from, roughly, the New Deal to the present, with occasional reminiscences of earlier times. The form of the book is chaotic. There are prose poems in italics, short impressionistic biographies of actual public figures, several fictional narratives in which various men and women are victimized by labor unions. And of course his patented device from *USA*: using newspaper headlines and fragments of news stories to act as counterpoint to the narration, to give a sense of time and place.

To deal with this last device first. In *USA* it was effective. In that book, Dos Passos stumbled on an interesting truth: nearly all of us are narcotized by newspapers. There is something about the way a newspaper page is set which, if only from habit, holds the attention no matter how boring the matter. One does read on, waiting for surprise or titillation. The success of the gossip column is no more than a crude exploitation of newspaper addiction. Even if you don't want to know what the Duchess of Windsor said to Elsa Maxwell or learn what stranger in the night was visited by Sir Stork, if your eye is addicted you will read on numbly.

(Parenthetic note to writers on the make and a warning to exploited readers: any column of text, even this one, will hold the eye and the attention of the reader if there are sufficient familiar proper names. Nat King Cole, Lee Remick, Central

Park, Marquis de Sade, Senator Bourke Hickenlooper, Marilyn Monroe. See? I trapped a number of you who'd skimmed the denser paragraphs above, deciding it was pretty dull literary stuff. "Marquis de Sade? Must've skipped something. Let's see, there's 'titillation' . . . no, 'Hollywood' . . . no.")

Also, dialogue has almost the same effect on the eye as names and newspaper headlines. In an age of worsening prose and declining concentration, most readers' attention will wander if there is too much unbroken text. On the other hand, even the most reluctant reader enjoys descending the short sprightly steps of dialogue on the page, jumping the descriptions, to shift the metaphor, as a skilled rider takes hedges in a steeplechase.

The newspaper technique is a good one; but to make it work the excerpts ought, minimally, to have some bearing on the narrative. In *Midcentury* one has the impression that Dos Passos simply shredded a few newspapers at random and stuffed them between the chapters as a form of excelsior to keep the biographies from bumping into one another. On the whole these biographies provide the book with its only interest, although the choice of subjects is inscrutable. Walter Reuther, John L. Lewis, James Hoffa are relevant to a novel dealing with organized labor, but then why include Robert Oppenheimer and Eleanor Roosevelt? And what exactly *is* Sam Goldwyn doing in the book? Or James Dean, that well-known statesman of organized labor? But, disregarding the irrelevance of many of the subjects, Dos Passos handles his impressionistic technique with a good deal of cunning. It is a tribute to his method that I was offended by the job he did on Mrs. Roosevelt. He is wonderfully expert at the precise, low blow. Thus, referring to Oppenheimer's belated political awakening (and turn to the Left): "Perhaps he felt the need to expiate the crime of individuality (as much of a crime to the solid citizens of the American Legion posts as to party functionaries Moscow-trained in revolution)." That's good stuff. He may not make the eagle scream, but he can certainly get the geese to honking. Yet despite his very pretty malice, the real reason the biographies work is again newspaper addiction: we know the subjects already. Our memories round the flat portraits; our prejudices do the author's work.

Finally, we come to the fictional characters, buried beneath headlines, feature stories and prose poems. (*Walking the earth under the stars, musing midnight in midcentury, a man treads the road with his dog; the dog, less timebound in her universe of stench and shrill, trots eager ahead....* Not since Studs Lonigan's old buddy Weary Reilley was making the scene has there been such word-music, I mean wordmusic.) Excepting one, the invented characters are cast in solid cement. Dos Passos tells us this and he tells us that, but he never shows us anything. He is unable to let his characters alone to see which will breathe and which will not. The only story which comes alive is a narrative by a dying labor organizer and onetime Wobbly who recalls his life; and in those moments when Dos Passos allows him to hold the stage, one is most moved. If Dos Passos were a novelist instead of a pamphleteer he would have liberated this particular character from the surrounding cement and made a book of him, and in that book, simply told, not only made all his urgent polemical points but art as well. As it is, Dos Passos proves a point well taken by Stendhal: "Politics, amidst the interests of the imagination, are a pistol shot in the middle of a concert. This noise is ear-rending, without being forceful. It clashes with every instrument."

Dos Passos ends his book with a sudden lashing out at the youth of the day. He drops the labor movement. He examines James Dean. Then he does a Salingeresque first-person narrative of an adolescent who stole some credit cards (remember a similar story in *Life*?) and went on a spree of conspicuous consumption. Despite stylistic confusions, Dos Passos is plain in his indictment: doomed is our pleasure-loving, scornful, empty, flabby modern youth, product of that midcentury dream in which, thanks to the do-gooders, we have lost our ancient Catonian virtue. I found the indictment oddly disgusting. I concede that there is some truth in everything Dos Passos says. But his spirit strikes me as sour and mean and, finally, uncomprehending. He has mistaken the decline of his own flesh and talent for the world's decline. This is the old man's folly, which a good artist or a generous man tries to avoid. Few of us can resist celebrating our own great days or finding fault with those who do not see in us now what we were or might have been. Nor is it unnatural when contemplating extinction to want, in sudden raging moments, to take the light with one. But it is a sign of wisdom to recognize one's own pettiness and not only to surrender vanity to death, which means to take it anyway, but to do so with deliberate grace as exemplar to the young upon whom our race's fragile continuity, which is all there is, depends. I should have thought that that was why one wrote—to make something useful for the survivors, to say: I was and now you are, and I leave you as good a map as I could make of my own traveling.

Esquire, May 1961

BARRY GOLDWATER:
A CHAT

Julius Caesar stood before a statue of Alexander the Great and wept, for Alexander at twenty-nine had conquered the world and at thirty-two was dead, while Caesar, a late starter of thirty-three, had not yet subverted even his own state. Pascal, contemplating this poignant scene, remarked rather sourly that he could forgive Alexander for wanting to own the earth because of his extreme youth, but Caesar was old enough to have known better.

I suggest, with diffidence, that Pascal did not entirely understand the nature of the politician; and the inner mechanism of a Caesar is no different in kind from that of an Alfred M. Landon. The aim of each is power. One would achieve it through military conquest, the other through what it pleases us to call the democratic process. It is natural for men to want power. But to seek power actively takes a temperament baffling to both the simple and the wise. The simple cannot fathom how any man would dare presume to prevail, while the wise are amazed that any reasonable man would *want* the world, assuming he could get it.

Suspended then between simplicity and wisdom, self-delusion and hard practicality, is the operative politician. He is not at all like other men, though he must acquire as protective coloration the manners of his society, join in its rituals (Caesar, the atheist, was a solemn high priest and our own Calvin Coolidge wore an Indian war bonnet), exploit its prejudices and anticipate its hungers.

Like his predecessors, an American politician in the midtwentieth century must conform to certain conventions. He must be gregarious (or seem to be), candid (but never give the game away), curious about people (otherwise, he would find his work unendurable). An American politician must not seem too brainy. He must put on no airs. He must smile often but at the same time appear serious. Most disagreeable of all, according to one ancient United States Senator, wise with victory, "is when you got to let some s.o.b. look you straight in the eye and think he's making a fool of you. Oh, that is gall and wormwood to the spirit!" Above all, a politician must not sound clever or wise or proud.

Finally, the politician must have that instinctive sense of occasion which is also the actor's art. To the right challenge he must have the right response. He is, in the purest sense, an opportunist. He must be an accurate barometer to the weather of his time. He must know the phases of the political moon and the hour of the tides. He must be ready at a moment's notice to seize that prize which is the game's reward, power. He must know in the marrow of his bones when it is right to make the large effort. For example, at the Democratic convention of 1956 the Vice-Presidential nomination was unexpectedly thrown open to the floor. The young Senator from Massachusetts went for the prize. The moment was wrong but the move was right. In a car on his way to the convention the day of the voting, John Kennedy was heard muttering grimly to himself, "Go, go, go!" When to go, when to stay; that is the art.

Even those who write knowledgeably about politics tend to

make certain fundamental errors. They look for subtle motives where there are none. They believe there is a long-range plan of war when there is seldom anything more than quick last-minute deployments of troops before unscheduled battle. In a society like ours, politics is improvisation. To the artful dodger rather than the true believer goes the prize.

The junior Senator from Arizona, Barry Goldwater, is a politician of some grace and skill who at this moment is studying the political sky for omens, waiting for a sign in which to conquer. His moment may come in the Presidential election of 1964, or of 1968 or never. There is every evidence that he is, this year, a divided man, uncertain how to proceed. His sense of occasion is keen; his sense of history is practical. He knows perfectly well that his views are at variance with the majority views of his time. To do great deeds, to take the prize, he must, paradoxically, surrender many of those positions he has so firmly taken in his reaction to a society he neither likes nor, many feel, understands. Yet, again paradoxically, his entire celebrity is due to his appealingly cranky rejection of those positions the majority reveres. In short, he is loved for those very attitudes which a majority of the electorate does not accept.

Goldwater's success is phenomenal considering that he is only a second-term Senator with no significant legislation to his name. He comes from a politically unimportant state. By his own admission he is not a profound thinker. His success in Arizona was due not only to his charm and hard campaigning in a state usually Democratic but also to the popularity of his family, one of the oldest in the state, whose business, Goldwater's department stores, is to Arizona what Macy's is to New York.

It is a clue to Goldwater's recent success that he was primarily a salesman in the family business (his one creative contribution was the invention and promotion of men's shorts decorated with large red ants in the pants) and he considers his role at the moment as salesman for the conservative point of view, which is not necessarily the Republican view. But, spokesman for the majority of his party or not, bumper stickers with GOLDWATER IN '64 are beginning to appear around the country (as well as a few GOLDWATER IN 1864 stickers).

Goldwater's path to higher office is strewn with many hazards, not all of his own making. His father was Jewish (the family name originally was Goldwasser), yet he is an Episcopalian. Since he favors right-to-work laws and limitations on unions, organized labor is against him. Personally, he sees nothing wrong with Negro and white children together in the same schools. But he opposes any Federal interference with the rights of the Southern states to maintain segregation, even in the face of the recent Supreme Court decision. Goldwater has about as much chance of getting the Negro vote, according to one Tennessee politician, as "a legless man in a pants-kicking contest." Reluctantly, Goldwater realizes that Social Security is here to stay—it is too late to take it away—but he does think the program should be voluntary and certainly not enlarged to include medical care for the aged or anything else. He favors breaking off diplomatic relations with the Russians; he wants to present them wherever possible with a take-it-or-leave-it, peace-or-war attitude which many thoughtful conservatives who approve his domestic program find disquietingly like brinkmanship. In his own party he is blocked not only by Nelson Rockefeller but by Richard Nixon.

As if all these difficulties, inherent and assumed, were not enough, he is now seriously endangered by his admirers. Like most radicals of Right or Left, he is attractive to every sort of extremist. His most compromising support comes from the mysterious John Birch Society, whose beleaguered "Founder" (a title last used by the creator of Hollywood's Forest Lawn Cemetery), Robert Welch, is firmly convinced that forty million Americans are Communists, including such unexpected conspirators as Milton and Dwight D. Eisenhower. Stubbornly, Goldwater has refused to repudiate the Birch Society, a stand which has led one Republican leader to say, "That's the end of Barry."

Yet, despite great handicaps, Goldwater is perhaps the

country's most popular politician, after Kennedy. He gets enormous crowds wherever he goes. They are enthusiastic and —hopeful sign—they include many young people. He has caught on as a personality even if his policies have not. It is common to hear, "O.K., so a lot of his ideas are cockeyed, but at least he tells you where he stands. He isn't afraid to speak up, the way the others are." That many of Goldwater's ideas are in a state of flux and that many of his positions are quite as obscure as those of any other politician does not penetrate. Once a man's "image," good or ill, is set in the public's mind, he can contradict himself every day and still be noted for consistency.

Yet Goldwater *is* something new on the scene. He is per- haps the first American politician who, though spokesman for an unpopular minority, finds himself personally popular for reasons irrelevant to his politics. He is forgiven by admirers when he speaks against the $1.25 minimum wage, union activi- ties or the Supreme Court's power to integrate schools. So what? He's a nice guy, and nice guys are not dangerous. He is also sincere, a vague quality far more admired by the lonely crowd than competence or intelligence.

Barry Goldwater's office is on the fourth floor of the old Senate Office Building. The corridors are marble with high ceilings and enormous doors which tend to dwarf not only visitors but Senators. There is an air of quiet megalomania which is beguiling in its nakedness.

Behind the great mahogany door with its sign MR. GOLDWA- TER, ARIZONA is the outer office: wooden paneling, a view through large windows of the Capitol grounds. I was greeted by the Senator's secretary, Mrs. Coerver. She is small, amiable, gray, with that somewhat fixed smile politicians and their aides develop. (One smile is a vote gained, maybe. One frown is a vote lost, definitely.) "The Senator will see you in just a moment." She beamed.

I approached this meeting with curiosity. For one thing, since his book, *The Conscience of a Conservative*, Goldwater's fundamentalist ideas about the Constitution and society had undergone changes. When the Presidential virus attacks the system there is a tendency for the patient in his fever to move from the Right or the Left to the Center where the curative votes are, where John Kennedy now is. Other observers of Goldwater had also detected a perceptible shift to the Center. Further shifts would depend entirely on whether the patient took a turn for the White House. I wanted, simply, to take his temperature as of that day, for like all illnesses the Presidential virus has its own peculiar ebb and flow. At night in the company of good friends the fever blazes. In a cold dawn on the way to an airport to speak in some far-off town the virus is at its lowest point: To hell with it! thinks the patient, almost cured.

Also, I wanted to get an impression of character. I have often thought and written that if the United States were ever to have a Caesar, a true subverter of the state, (1) he would attract to himself all the true believers, the extremists, the hot-eyed custodians of the Truth; (2) he would oversimplify some difficult but vital issue, putting himself on the side of the majority, as Huey Long did when he proclaimed every man a king and proposed to divvy up the wealth; (3) he would not in the least resemble the folk idea of a dictator. He would not be an hysteric like Hitler. Rather, he would be just plain folks, a regular guy, warm and sincere, and while he was amusing us on television storm troopers would gather in the streets.

Now I have put the case extremely only because in recent months there has been an unusual rash of extremist groups like the John Birch Society, reminding us that there is a totalitarian potential in this country just as there is in every country. Fortunately, barring military or economic disaster, none of these groups is apt to come to much without a leader who could appeal personally to a majority. It seemed to me that Goldwater was perhaps such a man: (1) He has already attracted many extremists, and he has not denied them; (2) he oversimplifies a great many issues (getting "tough" with the Russians is fine and getting rid of the income tax is fine, too, but toughness costs money; where will it come from?); (3) he

is exactly the sort of charming man whom no one would
suspect of Caesarism, least of all himself.

Barry Goldwater entered Mrs. Coerver's office in his shirt
sleeves and said, "Come on in." At the door to his own office
he turned to a departing interviewer and said, finishing some
earlier thought: "You know, of all the untrue things they
write, the wildest one is how I'm a millionaire. I've been called
that now so many times I'm beginning to feel like I ought to
live like one." Chuckling at his own hyperbole (he is a millionaire; he does live like one), he led me to his office. The large
desk was catercornered so that the light from the windows was
in the visitor's face. Beside the desk was a bookcase containing,
among other works, a leather-bound set of the speeches of
Barry Goldwater. On the mantel of the fireplace was a bust of
Lincoln. In the far corner of the room stood three flags. One
of them was the Senator's own flag: he is a brigadier general
in the Air Force Reserve. On the walls were photographs of
the Arizona landscape, as beautiful and empty as a country of
the moon.

We sat and looked at each other a moment. At fifty-two, he
is lean and obviously in fine condition. The hair is gray. The
eyes are small, alert, dark blue; the face tanned from a recent
trip home. The nose is pleasantly crooked. The nostrils are
odd, visible only when he tilts his head back, like the small
neatly round punctures in a child's rubber mask. The mouth
is wide and thin-lipped, the jaw square. The smile is attractive
but when his face is in repose there is an unexpected hardness,
even harshness. Neither of us, I noticed, was very good at
looking straight at the other. Simultaneously, each looked
away. I looked out the window. Goldwater examined his
brigadier general's flag (for those who believe the old saw that
an honest man must have a direct gaze, I refer them to a
contemporary's report that the shiftiest-eyed man he had ever
met was Thomas Jefferson).

I began compassionately: "You must get awfully tired of
being interviewed." He smiled. "It's repetitive, but . . ." His
voice trailed off. It is a good voice for politics, light but earnest,

with a slight rural accent of the sort made familiar by television Westerns.

I had debated whether to bring a tape recorder. I knew that Goldwater had a small wrist-watch recorder which he used gleefully to disconcert others as well as to protect himself from misquotation. I decided to take notes instead. On a small pad of paper I had written a few topics. First, the John Birch Society. Recently Goldwater had said that "a great many fine people" were members, including "Republicans, liberal Democrats, conservatives," and he thought it would cause considerable political embarrassment if they were attacked en masse. He had also implied that besides the two known Birchers in Congress, Representatives Edgar Hiestand and John Rousselot, both Republicans of California, there were others. In one interview, however, he suggested that Robert Welch resign. Later he denied he had said this. I asked him how well he knew Welch. He frowned thoughtfully.

"Well, I've known Bob Welch five, maybe six years. But I didn't really get to him until that summit business, you know, when we all tried to keep Eisenhower from meeting Khrushchev. Welch and I worked together then. Of course all that stuff of his about Eisenhower being a Communist and so on was silly. Fact, I told him when he gave me that book of his [*The Politician*] to read, I said: 'Unless you can prove every one of those statements about people being Communists is true, you better go destroy every single copy of that book.'"

"Do you think Welch should resign as head of the society?"

The answer was quick: "I do. Just the other day I sent somebody over to the Library of Congress to get me the bylaws of the Birch Society, and I was disturbed about this dictatorial thing, how he personally can chuck people out any time he pleases. I didn't like it."

"What did you mean when you said there were liberal Democrats in the Birch Society?"

"Because there are. There're all kinds of people in that group. I know. I've met 'em and a nicer-looking bunch you never saw. That thirty- to forty-five-year-old group you want in politics. They're thoughtful people and they're concerned. But don't get the idea they're all conservatives because they're fighting Communism. A lot of people are fighting Communism who aren't conservative." I had the impression he wanted it made clear that his own conservative position was one thing and the fight against Communism was another thing. Most conservatives regard the two as synonymous. Goldwater does ordinarily, but this day I felt he was preparing a possible escape hatch.

I asked him if he knew of any members of Congress who belonged to the society, other than the two Californians. He paused. Then he said, "No." It was a slow, thoughtful "no," hard to interpret. Then: "You know, I don't really know that much about those people."

I asked him if he approved of their methods, as outlined in Welch's *Blue Book*. "Never read it. I don't know." It seemed to me strange that he would read the bylaws and *The Politician* yet not read the *Blue Book*, which contains not only the bylaws but a ten-point program on how to expose and discourage "Communists."

I mentioned some of Welch's gambits: infiltrating school boards and library boards, getting "mean and dirty" with known liberals, encouraging students to spy on teachers.

Goldwater interrupted. No, he didn't like that, of course. "In fact, I've always been in favor of teaching Communism in schools. Show the kids what we're up against. Naturally I'd want a good course in American history to balance it. After all, the only way you're going to beat Communism is with a better idea, like Nero and the Christians . . . you know? He couldn't stamp 'em out, because there was that idea they had. Well, that's what we've got to have."

Goldwater had been against Federal aid to education. First, he is not convinced any aid is needed. Second, he feels that to give money to the states is an invasion of states' rights. Recently he testified before a House Education subcommittee in the interests of a bill of his own which he said would solve the whole problem. He proposed giving property owners a rebate on their Federal income tax up to one hundred dollars, the amount to represent what the property owner had paid in local school taxes. Even Goldwater's admirers found this solution baffling. His exchange with Representative John Brademas in committee had a good deal of unconscious humor in it.

Brademas asked Goldwater why he had proposed a bill to answer a problem which he did not believe existed. Soon both men were lost in a maze of: "I said 'if.' Well, if there is a problem, which I don't believe, then here's the answer. . . . All right, but if there is *not* a problem, then why propose . . . ?"

In the course of his testimony, Goldwater unexpectedly came out for minimum academic standards to be set by the Federal government for the entire country. Brademas pointed out the contradiction: to set such standards and requirements would mean government intervention of the most extreme sort. Goldwater saw no contradiction: the government's minimum standards would not be compulsory; they would be "guide lines." He felt, too, that although Federal aid to education was unconstitutional, *if* there was to be such aid parochial and private schools should be included.

I teased Goldwater about his exchange with Brademas. He laughed. He then repeated his position: There was no problem, and it was growing less. He quoted statistics. . . . Neither of us listened. I had touched a familiar button. He was responding as he had many times before.

I was amused during the Nixon-Kennedy debates by those who were astonished at the wide range of knowledge displayed by the two men, at their "mastery" of detail. Actually, neither was asked a question he had not already answered on an average of a dozen times a day for months. After such rehearsal any politician can discuss a number of subjects with what seems encyclopedic detail. It is a trick of the trade but a dangerous one, for answering the same questions over and over interferes with thought. Goldwater finished his statistics and waited for me to press the next button.

Not wanting to get him on a familiar track, I thought quickly, a little desperately. I wanted a general subject. The idea of the presidency occurred to me. What would *he* do if he were president? Goldwater had once said to a journalist that, all in all, he preferred the Senate to the White House because as a Senator he could speak his mind, "where if you're president you can't. You got to be cautious and watch what you say." When the journalist asked Goldwater what he had been saying as a Senator that he would not feel free to say as president, he had looked baffled and finally said, "Well, damned if I know."

On the word "president" I noticed a faint flush of the fever. His eyes glittered. He sat back in his chair. "If I was president," he began with a new weight and authority, "I'd move slowly, cautiously at first. You'd have to feel your pathway. Not that my ideas are new ideas. No, they're old, old ideas."

Then he talked of government farm supports. In the campaign, he had demanded "prompt and final termination of all subsidy." But he has changed. He would still eliminate supports, but gradually. I mentioned that only about half of the nation's farmers are needed to grow most of our food. Without supports a lot of people would be thrown on the labor market —in addition to the five million already unemployed. This, I suggested, was a real crisis. He agreed. They would have to be absorbed gradually. But how? Well, management and labor would get together (*without* the government) and set up a joint program to retrain and reallocate displaced people, "Not just farmers either, anybody who's been displaced by mechanization, and so on," and to sponsor "basic research for new gadgets—you know, for a lot of things like that we need."

Could labor and management be relied upon to do the job without some urging from the government? He thought they could. "Of course back in the 1920's management was pretty stupid, but I think they've come of age now, lot of fine new people at the top. The day of those self-made men, the founders, all that's over. In fact, labor's at the same place today management was in the 1920's. All those labor leaders, they're the same type of self-made man ran big business in the old days."

I asked him about his quarrel with Reuther. ("I would rather have Jimmy Hoffa stealing my money than Walter Reuther stealing my freedom.") He shook his head. "It's not personal. I just don't believe labor should be in politics." I was about to ask him what he thought of management in politics (the N.A.M., the Chamber of Commerce) when we were interrupted. A visiting lawyer was outside. He would like to shake the Senator's hand. He was ushered in.

The lawyer was a pleasant-looking, somewhat tense young man who was in Washington for the American Bar Association's antitrust conference. Goldwater came around from behind his desk. He smiled warmly. They shook hands. The young lawyer said in a voice shaking with emotion, "I just wanted you to know, Senator, there are a lot of people over in that Justice Department who better get off their fud and realize we've got some states that can do the job." Goldwater was sympathetic. I turned away, embarrassed. Two conservatives had met and I felt their intensity, their oneness. They spoke in their own shorthand and they knew the enemy.

I made notes while they talked. I wondered idly if I should ask Goldwater what he liked to eat and whether or not he wore pajamas and if he liked movies. I have always enjoyed reading those interviews which are made up of an incredible amount of minutiae; like coral islands they rise bit by bit out of the sea of personality, formed of dead facts. Absently, with what I hoped was the eye of a naturalist-novelist, I began to record the objects on his desk: a large transparent plastic duck mysteriously containing a small metal elephant, all mounted rather disagreeably on a penholder. Next to the duck was a clipping from a Hartford newspaper whose editorial began, *Well, What About Goldwater?* On the wall behind the desk hung a number of small photographs. There was one of Nixon, smiling, with a long inscription which I was too far away to read. There was a similar photograph of Eisenhower, also smiling, also inscribed. Why are politicians so happy when on view? "Always smiling," I wrote neatly on the pad. Then the young lawyer shook hands again. Goldwater smiled. I smiled.

The photographs smiled. Only the young lawyer did not smile. He knew the Republic was in danger. He left. Goldwater and I put our smiles away and resumed the interview.

I had been told that the one question which made him uncharacteristically edgy was: Who wrote his book, *The Conscience of a Conservative?* I asked it. He frowned. "That's what wrote it," he said, somewhat irrelevantly. He ran his hand across the row of leather-bound books. "My speeches. The book's nothing but a selection from speeches, from a lot of the things I've been saying for years. After all, I've written four books, a lot of magazine articles, my column."

I had been told that among his literary ghosts were Steve Shadegg and L. Brent Bozell. I started to ask him about them but decided not to. It was cruel. It was pointless. We live in an age of ghosts: singers whose high notes are ghosted by others; writers whose works are created by editors; actors whose performances are made out of film by directors. Why should one harry politicians for not writing their own books and speeches? Few have the time or the talent. In any case the work published must necessarily reflect the views of its "author."

I was ready to drop the subject, but Goldwater was not. He told me he was planning another book. He was going on a cruise with his wife in the fall. While traveling, he would write the first draft. Then he would go over it carefully for "improvement in expression. Then after that I'll submit it to an author . . . I mean publisher." I suspect that Goldwater knows even less about Freud than I do, which is little, but we both know a Freudian slip when we hear one. The dark eyes darted anxiously in my direction. Had I caught the slip? I had.

He talked about conservatism. "Bunch of us got together after the convention and we all agreed we'd never heard such conservative speeches get so much applause, and then they go and accept that platform which 95 per cent of them were against." He sighed. "I don't know. What's wrong with the word 'conservative' anyway? Must be something." He said he had been impressed by the British Conservatives' comeback in

1951. They had got out and sold the party to the young people. This was his own plan. He would sell conservatism wherever he could, preferably to the young and uncommitted. "Of course the Conservative Party in England is about like the New Deal was here."

I asked him his impression of Kennedy. "Well, I guess I know him about as well as anybody around here. I like him. Of course we disagree on a lot of things. He thinks the government should do a lot more for people than I do." He mused about the campaign. He had advised against Nixon's television debates with Kennedy. "Funny, when my sister saw the first one, she said, 'Why, that Kennedy isn't so young!' And I knew then and there that was it. Of course, on sheer debating points Nixon took Kennedy every time. Anybody who knows about these things could see that. Especially on Quemoy and Matsu. Boy, if *I* had been debating Kennedy, I sure would have jazzed him all over the lot—Berlin, Laos, everything!"

I commented that Nixon had been a victim of his own legend. He had been pictured by both admirers and enemies as a rough infighter, a merciless debater, a ruthless killer, yet in the campaign and in the television debates it was quite clear that of the two, Kennedy was by far the tougher fighter. Goldwater nodded. "I warned Nixon about that a long time ago when the real mistake was made, 'way back there in California in that Senate election. You see, Nixon was sold by these people on putting himself over as a real gut fighter. They figured it would do him good against Helen Gahagan Douglas. So they built him up tough and mean, when of course he wasn't, when all he ever did was just tell the truth about that woman. The whole thing about him being so mean was nothing but publicity. So I told him: 'You wait and see, when you get to running for President and you start getting rough, the way you *got* to, they'll jump on you and say it's the old Nixon.' And they did. And then he'd pussyfoot." Goldwater shook his head sadly.

We talked about medical care for the aged to be paid through Social Security. The Senator was against it. He said that at the

Arizona hospital of which he was a director, only one elderly person had been unable to pay. He had also seen a poll from western Florida where the elderly people had voted firmly against Federal aid. I suggested that those who could afford to retire to Arizona and Florida might be comfortably off. He said no, their average income was about $300 a month. Anyway, people ought to look after themselves either through their own foresight or through help from their families. Failing that, indigence should be handled the way it has always been: at the local level, by charities and so on.

I suggested that with taxes as high as they are, and longer life expectancies, there would be more rather than fewer programs for state and Federal aid in the coming years. He agreed. That was why he felt the whole tax structure had to be overhauled. And though he no longer favors repealing the graduated income tax, as he suggested in his book, he did feel that taxes on business should be reduced and greater allowance made for depreciation. "I told Jack Kennedy: you could be President for life if you'd just lift some of those taxes so that businessmen—and I know hundreds of 'em—would have some incentive to get new machinery, to overhaul their plants, to *really* start producing."

Publicly, no American politician can admit that we have anything to learn from the experiments of any other society. The ritual dialogue between office seeker and electorate is one of mutual congratulation, and to suggest that perfection has another home is treasonable. But privately our more conscientious legislators do ponder other countries' penal reforms, medical programs, educational methods. From his book and speeches I suspected Goldwater had done little or no homework. He was firmly against socialized medicine, but he seemed to know nothing about how it worked in Scandinavia, West Germany, England.

Goldwater was honest. No, he didn't know much about European socialism. "But I did meet this Norwegian doctor, matter of fact her name was Goldwater, which is how she happened to get in touch with me. She said the thing *seemed* to work all right, but that being assured of a certain income every month from the government kept her from feeling any real urge to study harder—you know, keep up at her profession. There was no incentive." I asked him if he thought that the desire to be good was entirely economic in origin. He said of course it was. I then asked him to explain how it was that two people as different as ourselves worked hard, though in neither case was money the spur. He was startled. Then he murmured vaguely and slipped away from the subject.

I asked him what he felt about some of his more oddball admirers. Goldwater became suddenly cautious. The quick, easy responses were replaced by a slow, careful measuring of words. He knew, he said, of some 250 organizations either conservative or anti-Communist. He admitted it was often difficult to figure out who was what. "Every invitation I get to speak, I have to check it for this and check it for that, make absolutely sure they're O.K. You never know what you may be getting into. Some are first-rate, like this fellow in New Orleans, Ken Courtney. He publishes a magazine down there. He's quite a guy." He asked on the phone for the magazine's name. I mentioned the Young Americans for Freedom, an organization founded by those who had been involved in the Youth for Goldwater movement at the Chicago convention. He approved of them highly, especially of "What's his name—Gaddy? Caddy, that's right. Nice kid, a real savvy guy with a lot on the ball."

Mrs. Coerver entered. "The magazine's called *Independent American*, and his name is Kent, not Ken, Courtney." She left.

More than once, Goldwater has complained that though the Republican Party's leaders are conservative they invariably choose liberal or moderate candidates to run for president on the false (to him) premise that a true conservative could never win. I asked him, Why not start a third party?

Goldwater sat up briskly. "If I thought it would work, I might. But I don't know . . . third parties never get off the ground in this country. There was Teddy Roosevelt, and there was . . ." He shook his head. "No, I don't see it. For one thing, conservatism is pretty divided. Suppose I started a party. Then somebody would come along and say, 'Well, look here, you're not *my* kind of conservative,' and then he'd go off and start *his* party and you'd end up like France. That's the trouble with the conservatives. They've got this all-or-nothing attitude." He sighed. "Why, I got booed in New York when I said if it was between Rockefeller and Harriman I'd be for Rockefeller. I tried to explain how at least Rockefeller was a Republican and you got your foot in the door. . . . No. A political party can only start around a strong individual." He looked past me at the bust on the mantelpiece; his jaw had set. "Like Lincoln. The people were there looking for a party, looking for this strong individual. And there he was and that's how the Republican Party started. A strong individual."

The next question was obvious. Was Goldwater that "strong individual"? Could he lead his people out of the wilderness? Were there enough of them to allow him to re-create that dream of Eden which conservatives evoke whenever they recall the bright simple days of our old agrarian Republic? But I let it go. Neither of us knew the answer. He had his hopes, and that was enough.

I rose to go. He walked me to the door. We exchanged impieties, each about his own political party, then said goodby.

"Ignorant but shrewd" was the verdict of one colleague of Goldwater. "He's read very little. He has no knowledge of economics. He's completely outside the world of ideas. Even his passion for the Constitution is based upon a misunderstanding of its nature." I am not sure I would agree that Goldwater's ignorance of ideas is necessarily relevant to his ability or his capacity for growth.

I was impressed by his charm, which, even for a politician, is considerable. More than that, in his simplifying of great issues Goldwater has a real appeal for a nation which is not at all certain about its future either as a society or as a world power. Up and down the land there are storm warnings. Many look nervously for shelter, and Goldwater, in the name of old-time virtue and ruggedness and self-reliance, offers them refuge beneath the venerable great roof of the Constitution. True or not, his simplifications are enormously appealing and, who knows, in a time of crisis he might seize the prize.

But I make no predictions. I would only recommend to Goldwater Cicero's warning to a fellow political adventurer, in a falling year of the Roman Republic: "I am sure you understand the political situation into which you have . . . no, not stumbled, but stepped; for it was by deliberate choice and by no accident that you flung your tribunate into the very crisis of things; and I doubt not that you reflect how potent in politics is opportunity, how shifting the phases, how incalculable the issues of events, how easily swayed are men's predilections, what pitfalls there are and what insincerity in life."

Life, June 9, 1961

This interview received a great deal of attention. Henry Luce complimented the editor, adding that he never again wanted to see a piece like that in *Life*.

POLICE BRUTALITY

For some time now our leaders, both demagogic and honest, have been telling us to rouse ourselves to greater purpose, national and private. Walter Lippmann suggests that the United States behaves like a society which thinks it is complete, with no more to accomplish; that, for better or worse, we are what we are, and the only danger to our comfort is external. President Kennedy's exhortations to self-sacrifice are becoming ever more urgent, even shrill. Yet his critics point out that he has not done much to show us how we might best serve our society. To which the answer of the Administration, at least privately, is that until Americans understand those things that threaten us, both from without and within, any presidential program demanding the slightest sacrifice would be demolished by Congress and the jingo press. After all, things do look all right if you don't look too carefully, and no one can accuse us of ever looking carefully at an unpleasant sight, whether it is Soviet superiority in space or chronic unemployment at home. Now I don't want to add my voice to the general keening. American society has many virtues which we should never underestimate. By fits and starts, we are attaining a civilization and, barring military accident, we shall certainly attain one before the Soviets. "Be the First into Civilization!" Now *there's* a slogan for the two competitors.

Yet for those who are puzzled at how to respond to Presidential cries for action, vigor and movingaheadness, I propose that there are certain very practical things we can do in a society that is by no means complete. I might add that those professional patriots who trumpet that this is the new Eden and only traitors would change it or downgrade it are declaring, of course, that the society is closed and therefore decadent and soon to fall. I vote No to "perfection," and Yes to change and survival. Most of us spend too much time solving international problems at cocktail parties, rather than dealing with those things which we might affect and change, the tying up of the loose ends in our own society. There are many of them, ranging from the abolition of capital punishment to school integration. On either of those great matters any citizen can be usefully engaged. He can also be useful in social and moral legislation, where there is much work to be done. As for civil liberties, anyone who is not vigilant may one day find himself living, if not in a police state, at least in a police city. Now I will tell a horror story which has haunted me for several months, something that, I am told, is common but which I witnessed for the first time, reacting as deeply as the writer in Angus Wilson's novel *Hemlock and After.*

I was in Washington for a few days last spring. At about ten o'clock in the evening of my last day in town, I took a taxicab to the Union Station. It was a mild, drizzly night. Traffic in the side streets near Pennsylvania Avenue was tied up. My cab was stopped in front of the YMCA, a large building a half-block from the Old State Department and two blocks from the White House. The sidewalk was deserted. As we sat there, out of the building marched four men, wearing light raincaps with upturned brims and trench coats. There were two men with them. One was well dressed, perhaps sixty; he wore a white raincoat. The other was young and thin and shabby, and he wore no raincoat. I watched as this odd company moved seven or eight yards along the sidewalk toward the traffic light, which was now red. In front of a deserted shop, the trench-coats stopped and methodically began to beat up the two men with them. I sat there stunned. There had been no provoca-tion. As suddenly and pointlessly as a nightmare, the attack began; and there, right in front of me on the black wet side-walk, the older man lay as two men kicked him, while the other two shoved the young man into the doorway of the shop and began to beat him across the face.

The cab driver, an old Negro, said, "I hate to see anybody do that to another man. I do." The light was now green, but I told him to wait. I got out and crossed to the nearest trench-coat. He was, at the moment, disengaged. He had been work-ing the younger man over and he now stood a few feet away, breathing hard. I asked him who he was and what he was doing. He turned on me and I have never seen such a savage, frightening little face. It was plump, flushed, with popping eyes; the face of a young pig gone berserk. He began to scream at me to get out of there or I'd be arrested. Threats and ob-scenities poured out of him in one long orgiastic breath. I looked away and saw that the older man was now on his stomach, trying to shield his head from the kicks of the men standing over him. His raincoat was streaked with mud. The younger man was silent, except for the whacking noise his face made when it was struck—first left, then right, like a punching bag. In my hardest voice I said: "You're going to be the one in trouble if you don't tell me who you are." The dark one came over to me at this point; he showed me his detective's badge, and suggested I get lost. Then he returned to his sport. The plump one was now longing (and I do not exaggerate by using a verb of judgment) to get back to the man in the door-way. But before he could, I asked him for his name. He started to curse again, but a look from his companion stopped him. He gave me his name and then with a squeal leaped on the man in the doorway and began hitting him, making, as he did, obscene gasping noises.

I stood there dumbly wondering what to do. Right in front of me, two men were being knocked about by four men who were, quite simply, enjoying their work. I was also witness to the fact that the victims had *not* resisted arrest, which would of course be the police explanation of what had happened. Cravenly, I got back into the cab. I asked my driver if he would be a witness with me. He shook his head sadly. "I don't want no trouble. This is a mighty dirty town."

At Union Station I telephoned the *Washington Post and Times-Herald* and talked to the night editor. I gave him my name. Yes, he knew who I was. Yes, the story interested him. I gave him the detective's name, which I had thought was probably false. He said no, there was such a man. I gave him the cab driver's license number, in case the driver changed his mind. Then the editor asked me what I intended to do about it. I shouted into the receiver, "This is your town. Your scandal. Your newspaper. *You* do something about it, I'm catching a train." He asked if they could use my name. I said of course, and hung up.

But that was the end of it.

I got back to New York to read that a Southern editor had written an editorial attacking the John Birch Society. In the course of his editorial, he quoted the F.B.I. as saying that the Birchers were "irresponsible." Some hours *before* the editorial was published, two men from the F.B.I. arrived at the editor's office and asked him on what authority he could quote the F.B.I. as terming the Birch Society "irresponsible." The editor's sources were not, as it turned out, reliable. But then the editor, quite naturally, asked how it was that the F.B.I. knew the contents of his editorial before it was published. He got no answer.

Now the point to these two stories is that here is something we *can* do: guard our own liberties. We may not be able to save Laos; but we can, as individuals, keep an eye on local police forces, even if it means, as some have proposed, setting up permanent committees of appeal in every city to hear cases of police brutality, or to consider infractions of our freedom to speak out in the pursuit of what our founders termed happiness—two rights always in danger, not only at the local but at the Federal level.

Esquire, August 1961

NASSER'S EGYPT

"Are you German, sir?" A small, dark youth stepped from behind a palm tree into the full light of the setting sun which turned scarlet the white shirt and albino red the black eyes. He had been watching me watch the sun set across the Nile, now blood-red and still except for sailboats tacking in a hot, slow breeze. I told him that I was American but was used to being mistaken for a German: in this year of the mid-century, Germans are everywhere, and to Arab eyes we all look alike. He showed only a moment's disappointment.

"I have many German friends," he said. "Two German friends. *West* German friends. Perhaps you know them?" He pulled a notebook out of his pocket and read off two names. Then, not waiting for an answer, all in a rush, he told me that he was a teacher of Arabic grammar, that he was going to Germany, *West* Germany (he emphasized the *West* significantly), to write a book. What sort of book? A book about West Germany. The theme? He responded with some irritation: "A

Book About West Germany." That was what the book would be about. He was a poet. His name was Ahmed. "Welcome," he said, "welcome!" His crooked face broke into a smile. "Welcome to Luxor!" He invited me to his house for mint tea.

As we turned from the bank of the Nile, a long, haunting cry sounded across the water. I had heard this same exotic cry for several evenings, and I was certain that it must be of ancient origin, a hymn perhaps to Ikhnaton's falling sun. I asked Ahmed what this lovely aria meant. He listened a moment and then said, "It's this man on the other side who says: will the ferryboat please pick him up?" So much for magic.

Ahmed led the way through narrow streets to the primary school where he taught. It was a handsome modern building, much like its counterparts in Scarsdale or Darien. He took me inside. "You must see what the children make themselves. Their beautiful arts." On the entrance-hall table their beautiful arts were exhibited: clay figures, carved wood, needlework, all surrounding a foot-long enlargement in clay of the bilharzia, a parasite which is carried by snails in the irrigation ditches; once it invades the human bloodstream, lungs and liver are attacked and the victim wastes away; some ninety per cent of the fellahin suffer from bilharzia. "Beautiful?" he asked. "Beautiful," I said.

On the wall hung the exhibit's masterpiece, a larger than life-size portrait of Nasser, painted in colors recalling Lazarus on the fourth day. A somewhat more talented drawing next to it showed students marching with banners in a street. I asked Ahmed to translate the words on the banners. "Our heads for Nasser," he said with satisfaction. I asked him if Nasser was popular with the young. He looked at me as though I had questioned the next day's sunrise. Of course Nasser was loved. Had I ever been in Egypt before? Yes, during the winter of 1948, in the time of the bad fat King. Had things improved? I told him honestly that they had indeed. Cairo had changed from a nineteenth-century French provincial capital surrounded by a casbah to a glittering modern city, only partially surrounded by a casbah. He asked me what I was doing in

Egypt, and I told him I was a tourist, not mentioning that I had an appointment to interview Nasser the following week for an American magazine.

Ahmed's house is a large one, four stories high; here he lives with some twenty members of his family. The parlor is a square room with a high ceiling from which hangs a single unshaded light bulb. Two broken beds serve as sofas. I sat on one of the beds while Ahmed, somewhat nervously, ordered mint tea from a sister who never emerged from the dark hall. Then I learned that his father was also a teacher, and that an uncle worked in Nasser's office; obviously a prosperous family by Luxor standards.

I was offered the ceremonial cigarette. I refused; he lit up. He was sorry his father was not there to meet me. But then again, puffing his cigarette, he was glad, for it is disrespectful to smoke in front of one's father. Only recently the father had come unexpectedly into the parlor. "I was smoking a cigarette and when he came in, oh! I bit it hard, like this, and have to swallow it down! Oh, I was sick!" We chuckled at his memory.

When the mint tea arrived (passed to us on a tray from the dark hall, only bare arms visible), Ahmed suggested we sit outside where it was cool. Moonlight blazed through a wooden trellis covered with blossoming wisteria. We sat on stiff wooden chairs. He switched on a light momentarily to show me a photograph of the girl he was to marry. She was pretty and plump and could easily have been the editor of the year-book in any American high school. He turned off the light. "We modern now. No more arranged marriages. Love is everything. Love is why we marry. Love is all." He repeated this several times, with a sharp intake of breath after each statement. It was very contagious, and I soon found myself doing it. Then he said, "Welcome," and I said, "Thank you."

Ahmed apologized for the unseasonable heat. This was the hottest spring in years, as I had discovered that day in the Valley of the Kings where the temperature had been over a hundred and the blaze of sun on white limestone blinding. "After June, Luxor is *impossible!*" he said proudly. "We all go

who can go. If I stay too long, I turn dark as a black in the sun."
Interestingly enough, there is racial discrimination in Egypt.
"The blacks" are second-class citizens: laborers, servants, minor government functionaries. They are the lowest level of
Egyptian society in every way except one: there are no Negro
beggars. That is an Arab monopoly. Almsgivers are blessed by
the Koran, if not by Nasser, who has tried to discourage the
vast, well-organized hordes of beggars.

"To begin with, I had naturally a very light complexion,"
said Ahmed, making a careful point, "like the rest of my
family, but one day when I was small the nurse upset boiling
milk on me and ever since that day I have been somewhat
dark." I commiserated briefly. Then I tried a new tack. I asked
him about his military service. Had he been called up yet? A
new decree proposed universal military service, and I thought
a discussion of it might get us onto politics. He said that he had
not been called up because of a *very interesting story*. My heart
sank, but I leaned forward with an air of sympathetic interest.
Suddenly, I realized I was impersonating someone. But who?
Then when he began to talk and I to respond with small nods
and intakes of breath, I realized that it was E. M. Forster. I was
the Forster of *A Passage to India* and this was Dr. Aziz. Now
that I had the range, my fingers imperceptibly lengthened into
Forsterian claws; my eyes developed an uncharacteristic twin-
kle; my upper lip sprouted a ragged gray moustache, while all
else turned to tweed.

"When the British attacked us at Suez, I and these boys from
our school, we took guns and together we marched from Alexandria to Suez to help our country. We march for many days
and nights in the desert. We have no food, no water. Then we
find we are lost and we don't know where we are. Several die.
Finally, half dead, we go back to Alexandria and we march in
the street to the place where Nasser is. We ask to see him, to
cheer him, half dead all of us. But they don't let us see him.
Finally, my uncle hears I am there and he and Nasser come
out and, ah, Nasser congratulates us, we are heroes! Then I
collapse and am unconscious one month. That is why I have

not to do military service." I was impressed and said so, especially at their getting lost in the desert, which contributed to my developing theory that the Arabs are disaster-prone: they *would* get lost, or else arrive days late for the wrong battle.

Ahmed told me another story of military service, involving friends. "Each year in the army they have these . . . these . . ." We searched jointly—hopelessly—for the right word until E. M. Forster came up with "maneuvers," which was correct. I could feel my eyes twinkling in the moonlight.

"So these friends of mine are in this maneuvers with guns in the desert and they have orders: *shoot to kill.* Now one of them was Ibrahim, my friend. Ibrahim goes to this outpost in the dark. They make him stop and ask him for the password and he . . ." Sharp intake of breath. "He has *forgotten* the password. So they say, 'He must be the enemy.' " I asked if this took place in wartime. "No, no, *maneuvers.* My friend Ibrahim say, 'Look, I forget. I *did* know but now I forget the password but you know me, anyway, you know it's Ibrahim.' And he's right. They do know it was Ibrahim. They recognize his voice but since he cannot say the password they shot him."

I let E. M. Forster slip to the floor. "Shot him? Dead?"

"Dead," said my host with melancholy satisfaction. "Oh, they were very sorry because they knew it was Ibrahim, but, you see, *he did not know the password,* and while he was dying in the tent they took him to, he said it was all right. They were right to kill him."

I found this story hard to interpret. Did Ahmed approve or disapprove what was done? He was inscrutable. There was silence. Then he said, "Welcome," and I said, "Thank you." And we drank more mint tea in the moonlight.

I tried again to get the subject around to politics. But beyond high praise for everything Nasser has done, he would volunteer nothing. He did point to certain tangible results of the new regime. For one thing, Luxor was now a center of education. There were many new schools. All the children were being educated. In fact he had something interesting to show me. He turned on the lamp and opened a large scrapbook conveniently at hand. It contained photographs of boys and girls, with a scholastic history for each. Money had to be raised to educate them further. It *could* be done. Each teacher was obliged to solicit funds. "Look what my West German friends have given," he said, indicating amounts and names. Thus I was had, in a good cause. I paid and walked back to the hotel.

On the way back, I took a shortcut down a residential street. I had walked no more than a few feet when an old man came rushing after me. "Bad street!" he kept repeating. I agreed politely, but continued on my way. After all, the street was well lit. There were few people abroad. A shout from an upstairs window indicated that I should halt. I looked up. The man in the window indicated I was to wait until he came downstairs. I did. He was suspicious. He was from the police. *Why* was I in that street? I said that I was taking a walk. This made no sense to him. He pointed toward my hotel, which was in a slightly different direction. That was where I was supposed to go. I said yes, but I wanted to continue in *this* street, I liked to walk. He frowned. Since arrest was imminent, I turned back. At the hotel I asked the concierge why what appeared to be a main street should be forbidden to foreigners. "Oh, 'they' might be rude," he said vaguely. "You know. . . ." I did not know.

In the diner on the train south to Aswan I had breakfast with a young government official from the Sudan. He was on his way home to Khartoum. He had a fine smile and blue-black skin. On each cheek there were three deep scars, the ritual mark of his tribe—which I recognized, for I had seen his face only the day before on the wall of the Temple of Luxor. Amenhotep III had captured one of his ancestors in Nubia; five thousand years ago the ritual scars were the same as they are now. In matters of religion Africans are profound conservatives. But otherwise he was a man of our time and world. He was dressed in the latest French fashion. He had been for two years on an economic mission in France. He spoke English, learned at the British school in Khartoum.

We breakfasted on musty-tasting dwarfish eggs as dust

filtered slowly in through closed windows, covering table, plates, eggs with a film of grit. A fan stirred the dusty air. Parched, I drank three Coca-Colas—the national drink—and sweated. The heat outside was already 110 degrees, and rising. For a while we watched the depressing countryside and spoke very little. At some points the irrigated land was less than a mile wide on our side of the river: a thin ribbon of dusty green ending abruptly in a blaze of desert where nothing at all grew, a world of gray sand as far as the eye could see. Villages of dried-mud houses were built at the desert's edge so as not to use up precious land. The fellahin in their ragged clothes moved slowly about their tasks, quite unaware of the extent of their slow but continual decline. In the fifth century B.C., Herodotus was able to write: "As things are at present these people get their harvest with less labor than anyone else in the world; they have no need to work with plow or hoe, or to use any other of the ordinary methods of cultivating their land; they merely wait for the river of its own accord to flood the fields." But all that has changed. Nearly thirty million people now live in a country whose agriculture cannot support half that number.

"I used to think," said the Sudanese at last, "that Egypt was a fine place, much better than the Sudan. A big country. Rich. But now I know how lucky we are. There is no one at home poor like this." He pointed to several ragged men in a field. Two lay listlessly in the sun. The others worked slowly in the field, narcotized by the heat; the diet of the fellahin is bread and stewed tea and not much of that. I asked him what he thought of Nasser's attacks on his government (recently there had been a disagreement over Nile water rights and Nasser had attacked the Sudanese President with characteristic fury). "Oh, we just laugh at him. We just laugh at him," he repeated as though to convince himself. I asked him why Nasser was continuously on the offensive not only against the West but against the rest of the Arab world. He shrugged. "To impress his own people, I suppose. We don't like it, of course. But perhaps it makes him feel big. Makes them . . ." He pointed to a group of villagers drawing water from a canal. "Makes them forget."

Aswan is the busiest and most optimistic of Egypt's cities. On its outskirts a brand-new chemical factory employs several thousand people. There is a sense of urgency in the city's life, for it is here that all of Egypt's hopes are concentrated: the High Dam is being built. When the dam—the world's largest —is completed in 1970, vast tracts of desert will be made arable and electrical power will be supplied cheaply for the whole country. It should be recalled that the United States had originally agreed to finance a part of the dam, but in 1956 John Foster Dulles withdrew our support and the Soviet obligingly filled the vacuum. Not only are the Russians now financing the dam, but their engineers are building it.

The government had arranged that I be shown around by one of the Egyptian engineers, a cautious, amiable man who spoke not only English but Russian. "I like the Russians very much," he announced firmly as we got into his car. He would show me everything, he said. Nothing to hide.

It was sundown as we approached the barren hills where a huge channel is being cut contiguous to the Nile. Ten thousand men work three eight-hour shifts. Most of the heavy work is done in the cool of the night. Off to the left of the road I noticed a fenced-in compound containing a number of small, modern apartment houses. "The Russians," said my guide. It was a pleasant scene: women chatted in doorways while through uncurtained windows one could see modern kitchens where dinners were cooking. A large sign forbade the taking of photographs.

"How many Russians are there in Aswan?" I asked. He looked at me bewildered. "What you say?" He took refuge in pidgin English. I repeated the question very slowly and distinctly. He looked puzzled. He lost all his English until I made it impossible for him not to understand me.

"You mean how many Russians altogether? Or how many Russian *engineers?*" he countered, playing for time. "After all, there are wives and children, and sometimes visitors and

. . . " I told him carefully and slowly that I would like to know, first, how many Russians altogether; then I would like to know how many of those were engineers. Of course he had thought that what I wanted to know was the actual number of technicians, and in what categories. After all, there were civil engineers, electrical engineers, and so on, but none of *that* was secret. "We have no secrets! Everything open! Anything you want to know we tell you!" He beamed expansively and parked the car in front of a small circular building. Not until I got out did I realize he had not answered the question.

We now stood on a low hill with a long view of the digging. It was a startling sight. Beneath us was the vast channel already cut from the rock. The sun was gone by now, and the channel—more like a crater—was lit by hundreds of electric lights strung on poles. A perpetual haze of dust obscured the view. Russian diesel trucks roared up and down the sides of the crater, adding to the shrill chatter of drills in stone. Behind us a whole town of new buildings had been somewhat casually assembled: machine shops, technical schools, a hospital. In the desert beyond these buildings, a thousand low black tents were pitched, each with its own campfire. Here the workers lived in stern, nomadic contrast to the modern world they were making.

We entered the circular building which contained a large detailed model of the completed dam. On the walls, diagrams, maps, photographs demonstrated the work's progress and dramatized the fertile Egypt-to-be. I met more Egyptian engineers.

We studied the models and I tried unsuccessfully to sound knowledgeable about turbines. I asked how the workers were recruited. Were they local? How quickly could people who had never used machinery be trained? I was told that the fellahin were surprisingly adaptable. They were trained in schools on the spot. Most of the workers are recruited locally. "But the main thing," said my guide, "is that they know how important all this is. And they do."

I had been told that the dam was some forty weeks behind

in its current schedule. But not being an expert in these matters, I could not tell from looking at what I was shown if things were going well or badly, behind or on schedule. The most I could gather was that the engineers were genuinely enthusiastic about their work. Morale is high. And I am ready to testify that they have dug a fine big hole.

We drove to the center of the channel, a good mile from the exhibition hall and at least a hundred yards below the surface of the desert. The air in the crater is almost unbreathable: part dust, part exhaust. A constant haze dims the lights on their poles. The noise is continual and deafening. Hundreds of drills in long, chattering rows break the sandstone floor of the crater, while Russian steam shovels tear at the cliff. I noticed that all the Russian machines looked improvised. No two steam shovels were alike.

We made our way to the entrance of a tunnel cut into a sandstone hill. This was a shortcut to the place where the first turbines were to be set up. At the entrance of the tunnel we were stopped by the only Russian I was to see: a gray, middle-aged man with a tired face. After a long discussion, he gave permission for me to enter the tunnel. "With every Egyptian engineer," said my guide, "there is also a Russian engineer." It was obvious who was in charge.

The tunnel was brightly lit; the noise of drilling was stunningly amplified by stone walls. I was surprised to see occasional puddles of water on the tunnel floor. I daydreamed: The diggers had struck underground springs. That meant there was water in the desert, deep down, and if there was water deep down, all of Egypt's problems were solved. Obviously no one else had figured out the true meaning of the puddles. I turned to my guide. We shouted at one another and I learned that the puddles were caused not by springs but by seepage from the nearby Nile. The nightmare of the dam builders is that the Nile's water might begin to seep at too great a rate through the sandy walls of the crater, wrecking not only the project but possibly diverting the river's course as well.

Finally, lungs protesting, I said that I had seen enough. This time two engineers drove me back to the hotel, where we drank a ceremonial beer together and I complimented them not only on their enthusiasm but on their courage. At the earliest, the dam will be completed in 1970, which means that these men are dedicating their professional lives to a single project. "But we do this, as Nasser says, for the good of our people," said my original guide solemnly. The other engineer was equally solemn: "No, for the good of all humanity." Taking advantage of this suddenly warm mood, I asked again how many Russians were working on the dam. I got two blank looks this time. "What you say?" And I was no wiser when they left.

The next day in Aswan I was able to obtain an unofficial view of what is really going on. There is a good deal of friction between Egyptians and Russians. Much of it is due to the language barrier. The Russians speak only Russian, the Egyptians speak English or French, sometimes both, but few have learned Russian. The professional interpreters are hopeless because, though they can cope with ordinary conversation, they do not know the technical terms of either language. "We use sign language mostly," said one technician glumly. "Everything is too slow."

Another problem is machinery. It is well known that the Soviet has always had a somewhat mystical attitude toward that sine qua non of the machine age: the interchangeable part. It seems to go against the Slavic grain to standardize. Consequently, when a machine breaks down (usually in six months' time) it must be replaced entirely. Efforts to "cannibalize," as the mechanics put it, are futile since a part from one drill will not fit another drill. As a result, Swedish drills are now being imported, at considerable cost.

Humanly, the Russians are praised for their ability to survive without complaint the terrible heat. "But," said one Egyptian, "heat is bad for their babies. They turn all red and get sick so they have to send them home." The Russians keep almost entirely to themselves. One of the livelier engineers was the most critical: "They don't go out; they don't dance;

they don't do nothing. Just eat and drink!" He shook his head disapprovingly, for the Egyptian with any money is a happy fellow who wants to have a good time in whatever is the going way: alcohol has lately caught on, despite the Prophet's injunction, while the smoking of hashish and kif has gone into decline, the result of stringent new laws against their sale and use. Also the emancipation of women is progressing nicely and women are to be seen in public places. Dancing is popular. In fact, the twist was the rage of Cairo's nightclubs until Nasser banned it.

Sooner or later every Egyptian connected with the High Dam denounces John Foster Dulles. He is the principal demon in the Egyptian hell, largely because the engineers still wish the Americans would come in on the dam—speaking only as technicians, they add quickly, reminding one that they are, after all, Western-trained and used to Western machinery and procedures. Also they find Western life sympathetic. But what's done is done . . . and we would look sadly at one another . . . such is Allah's will. The Soviet is committed to the dam to the end. I suspect that they wish they were out of it: spending four hundred million dollars to build the largest dam in the world in the midst of a desert is a venture more apt than not to leave all participants exhausted and disenchanted with one another. And there, but for the grace of John Foster Dulles, go we.

At my hotel in Cairo I found a message from the President's office. My appointment was canceled, but His Excellency would see me in the next few days. I telephoned the Appointments Secretary. When? They would let me know. I was to stand by. Meanwhile, there were many people in and out of the Cabinet I could see. Name anyone. I picked Mohammed Hassanein Heikal. He is editor of Cairo's chief newspaper, *Al Abram*. He is supposed to have written *The Philosophy of the Revolution*, Nasser's *Mein Kampf* (a rather touching work reminiscent more of Pirandello than of Hitler). Heikal is the President's alter ego. An appointment was made for late that afternoon.

I had a drink in a nearby hotel bar with an English journalist who had been some years in Egypt. He is a short, red-faced man who speaks Arabic; he demonstrates the usual love-hate for Nasser which one soon gets used to. "He's a dictator, but then they all are. They have to be. He's personally honest, which few of them are. But the main thing is he's the first man ever to try to do anything for the people here. *The first.* Ever! And it's not just demagoguery. He means it. But the problems! He's inherited the old bureaucracy, the most corrupt in the world. On top of that there aren't enough trained people to run the country, much less all the new business he confiscated last year. The foreigners who used to manage things are gone. Alexandria's a ghost town. Even so, in spite of everything, he's made these people proud to be Egyptians." I said that I thought nationalistic pride, of de Gaulle's *la gloire* sort, too luxurious an emotion in a dangerous world.

"That's not the point. This isn't manifest-destiny stuff. It's that these people really believed they were inferior to everybody else. They thought they really were scum . . . wogs. For centuries. Well, Nasser's changed all that. He's shown them they're like anybody else. We said Egyptians could never run the Suez Canal. Remember? Well, they run it a lot better than we ever did." I asked him about Arab imperialism. Nasser has proposed himself as leader of the Arab world, a new Saladin. Through his radio and through the thousands of Cairo-trained schoolteachers sent out to the various Arab countries, Nasser has tried to incite the people to overthrow their "reactionary" governments and to unite with him in some vague but potent hegemony.

The Englishman laughed. "The joke of course is the Egyptians aren't Arab at all. The Arabs conquered Egypt and stayed. But so have a lot of other races. Nasser himself is only part Arab. The Copts have no Arab blood, while everyone else is a mixture. The Egyptians used to be contemptuous of the Arabs. In fact, their word for Arab means a nomad, a wild man, a . . . " "Hick?" I supplied, and he nodded. "Now everyone's trying to claim pure Arab descent."

We spoke of the more ruthless side of Nasser's reign. Egypt is a police state. Arrests are often indiscriminate. Currently, a journalist is in jail for having provided an American newspaper with the information—accurate—that Nasser is a diabetic. There is nothing resembling representative government. The middle class is in a state of panic.

I asked him about Nasser personally. What sort of a man was he? I got the familiar estimate: great personal charm, most reasonable in conversation, entirely lacking in personal vanity and ostentation . . . he still lives at Heliopolis in the house he owned as a colonel. He tends to be nervous with foreigners, especially with the British and the French. They put him on the defensive. He is a devoted family man, a puritan who was profoundly shocked during his first Cairo meeting with Indonesia's President Sukarno, who gaily asked, "Now, where are the girls?" He worries about gaining weight. He admires Tito because he "showed me how to get help from both sides —without joining either." Nasser in his passion for Egypt has also declared, "I will treat with the devil himself if I have to for my country." But he is wary of foreign commitments. He has said: "An alliance between a big and a small power is an alliance between the wolf and the sheep, and it is bound to end with the wolf devouring the sheep." His relations with the Soviet are correct but not warm. He has imprisoned every Egyptian Communist he can find. He took advantage of a Soviet offer to give technical training to Egyptian students, but when he discovered that their first six months in Moscow were devoted to learning Marxist theory, he withdrew the students and rerouted them to the West. He is thought to be genuinely religious. He is obsessed, as well he might be, by the thought of sudden death.

"He's at the Barrage right now. That's his place downriver. You may as well know you're going to have a hard time seeing him." He looked about to make sure that the ubiquitous barman—a government informer—was out of earshot. Then he whispered: "Nasser was shot at yesterday." I contained my surprise and the Englishman played this dramatic scene with admirable offhandedness. "Complete censorship, of course. It won't hit the papers. He wasn't hurt, but his body-guard was killed. So he's holed up at the Barrage for the rest of this week." Who shot at him? The Englishman shrugged. Saudi Arabia, Yemen, Syria, Iraq, Israel—any number of governments would like Nasser dead.

I sat in the anteroom of the editor of *Al Ahram*. His secretary went on with her work. I glanced at her desk (I can read upside down if the type is sufficiently large) and noted a copy of the American magazine *Daedalus*. Seeing my interest, she gave it to me. It featured an article on birth control. Heikal himself had made many marginal notes. "A problem, isn't it?" I said. She nodded. "A problem."

I was shown into the editor's office. Heikal is a short, lean man, handsome in the way that certain actors of the 30's who played suave villains with pencil moustaches were handsome. He smokes cigars. He gives an impression of great energy. He shook my hand; then he darted back to his desk where he was correcting proofs of an editorial. Would I mind? He always liked to go over them at the last minute. He made marginal notes. He puffed cigar smoke. He is an actor, I decided, giving a performance: Malraux without genius. He has the half-challenging, half-placating manner of those men who are close to a prince.

I waited patiently for quite a few minutes. Finally, he slapped his pencil down with a flourish. He was mine. I asked him how many printer's errors he had found. "Eight," he said precisely, "but mostly I like to change at the last minute." I mentioned *Daedalus* and birth control. "A problem," he said. They were doing their best, of course, but it would take twenty years to educate the people. It was a formidable task.

I then made the error of referring to *The Philosophy of the Revolution* as his book. "My book? *My* book? It is Nasser's book." I said that I had thought it was at least a joint effort. "You've been reading Robert St. John's *The Boss*," which indeed I had. "Well, that is not the only mistake in that book," he said drily. I remarked that it was neither shameful nor unusual for politicians to be helped in their literary work. Even President Kennedy had once been accused of having used a ghost to write an entire book. "Yes," said Heikal knowledgably, "but Sorensen works for Kennedy. I don't work for Nasser. He is my friend. My leader. But I don't work for him." He discussed American politics for a moment; he was the only Egyptian politician or editor I met who knew much about American affairs. I mentioned the recent letter Kennedy had written to Nasser, a personal letter whose contents were more or less known to everyone. Nasser had been sufficiently moved to answer Kennedy personally, not going through the usual Foreign Office machinery. This exchange had been much discussed in Cairo. It was believed that a new era had begun; that the two young Presidents would understand one another. But the crux to the renewed dialogue was unchanged: What about Israel? Was there a solution to the Arab-Israel conflict?

"None," said Heikal firmly, ending all debate. "How can there be?" Before I could stop him, he was off in full tirade. I was reminded of 1948, of the seven hundred thousand Arabs driven from their Palestinian homes, of the predatoriness of Israeli foreign policy, and how it is written on the wall of the Knesset that there would one day be a Jewish empire from the Mediterranean to the Euphrates. He spoke of Jewish ingratitude. "The Arabs are the only people *never* to persecute Jews," he said with some accuracy. "English, French, Germans, Spanish, at one time or another every country in Europe persecuted them, but never we. During the last war, we were friends to them. Then they do this! They dispossess Arabs from their homes. They move into a land which isn't theirs. The Jews," he said, with a note of triumph, "are not a race, they're a religion." There is nothing quite so chilling as to hear a familiar phrase in a new context. I relished it. "They are *Europeans*," he said grimly, coming to the point, "setting themselves up in *our* world. No, there is no solution!" But then he became reasonable. "The real fault of course is our weakness, and their strength. Our policy now is to build up Egypt. Perhaps when we are stronger economically there will be less to fear from the Israelis." This seems to be current Egyptian policy.

We discussed Nasser's "Arab socialism." Heikal was emphatic: it was not doctrinaire socialism. It was improvisational. Point-to-point navigation, as it were. I said that despite some of the methods used to expropriate businesses, there was no doubt that some kind of socialism was inevitable for Egypt and that Nasser had merely done the inevitable. But Heikal would not accept this small compliment. "Methods? Methods? You make us sound like Stalin, with your 'methods'!" I said I had not meant to compare Nasser to Stalin. He cut me off. "What we do is legal. Open. It is for the people. How can you accuse us of 'methods' . . ." This time I cut *him* off. With some irritation, I told him that I had no intention of repeating the various horror stories told me by those who had been ruined by his government, their businesses seized, their livelihoods ended. Even allowing for the natural exaggeration of victims, such methods were not apt to please those who were ruined by them. Nor was it only the large corporations which had been nationalized. Innumerable small businesses had also been taken over. An owner would come to work one morning to find an army officer sitting at his desk, directing what had been his business the day before.

Heikal was scornful. "So we take their money. So they are not happy. So what? At least they are still alive! That's something!" He felt this showed great restraint on the part of the government and perhaps he was right. I was reminded of Joseph Stalin's answer to Lady Astor when she asked him, "When are you going to stop killing people?" "The undesirable classes," said the tyrant, turning upon her his coldest eye, "never liquidate themselves."

Wanting to needle Heikal—an irresistible impulse—I said I didn't think that the endlessly vituperative style of Egypt's newspapers was very apt to win them any friends. Israel is the principal victim of these attacks, but any government which does not momentarily please Nasser will get the full treatment from the Arab press and radio.

Heikal took my question personally, as well he might. His voice slipped automatically into the singsong of rhetoric and denunciation. "We write this way because we feel this way. How can we help it? How can we be asked not to say what we feel so strongly? Take the British, *I hate the British*. I can't help it. I saw them. I know them. Their contempt for us. Their treachery. And over Suez they were not . . . kind." This was an unexpected word. "You came into Suez with force." "They," I murmured. "You tried to destroy us." "They," I said somewhat more loudly. "All right," he said irritably, the tide of his rhetoric briefly stemmed. "*They* wanted to destroy us. So how can we feel anything but hate for them? Look what they did to the Arab world after 1918. They brought back the kings, the sheiks, to keep us medieval. As if we were to occupy England and restore the lords, break the country up into Saxon kingdoms. So how can we express ourselves in any way except the way we do?" Like most rhetorical questions, no answer was desired.

Actually, the fulminating style is inherent in the language (*vide* the Old Testament). Semitic languages are curiously suited to the emotional tirade, even when the speaker is not himself an emotional man. By nature Nasser is an unemotional speaker. As a rule he will bore his audiences for an hour or two, droning on sensibly about the state of the nation. Then when he is in danger of losing them entirely, he allows the language to do its natural work; he proposes that all Egypt's enemies "choke in their rage" as well as other gaudy sentiments calculated to keep his torpid audience awake. Yet to give Nasser his due he is, verbally, one of the most continent of Arab leaders.

Heikal reverted to Israel. Did I realize that thirty-eight per cent of their budget went for the military as opposed to thirteen per cent of Egypt's budget? Having spent several days poring over the Egyptian budget, I was surprised that anyone could have come up with any figure for any department. The only ascertainable fact is that Egypt is flat broke. But I accepted his figures. I did remark that it must be distressing for Israel—for any country—to be reminded daily that its neighbors, once they awaken from their "deep slumber," will drive them into the sea. After all, no one wants to be drowned. Heikal shook his head sadly: didn't I realize that the Israeli military expenditure was for offense, not defense? I asked him point-blank: "Do you think Israel is planning an offensive war against Egypt?" He shrugged. I then mentioned his own press's continual reminder of Israel's financial dependence on the United States. This being true, did he really think that the United States would permit Israel to embark on a military adventure? We had effectively stopped Israel, France, and England at the time of Suez. Did he honestly believe that we would now allow Israel, by itself, to launch an attack on Egypt? He edged away. No, he did not think the United States would allow a unilateral action. "But," he added quickly, "you can't blame us for being on guard." Then again he reverted to what is the government's present line: we must strengthen Egypt, concentrate on home problems, create "Arab socialism," become a model for the rest of the Arab world.

As I left, I told him that if I saw Nasser at the end of the week I was perfectly willing to present to the American public Egypt's case against Israel, just as Egypt would like it presented. Partly out of a sense of mischief (we hear altogether too much of the other side) and partly out of a sense of justice, I thought that the Arab case *should* be given attention in the American press. As of now it has been disregarded. In fact, a few years ago the Egyptians, despairing of ever seeing their cause presented impartially in the usual news columns, tried to buy an advertisement in the New York *Times.* They were turned down. As a result, the Egyptians are somewhat cynical about our "free press." They are also quite aware that when Israel was being founded in 1948 and the Arabs protested to Harry Truman, he told them with characteristic bluntness: "I do not have hundreds of thousands of Arabs among my constituents." Heikal laughed when I told him that the Arab point of view might one day be given in the American national press. "Your press would never let you," he said with finality, as one journalist to another. "Don't even try."

Another week passed. More appointments were made with Nasser. Each was broken at the last minute, and I was advised to be patient. He would see me soon. But then the Syrian comedy began, disrupting Nasser's schedule. The President of Syria was removed by some army colonels in Damascus. A few days later the young captains in Aleppo tried to overthrow the older officers in Damascus who had overthrown the President. The young men in Aleppo declared that they were for Nasser; they wanted union again with Egypt. Was Nasser behind this plot? Some think yes. Some think no. I suspect no. As one of his closest advisers said, with what seemed candor: "We don't even know these boys in Aleppo. They're much younger than our group." It is protocol in the Middle East that only colonels may start revolutions. Generals are too old, captains too young. In any case, the colonels in Damascus triumphed over the captains in Aleppo and then in a marvelous gesture of frustration the colonels restored the President they had overthrown in the first place. There was no one else, apparently, available for the job. But by the time this comedy had run its course I had fled Egypt, though just as I was getting on the plane to Beirut there was yet another telephone message from the President's office: "His Excellency will definitely see you tomorrow." But I was ready to go, shamefully demonstrating the difference between the amateur and the professional journalist. The professional would have remained, as Hans Von Kaltenborn once remained six weeks, to obtain an interview with Nasser. The amateur moves on.

"The Arabs are their own worst enemies," said a foreign diplomat in Beirut. "They can't present anything to anyone without undermining themselves. They are self-destructive. In fact, many of them actually believe that since this world is a mess, why bother to alter it when what really matters is the Paradise to come." I was reminded of the Koran, where it is written that "The life of the world is only play and idle talk and pageantry."

The Arabs' religion contributes greatly to the difficulties

they are experiencing in the modern world. Americans tend to believe, in a vague, soupy way, that all religion is A Good Thing. Richard Nixon was much applauded when he said that a man's religion should never be a matter of concern in politics, *unless of course he had no religion.* Nixon shook his head gravely on that one. Yet some religions are more useful than others, and some religions are downright dangerous to the human spirit and to the building of a good society.

To understand the Arab world one must understand the Koran, a work Goethe described as "A holy book which, however often we approach it, always disgusts us anew, but then attracts, and astonishes and finally compels us to respect it." It is a remarkable work which I shall not go into here except to note that its Five Pillars are: (1) the creed; (2) the prayer; (3) the fast; (4) the pilgrimage to Mecca; (5) almsgiving. One unfortunate result of the last: the holiness which accrues to almsgivers has fostered a demoralizing tradition of beggars. Also, in requesting aid of other countries, the Arab nations are profoundly self-righteous and demanding, on the high moral ground that they are doing the giver a favor by taking his money and making him more holy. The result has been that until very recently American aid to Egypt was almost never acknowledged in the press or noted in any other way, except by complaints that the giver, if he weren't so selfish, ought to come through with ever more cash, making himself that much worthier in Allah's eyes. In any event, no quo for the quid is Arab policy, as both the Soviet and ourselves have discovered.

I found myself continually asking diplomats, journalists, and old Arab hands: Why should we give *any* aid to Egypt? What do we gain by it? What should we get from it? Answers were never very precise. Naturally, there was "the Soviet threat." If we don't help Egypt, the Russians will and the Middle East will come into "the Soviet sphere." For a number of reasons this is not likely to happen. Soviet policy in the Arab world has been even more unsuccessful than our own. In 1956, after jailing the local Communists (while accepting Soviet aid for the High Dam), Nasser said quite explicitly:

"The Communists have lost faith in religion, which in their opinion is a myth. . . . Our final conclusion is that we shall never repudiate it in exchange for the Communist doctrine." The Moslem world and the Marxist world are an eternity apart. Paradise here and now on earth, as the result of hard work and self-sacrifice, is not a congenial doctrine to the Arab. Also, of some importance is the Egyptian's human response to the Russians: they find them austere, dogmatic, and rather alarming.

One is also reminded that whether Nasser chooses to be absorbed by the Soviet bloc or not, at a time of chaos the Soviets *might* move in and take the country by force. This drastic shift in the world balance of power is not easy to visualize. The Soviets, already overextended financially, are not apt to take on (any more than we are) the burden of governing a starving Egypt. But if they did, it is unlikely that they would then shut down the Suez Canal (England's old nightmare), since, after cotton, the canal is the main source of Egypt's revenue. I would suggest that the strategic value of Egypt to the West is very small, and it merely turns Nasser's head and feeds his sense of unreality for us to pretend that Egypt is of great consequence. Yet it is of *some* consequence, especially now.

The principal source of irritation between Nasser and the United States is Israel, a nation in which we have a large economic and emotional interest. But I got the impression from members of the Egyptian government that the continual tirades against Israel are largely for home consumption. Nations traditionally must have the Enemy to prod them into action. President Kennedy finds it difficult to get any large appropriation bill through our Congress unless he can first prove that it will contribute to the holy war against Communism. Once he has established that he is indeed striking a blow at the Enemy, he can get any money he needs, whether it is to explore the moon or to give assistance to the public schools. In the same way, Nasser needs the idea of Israel to goad his own people into the twentieth century.

Nasser once said to Miles Copeland, "If you want the cooperation of any Middle Eastern leader you must first understand his limitations—those limitations placed on him by the emotions and suspicions of the people he leads—and be reconciled to the fact that you can never ask him to go beyond those limitations. If you feel you *must* have him go beyond them, you must be prepared to help him lessen the limitations." A most rational statement of any politician's dilemma; and one which Dulles in his blithely righteous way ignored, causing Nasser to observe with some bitterness in 1956: "Dulles asked me to commit suicide." National leaders are always followers of public opinion. No matter how well-intentioned they might be privately, they are limited by those they govern. Paradoxically, this is truest of dictators.

Our current policy toward Nasser is sympathetic. It is hard to say to what extent he can or will respond, but it is evident that he is trying. His value to us is much greater now that he has, temporarily, given up hope of leading the Arab world, of becoming the new Saladin. He must make Egypt work first. He is perfectly—sadly—aware that Algeria and Morocco, two Arab nations potentially richer and politically more sophisticated than Egypt, may well provide new leadership for the Moslem world. His only remaining hope is to make "Arab socialism" a success. If it is, then the kings and the sheiks will eventually fall of their own corruption and incompetence, and Nasser's way will be the Arab's way.

What is our role? Since 1952 our assistance to Egypt has totaled $705,000,000. Over half this amount was given or loaned in the last three years. So far the Egyptian government has been most scrupulous in its interest payments, etc. However, since July, 1961, when Nasser seized most of the nation's industries and businesses, he has opposed all private investment. The only assistance he will accept (the weak must be firm!) is government-to-government, with no political strings. Again, why should we help him?

"Because," said an American economist, "any aid ties him to us, whether he likes it or not, whether he acknowledges it or not. If we help him build the new power plant in Cairo (with Westinghouse assistance), he will have to come to us in the future for parts and technicians. That's good business for us. That keeps *our* economy expanding." This, of course, is the standard rationale for America's foreign-aid program, and up to a point it is valid. Today's empires are held not with the sword but the dollar. It is the nature of the national organism to expand and proliferate. We truly believe that we never wanted a world empire simply because we don't suffer (since Teddy Roosevelt, at least) from a desire to see Old Glory waving over the parliaments of enslaved nations. But we do want to make a buck. We do want to maintain our standard of living. For good or ill, we have no other true national purpose. There is no passion in America for military glory, at least outside of Texas and Arizona. Our materialistic ethos is made quite plain in the phrase "the American way of life."

I submit that our lack of commitment to any great mystique of national destiny is the healthiest thing about us and the reason for our current success. We are simple materialists, not bent on setting fire to the earth as a matter of holy principle, unlike the True Believers with their fierce Either-Ors, their Red or Dead absolutes, when the truth is that the world need be neither, just comfortably pink and lively. Even aid to such a disagreeable and unreliable nation as Nasser's Egypt increases our sphere of influence, expands our markets, maintains our worldly empire. And we are an empire. Americans who would not have it so had best recall Pericles' admonition to those Athenians who wished to shirk imperial responsibilities. We may have been wrong to acquire an empire, Pericles said, but now that we possess one, it is not safe for us to let it go. Nor is it safe for the United States to opt out now. Luckily, our passion for trade and moneymaking and our relatively unromantic view of ourselves has made us surprisingly attractive to the rest of the world,* especially to those countries whose rulers suffer from *folie de grandeur*.

*Those were the days!

Historians often look to the Roman Empire to find analogies with the United States. They flatter us. We live not under the Pax Americana, but the Pax Frigida. I should not look to Rome for comparison but rather to the Most Serene Venetian Republic, a pedestrian state devoted to wealth, comfort, trade, and keeping the peace, especially after inheriting the wreck of the Byzantine Empire, as we have inherited the wreck of the British Empire. Venice was not inspiring but it worked. Ultimately, our danger comes not from the idea of Communism, which (as an Archbishop of Canterbury remarked) is a "Christian heresy" whose materialistic aims (as opposed to means) vary little from our own; rather, it will come from the increasing wealth and skill of other Serene Republics which, taking advantage of our increasing moral and intellectual fatness, will try to seize our markets in the world. If we are to end, it will not be with a Bomb but a bigger Buck. Fortunately, under that sanctimoniousness so characteristic of the American selling something, our governors know that we are fighting not for "the free world" but to hold onto an economic empire not safe or pleasant to let go. The Arab world—or as salesmen would say, "territory"—is almost ours, and we must persevere in landing that account. It will be a big one some day.

Esquire, October 1963

EDMUND WILSON, TAX DODGER

"Between the year 1946 and the year 1955, I did not file any income tax returns."

With that blunt statement, Edmund Wilson embarks on a most extraordinary polemic.* He tells us why he did not pay his taxes. Apparently he had never made much money. He was generally ignorant of the tax laws. In 1946, when his novel *Memoirs of Hecate County* was published, his income doubled. Then the book was suppressed by court order and the income stopped. While all this was going on, he was much distracted by a tangled private life. So what with one thing and another, Mr. Wilson never got around to filing a return.

"It may seem naïve, and even stupid, on the part of one who had worked for years on a journal which specialized in public affairs (the *New Republic*) that he should have paid so little

---

* *The Cold War and the Income Tax* (1963).

attention to recent changes in the income tax laws . . ." It does indeed seem naïve and stupid, and one cannot help but think that our premier literary critic (who among other great tasks of illumination explained Marxian economics to a generation) is a bit of a dope. But with that harsh judgment out of the way, one can only admire his response to the American bureaucracy.

Mr. Wilson originally owed $20,000 in unpaid taxes. With interest and fines, the $20,000 became $60,000. The Internal Revenue Service then went into action, and Mr. Wilson learned at first hand just how much power the IRS exerts. Royalties, trust funds, bank accounts can be attached; automobiles may be seized and sold at auction. Nothing belongs to the victim until the case is settled. Meanwhile, his private life is ruthlessly invaded in order to discover if he is of criminal intent (and therefore willfully bilking the nation of its rightful revenue). In Mr. Wilson's case, much was made of the fact that he had been married four times (a sign of unstable temperament); that he had written, Heaven help him, *books*! In a passage of exquisite irony, Mr. Wilson describes how one of the agents was put to work reading the master's complete *oeuvre* in order to prove that his not paying taxes was part of a sinister design to subvert a great nation. Did they find anything? Yes. In a journalistic piece, Mr. Wilson seemed to admire a man who had, among other crimes, not paid a Federal tax.

Even more unpleasant than the bureau's legitimate investigation was the unrelenting impertinence of the investigators. Why did Mr. Wilson spend six dollars to buy a cushion for his dog to sleep on? Why did he keep three places to live when the investigator (who earned a virtuous $7,500 a year) needed only one place to live in? Why was Mr. Wilson's daughter in a private school? Even worse than this sort of harassment was the inefficiency and buck-passing of the bureau. No one seemed able to make a decision. Regional office A had no idea what regional office B had decided. Then, just as progress was about to be made, a new investigator would be assigned the case and everyone had to go back to "Start." Kafka inevitably comes to mind; also, the bureaucracy of the Soviet Union which Mr. Wilson once contrasted—to his regret—unfavorably with our own.

After describing his own particular predicament, Mr. Wilson then discusses the general question of the income tax and the free society. He records in detail the history of the tax since the 1913 Constitutional amendment which made it legal (in 1895 the Supreme Court had ruled that President Lincoln's wartime tax on personal income was unconstitutional). Inexorably, the Federal tax has increased until today we pay more tax than we did during the Second World War. And there is no end in sight.

Mr. Wilson then asks a simple question: Why must we pay so much? He notes the conventional answer: Since the cold war, foreign aid, and defense account for seventy-nine per cent of all Federal expenditures, putting the nation in permanent hock to that economic military complex President Eisenhower so movingly warned us against after a lifetime's loyal service to it. There is of course some consolation in the fact that we are not wasting our billions weakening the moral fiber of the American yeoman by building him roads and schools, or by giving him medical care and decent housing. In public services, we lag behind all the industrialized nations of the West, preferring that the public money go not to the people but to big business. The result is a unique society in which we have free enterprise for the poor and socialism for the rich. This dazzling inequity is reflected in our tax system where the man on salary pays more tax than the man who lives on dividends, who in turn pays more tax than the wheeler-dealer who makes a capital-gains deal.

How did we get into this jam? Admittedly, the Soviet is a formidable enemy, and we have been well advised to protect ourselves. Empires traditionally must buy not only weapons but allies, and we are, like it or not, an empire. But there is no evidence that we need spend as much as we do spend on atomic overkill, on foreign aid, on chemical and bacteriological warfare (we are now reactivating at great expense diseases that the human race has spent centuries attempting to wipe out).

Mr. Wilson is excellent at describing the mad uses to which our tax money is being put ($30 billion to get a man on the moon is lunacy), but he seems not to be aware of the original policy behind the cold war. It was John Foster Dulles's decision to engage the Soviet in an arms race. Dulles figured, reasonably enough, that the Soviet economy could not endure this sort of competition. It was also believed that even if they should achieve military parity, their people, hungering for consumer goods, would revolt. This policy was successful for a time. But it worked as much hardship on our free society as it did on their closed one. We have become a garrison state, frightened of our own government and bemused by a rhetoric in which all is appearance, nothing reality. Or, as Mr. Wilson puts it:

"The truth is that the people of the United States are at the present time dominated and driven by two kinds of officially propagated fear: fear of the Soviet Union and fear of the income tax.

"These two terrors have been adjusted so as to complement one another and thus to keep the citizen of our free society under the strain of a double pressure from which he finds himself unable to escape—like the man in the old Western story who, chased into a narrow ravine by a buffalo, is confronted with a grizzly bear. If we fail to accept the tax, the Russian buffalo will butt and trample us, and if we try to defy the tax, the Federal bear will crush us."

Is there a way out? Mr. Wilson is not optimistic. Opponents of the income tax tend to be of the Far Right, where they fear the buffalo even more than they do the bear. There is nothing quite so engaging in our public life today as to hear Barry Goldwater tell us how we can eventually eliminate the graduated income tax *while* increasing military expenditures. Also, the militant conservative, though he will go to the barricades to keep a Federal dollar from filtering down to a state school, sees nothing wrong with Federal billions subsidizing a corporation in which he owns stock. As for the politicians, they tend to be too much part of the system to try and change it. The most passionate Congressional budget cutter will do all that he can to get Federal money for his own district. Between the pork barrel and the terrible swift sword, Pentagon, Congress, and industry are locked together, and nothing short of a major popular revolt can shatter their embrace.

Mr. Wilson discusses in some detail various attempts made by individuals (mostly pacifists) to thwart the IRS. But the results have not been happy. The line between Thoreau and Poujade is a delicate one. Yet it is perfectly clear that it must one day be drawn if the United States is not to drift into a rigid Byzantine society where the individual is the state's creature (yes, liberals worry about this, too), his life the property of a permanent self-perpetuating bureaucracy, frozen in some vague never-ending cold war with an enemy who is merely a reflection of itself.

Edmund Wilson's personal conclusion is a sad one. He points out that at the age of sixty-eight he can never hope to pay the government what he owes. According to his settlement with the IRS, everything that he makes over a certain amount goes automatically toward settling the debt. On principle, he hopes to keep his income below the taxable level. More to the point, as a result of his experience with the New America, "I have finally come to feel that this country, whether or not I live in it, is no longer any place for me." That is a stunning indictment of us all. Edmund Wilson is our most distinguished man of letters. He has always been (though the bureaucrats may not know it) something of a cultural America Firster. To lose such a man is a warning signal that our society is approaching that shadow line which, once crossed, means an end to what the makers of the country had hoped would be a place in which happiness might be usefully pursued. Yet Mr. Wilson's grim pamphlet may be just the jolt we need.

Not since Thomas Paine has the drum of polemic sounded with such urgency through the land, and it is to be hoped that every citizen of the United States will read this book.

Book Week, November 3, 1963

Few matters of a substantive nature can be discussed in the United States. Wilson's extraordinary book was regarded as a joke at the time. In the ten years that have passed, the injustice of our tax system and the evil and foolish uses to which the national income is put are at last, most timidly, being noted.

TARZAN REVISITED

There are so many things that people who take polls never get around to asking. Fascinated as we all are to know what our countrymen think of great issues (approving, disapproving, don't-knowing, with that native shrewdness which made a primeval wilderness bloom with Howard Johnson signs), the pollsters never get around to asking the sort of interesting personal questions our new Romans might be able to answer knowledgeably. For instance, how many adults have an adventure serial running in their heads? How many consciously daydream, turning on a story in which the dreamer ceases to be an employee of IBM and becomes a handsome demigod moving through splendid palaces, saving maidens from monsters (or monsters from maidens: this is a jaded time). Most children tell themselves stories in which they figure as powerful figures, enjoying the pleasures not only of the adult world as they conceive it but of a world of wonders unlike dull reality. Although this sort of Mittyesque daydreaming is supposed to cease in maturity, I suggest that more adults than we suspect are dazedly wandering about with a full Technicolor extravaganza going on in their heads. Clad in tights, rapier in hand, the daydreamers drive their Jaguars at fantastic speeds through a glittering world of adoring love objects, mingling anachronistic historic worlds with science fiction. "Captain, the time-warp's been closed! We are now trapped in a parallel world, inhabited entirely by women with three breasts!" Though from what we can gather about these imaginary worlds, they tend to be more Adlerian than Freudian: the motor drive is the desire not for sex (other briefer fantasies take care of that) but for power, for the ability to dominate one's environment through physical strength, best demonstrated in the works of Edgar Rice Burroughs, whose books are enjoying a huge revival.

When I was growing up, I read all twenty-three Tarzan books, as well as the ten Mars books. My own inner story-telling mechanism was vivid. At any one time, I had at least three serials going as well as a number of tried and true reruns. I mined Burroughs largely for source material. When he went to the center of the earth à la Jules Verne (much too fancy a writer for one's taste), I immediately worked up a thirteen-part series, with myself as lead and various friends as guest stars. Sometimes I used the master's material, but more often I adapted it freely to suit myself. One's daydreams tended to be Tarzanish pre-puberty (physical strength and freedom) and Martian post-puberty (exotic worlds and subtle *combinazione* to be worked out). After adolescence, if one's life is sufficiently interesting, the desire to tell oneself stories diminishes. My last serial ran into sponsor trouble when I was in the Second World War, and it was never renewed.

Until recently I assumed that most people were like myself: daydreaming ceases when the real world becomes interesting and reasonably manageable. Now I am not so certain. Pondering the life and success of Burroughs leads one to believe that a good many people find their lives so unsatisfactory that they go right on year after year telling themselves stories in which they are able to dominate their environment in a way that is not possible in the overorganized society.

According to Edgar Rice Burroughs, "Most of the stories I wrote were the stories I told myself just before I went to sleep." He is a fascinating figure to contemplate, an archetypal American dreamer. Born in 1875 in Chicago, he was a drifter until he was thirty-six. He served briefly in the U.S. Cavalry; then he was a gold miner in Oregon, a cowboy in Idaho, a railroad policeman in Salt Lake City; he attempted several businesses that failed. He was perfectly in the old-American grain: the man who could take on almost any job, who liked to keep moving, who tried to get rich quick but could never pull it off. And while he was drifting through the unsatisfactory real world, he consoled himself with an inner world where he was strong and handsome, adored by beautiful women and worshiped by exotic races. His principal source of fantasy was Rider Haggard. But even that rich field was limited, and so, searching for new veins to tap, he took to reading the pulp magazines, only to find that none of the stories could compare for excitement with his own imaginings. Since the magazine writers could not please him, he had no choice but to please himself, and the public. He composed a serial about Mars and sold it to *Munsey's*. The rest was easy, for his fellow daydreamers recognized at once a master dreamer.

In 1914 Burroughs published *Tarzan of the Apes* (Rousseau's noble savage reborn in Africa), and history was made. To date the Tarzan books have sold over twenty-five million copies in fifty-six languages. There is hardly an American male of my generation who has not at one time or another tried to master the victory cry of the great ape as it issued from the androgynous chest of Johnny Weissmuller, to the accompaniment of thousands of arms and legs snapping during attempts to swing from tree to tree in the backyards of the Republic. Between 1914 and his death in 1950, the squire of Tarzana, California (a prophet more than honored in his own land), produced over sixty books, while enjoying the unique status of being the first American writer to be a corporation. Burroughs is said to have been a pleasant, unpretentious man who liked to ride and play golf. Not one to compromise a vivid unconscious with dim reality, he never set foot in Africa.

With a sense of recapturing childhood, I have just reread several Tarzan books. It is fascinating to see how much one recalls after a quarter century. At times the sense of *déjà vu* is overpowering. It is equally interesting to discover that one's memories of Tarzan of the Apes are mostly action scenes. The plot had slipped one's mind . . . and a lot of plot there is. The beginning is worthy of Conrad. "I had this story from one who had no business to tell it to me, or to any other. I may credit the seductive influence of an old vintage upon the narrator for the beginning of it, and my own skeptical incredulity during the days that followed for the balance of the strange tale." It is 1888. The young Lord and Lady Greystoke are involved in a ship mutiny ("there was in the whole atmosphere of the craft that undefinable something which presages disaster"). The peer and peeress are put ashore on the west coast of Africa, where they promptly build a tree house. Here Burroughs is at his best. He tells you the size of the logs, the way to hang a door when you have no hinges, the problems of roofing. One of the best things about his books is the descriptions of making things. The Greystokes have a child, and conveniently die. The "man-child" is discovered by Kala, a Great Ape, who brings him up as a member of her tribe. As anthropologist, Burroughs is pleasantly vague. His apes are carnivorous, and they are able, he darkly suspects, to mate with human beings.

Tarzan grows up as an ape, kills his first lion (with a full nelson), teaches himself to read and write English by studying some books found in the cabin. The method he used, sad to say, is the currently fashionable "look-see." Though he can read and write, he cannot speak any language except that of the apes. He also gets on well with other members of the animal kingdom, with Tantor the elephant, Ska the vulture, Numa the lion (Kipling was also grist for the Burroughs dream mill). Then white folks arrive: Professor Archimedes Q. Porter and his daughter Jane. Also, a Frenchman named D'Arnot who teaches Tarzan to speak French, which is confusing. By an extraordinary coincidence, Jane's suitor is the current Lord Greystoke, who thinks the Greystoke baby is dead. Tarzan saves Jane from an ape. Then he puts on clothes and goes to Paris, where he drinks absinthe. Next stop, America. In Wisconsin, he saves Jane Porter from a forest fire: only to give her up nobly to Lord Greystoke, not revealing the fact that *he* is the real Lord Greystoke. Fortunately in the next volume, *The Return of Tarzan*, he marries Jane and they live happily ever after in Africa, raising a son John, who in turn grows up and has a son. Yet even as a grandfather, Tarzan continues to have adventures with people a foot high, with descendants of Atlantis, with the heirs of a Roman legion who think that Rome is still a success. All through these stories one gets the sense that one is daydreaming, too. Episode follows episode with no particular urgency. Tarzan is always knocked on the head and taken captive; he always escapes; there is always a beautiful princess or high priestess who loves him and assists him; there is always a loyal friend who fights beside him, very much in that Queequeg tradition which, Professor Leslie Fiedler assures us, is the urning in the fuel supply of the American psyche. But no matter how difficult the adventure, Tarzan, clad only in a loincloth with no weapon save a knife (the style is comforting to imitate), wins against all odds and returns to his shadowy wife.

Stylistically, Burroughs is—how shall I put it?—uneven. He has moments of ornate pomp, when the darkness is "Cimmerian"; of redundancy, "she was hideous and ugly"; of extraordinary dialogue: "Name of a name," shrieked Rokoff. "Pig, but you shall die for this!" Or Lady Greystoke to Lord G.: "Duty is duty, my husband, and no amount of sophistries may change it. I would be a poor wife for an English lord were I to be responsible for his shirking a plain duty." Or the grandchild: "Muvver," he cried, "Dackie doe? Dackie doe?" "Let him come along," urged Tarzan. "Dare!" exclaimed the boy, turning triumphantly upon the governess, "Dackie do doe yalk!" Burroughs's use of coincidence is shameless even for a pulp writer. In one book he has three sets of characters shipwrecked at exactly the same point on the shore of Africa. Even Burroughs finds this a bit much. "Could it be possible [muses Tarzan] that fate had thrown him up at the very threshold of his own beloved jungle?" It was possible since anything can happen in a daydream.

Though Burroughs is innocent of literature and cannot reproduce human speech, he does have a gift very few writers of any kind possess: he can describe action vividly. I give away no trade secrets when I say that this is as difficult for a Tolstoi as it is for a Burroughs (even William). Because it is so hard, the craftier contemporary novelists usually prefer to tell their stories in the first person, which is simply writing dialogue. In character, as it were, the writer settles for an impression of what happened rather than creating the sense of the thing happening. In action Tarzan is excellent.

There is something basic in the appeal of the 1914 Tarzan which makes me think that he can still hold his own as a daydream figure, despite the sophisticated challenge of his two young competitors, James Bond and Mike Hammer. For most adults, Tarzan (and John Carter of Mars) can hardly compete with the conspicuous consumer consumption of James Bond or the sickly violence of Mike Hammer, but for children and adolescents the old appeal continues. All of us need the idea of a world alternative to this one. From Plato's Republic to Opar to Bondland, at every level, the human imagination has tried to imagine something better for itself than the existing society. Man left Eden when he got up off all fours, endowing his descendants with nostalgia as well as chronic backache. In its naïve way, the Tarzan legend returns us to that Eden where, free of clothes and the inhibitions of an oppressive society, a man is able, as William Faulkner put it in his high Confederate style, to prevail as well as endure. The current fascination with LSD and nonaddictive drugs—not to mention alcohol—is all a result of a general sense of boredom. Since the individual's desire to dominate his environment is not a desirable trait in a society that every day grows more and more confining, the average man must take to daydreaming. James Bond, Mike Hammer, and Tarzan are all dream selves, and the aim of each is to establish personal primacy in a world that, more and more, diminishes the individual. Among adults, the current popularity of these lively fictions strikes me as a most significant and unbearably sad phenomenon.

Esquire, December 1963

JOHN O'HARA

In 1938, writing to a friend, George Santayana described his first (and presumably last) encounter with the writing of Somerset Maugham. "I could read these [stories], enticed by the familiarity he shows with Spain, and with Spanish Americans, in whose moral complexion I feel a certain interest; but on the whole I felt . . . wonder at anybody wishing to write such stories. They are not pleasing, they are not pertinent to one's real interests, they are not true; they are simply graphic or plausible, like a bit of a dream that one might drop into in an afternoon nap. Why record it? I suppose it is to make money, because writing stories is a profession . . ." In just such a way, the Greek philosophers condemned the novels of the Milesian school. Unpleasing, impertinent, untruthful—what else can one say about these fictions except to speculate idly on why grown men see fit to write them. Money? There seems nothing more to be said.

Yet there is at least one good reason for a serious consideration of popular writing. "When you are criticizing the Philosophy of an epoch," wrote Alfred Whitehead in *Adventures Of Ideas*, "do not chiefly direct your attention to those intellectual positions which its exponents feel it necessary to defend. There will be some fundamental assumption which adherents of all the various systems within the epoch unconsciously presuppose." Writers of fiction, even more than systematic philosophers, tend to reveal unconscious presuppositions. One might even say that those writers who are the most popular are the ones who share the largest number of common assumptions with their audience, subliminally reflecting prejudices and aspirations so obvious that they are never stated and, never stated, never precisely understood or even recognized. John O'Hara is an excellent example of this kind of writer, and useful to any examination of what we are.

Over the last three decades, Mr. O'Hara has published close to thirty volumes of stories, plays, essays and novels. Since 1955 he has had a remarkable burst of activity: twelve books. His most recent novel, *Elizabeth Appleton*, was written in 1960 but kept off the market until 1963 in order that five other books might be published. His latest collection of short stories, *The Hat on the Bed*, is currently a best seller and apparently gives pleasure to the public. In many ways, Mr. O'Hara's writing is precisely the sort Santayana condemned: graphic and plausible, impertinent and untrue. But one must disagree with Santayana as to *why* this sort of work is done (an irrelevant speculation, in any case). Money is hardly the motive. No man who devotes a lifetime to writing can ever be entirely cynical, if only because no one could sustain for a lifetime the pose of being other than himself. Either the self changes or the writing changes. One cannot have it both ways. Mr. O'Hara uses himself quite as fully and obsessively as William Faulkner. The difference between them lies in capacity, and the specific use each makes of a common obsession to tell what it is like to be alive. But where Faulkner re-created his society through a gifted imagination, Mr. O'Hara merely reflects that society, making him, of the two, rather the more interesting for our immediate purpose, which is to examine through certain popular works the way we live now.

Mr. O'Hara's work is in the naturalistic tradition. "I want to get it all down on paper while I can. The U. S. in this century, what I know, and it is my business to write about it to the best of my ability with the sometimes special knowledge that I have." He also wants "to record the way people talked and thought and felt, and to do it with complete honesty and variety." In this, he echoes Sinclair Lewis, Emile Zola, and (rather dangerously) the brothers Goncourt.

The Hat on the Bed is a collection of twenty-four short stories. They are much like Mr. O'Hara's other short stories, although admirers seem to prefer them to earlier collections. Right off, one is aware of a passionate interest in social distinctions. Invariably we are told not only what university a character attended but also what prep school. Clothes, houses, luggage (by Vuitton), prestigious restaurants are all carefully noted, as well as brand names. With the zest of an Internal Revenue man examining deductions for entertainment, the author investigates the subtle difference between the spending of old middle-class money and that of new middle-class money. Of course social distinctions have always been an important aspect of the traditional novel, but what disturbs one in reading Mr. O'Hara is that he does so little with these details once he has noted them. If a writer chooses to tell us that someone went to St. Paul's and to Yale and played squash, then surely there is something about St. Paul's and Yale and squash which would make him into a certain kind of person so that, given a few more details, the reader is then able to make up his mind as to just what that triad of experience means, and why it is different from Exeter-Harvard-lacrosse. But Mr. O'Hara is content merely to list schools and sports and the makes of cars and the labels on clothes. He fails to do his own job in his own terms, which is to show us *why* a character who went to Andover is not like one who went to Groton, and how the two schools, in some way, contributed to the difference. It would seem that Mr. O'Hara is excited by fashionable schools in much the same way that Balzac was by money, and perhaps for the same reason, a cruel deprivation. Ernest Hemingway (whose malice was always profound) once announced that he intended to take up a collection to send John O'Hara through Yale. In his own defense, Mr. O'Hara has said that his generation did care passionately about colleges. Granting him this, one must then note that the children and grandchildren of his contemporaries do not care in the *same* way, a fact he seems unaware of.

The technique of the short stories does not vary much. The prose is plain and rather garrulous; the dialogue tends to run on, and he writes most of his stories and novels in dialogue because not only is that the easiest kind of writing to read but the easiest to do. In a short story like "The Mayor" one sees his technique at its barest. Two characters meet after three pages of setting up the scene (describing a hangout for the town's politicians and setting up the personality of the mayor, who often drops in). Then two characters start to talk about a third character (the mayor) and his relationship with a fourth, and after some four pages of dialogue—and one small uninteresting revelation—the story is over. It has been, in Santayana's image, a daydream. One has learned nothing, felt nothing. Why record it?

Another short story, "How Can I Tell You?" is purest reverie. Once upon a time there was a car salesman who by all worldly standards is a success; he even gets on well with his wife. All things conspire to make him happy. But he suffers from accidie. The story begins *in medias res*. He is making an important sale. The woman buying the car talks to him at great length about this and that. Nothing particularly relevant to the story is said. The dialogue wanders aimlessly in imitation of actual speech as it sounds to Mr. O'Hara's ear, which is good but unselective, with a tendency to use arcane slang ("plenty of glue") and phonetic spellings ("wuddia"). Yet despite this long conversation, the two characters remain vague and undefined. Incidentally, Mr. O'Hara almost never gives a physical description of his characters, a startling continence for a naturalistic writer, and more to be admired than not.

The woman departs. The salesman goes to a bar, where the bartender immediately senses that "You got sumpn eatin' you, boy." The salesman then goes home. He looks at his sleeping wife, who wakes up and wants to know if something is wrong. "How the hell can I tell you when I don't know myself?" he says. She goes back to sleep. He takes down his gun. He seems about to kill himself when his wife joins him and says, "Don't. Please?" and he says, "I won't." And there the story ends. What has gone wrong is that one could not care less about this Richard Cory (at least we were told that the original was full of light and that people envied him), because Mr. O'Hara's creation has neither face nor history. What the author has shown us is not a character but an event, and though a certain kind of writing can be most successful dealing only with events, this particular story required character shown from the inside, not a situation described from the outside and through dialogue.

Elizabeth Appleton, O'Hara's latest novel, takes place in a Pennsylvania university town. Will the dean, Elizabeth's husband, be made president of the college? He is a popular choice, and in line for the post. Elizabeth has been a conscientious faculty wife, in spite of being "aristocratic" (her family used to go to Southampton in the summer). Elizabeth also has money, a fact which her patrician good taste insists she hide from her husband's world. But hidden or not, for those who know true quality Elizabeth is the real thing. She even inspires the reverence of a former New York policeman who happens to be sitting next to her during a plane trip. There has been bad weather. Danger. Each is brave. The danger passes. Then they talk of . . . what else do Mr. O'Hara's people talk of in a pinch? Schools. "You're a New York girl, even if you did get on at Pittsburgh." Elizabeth allows that this is so. Then with that uncanny shrewdness the lower orders often demonstrate when they are in the presence of their betters, the flatfoot asks, "Did you ever go to Miss Spence's Finishing School? I used to help them cross the street when I was in that precinct." No

Franklin High School for him. "I went to Miss Chapin's," says Elizabeth quietly, as if declaring, very simply, that she is a Plantagenet. Needless to say, the fuzz knows all about Chapin, too. He is even more overcome when he learns her maiden name. He knows exactly who her father was. He even recalls her family house "on the north side of Fifty-Sixth between Madison and Park. Iron grillwork on the ground floor windows. . . . Those were the good days, Mrs. Appleton, no matter what they say," he declares in an ecstasy of social inferiority.

Like so many of O'Hara's novels, the book seems improvised. The situation is a simple one. Appleton is expected to become Spring Valley's next president. He wants the job, or nearly (readers of the late John P. Marquand will recognize with delight that hesitancy and melancholy which inevitably attend success in middle age. Is this all there is to it? Where are my dreams, my hopes, my love?). Elizabeth wants the promotion, partly for her husband's sake, partly because she is guilty because *she has had an affair*. It is over now, of course. Her lover has taken to drink. But with the aid of flashbacks we can savor the quality of their passion, which turns out to have been mostly talk. Sometimes they talked about schools, sometimes about games; occasionally they discussed the guilt each feels toward her husband, and the possibility of their own marriage one day. But aside from talk nothing happens. In fact, there is almost no action in Mr. O'Hara's recent work. Everything of consequence takes place offstage, to be reported later in conversation—perhaps his only resemblance to classical literature.

To be effective, naturalistic detail must be not only accurate but relevant. Each small fact must be fitted to the overall pattern as tightly as mosaic. This is a tiresomely obvious thing to say, but repetition does not seem to spoil the novelty of it as criticism. Unfortunately Mr. O'Hara does not relate things one to the other, he simply puts down the names of schools, resorts, restaurants, hotels for the simple pleasure of recording them (and perhaps, magically, possessing them in the act of naming). If he can come up with the name of an actual entertainer who performed in a real club of a known city in a particular year, he seems to feel that his work as recorder has been justified. This love of minutiae for their own sake can be as fatal to the serious novelist as it is necessary to the success of the popular writer . . . which brings us to the audience and its unconscious presuppositions.

Right off, one is struck by the collective narcissism of those whose tastes create the best-seller lists. Until our day, popular writers wrote of kings and queens, of exotic countries and extreme situations, of worlds totally unlike the common experience. No longer. Today's reader wants to look at himself, to find out who *he* is, with an occasional glimpse of his next-door neighbor. This self-absorption is also reflected in the ubiquitous national polls which fascinate newspaper readers and in those magazine articles that address themselves with such success to the second person singular. Certainly, fiction is, to a point, an extension of actual life, an alternative world in which a reader may find out things he did not know before and live in imagination a life he may not live in fact. But I suggest that never before has the alternative world been so close to the actual one as it is today in the novels of John O'Hara and his fellow commercialites. Journalism and popular fiction have merged, and the graphic and the plausible have become an end in themselves. The contemporary public plainly prefers mirrors to windows.

The second unconscious presupposition Mr. O'Hara reveals is the matter of boredom. Most of the people he describes are bored to death with their lives and one another. Yet they never question this boredom, nor does their author show any great awareness of it. He just puts it all down. Like his peers, he reflects the *taedium vitae* without seeming to notice it. Yet it lurks continually beneath the surface, much the way a fear of syphilis haunted popular writing in the nineteenth century. One can read O'Hara by the yard without encountering a single character capable of taking pleasure in anything. His creatures are joyless. Neither art nor mind ever impinges on their garrulous self-absorption. If they read books, the books are by writers like Mr. O'Hara, locked with them in a terrible self-regard. Strangely enough, they show little true curiosity about other people, which is odd since the convention of each story is almost always someone telling someone else about so-and-so. They want to hear gossip but only in a desultory, time-passing way.

Finally, there is the matter of death. A recent survey among young people showed that since almost none believed in the continuation of personality after death, each felt, quite logically, that if this life is all there is, to lose it is the worst that can happen to anyone. Consequently, none was able to think of a single "idea," political or moral, whose defense might justify no longer existing. To me this is the central underlying assumption of our society and one which makes us different from our predecessors. As a result, much of the popular writers' glumness reflects the unease of a first generation set free from an attitude toward death which was as comforting as it was constraining. Curiously enough, this awareness is responsible for one of Mr. O'Hara's few entirely successful works, the short story "The Trip," from *Assembly.*

An elderly New York clubman is looking forward to a boat trip to England, the scene of many pleasures in his youth (the Kit Kat Club with the Prince of Wales at the drums, etc.). He discusses the trip with his bridge partners, a contented foursome of old men, their pleasant lives shadowed only by the knowledge of death. An original member of the foursome died some years earlier, and there had been some criticism of him because he had collapsed "and died while playing a hand. The criticism was mild enough, but it was voiced, one player to another; it was simply that Charley had been told by his doctor not to play bridge, but he had insisted on playing, with the inevitable, extremely disturbing result." But there were those who said how much better it was that Charley was able to die among friends rather than in public, with "policemen going through his pockets to find some identification. Taxi drivers pointing to him. Look, a dead man." Skillfully O'Hara weaves his nightmare. Shortly before the ship is to sail for England, one of the foursome misses the afternoon game. Then it is learned that he has died in a taxicab. Once again the "inevitable, extremely disturbing" thing has happened. The trip is called off because "I'd be such a damn nuisance if I checked out in a London cab." This particular story is beautifully made, and completely effective. Yet Boccaccio would have found it unfathomable: isn't death everywhere? and shouldn't we crowd all the pleasure that we can into the moment and hope for grace? But in Mr. O'Hara's contemporary mirror, there is neither grace nor God nor—one suspects—much pleasure in living.

Why our proud Affluency is the way it is does not concern us here. Enough to say that Mr. O'Hara, for all his faults, is a reliable witness to our self-regard, boredom, and terror of not being. Nor is he without literary virtues. For one thing, he possesses that rare thing, the narrative gift. For another, he has complete integrity. What he says he sees, he sees. Though his concern with sex used to trouble many of the Good Gray Geese of the press, it is a legitimate concern. Also, his treatment of sexual matters is seldom irrelevant, though touchingly old-fashioned by today's standards, proving once again how dangerous it is for a writer to rely too heavily on contemporary sexual mores for his effects. When those mores change, the moments of high drama become absurd. "Would you marry me if I weren't a virgin?" asks a girl in one of the early books. "I don't know. I honestly don't know," is the man's agonized response, neither suspecting that even as they suffer, in literature's womb Genet and Nabokov, William Burroughs and Mary McCarthy are stirring to be born. But despite Mr. O'Hara's passionate desire to show things as they are, he is necessarily limited by the things he must look at. Lacking a moral imagination and not interested in the exercise of mind or in the exploration of what really goes on beneath that Harris tweed suit from J. Press, he is doomed to go on being a writer of gossip who is read with the same mechanical attention any newspaper column of familiar or near-familiar names and places is apt to evoke. His work, finally, cannot be taken seriously as literature, but as an unconscious record of the superstitions and assumptions of his time, his writing is "pertinent" in Santayana's sense, and even "true."

The New York Review of Books, April 16, 1964

E. NESBIT'S MAGIC

After Lewis Carroll, E. Nesbit is the best of the English fabulists who wrote about children (neither wrote *for* children), and like Carroll she was able to create a world of magic and inverted logic that was entirely her own. Yet Nesbit's books are relatively unknown in the United States. Publishers attribute her failure in these parts to a witty and intelligent prose style (something of a demerit in the land of the dull and the home of the literal) and to the fact that a good many of her books deal with magic, a taboo subject nowadays. Apparently, the librarians who dominate the "juvenile market" tend to the brisk tweedy ladies whose interests are mechanical rather than imaginative. Never so happy as when changing a fan belt, they quite naturally want to communicate their joy in practical matters to the young. The result has been a depressing literature of how-to-do things while works of invention are sternly rejected as not "practical" or "useful." Even the Oz books which had such a powerful influence on three generations of

Americans are put to one side in certain libraries, and children are discouraged from reading them because none of the things described in those books could ever have happened. Even so, despite such odds, attempts are being made by gallant publishers to penetrate the tweed curtain, and a number of Nesbit's books are currently available in the United States, while in England she continues to be widely read.

Born in 1858, Edith Nesbit was the daughter of the head of a British agricultural college. In 1880 she married Hubert Bland, a journalist. But though they had a good deal in common—both were socialists, active in the Fabian Society—the marriage was unhappy. Bland was a philanderer; worse, he had no gift for making a living. As a result, simply to support her five children, Nesbit began to write books about children. In a recent biography, *Magic and the Magician,* Noel Streatfeild remarks that E. Nesbit did not particularly like children, which may explain why those she created in her books are so entirely human. They are intelligent, vain, aggressive, humorous, witty, cruel, compassionate . . . in fact, they are like adults, except for one difference. In a well-ordered and stable society (England in the time of the gross Edward), children are as clearly defined a minority group as Jews or Negroes in other times and places. Physically small and weak, economically dependent upon others, they cannot control their environment. As a result, they are forced to develop a sense of communality; and though it does not necessarily make them any nicer to one another, at least it helps them to see each other with perfect clarity. Nesbit's genius is to see them as clearly and unsentimentally as they see themselves, thus making for that sense of life upon the page without which no literature.

Nesbit's usual device is to take a family of children ranging in age from a baby to a child of ten or eleven and then involve them in adventures, either magical or realistic (never both at the same time). *The Story of the Treasure Seekers, The Wouldbegoods,* and *The New Treasure Seekers* are realistic books about the Bastable children. They are told by Oswald Bastable, whose style owes a great deal to that of Julius Caesar. Like the conqueror, Oswald is able through a cunning use of the third person to establish his marked superiority to others. Wondering if his younger brother H. O. is mentally retarded, he writes, "H. O. is eight years old, but he cannot tell the clock yet. Oswald could tell the clock when he was six." Oswald is a delightful narrator and the stories he tells are among Nesbit's best. For the most part they deal with scrapes the children get into while searching for treasure in familiar surroundings, and the strategies they employ in coping as sensibly as possible with the contrary world of grown-ups. In a Nesbit book there is always some sort of domestic trouble. One parent is usually missing, and there is never enough money—although to the twentieth-century reader, her "impoverished" middle-class households, each with its three servants and large house, suggest an entirely golden aristocratic age. Yet many of the children's adventures have to do with attempts to improve the family's finances.

To my mind, it is in the "magic books" that Nesbit is at her best, particularly the trilogy which involves the Five Children. In the first volume, *Five Children and It*, they encounter the Psammead, a small bad-tempered, odd-looking creature from pre-history. The Psammead is able to grant wishes by first filling itself with air and then exhaling. ("If only you knew how I hate to blow myself out with other people's wishes, and how frightened I am always that I shall strain a muscle or something. And then to wake up every morning and know that you've got to do it. . . .")

But the children use the Psammead relentlessly for their wishes, and something almost always goes wrong. They wish "to be more beautiful than the day," and find that people detest them, thinking they look like Gypsies or worse. Without moralizing, Nesbit demonstrates, literally, the folly of human wishes, and amuses at the same time. In *The Phoenix and the Carpet*, they become involved with the millennial phoenix, a bird of awesome vanity ("I've often been told that mine is a valuable life"). With the use of a magic carpet, the phoenix and the children make a number of expeditions about the world.

Yet even with such an ordinary device as a magic carpet, Nesbit's powers of invention are never settled easily. The carpet has been repaired, and the rewoven section is not magic; whoever sits on that part travels neither here nor there. Since most intelligent children are passionate logicians, the sense of logic is a necessary gift in a writer of fantasy. Though a child will gladly accept a fantastic premise, he will insist that the working out of it be entirely consistent with the premise. Careless invention is immediately noticed; contradiction and inconsistencies irritate, and illusion is destroyed. Happily, Nesbit is seldom careless and she anticipates most questions which might occur to a child. Not that she can always answer him satisfactorily. A condition of the Psammead's wishes is that they last only for a day. Yet the effects of certain wishes in the distant past did linger. Why was this? asked one of the children. *"Autres temps,"* replied the Psammead coolly, *"autres moeurs."*

In *The Story of the Amulet*, Nesbit's powers of invention are at their best. It is a time-machine story, only the device is not a machine but an Egyptian amulet whose other half is lost in the past. By saying certain powerful words, the amulet becomes a gate through which the children are able to visit the past or future. Pharaonic Egypt, Babylon (whose dotty queen comes back to London with them and tries to get her personal possessions out of the British Museum), Caesar's Britain— they visit them all in search of the missing part of the amulet. Nesbit's history is good. And there is even a look at a Utopian future, which turns out to be everything a good Fabian might have hoped for. Ultimately, the amulet's other half is found, and a story of considerable beauty is concluded in a most unexpected way.

There are those who consider *The Enchanted Castle* Nesbit's best book. J. B. Priestley has made a good case for it, and there *is* something strange about the book that sets it off from the bright world of the early stories. Four children encounter magic in the gardens of a great deserted house. The mood is midnight. Statues of dinosaurs come alive in the moonlight, the gods of Olympus hold a revel, Pan's song is heard. Then things go inexplicably wrong. The children decide to give a play. Wanting an audience, they create a number of creatures out of old clothes, pillows, brooms, umbrellas. To their horror, as the curtain falls, there is a ghastly applause. The creatures have come alive, and they prove to be most disagreeable. They want to find hotels to stay at. Thwarted, they turn ugly. Finally, they are locked in a back room, but not without a scuffle. It is the sort of nightmare that might have occurred to a high-strung child, perhaps to Nesbit herself. And one must remember that a nightmare was a serious matter for a child who had no electric light to switch on when a bad dream awakened him; he was forced to continue in darkness, the menacing shadows undispelled.

My own favorites among Nesbit's work are *The House of Arden* and *Harding's Luck*, two books that comprise a diptych, one telling much the same story as the second, yet from a different point of view. The mood is somewhere between that of *The Enchanted Castle* and of the *Five Children*, not midnight yet hardly morning. Richard Harding, a crippled boy, accompanies an old tramp about England. The Dickensian note is struck but without the master's sentimentality. Through magic, Harding is able to go into the past where he is Sir Richard Harding in the age of Henry VIII, and not lame. But loyalty to the tramp makes him return to the present. Finally he elects to remain in the past. Meanwhile in *The House of Arden* a contemporary boy, Edred, must be tested before he can become Lord Arden and restore the family fortunes. He meets the Mouldiwarp (a mole who appears on the family coat of arms). This magic creature can be summoned only by poetry, freshly composed in its honor—a considerable strain on Edred and his sister Elfrida, who have not the gift. There are adventures in the past and the present, and the story of Richard Harding crosses their own. The magic comes and goes in a most interesting way.

As a woman, E. Nesbit was not to everyone's taste. H. G. Wells described her and Hubert Bland as "fundamentally intricate," adding that whenever the Blands attended meetings of the Fabian Society "anonymous letters flitted about like bats at twilight" (the Nesbit mood if not style is contagious). Yet there is no doubt that she was extraordinary. Wanting to be a serious poet, she became of necessity a writer of children's books. But though she disdained her true gift, she was peculiarly suited by nature to be what in fact she was. As an adult writing of her own childhood, she noted, "When I was a little child I used to pray fervently, fearfully, that when I should be grown up I might never forget what I thought and felt and suffered then." With extraordinary perceptiveness, she realized that each grown-up must kill the child he was before he himself can live. Nesbit's vow to survive somehow in the enemy's consciousness became, finally, her art—when this you see remember me—and the child continued to the end of the adult's life.

E. Nesbit's failure in the United States is not entirely mysterious. We have always preferred how-to-do to let's-imagine-that. As a result, in the last fifty years we have contributed relatively little in the way of new ideas of any sort. From radar to rocketry, we have had to rely on other societies for theory and invention. Our great contribution has been, characteristically, the assembly line.

I do not think it is putting the case too strongly to say that much of the poverty of our society's intellectual life is directly due to the sort of books children are encouraged to read. Practical books with facts in them may be necessary, but they are not everything. They do not serve the imagination in the same way that high invention does when it allows the mind to investigate *every* possibility, to set itself free from the ordinary, to enter a world where paradox reigns and nothing is what it seems. Properly engaged, the intelligent child begins to question all presuppositions, and thinks on his own. In fact, the moment he says, "Wouldn't it be interesting if . . . ?" he is on his way and his own imagination has begun to work at a level considerably more interesting than the usual speculation on what it will be like to own a car and make money. As it is, the absence of imagination is cruelly noticeable at every level of the American society, and though a reading of E. Nesbit is hardly going to change the pattern of a nation, there is some evidence that the child who reads her will never be quite the same again, and that is probably a good thing.

The New York Review of Books, December 3, 1964

JOHN HORNE BURNS

In 1947 *The Gallery* by John Horne Burns was published, to great acclaim: the best book of the Second War. That same year Burns and I met several times, each a war novelist and each properly wary of the other. Burns was then thirty-one with a receding hairline above a face striking in its asymmetry, one ear flat against the head, the other stuck out. He was a difficult man who drank too much, loved music, detested all other writers, and wanted to be great (he had written a number of novels before the war, but none was published). He was also certain that to be a good writer it was necessary to be homosexual. When I disagreed, he named a half dozen celebrated contemporaries, "A Pleiad," he roared delightedly, "of pederasts!" But what about Faulkner, I asked, and Hemingway. He was disdainful. Who said *they* were any good? And besides, hadn't I heard how Hemingway once . . .

I never saw Burns after 1947. But we exchanged several letters. He was going to write a successful play and become rich. He was also going to give up teaching in a prep school and go live in Europe. He did achieve Europe, but the occasion of the return was not happy. His second novel, *Lucifer with a Book* (1949), was perhaps the most savagely and unjustly attacked book of its day. Outraged, and with good reason, Burns exchanged America for Italy. But things had started to go wrong for him, and Italy did not help. The next novel, *A Cry of Children* (1952), was bad. He seemed to have lost some inner sense of self, gained in the war, lost in peace. He disintegrated. Night after night, he would stand at the Excelsior Hotel bar in Florence, drinking brandy, eating hard candy (he had a theory that eating sugar prevents hangovers . . . it does not), insulting imagined enemies and imagined friends, and all the while complaining of what had been done to him by book reviewers. In those years one tried not to think of Burns: it was too bitter. The best of us all had taken the worst way. In 1958 when I read that he was dead, I felt no shock. It seemed right. One only wondered how he had achieved extinction. Sunstroke was the medical report. But it being Burns, there were rumors of suicide, even of murder; however, those who knew him at the last say that his going was natural and inevitable. He was thirty-seven years old.

Twenty-one years ago the U. S. Army occupied Naples and John Horne Burns, a young soldier from Boston—Irish, puritan, unawakened—was brought to life by the human swarm he encountered in the Galleria Umberto, "a spacious arcade opening off Via Roma. . . . It was like walking into a city within a city." From this confrontation Burns never recovered. As he put it, "I thought I could keep a wall between me and the people. But the monkeys in the cage reach out and grab the spectator who offers them a banana." It was the time when cigarettes, chocolate, and nylons were exchanged for an easy sex that could become, for a man like Burns, unexpected love. He was startled to find that Italians could sell themselves with no sense of personal loss and, unlike their puritan conquerors, they could even take pleasure in giving pleasure; their delight in the fact of life persisted, no matter how deep the wound. Unlike "the Irish who stayed hurt all their lives, the Italians had a bounce-back in them."

The Gallery is a collection of "Portraits" and "Promenades"; a study of men and women brought together in one way or another by the fact of the Galleria and war. The characters, some shadowy, some startlingly brilliant, have sex, make love, lose themselves, find themselves. A young soldier retreats into visions of himself as Christ; a major in censorship builds himself a bureaucratic empire; a Catholic chaplain quibbles with a Protestant chaplain; a soldier grimly endures the VD ward and wonders how he could ever have loved the girl who put him there; and Momma, a genial Italian lady, presides over the Galleria's queer bar, finding her charges mysteriously *simpatico*, quite unlike the other conquerors. Finally, it is not so much what these characters do as the effect that Naples has on them. One discovers "the difference between love and Having Sex." To another: "It seemed that in our lethargic and compassionate caresses we were trying to console each other for every hurt the world had ever inflicted." To the demented visionary: "These people are all in search of love. The love of God, or death, or of another human being. They're all lost. That's why they walk so aimlessly. They all feel here that the world isn't big enough to hold them—and look at the design of this place. Like a huge cross laid on the ground, after the corpus is taken off the nails."

In the classic tradition of northern visitors to the South, Burns is overwhelmed by the spontaneity of the Italians. Even their rapacity and cruelty strike him as being closer to some ideal of the human than the moral numbness of the Americans. He contrasts Italian delicacy in human matters with the harshness of our own soldiers and their pathological loathing of the "inferior" races which war forced them to deal with. For the thousandth time in history, gross northern warriors were loose among the ancient civilization at the edge of the middle sea, and for Burns it was a revelation to realize that he belonged not to an army of civilized liberators but to a barbarian horde humanly inferior to the conquered.

Burns's style is energetic, very much that of the 40's, with distracting attempts at phonetic spelling ("furren" for "foreign") and made-up verbs ("he shrilled"). Burns's ear for dialogue was not always true; his dislike of those speaking often came between him and accuracy. He was also sometimes operatic in his effects (penicillin hurled at the Galleria: symbolic revenge). But when he is good, the style has a compelling drive that displays the national manner at its best. "Their faces complemented one another as a spoon shapes what it holds," thinks a character who has "contracted a bad case of irrelevance."

Of the well-known books of the Second War, I have always thought that only Burns's record was authentic and felt. To me the others are redolent of ambition and literature. But for Burns the war was authentic revelation. In Naples he fell in love with the idea of life. And having obtained a sense of his own identity, he saw what life might be. That the vision was a simple one makes no difference. It was his. "There'll be Neapolitans alive in 1960. I say, more power to them. They deserve to live out the end of their days because they caught on sooner than we how simple human life can be, uncomplicated by advertising and Puritanism and those loathsome values of a civilization in which everything is measured in terms of commercial success." His indictment is now a cliché, but it struck a nerve twenty years ago. Also I suspect he never understood his own people very well; nor do I think he would have been so entirely pleased by the Neapolitans of 1960 who, in their relative affluence, have begun to resemble us. But the spirit of his revelation remains true. "For I got lost in the war in Naples in August 1944. Often from what I saw I lost the power of speech. It seemed to me that everything happening there could be happening to me. A kind of madness, I suppose. But in the twenty-eighth year of my life I learned that I too must die. Until that time the only thing evil that could be done to me would be to hurry me out of the world before my time. Or to thwart my natural capacities. If this truth held for me, it must be valid for everybody else in the world."

Burns hurried himself out of the world before his time. But he had had his moment. And now that the war we lived through is history, we are able to recognize that the novel he wrote about it is literature. Burns was a gifted man who wrote a book far in excess of his gift, making a masterpiece that will endure in a way he himself could not. Extreme circumstances made him write a book which was better than his talent, an unbearable fate for an ambitious artist who wants to go on, but cannot—all later work shadowed by the splendid accident of a moment's genius. I suspect that once Burns realized his situation, he chose not to go on, and between Italian brandy and Italian sun contrived to stop.

As for the man, Burns had the luck to know, if only briefly, what it was to be alive with all senses responsive to all things; able to comprehend another person and to share that truth which is "valid for everybody else." Describing a soldier much like himself, even to the first name, Burns shows us a man discovering himself for the first time in the act of love on a hot August night. But then, love made, he is too keyed up to fall asleep, too restless with discovery; and so he is soothed and comforted in the dark, and the whispered Italian of his companion strikes the note of epitaph: "Buona notte e sogni d'oro. . . . Dormi, John."

The New York Times Book Review, May 30, 1965

SEX AND THE LAW

In 1963, H. L. A. Hart, Oxford Professor of Jurisprudence, gave three lectures at Stanford University. In these lectures (published by the Stanford University Press as *Law, Liberty and Morality*) Professor Hart attempted to answer an old question: Is the fact that certain conduct is by common standards immoral a sufficient cause to punish that conduct by law? A question which leads him to what might be a paradox: "Is it morally permissible to enforce morality as such? Ought immorality as such to be a crime?" Philosophically, Professor Hart inclines to John Stuart Mill's celebrated negative. In *On Liberty*, Mill wrote, "The only purpose for which power can rightfully be exercised over any member of a civilized community against his will is to prevent harm to others"; and to forestall the arguments of the paternally minded, Mill added that a man's own good, either physical or moral, is not sufficient warrant. He cannot rightfully be compelled to do or forbear because it will be better for him to do so, because it will make him happier, because in the opinions of others, to do so would be wise or even right.

Now it would seem that at this late date in the Anglo-American society, the question of morality and its relation to the law has been pretty much decided. In general practice, if not in particular statute, our society tends to keep a proper distance between the two. Yet national crisis may, on occasion, bring out the worst in the citizenry. While our boys were Over There, a working majority of the Congress decided that drink was not only bad for morals but bad for health. The result was Prohibition. After a dozen years of living with the Great Experiment, the electorate finally realized that moral legislation on such a scale is impossible to enforce. A lesson was learned and one would have thought it unlikely that the forces which created the Volstead Act could ever again achieve a majority. But today strange things are happening in the American Empire, as well as in the Kingdom across the water where Professor Hart detects a revival of what he calls "legal moralism," and he finds alarming certain recent developments.

In the days of the Star Chamber, to conspire to corrupt public morals was a common-law offense. Needless to say, this vague catchall turned out to be a useful instrument of tyranny and it was not entirely abandoned in England until the eighteenth century. Now it has been suddenly revived as a result of the 1961 case *Shaw* v. *Director of Public Prosecutions.* Shaw was an enterprising pimp who published a magazine called *Ladies Directory*, which was just that. Despite this useful contribution to the gallantry of England, Shaw was found guilty of three offenses: publishing an obscene article, living on the earnings of prostitutes, and conspiring to corrupt public morals. The last offense delighted the legal moralists. There was much satisfied echoing of the eighteenth-century Lord Mansfield's statement, "Whatever is *contra bonos mores et decorum* the principles of our laws prohibit and the King's Court as the general censor and guardian of the public morals is bound to restrain and punish." As a result of the decision against Mr. Shaw, the possibilities of banning a book like *Lady Chatterley's Lover* on the imprecise grounds that it will corrupt public morals (themselves ill-defined) are endless and alarming. Though various American states still retain "conspiring to corrupt" statutes, they are largely cherished as relics of our legal origins in the theocratic code of Oliver Cromwell. The last serious invoking of this principle occurred in 1935 when the Nazis solemnly determined that anything was punishable if it was deserving of punishment according "to the fundamental conceptions of penal law and sound popular feeling."

Defining immorality is of course not an easy task, though English judges and American state legislatures seem not to mind taking it on. Lord Devlin, a leader of the legal moralists, has said that "the function of the criminal law is to enforce a moral principle and nothing else." How does Lord Devlin arrive at a moral principle? He appeals to the past. What is generally said to be wrong is wrong, while "a recognized morality is as necessary to society's existence as a recognized government." Good. But Lord Devlin does not acknowledge that there is always a considerable gap between what is officially recognized as good behavior and what is in actual fact countenanced and practiced. Though adultery in England is thought to be morally wrong, there are no statutes under which a man may be punished for sleeping with someone else's wife. Adultery is not a legal offense, nor does it presumably arouse in the public "intolerance, indignation, and disgust," the three emotions which Lord Devlin insists are inevitably evoked by those acts which offend the accepted morality. Whenever this triad is present, the law must punish. Yet how is one to measure "intolerance, indignation, and disgust"? Without an appeal to Dr. Gallup, it would be difficult to decide what, if anything, the general public really thinks about these matters. Without a referendum, it is anyone's guess to what degree promiscuity, say, arouses disgust in the public. Of course Lord Devlin is not really arguing for this sort of democracy. His sense of right and wrong is based on what he was brought up to believe was right and wrong, as prescribed by church and custom.

In the realm of sexual morals, all things take on a twilight shade. Off and on for centuries, homosexuality has aroused the triple demon in the eyes of many. But a majority? It would be surprising if it did, knowing what we now know about the extent—if not the quality—of human sexual behavior. In any case, why should homosexual acts between consenting adults be considered inimical to the public good? This sort of question raises much heat, and the invoking of "history." According to Lord Devlin, "the loosening of moral bonds is often the first stage of [national] disintegration." Is it? The periods in history which are most admired by legal moralists tend to be those vigorous warlike times when a nation is pursuing a successful and predatory course of military expansion, such as the adventures of the Spartans and Alexander, of Julius Caesar and Frederick of Prussia. Yet a reading of history ought to convince Lord Devlin that these militaristic societies were not only brutish and "immoral" by any standard but also startlingly homosexual. Yet what was morally desirable in a clean-limbed Spartan army officer is now punished in Leicester Square. Obviously public attitudes have changed since those vigorous days. Does that then mean that laws should alter as old prejudices are replaced by new? In response to public opinion, the Emperor Justinian made homosexuality a criminal offense on the grounds that buggery, as everyone knew, was the chief cause of earthquakes.*

With the decline of Christianity, western moralists have more and more used the state to punish sin. One of Lord Devlin's allies, J. G. Stephen, in *Liberty, Equality, Fraternity*, comes straight to the point. Referring to moral offenders, he writes, "The feeling of hatred and the desire of vengeance are important elements to human nature which ought, in such cases, to be satisfied in a regular public and legal manner." There is the case not only for capital punishment but for

---

*Actually Justinian had little interest in public opinion on sexual morality. He was interested in removing an Archbishop who happened to be a pederast. Hence the statute.

public hangings, all in the name of the Old Testament God of vengeance. Or as Lord Goddard puts it, "I do not see how it can be either non-Christian, or other than praiseworthy, that the country should be willing to avenge crime." Yet Mr. Stephen also realizes that for practical purposes "you cannot punish anything which public opinion as expressed in the common practice of society does not strenuously and unequivocally condemn. To be able to punish a moral majority must be overwhelming." But is there such a thing as moral majority in sexual matters? Professor Hart thinks not. "The fact that there is lip service to an official sexual morality should not lead us to neglect the possibility that in sexual, as other matters, there may be a number of mutually tolerant moralities, and that even where there is some homogeneity of practice and belief, offenders may be viewed not with hatred or resentment, but with amused contempt or pity."

In the United States the laws determining correct human behavior are the work of the state legislatures. Over the years these assemblies have managed to make a complete hash of things, pleasing no one. The present tangled codes go back to the founding of the country. When the Cromwells fell, the disgruntled Puritans left England for Holland (not because they were persecuted for their religious beliefs but because they were forbidden to persecute others for *their* beliefs). Holland took them in, and promptly turned them out. Only North America was left. Here, as lords of the wilderness, they were free to create the sort of quasi-theocratic society they had dreamed of. Rigorously persecuting one another for religious heresies, witchcraft, sexual misbehavior, they formed that ugly polity whose descendants we are. As religious fundamentalists, they were irresistibly drawn to the Old Testament God at his most forbidding and cruel, while the sternness of St. Paul seemed to them far more agreeable than the occasional charity of Jesus. Since adultery was forbidden by the Seventh Commandment and fornication was condemned in two of St. Paul's memos, the Puritans made adultery and fornication criminal offenses even though no such laws existed in England, before or after Cromwell's reign. As new American states were formed, they modeled their codes on those of the original states. To this day, forty-three states will punish a single act of adulterous intercourse, while twenty-one states will punish fornications between unmarried people. In no other western country is fornication a criminal offense. As for adultery, England, Japan, and the Soviet Union have no such statutes. France and Italy will punish adultery under special conditions (e.g., if the man should establish the mistress in the family home). Germany and Switzerland punish adultery only if a court can prove that a marriage has been dissolved because of it.

In actual practice, the state laws are seldom invoked, although two hundred and forty-two Bostonians were arrested for adultery as recently as 1948. These statutes are considered "dead-letter laws" and there are those who argue that since they are so seldom invoked, why repeal them? One answer came in 1917 when a number of racketeers were arrested by the Federal government because they had taken girl friends to Florida, violating the Mann Act as well as the local fornication-adultery statutes. This case (*Caminetti* v. *U.S.*) set a dangerous precedent. Under a busy Attorney General, the "dead-letter laws" could be used to destroy all sorts of dissidents, villainous or otherwise.

Rape is another offense much confused by state laws. During the thirties, out of 2,366 New York City indictments for rape, only eighteen per cent were for forcible rape. The remaining eighty-two per cent were for statutory rape, a peculiar and imprecise crime. For instance, in Colorado it is statutory rape if intercourse takes place between an unmarried girl under eighteen and a man over eighteen. In practice this means that a boy of nineteen who has an affair with a consenting girl of seventeen is guilty of statutory rape. All the girl needs to do is to accuse her lover of consensual relations and he can be imprisoned for as long as fifty years. There are thousands of "rapists" serving time because, for one reason or another, they were found guilty of sexual intercourse with a willing partner.

In nearly every state fellatio, cunnilingus, and anal intercourse are punished. Not only are these acts forbidden between men, they are forbidden between men and women, within as well as without wedlock. As usual, the various state laws are in wild disarray. Ohio deplores fellatio but tolerates cunnilingus. In another state, sodomy is punished with a maximum twenty-year sentence, while fellatio calls for only three years, a curious discrimination. Deviate sexual acts between consenting adults are punished in most states, with sentences running from three years to life imprisonment. Of the other countries of the West, only the Federal German Republic intrudes itself upon consenting adults.

Elsewhere in the field of moral legislation, twenty-seven states forbid sexual relations and/or marriage between the white race and its "inferiors": blacks, American Indians, Orientals. And of course our narcotics laws are the scandal of the world. With the passage in 1914 of the Harrison Act, addiction to narcotics was found to be not the result of illness or bad luck but of sin, and sin must of course be punished by the state. For half a century the Federal government has had a splendid time playing cops and robbers. And since you cannot have cops without robbers, they have created the robbers by maintaining that the sinful taking of drugs must be wiped out by law. As a result, the government's severity boosts the price of drugs, makes the game more desperate for addicts as well as pushers, and encourages crime which in turn increases the payroll of the Narcotics Bureau. This lunatic state of affairs could exist only in a society still obsessed by the idea that the punishing of sin is the responsibility of the state. Yet in those countries where dope addiction is regarded as a matter for the doctor and not the police, there can be no criminal traffic in drugs. In all of England there are 550 drug addicts. In New York City alone there are 23,000 addicts.*

Theoretically, the American separation of church and state should have left the individual's private life to his conscience.

---

*Figures have gone up in both countries. In the entire United Kingdom, as of December 31, 1970, there were 1,430 addicts. In New York City there are 300,000. The English system is better than ours. See p. 373.

But this was not to be the case. The states promptly took it upon themselves to regulate the private lives of the citizens, flouting, many lawyers believe, the spirit if not the letter of the Constitution. The result of this experiment is all around us. One in eight Americans is mentally disturbed, and everywhere psychiatry flourishes. Our per capita acts of violence are beyond anything known to the other countries of the West. Clearly the unique attempt to make private morality answerable to law has not been a success. What to do?

On April 25, 1955, a committee of the American Law Institute presented a Model Penal Code (tentative draft No. 4) to the Institute, which was founded some forty years ago "to promote the clarification and simplification of the law and its better adaptation to social needs." This Code represented an attempt to make sense out of conflicting laws, to remove "dead-letter laws" which might, under pressure, be used for dark ends, and to recognize that there is an area of private sexual morality which is no concern of the state. In this the Code echoed the recommendation of the British Wolfenden Report, which said: "Unless a deliberate attempt is to be made by society, acting through the agency of the law, to equate the sphere of crime with that of sin, there must remain a realm of private morality and immorality which is, in brief and crude terms, not the law's business."

The drafters of the Code proposed that adultery and sodomy between consenting adults be removed from the sphere of the law on the grounds that "the Code does not attempt to use the power of the state to enforce purely moral or religious standards. We deem it inappropriate for the government to attempt to control behavior that has no substantial significance except as to the morality of the actor. Such matters are best left to religious, educational and other influences." The Committee's recommendation on adultery was accepted. But on sodomy, Judge John J. Parker spoke for the legal moralists: "There are many things that are denounced by the criminal civil code in order that society may know that the state disapproves. When we fly in the face of public opinion, as evidenced by the code of every state in this union, we are not proposing a code which will commend itself to the thoughtful." Judge Parker was answered by Judge Learned Hand, who said, "Criminal law which is not enforced practically is much worse than if it was not on the books at all. I think homosexuality is a matter of morals, a matter very largely of taste, and it is not a matter that people should be put in prison about." Judge Hand's position was upheld by the Institute.

As matters now stand, only the state of Illinois has attempted to modify its sex laws. As of 1962 there is no longer any penalty in Illinois for the committing of a deviate sexual act. On the other hand, an "open and notorious" adulterer can still be punished with a year in prison and fornication can be punished with six months in prison. So it is still taken for granted that the state has the right to regulate private behavior in the interest of public morality.

One postwar phenomenon has been the slowness of the liberal community to respond to those flaws in our society which might be corrected by concerted action. It would seem to me that a change in the legal codes of the fifty American states might be an interesting occupation for the liberally inclined. As the laws stand, they affect nearly everyone; implemented, they would affect millions. Originally, the United States made a brave distinction between church and state. But then we put within the legal province of the states that which was either the concern of religion or of the moral conscience of the individual. The result has caused much suffering. The state laws are executed capriciously and though in time they may fade away, without some organized effort they could continue for generations. In fact, there are signs today that the legal conservatives are at work strengthening these laws. In Florida the administration has distributed an astonishing pamphlet denouncing homosexualists in terms of seventeenth-century grandeur. In Dallas a stripper named Candy Barr was given an unprecedented fifteen-year prison term, ostensibly because she was found with marijuana in her possession but actually because she was a sinful woman. In the words of a

Dallas lawyer (Warren Leslie in *Dallas, Public and Private*), the jury was "showing the world they were in favor of God, heaven, and sending to hell-fire a girl who violated their sense of morality."

In these lowering days, there is a strong movement afoot to save society from sexual permissiveness. Guardians of the old-time virtue would maintain what they believe to be the status quo. They speak of "common decency" and "accepted opinion." But do such things really exist? And if they do, are they "right"? After all, there is no position so absurd that you cannot get a great many people to assume it. Lord Maugham, a former Lord Chancellor (where do they find them?), was convinced that the decline of the Roman Empire was the result of too frequent bathing. Justinian *knew* there was a causal link between buggery and earthquakes, while our grandparents, as Professor Steven Marcus recently reminded us, believed that masturbation caused insanity. I suspect that our own faith in psychiatry will seem as touchingly quaint to the future as our grandparents' belief in phrenology seems now to us. At any given moment, public opinion is a chaos of superstition, misinformation, and prejudice. Even if one could accurately interpret it, would that be a reason for basing the law upon a consensus?

Neither Professor Hart nor the legal moralists go that far. The conservatives are very much aware that they are living in an age of "moral decline." They wish to return to a stern morality like that of Cato or of Calvin. Failing that, they will settle for maintaining existing laws, the harsher the better. Professor Hart, on the other hand, believes that between what the law says people ought to do in their private lives and what they in fact do, there is a considerable division. To the degree that such laws ought, ideally, to conform with human practice, he is a democrat. In answering those who feel that despite what people actually do, they ought not to do it, he remarks that this may be true, yet "the use of legal punishment to freeze into immobility the morality dominant at a particular time in a society's existence may possibly succeed, but even where it does it contributes nothing to the survival of the animating spirit and formal values of social morality and may do much harm to them."

There is some evidence that by fits and starts the United States is achieving a civilization. Our record so far has not been distinguished, no doubt because we had a bad beginning. Yet it is always possible to make things better—as well as worse. Various groups are now at work trying to make sense of the fifty state codes. New York and California are expected to have improved codes by the end of this decade. But should there be a sudden renewal of legal moralism, attempts to modify and liberalize will fail. What is needed, specifically, is a test case before the Supreme Court which would establish in a single decision that "sin," where it does not disturb the public order, is not the concern of the state. This conception is implicit in our Constitution. But since it has never been tested, our laws continue to punish the sinful as though the state were still an arm of Church Militant. Although a Great Society is more easily attained in rhetoric than in fact, a good first step might be the removal from our statute books of that entirely misplaced scarlet letter.

Partisan Review, Summer 1965

THE *SEXUS* OF
HENRY MILLER

In 1949 Henry Miller sent his friend Lawrence Durrell the two volumes of *Sexus* that together comprise one of the seven sections of his long-awaited masterwork, *The Rosy Crucifixion* (Rosicrucian?). The other parts are titled *Nexus, Plexus,* and presumably anything else that ends in "exus." Durrell's reaction to *Sexus* has been published in that nice book, *Lawrence Durrell and Henry Miller: A Private Correspondence:* "I must confess I'm bitterly disappointed in [*Sexus*], despite the fact that it contains some of your very best writing to date. But, my dear Henry, the moral vulgarity of so much of it is artistically painful. These silly meaningless scenes which have no *raison d'être*, no humor, just childish explosions of obscenity—what a pity, what a terrible pity for a major artist not to have a critical sense enough to husband his force, to keep his talent aimed at the target. What on earth possessed you to leave so much twaddle in?"

Miller's response was serene and characteristic. "I said it

before and I repeat it solemnly: I am writing exactly what I want to write and the way I want to do it. Perhaps it's twaddle, perhaps not. . . . I am trying to reproduce in words a block of my life which to me has the utmost significance—every bit of it. Not because I am infatuated with my own ego. You should be able to perceive that only a man without ego could write thus about himself. (Or else I am really crazy. In which case, pray for me.)"

Sexus is a very long book about a character named Henry Miller (though at times his first name mysteriously changes to Val) who lives in Brooklyn (circa 1925) with a wife and daughter; he works for the Cosmodemonic Telegraph Company of North America (Western Union) and conducts an affair with a dance-hall girl named Mara (whose first name changes to Mona halfway through and stays Mona). In the course of six hundred and thirty-four pages, the character Henry Miller performs the sexual act many times with many different women, including, perversely, his wife, whom he does not much like. By the end of the book he has obtained a divorce and Mara-Mona becomes his second or perhaps third wife, and he dreams of freedom in another land.

Because of Miller's hydraulic approach to sex and his dogged use of four-letter words, *Sexus* could not be published in the United States for twenty-four years. Happily, the governors of the new American Empire are not so frightened of words as were the custodians of the old Republic. *Sexus* can now be dispensed in our drugstores, and it will do no harm, even without prescription.

Right off, it must be noted that only a total egotist could have written a book which has no subject other than Henry Miller in all his sweet monotony. Like shadows in a solipsist's daydream, the other characters flit through the narrative, playing straight to the relentless old exhibitionist whose routine has not changed in nearly half a century. Pose one: Henry Miller, sexual athlete. Pose two: Henry Miller, literary genius and life force. Pose three: Henry Miller and the cosmos (they have an understanding). The narrative is haphazard. Things usually get going when Miller meets a New Person at a party. New Person immediately realizes that this is no ordinary man. In fact, New Person's whole life is often changed after exposure to the hot radiance of Henry Miller. For opening the door to Feeling, Miller is then praised by New Person in terms which might turn the head of God—but not the head of Henry Miller, who notes each compliment with the gravity of the recording angel. If New Person is a woman, then she is due for a double thrill. As a lover, Henry Miller is a national resource, on the order of Yosemite National Park. Later, exhausted by his unearthly potency, she realizes that for the first time she has met Man . . . one for whom *post coitum* is not *triste* but rhetorical. When lesser men sleep, Miller talks about the cosmos, the artist, the sterility of modern life. Or in his own words: ". . . our conversations were like passages out of *The Magic Mountain*, only more virulent, more exalted, more sustained, more provocative, more inflammable, more dangerous, more menacing, and much more, ever so much more, exhausting."

Now there is nothing inherently wrong with this sort of bookmaking. The literature of self-confession has always had an enormous appeal, witness the not entirely dissimilar successes of Saints Augustine and Genet. But to make art of self-confession it is necessary to tell the truth. And unless Henry Miller is indeed God (not to be ruled out for lack of evidence to the contrary), he does not tell the truth. Everyone he meets either likes or admires him, while not once in the course of *Sexus* does he fail in bed. Hour after hour, orgasm after orgasm, the great man goes about his priapic task. Yet from Rousseau to Gide the true confessors have been aware that not only is life mostly failure, but that in one's failure or pettiness or wrongness exists the living drama of the self. Henry Miller, by his own account, is never less than superb, in life, in art, in bed. Not since the memoirs of Frank Harris has there been such a record of success in the sack. Nor does Miller provide us with any sort of relief. One could always skip Frank Harris's erotic scenes in favor of literary and political gossip. But Miller is much too important for gossip. People do not interest him. Why should they? They are mere wedding guests: he is Ancient Mariner.

At least half of *Sexus* consists of tributes to the wonder of Henry Miller. At a glance men realize that he *knows*. Women realize that he *is*. Mara-Mona: "I'm falling in love with the strangest man on earth. You frighten me, you're so gentle . . . I feel almost as if I were with a god." Even a complete stranger ("possibly the countess he had spoken of earlier") is his for the asking the moment she sees him. But, uniquely, they both prefer to chat. The subject? Let the countess speak for herself: "Whoever the woman is you love, I pity her . . . Nobody can hold you for long . . . You make friends easily, I'm sure. And yet there is no one whom you can really call your friend. You are alone. You will always be alone." She asks him to embrace her. He does, chastely. Her life is now changed. "You have helped, in a way . . . You always help, indirectly. You can't help radiating energy, and that is something. People lean on you, but you don't know why." After two more pages of this keen analysis, she tells him, "Your sexual virility is only the sign of a greater power, which you haven't begun to use." She never quite tells him what this power is, but it must be something pretty super because everyone else can also sense it humming away. As a painter friend (male) says, "I don't know any writer in America who has greater gifts than you. I've always believed in you—and I will even if you prove to be a failure." This is heady praise indeed, considering that the painter has yet to read anything Miller has written.

Miller is particularly irresistible to Jews: "You're no Goy. You're a black Jew. You're one of those fascinating Gentiles that every Jew wants to shine up to." Or during another first encounter with a Jew (Miller seems to do very well at first meetings, less well subsequently): "I see you are not an ordinary Gentile. You are one of those lost Gentiles—you are searching for something . . . With your kind we are never sure where we stand. You are like water—and we are rocks. You eat us away little by little—not with malice, but with kindness

. . ." Even when Miller has been less than loyal in his relations with others, he is forgiven. Says a friend: "You don't seem to understand what it means to give and take. You're an intellectual hobo . . . You're a gangster, do you know that?" He chuckled. "Yes, Henry, that's what you are—you're a spiritual gangster." The chuckle saves the day for lovable Henry.

Yet Henry never seems to do anything for anyone, other than to provide moments of sexual glory which we must take on faith. He does, however, talk a lot and the people he knows are addicted to his conversation. "Don't stop talking now . . . please," begs a woman whose life is being changed, as Henry in a manic mood tells her all sorts of liberating things like "Nothing would be bad or ugly or evil—if we really let ourselves go. But it's hard to make people understand that." To which the only answer is that of another straight man in the text who says, "You said it, Henry. Jesus, having you around is like getting a shot in the arm." For a man who boasts of writing nothing but the truth, I find it more than odd that not once in the course of a long narrative does anyone say, "Henry, you're full of shit." It is possible, of course, that no one ever did, but I doubt it.

Interlarded with sexual bouts and testimonials are a series of prose poems in which the author works the cosmos for all it's worth. The style changes noticeably during these arias. Usually Miller's writing is old-fashioned American demotic, rather like the prose of one of those magazines Theodore Dreiser used to edit. But when Miller climbs onto the old cracker barrel, he gets very fancy indeed. Sentences swell and billow, engulfing syntax. Arcane words are put to use, often accurately: ectoplasmic, mandibular, anthropophagous, terrene, volupt, occipital, fatidical. Not since H. P. Lovecraft has there been such a lover of language. Then, lurking pale and wan in this jungle of rich prose, are the Thoughts: "Joy is founded on something too profound to be understood and communicated: To be joyous is to be a madman in a world of sad ghosts." Or: "Only the great, the truly distinctive individuals resemble one another. Brotherhood doesn't start at the bottom, but at the top." Or: "Sex and poverty go hand in hand." The interesting thing about the Thoughts is that they can be turned inside out and the effect is precisely the same: "Sex and affluence go hand in hand," and so on.

In nearly every scene of *Sexus* people beg Miller to give them The Answer, whisper The Secret, reveal The Cosmos; but though he does his best, when the rosy crucial moment comes he invariably veers off into platitude or invokes high mysteries that can be perceived only through Feeling, never through thought or words. In this respect he is very much in the American grain. From the beginning of the United States, writers of a certain kind, and not all bad, have been bursting with some terrible truth that they can never quite articulate. Most often it has to do with the virtue of feeling as opposed to the vice of thinking. Those who try to think out matters are arid, sterile, anti-life, while those who float about in a daffy daze enjoy copious orgasms and the happy knowledge that they are the salt of the earth. This may well be true but Miller is hard put to prove it, if only because to make a case of any kind, cerebration is necessary, thereby betraying the essential position. On the one hand, he preaches the freedom of the bird, without attachments or the need to justify anything in words, while on the other hand, he feels obligated to write long books in order to explain the cosmos to us. The paradox is that if he really meant what he writes, he would not write at all. But then he is not the first messiah to be crucified upon a contradiction.

It is significant that Miller has had a considerable effect on a number of writers better than himself—George Orwell, Anaïs Nin, Lawrence Durrell, to name three at random—and one wonders why. Obviously his personality must play a part. In the letters to Durrell he is a most engaging figure. Also, it is difficult not to admire a writer who has so resolutely gone about his own business in his own way without the slightest concession to any fashion. And though time may have turned the Katzenjammer Kid into Foxy Grandpa, the old cheerful anarchy remains to charm.

202

Finally, Miller helped make a social revolution. Forty years ago it was not possible to write candidly of sexual matters. The door was shut. Then the hinges were sprung by D. H. Lawrence, and Miller helped kick it in. Now other doors need opening (death is the new obscenity). Nevertheless, at a certain time and in a certain way, Henry Miller fought the good fight, for which he deserves not only our gratitude but a permanent place of honor in that not inconsiderable company which includes such devoted figures as Havelock Ellis, Alfred M. Kinsey, and Marie C. Stopes.

Book Week, August 1, 1965

BYZANTIUM'S FALL

One of the laws of physics as yet unrevised by the masters of the second of the two cultures is that in nature there can be no action without reaction. This law also appears to hold true in human nature. Praise Aristides too much for his justice and people will think him unjust. Evoke once too often a vision of golden youths listening to wise old men in the green shade of Academe and someone will snarl that those Athenian youths were a dreary lot taught by self-serving proto-fascists of whom Plato was the worst. Depict Byzantium as the last custodian of the Greek heritage, destroyed by barbarous Turks, and Professor H. Trevor-Roper will promptly ask the readers of the *New Statesman*: "As a living political system was the Byzantine Empire, at least in its decline, really better than the Ottoman Empire in its heyday?" Though Professor Trevor-Roper indicates that his own answer to the question is negative, the question itself is a useful one to ask, particularly now.

During the last forty years the attitude of the West toward

Byzantium (best expressed by Gibbon) has changed from indifferent contempt to a fascinated admiration for that complex and resourceful society which endured for a thousand years, governed by Roman Emperors in direct political descent from Constantine the Great who transformed the ruined village of Byzantium at the juncture of Europe and Asia into the New Rome. When the Western Empire broke up in the fifth century, Constantinople alone maintained the reality and the mystique of the Caesars. The city's long, perilous success story has so aroused the admiration of recent scholars that there is indeed a tendency to glorify Byzantium at the expense of the Ottoman Turks and, as Professor Trevor-Roper suggests, the Turks must have had virtues quite as notable as the legendary vices of the Byzantines.

Fortunately, a partial answer to Professor Trevor-Roper's question is provided by the book he was reviewing when he asked it, *The Fall of Constantinople, 1453*, by Sir Steven Runciman, a contemporary writer of history peculiarly unaffected by an age in which scholars quite as much as popularizers delight in publicity and perverse argument. Was Hitler mad? Evil? Neither, maintains one usually responsible historian: he was simply a better than average politician who nearly won a war made inevitable by a generation of political blunderers. Elsewhere, historians not content with telling what happened now reveal exactly *why* it happened, ordering events in such a way as to fit some overall and to them entirely satisfying theory of history. Alongside the publicists and grand designers, Sir Steven looks to be curiously demure. He tells his story plain. Since God has not revealed any master plan to him, he does not feel impelled to preach "truth" to us. He does make judgments but only after he has made his case. He likes a fact and distrusts a theory. He is always pleasurable to read, and his new book describing the conquest of Constantinople by the Turks is one of his best.

The end of the Byzantine Empire began in 1204, when the crusaders seized Constantinople and divided much of the Empire amongst themselves. This terrible deed was particularly dishonorable since the crusade's pious object had been the freeing of the holy sepulcher and the turning back of the Moslems. Instead, the crusaders greedily seized what belonged to their fellow Christians while making practical accommodations with the infidel. Simultaneously, the Pope did his best to bring the "schismatic" Greek church back into the fold. Not until 1264 were our ancestors ("those dark and wandering tribes . . . among whom neither grace nor muse takes shelter") driven out of Constantinople by Michael Palaeologus, founder of the last dynasty. But despite the vigor of that dynasty's domestic and foreign policies and the sudden artistic revival in the capital and at Mistra, the empire never recovered from the Fourth Crusade. By the end of the fourteenth century, only a part of the Morea, the cities of Constantinople and Thessalonica, and a few odd holdings remained to the Roman Emperors who, possibly as a result of their experience with contemporary Romans, took note at last that their culture as well as language was entirely Greek. Proudly, as Hellenes and not *Romaioi*, the last Byzantines now presented themselves to the world.

Two centuries after the Byzantine Hellenic revival under the Comneni and the Angeli, the Western Renaissance began and with it a new interest in matters Greek, both contemporary and ancient, as well as a new and perhaps guilty sympathy for the beleaguered Emperor. Much of this sympathy was due to the gradual dispersal of Byzantine scholars to Europe, a "brain drain" which began at least a generation before the city fell. As the bookish Pius II remarked, any man with a pretension to learning must not only know Greek but he would be well advised to say that he had attended the University of Constantinople.

At the beginning of the thirteenth century, Tartar victories in the East caused a great removal of Turks from Anatolia to the Balkans. By 1410 there were more Turks in Europe than in Asia Minor, further isolating the city from its old empire. Finally, with the fall of Thessalonica in 1430, it was plain that barring divine intervention, the absorption of Constantinople was only a matter of time. Although divine intervention was never entirely ruled out, human intervention was sought, particularly by John VIII Palaeologus, who made the round of European capitals, begging for aid. Although he was received respectfully, even warmly, his mission was a failure. For one thing, the Holy See had made it plain that the price of a new crusade would be the submission of the Greek church to Rome. Sir Steven is particularly illuminating as he describes the various wranglings at Constantinople for and against union, including the celebrated remark Lucas Notaras is supposed to have made: "Better the Sultan's turban than a Cardinal's hat."

In 1448 John VIII died and was succeeded by his forty-four-year-old brother Constantine XI, a shadowy figure whose fate it was to be the last Emperor of the East. At the time it was considered ominous that the new ruler's name was Constantine and that his mother's name was Helena; that the first and the last rulers of the city should have the same name is tribute to that neatness to which history is prone (the fact that the current King of the Hellenes is also named Constantine must give pause to the superstitious). Lacking money for mercenaries and a land empire for ordinary recruitment, the Emperor engaged in a desperate diplomacy to obtain Western aid, while spending the resources he did have on fortifying the city. Again the Pope insisted that the Greek church submit to Rome. For a time there was stalemate. Then Murad II, that most civilized of Sultans, died in 1451 to be succeeded by his son Mehmet II, a fierce youth of nineteen. When Mehmet's Vizier came to him with gifts, the new Sultan pushed them aside and said, "Only one thing I want. Give me Constantinople."

The siege began April 2, 1453. Four months earlier, Constantine had finally submitted to the Pope, but no aid came from Italy. Every advantage was now with the Turks, including a Hungarian armorer named Urban who had previously offered his services to the Emperor, who could not afford them. Urban then presented himself to the Sultan, who engaged him to build the cannon that shattered the walls. When the siege began, Mehmet's army numbered some eighty thousand men; the defenders numbered less than seven thousand. Nevertheless, the Christians fought valiantly and not until May 29 did the Turks break into the city through a gate left open by accident. Although Constantine's advisers wanted him to withdraw to the Morea, he chose to remain with the city. And so he vanishes, literally, from history, his body never found. "The last Christian Emperor standing in the breach," as Sir Steven records it, "abandoned by his Western allies, holding the infidel at bay until their numbers overpowered him and he died, with the Empire as his winding sheet."

It is a marvelous story, marvelously told. Sir Steven takes the traditional view that the fall of the city was indeed a great and significant event, and not merely a minor happening in some vast cyclic drama. But though his view is traditional, it is hardly romantic. He reminds us that the Turks though cruel conquerors were sensible governors. Unlike the Roman Catholics, they did not persecute others for their religion. By submitting politically to the Sultan, the Greek church was able to survive until the present day, while the Hellenic community, though politically enslaved, continued to maintain its identity in a way which might have proved impossible had the Westerners once more "saved" Constantinople.

Much of the old Byzantine Empire accepted the rule of the Sultans without protest, preferring political and economic stability to the sad and dangerous comings and goings of bankrupt Despots. Particularly in Thessaly was Turkish rule welcomed. It is at this point that one wishes that Sir Steven had gone into fuller detail. For it was at Thessalonica in the 1340's that the first recognizable class war of our era took place between aristocrats on the one hand and a well-organized communist-minded working class on the other, while a divided but powerful middle class representing "democratic" virtues vacillated between extremes. Significantly, the Palaeologi sided with the middle class, put down the revolution, and so maintained their dynasty for another century.

To read an historian like Sir Steven is to be reminded that history is a literary art quite equal to that of the novel. The historian must be a master not only of general narrative but of particular detail. He must understand human character. He must be able to describe physical action, a difficult task for any writer; and, finally, he must be, in the best sense, a moralist. Yet today the historian is not accorded the same artistic rank as the "serious" novelist. I suspect that much of this is due to the high value we place on "creativity," a vague activity that somehow has got mixed up with the idea of procreation. One ought to make something unique out of oneself, as opposed to assembling bits and pieces like Baron Frankenstein. But the art of a Runciman is certainly as creative as the art of the sort of novelist who tells us how his wife and his best friend betrayed him last summer. Both historian and novelist are describing actual events. Each must interpret those events in his own way. Finally, which is of greater significance: the work of private grievance or the work of history, which attempts to order fact in such a way as to show us what actually happened in the past and how what happened affects us still? Naturally, there is a place for both kinds of writing, but I consider it a sad commentary on our period that in the literary arts we tend to prefer gossip to analysis, personality to character, "creative writing" even at its worst to historical writing at its best.

Happily, works like *The Fall of Constantinople, 1453* continue to illuminate the present by recreating the past. For instance, when Zoë, the niece of Constantine XI, married the Grand Prince of Moscow, the masters of the Kremlin became not only defenders of the Greek Orthodox faith but by styling themselves Caesar (Tsar), they made it plain that as Emperors of the East they must one day liberate that imperial city to the south which they regarded as their rightful capital. And still do.

The Reporter, October 7, 1965

WRITERS
AND THE WORLD

Recently *Variety*, an American paper devoted to the performing arts, reviewed a television program about life inside the Harlem ghetto. The discussion was conducted "by literary oriented . . . Norman Podhoretz, editor of *Commentary* magazine, who initially tried to guide the colloquy along bookish lines. . . ." And apparently failed. "Podhoretz, who described himself as a 'cold, detached intellectual,' is given to verbosity and for about half the program was annoyingly the obtrusive interviewer, more eager to talk than to probe his subject. He receded in the second half, however, and overall was a good foil. . . ."

For several years, *Variety* has been reviewing television's talking writers in precisely the same terms that they review comedians and singers. Mary McCarthy, James Baldwin, Dwight Macdonald are now familiar actors in the world of *Variety*. Yet until this decade, no more than half a dozen writers were known to the mass audience at any given moment. It

took a generation of constant performing for someone like
Carl Sandburg to become a national figure. Today fame is the
work of a night. As a result, any number of contemporary
novelists, poets, and critics are known to the innocent millions, who value them not only as entertainers but seem to take
them seriously as public moralists. As resonant chorus to the
Republic's drama, the writers have replaced the clergy. It is to
Norman Mailer, not to Norman Vincent Peale, that the television producer turns when he wants a discussion of "America's
Moral Decline" or "The Meaning of Violence."

This dramatic change in literature's estate is not due to any
sudden passion for books among the people. Americans have
never liked reading. According to the ubiquitous Dr. Gallup,
fifty per cent of the adult population never reads a book once
school is done. Nor was the writers' condition altered by the
brief re-creation of Camelot beside the Potomac. It was reassuring to the intellectual community to know that the thirty-
fifth President knew the difference between Saul Bellow and
Irwin Shaw, but it was also true that he preferred Shaw to
Bellow and Ian Fleming to either. What he did respect was
success in the arts, which is not quite the same thing as excellence, though more easily identified. Finally, it was neither the
public nor the New Frontier which glorified the writers. It
was around-the-clock television and its horror of "dead air."

Producers discovered that one way of inexpensively enliv-
ening the air is to invite people to talk to one another while
the camera records. There are now literally thousands of talk
shows, national and local, ranging from the "Today Show,"
which commands the attention of most of the country's "opinion makers," to late-night educational symposia where literary
men deal with such knotty questions as "Has There Been a
Really Important American Novel Since *A Passage to India*?"
The thought of people sitting at home watching other people
talk is profoundly sad. But that is the way we live now, electronic villagers tuned in to the machine if not to the pundits.

In the search for talkers, it was soon discovered that movie
stars need a script and that politicians are not only evasive but

apt to run afoul of the "equal time for the opposition" statute. Of the well known, only the writers were entirely suitable and perfectly available. From poets (Auden haggling with Professor Trilling over who was older) to journalists (Walter Lippmann benignly instructing his countrymen in the ways of history), the writers responded to the Zeitgeist's call with suspicious alacrity. From the commercialite peddling his latest book-club choice to the serious critic getting in a good word for *Partisan Review*, the writers are now public in a way that they have never been before, and this has created all sorts of problems for them and their admirers, many of whom believe that it is degrading for a distinguished man of letters to allow himself to be questioned by an entertainer in front of an audience of forty million people who have not a clue as to who he is other than the vague knowledge that he has written a book.

To this charge, the highbrow writer usually replies that any sort of exhibitionism is good for selling books. After all, no one would criticize him for giving a paid reading at a university. The middlebrow murmurs something about educating the masses. The lowbrow echoes the highbrow: "exposure" is good for trade. Yet in actual fact, there is no evidence that television appearances sell novels as opposed to volumes of gossip or sex hygiene. Most people who watch television regularly do not read books or much of anything else. Yet this does not deter the talking writers. There are other pleasures and duties than trade. For one thing, those who have strong views of a political or moral nature are free to express them (aesthetic judgments are not encouraged by compères for obvious reasons). Finally if the writer talks often enough, he will acquire a movie-star persona which *ought* eventually to increase the audience for his books if, meanwhile, he has found the time to write them.

But even if the writer who talks well continues to write well, there are those who believe that publicness of any kind must somehow be corrupting, like Hollywood. Americans prefer their serious writers obscure, poor, and, if possible, doomed by drink or gaudy vice. It is no accident that those contemporary writers most admired within the Academy are the ones whose lives were disorderly and disastrous, in vivid contrast to their explicators, quietly desperate upon dull campuses.

From the beginning, the American civilization has been simultaneously romantic and puritan. The World is corrupt. If the virtuous artist does not avoid its pomps and pleasures, he will crack up like Scott Fitzgerald or shoot his brains out like Ernest Hemingway, whose sad last days have assured him a place in the national pantheon which his novels alone would not have done. Of living writers, only Norman Mailer seems willing to live a life that is bound to attract lengthy comment of a cautionary sort. America's literary critics and custodians are essentially moralists who find literature interesting only to the extent that it reveals the moral consciousness of the middle class. The limitations of this kind of criticism were remarked upon more than twenty years ago by John Crowe Ransom, who thought there was a place for at least one ontological critic in the American literary hierarchy. The place of course is still there; still vacant.

"I stayed home and wrote," Flaubert used to say, quoting Horace, and to the serious-minded this priestlike dedication is still the correct way for the good writer to live, even though it means that his biography will be disappointingly slim. Remote from public affairs, the unworldly American artist ought not to be concerned with aesthetic matters either. Whenever literary questions were put to William Faulkner, he would say, "I'm just a farmer," neglecting to add that for thirty years most of his farming was of a seasonal nature in Hollywood, writing films. Yet he was always given credit for having turned his back upon the World, like J. D. Salinger, who is regarded with a certain awe because he lives entirely withdrawn from everyone. Never photographed, never interviewed, perfectly silent (except when *The New Yorker* is attacked), Mr. Salinger turns out fictions which, for a time, were taken to be more serious than they are because of the entirely admirable way their author lives.

Except for a brief time during the 30's, the notion of the writer as citizen has not been popular. In fact, during the 40's, the intellectual catchword was "alienation." The writers simply ignored the Republic, their full attention reserved for those dramas of the interior where Greek myths are eternally re-enacted in vague places beyond time, and Alcestis wears seersucker and majors in Comp. Lit. at Princeton. The 50's were the time of the Great Golfer, and there was a death in the land to which the only response was the Beats. They were not even alienated. They just went. And felt. Then as swiftly as they appeared, they vanished; nothing but a whiff of marijuana upon the air to mark their exuberant passage. The 60's began with a flourish. The young President detested all rhetoric except his own, in which he resembled most of the writers. A quasi-intellectual, he knew how to flatter even the most irritable man of letters. A master of publicity, he realized the value of having well-known people support him. If James Baldwin was an effective and admired television performer, then it was only common sense to try to win his support.

In 1960 politics and literature officially joined forces. The politician had literary longings; the writer saw himself as president, leading the polity to the good life by means of lysergic acid or the more copious orgasm or whatever bee buzzed loudest in his bonnet. More to the point, through television, the talking writer was able to command an audience in a way few politicians can. Not only is the writer a celebrity, he is also a free agent who does not have to be re-elected or even to be responsible. And so, not unnaturally, writers have been drawn more and more to actual as opposed to symbolic politics. Many worked for the elections of both Kennedy and Johnson. Saul Bellow contemplated writing a biography of Hubert Humphrey. Norman Mailer took credit for Kennedy's election because at a crucial moment in the campaign he gave the candidate the moment's accolade; called him "hipster." After Kennedy's election, writers were regularly invited to the White House. It was a heady thousand days.

But since Johnson's accession, the links between poetry and power have snapped. Literary people annoy and confuse the President. The precise nature of Saul Bellow's achievement does not seem to weigh heavily with him. Nevertheless, like his predecessor, he knows the propaganda value of artists and he has somewhat wistfully tried to win them over. It has not been easy. Despite the good things he has done at home, the President's Asian adventures alarm the talking writers and they talk against him. In retaliation, he has refused to bestow Freedom Medals, Kennedy's order of merit for excellence in science and art. But this state of siege is hardly permanent. For better or worse, the writers are very much in the real world, and the politicians know it.

Simultaneously with their new-found celebrity, the writers have become the beneficiaries of a peculiar crisis in American publishing. Fifteen years ago the mass magazines lost much of their advertising revenue to television. To survive, they were forced to make radical changes. At the prodding of young editors, they began to raid the literary quarterlies. Overnight the work of writers like Bellow, Baldwin, and Paul Goodman replaced those cheerful fictions and bland commentaries that had made the popular magazines the despair of the intellectuals for half a century. All sorts of miracles began to occur: James Baldwin was allowed to deliver a sermon in *The New Yorker*, while Dr. Leslie Fiedler, having deserted raft, Huck, and Jim, became *Playboy's* "writer of the year." Curiously enough, the readers who had for so long been soothed by Clarence Budington Kelland seemed not to mind the abrasiveness of the new writers. More to the point, young people found them interesting, a matter of some importance to publishers, since the age of the average American is now twenty-seven and growing younger. In fact, those in college form the largest single subculture in the United States, far more numerous, say, than the organized-labor movement or nature's noblemen, the farmers. As a result, courses in contemporary literature have made a generation of young people aware of writers who ordinarily might have gone on to the end in

honorable obscurity. This new audience has at last been reflected in the publishing of books, both hard- and soft-cover.

For the first time since New England's brief Indian summer, good writers with some regularity outsell commercial
ones in hard cover. In recent years Mary McCarthy has outsold Daphne du Maurier; Bellow has outsold Uris; Auchincloss has outsold O'Hara. Financially, inflation has set in. The
paperback publishers are pursuing the new best sellers with
advances that go as high as a million dollars. No one knows
whether or not the publishers will ever earn back these huge
advances, but meanwhile they gain valuable newsstand space,
and in the wake of a famous book they can display their less
showy wares, which include, often as not, the best books. As
a result, a serious and well-reviewed novel which has sold
twenty-five hundred copies in hard cover can, in paperback,
reach an audience of many thousands of readers, mostly
young. This is the first sign that the novel, which has steadily
declined as a popular art form in this century, may be able at
last to hold its own not only with films and television but also
with that high journalism which has so distracted the intellectuals since the Second War.

Affluence, publicity, power, can these things be said to "corrupt" the artist? In themselves, no. Or as Ernest Hemingway
nicely put it: "Every whore finds his vocation." Certainly it is
romantic melodrama to believe that publicity in itself destroys
the artist. Too many writers of the first rank have been devoted self-publicists (Frost, Pound, Yeats), perfectly able to do
their work quite unaffected by a machine they know how to
run. Toughness is all. Neither Hollywood nor the World destroyed Scott Fitzgerald. He would have made the same mess
had he taught at a university, published unnoticed novels, and
lived in decorous obscurity. The spoiling of a man occurs long
before his first encounter with the World. But the romantic-
puritan stereotype dies hard. The misbehavior of the artist
thrills the romantic; his subsequent suffering and punishment
satisfy the puritan.

Yet today new situations exist, and the old archetypes, never

216

true, seem less relevant than ever. To be outside the World is not necessarily a virtue. To be in the World does not necessarily mean a loss of craft, a fall from grace, a fatness of soul. William Faulkner's thirty years as a movie writer affected his novels not at all. He could do both. Finally, it is truly impertinent to speculate as to whether or not the effect of this or of that on a writer's character is good or bad. What is pertinent is the work he does. Mary McCarthy is no less intelligent a literary critic because she plays games on television. But even if her work should show a sudden falling off, only the simplest moralist would be able to link her appearances as a talking writer to her work as a writing writer.

It has been observed that American men do not read novels because they feel guilty when they read books which do not have facts in them. Made-up stories are for women and children; facts are for men. There is something in this. It is certainly true that this century's romantic estrangement of writer from the World has considerably reduced the number of facts in the American novel. And facts, both literal and symbolic, are the stuff of art as well as of life. In *Moby Dick* Melville saw to it that the reader would end by knowing as much about whaling as he did. But today there are few facts in the American novel, if only because the writers do not know much about anything except their own immediate experience, which is apt to be narrow. It is no accident that the best of American writing since the war has been small, private, interior. But now that the writers have begun to dabble in the World, even the most solipsistic of them has begun to suspect that there are a good many things that other people know that he does not. Though senators tend to be banal in public statements, none is ever quite so wide of the mark as an impassioned novelist giving his views on public affairs, particularly if he accepts the traditional romantic view that passion is all, facts tedious, reflection a sign of coldness (even impotence) and the howl more eloquent than words. Fortunately, as writers come up against the actual World they are bound to absorb new facts, and this ought to be useful to them in their work. As for the

World, only good can come of the writers' engagement in public affairs. Particularly in the United States, a nation governed entirely by lawyers, those professional "maintainers of quarrels" whom Henry IV Plantagenet sensibly barred from sitting in Parliament. At last other voices are being heard, if only late at night on television.

The obvious danger for the writer is the matter of time. "A talent is formed in stillness," wrote Goethe, "a character in the stream of the world." Goethe, as usual, managed to achieve both. But it is not easy, and many writers who choose to be active in the World lose not virtue but time, and that stillness without which literature cannot be made. This is sad. Until one recalls how many bad books the World may yet be spared because of the busyness of writers turned Worldly. The romantic-puritans can find consolation in that, and take pleasure in realizing that there is a rude justice, finally, even in the best of worlds.

London *Times Literary Supplement*, November 25, 1965

PORNOGRAPHY

The man and the woman make love; attain climax; fall separate. Then she whispers, "I'll tell you who I was thinking of if you'll tell me who you were thinking of." Like most sex jokes, the origins of this pleasant exchange are obscure. But whatever the source, it seldom fails to evoke a certain awful recognition, since few lovers are willing to admit that in the sexual act to create or maintain excitement they may need some mental image as erotic supplement to the body in attendance. One perverse contemporary maintains that when he is with A he thinks of B and when he is with B he thinks of A; each attracts him only to the degree that he is able simultaneously to evoke the image of the other. Also, for those who find the classic positions of "mature" lovemaking unsatisfactory yet dare not distress the beloved with odd requests, sexual fantasy becomes inevitable and the shy lover soon finds himself imposing mentally all sorts of wild images upon his unsuspecting partner, who may also be relying on an inner theater of the mind to keep things going; in which case, those popular writers who deplore "our lack of communication today" may have a point. Ritual and magic also have their devotees. In one of Kingsley Amis's fictions, a man mentally conjugates Latin verbs in order to delay orgasm as he waits chivalrously for his partner's predictably slow response. While another considerate lover (nonfictional) can only reduce tempo by thinking of a large loaf of sliced white bread, manufactured by Bond.

Sexual fantasy is as old as civilization (as opposed to as old as the race), and one of its outward and visible signs is pornographic literature, an entirely middle-class phenomenon, since we are assured by many investigators (Kinsey, Pomeroy, et al.) that the lower orders seldom rely upon sexual fantasy for extra-stimulus. As soon as possible, the uneducated man goes for the real thing. Consequently he seldom masturbates, but when he does he thinks, we are told, of *nothing at all*. This may be the last meaningful class distinction in the West.

Nevertheless, the sex-in-the-head middle classes that D. H. Lawrence so despised are not the way they are because they want deliberately to be cerebral and anti-life; rather they are innocent victims of necessity and tribal law. For economic reasons they must delay marriage as long as possible. For tribal reasons they are taught that sex outside marriage is wrong. Consequently the man whose first contact with a woman occurs when he is twenty will have spent the sexually most vigorous period of his life masturbating. Not unnaturally, in order to make that solitary act meaningful, the theater of his mind early becomes a Dionysian festival, and should he be a resourceful dramatist he may find actual lovemaking disappointing when he finally gets to it, as Bernard Shaw did. One wonders whether Shaw would have been a dramatist at all if he had first made love to a girl at fourteen, as nature intended, instead of at twenty-nine, as class required. Here, incidentally, is a whole new line of literary-psychological inquiry suitable for the master's degree: "Characteristics of the Onanist as Dramatist." Late coupling and prolonged chastity certainly help explain much of the rich dottiness of those Victorians whose peculiar habits planted thick many a quiet churchyard with Rose La Touches.

Until recently, pornography was a small cottage industry among the grinding mills of literature. But now that sex has taken the place of most other games (how many young people today learn bridge?), creating and packaging pornography has become big business, and though the high courts of the American Empire cannot be said to be very happy about this state of affairs, they tend to agree that freedom of expression is as essential to our national life as freedom of meaningful political action is not. Also, despite our governors' paternalistic bias, there are signs that they are becoming less intolerant in sexual matters. This would be a good thing if one did not suspect that they may regard sex as our bread and circuses, a means of keeping us off the political streets, in bed and out of mischief. If this is so, we may yet observe the current President in his mad search for consensus settling for the consensual.

Among the publishers of pornography ("merchants of smut," as they say at the FBI), Maurice Girodias is uniquely eminent. For one thing, he is a second-generation peddler of dirty books (or "d.b.s," as they call them on Eighth Avenue). In the 1930's his English father, Jack Kahane, founded the Obelisk Press in Paris. Among Kahane's authors were Anaïs Nin, Lawrence Durrell, Cyril Connolly, and of course Henry Miller, whose books have been underground favorites for what seems like a century. Kahane died in 1939 and his son, Maurice Girodias (he took his mother's name for reasons not given), continued Kahane's brave work. After the war, Girodias sold Henry Miller in vast quantities to easily stimulated GIs. He also revived *Fanny Hill.* He published books in French. He prospered. Then the terror began. Visionary dictatorships, whether of a single man or of the proletariat, tend to disapprove of irregular sex. Being profoundly immoral in public matters, dictators compensate by insisting upon what they think to be a rigorous morality in private affairs. General de Gaulle's private morality appears to have been registered in his wife's name. In 1946 Girodias was prosecuted for publishing Henry Miller. It was France's first prosecution for obscenity since the trial of *Madame Bovary* in 1844. Happily, the world's writers rallied to Miller's defense, and since men of letters are taken solemnly in France, the government dropped its charges.

In a preface to the recently published *The Olympia Reader*, Girodias discusses his business arrangements at length; and though none of us is as candid about money as he is about sex, Girodias does admit that he lost his firm not as a result of legal persecution but through incompetence, a revelation that gives him avant-garde status in the new pornography of money. Girodias next founded the Olympia Press, devoted to the creation of pornography, both hard and soft core. His adventures as a merchant of smut make a nice story. All sorts of writers, good and bad, were set to work turning out books, often written to order. He would think up a title (e.g., *With Open Mouth*) and advertise it; if there was sufficient response, he would then commission someone to write a book to go with the title. Most of his writers used pseudonyms. Terry Southern and Mason Hoffenberg wrote *Candy* under the name of Maxwell Kenton. Christopher Logue wrote *Lust* under the name of Count Palmiro Vicarion, while Alex Trocchi, as Miss Frances Lengel, wrote *Helen and Desire*. Girodias also published Samuel Beckett's *Watt*, Vladimir Nabokov's *Lolita*, and J. P. Donleavy's *The Ginger Man*; perversely, the last three authors chose not to use pseudonyms.

Reading of these happy years, one recalls a similar situation just after the Second War when a number of New York writers were commissioned at so many cents a page to write pornographic stories for a United States Senator. The solon, as they say in smutland, never actually met the writers but through a go-between he guided their stories: a bit more flagellation here, a touch of necrophilia there. . . . The subsequent nervous breakdown of one of the Senator's pornographers, now a celebrated poet, was attributed to the strain of not knowing which of the ninety-six Senators he was writing for.*

*David Ignatius Walsh (Dem., Mass.).

In 1958 the Fourth French Republic banned twenty-five of Girodias's books, among them *Lolita*. Girodias promptly sued the Ministry of the Interior and, amazingly, won. Unfortunately, five months later, the General saw fit to resume the grandeur of France. De Gaulle was back; and so was Madame de Gaulle. The Minister of the Interior appealed the now defunct Fourth Republic's decision and was upheld. Since then, censorship has been the rule in France. One by one Girodias's books, regardless of merit, have been banned. Inevitably, André Malraux was appealed to and, inevitably, he responded with that elevated double-talk which has been a characteristic of what one suspects will be a short-lived Republic. Girodias is currently in the United States, where he expects to flourish. Ever since our Puritan republic became a gaudy empire, pornography has been a big business for the simple reason that when freedom of expression is joined with the freedom to make a lot of money, the dream of those whose bloody footprints made vivid the snows of Valley Forge is close to fulfillment and that happiness which our Constitution commands us to pursue at hand.

The Olympia Reader is a collection of passages from various books published by Maurice Girodias since 1953. Reading it straight through is a curiously disjointed experience, like sitting through a program of movie trailers. As literature, most of the selections are junk, despite the presence of such celebrated contemporary figures as Nabokov, Genet and Queneau; and of the illustrious dead, Sade and Beardsley.

Pornography is usually defined as that which is calculated to arouse sexual excitement. Since what arouses X repels Y, no two people are apt to respond in quite the same way to the same stimulus. One man's meat, as they say, is another man's poison, a fact now recognized by the American judiciary, which must rule with wearisome frequency on obscenity. With unexpected good sense, a judge recently observed that since the books currently before him all involved ladies in black leather with whips, they could not be said to corrupt the generality, since a taste for being beaten is hardly common and

223

those who are aroused by such fantasies are already "corrupted" and therefore exempt from laws designed to protect the young and usual. By their nature, pornographies cannot be said to proselytize, since they are written for the already hooked. The worst that can be said of pornography is that it leads not to "antisocial" sexual acts but to the reading of more pornography. As for corruption, the only immediate victim is English prose. Mr. Girodias himself writes like his worst authors ("Terry being at the time in acute financial need . . .") while his moral judgments are most peculiar. With reverence, he describes his hero Sir Roger Casement (a "superlative pederast," whatever that is) as "politically confused, emotionally unbalanced, maudlin when depressed and absurdly naïve when in his best form; but he was exceptionally generous, he had extraordinary courage and a simple human wisdom which sprang from his natural goodness." Here, Mr. Girodias demonstrates a harmony with the age in which he lives. He may or may not have described Sir Roger accurately, but he has certainly drawn an accurate portrait of the Serious American Novelist, 1966.

Of the forty selections Mr. Girodias has seen fit to collect, at least half are meant to be literature in the most ambitious sense, and to the extent that they succeed, they disappoint; Beckett's *Watt*, Queneau's *Zazie*, Donleavy's *The Ginger Man* are incapable of summoning up so much as the ghost of a rose, to appropriate Sir Thomas Browne's handsome phrase. There is also a good deal of Henry Miller, whose reputation as a pornographer is largely undeserved. Though he writes a lot about sex, the only object he seems ever to describe is his own phallus. As a result, unless one lusts specifically for the flesh of Henry Miller, his works cannot be regarded as truly edifying. Yet at Miller's best he makes one irritably conscious of what it is like to be inside his skin, no mean feat . . . the pornographic style, incidentally, is contagious: the stately platitude, the arch paraphrase, the innocent line which starts suddenly to buck with unintended double meanings.

Like the perfect host or madam, Mr. Girodias has tried to

provide something for everyone. Naturally there is a good deal of straightforward heterosexual goings-on. Mr. Girodias gives us several examples, usually involving the seduction of an adolescent male by an older woman. For female masochists (and male sadists) he gives us *Story of O.* For homosexual sadists (and masochists) *The Gaudy Image.* For negrophiles (and phobes) *Pinktoes*, whose eloquent author, Chester Himes, new to me, has a sense of humor which sinks his work like a stone. For anal eroticists who like science fiction there are passages from William Burroughs's *Naked Lunch* and *The Soft Machine.* For devotees of camp, new to the scene, the thirty-three-year-old *The Young and Evil* by Charles Henri Ford and Parker Tyler is a pioneer work and reads surprisingly well today. Parenthetically, it is interesting to note the role that clothes play in most of these works, camp, kinky, and straight. Obviously, if there is to be something for everyone, the thoughtful entrepreneur must occasionally provide an old sock or pair of panties for the fetishist to get, as it were, his teeth into. But even writers not aiming at the fetishist audience make much of the ritual taking off and putting on of clothes, and it is significant that the bodies thus revealed are seldom described as meticulously as the clothes are.

Even Jean Genet, always lyric and vague when celebrating cock, becomes unusually naturalistic and detailed when he describes clothes in an excerpt from *The Thieves' Journal.* Apparently when he was a boy in Spain a lover made him dress up as a girl. The experiment was a failure because "Taste is required . . . I was already refusing to have any. I forbade myself to. Of course I would have shown a great deal of it." Nevertheless, despite an inadequate clothes sense, he still tells us far more about the *travesti manqué* than he ever tells us about the body of Stilitano for whom he lusted.

In most pornography, physical descriptions tend to be sketchy. Hard-core pornographers seldom particularize. Inevitably, genitals are massive, but since we never get a good look at the bodies to which they are attached, the effect is so impersonal that one soon longs to read about those more mod-

225

est yet entirely tangible archetypes, the girl and boy next door, two creatures far more apt to figure in the heated theater of the mind than the voluptuous grotesques of the pulp writer's imagination. Yet by abstracting character and by keeping his human creatures faceless and vague, the pornographer does force the reader to draw upon personal experience in order to fill in the details, thereby achieving one of the ends of all literary art, that of making the reader collaborator.

As usual, it is the Marquis de Sade (here represented by a section from *Justine*) who has the most to say about sex—or rather the use of others as objects for one's own pleasure, preferably at the expense of theirs. In true eighteenth-century fashion, he explains and explains and explains. There is no God, only Nature, which is heedless of the Good as well as of the Bad. Since Nature requires that the strong violate the weak and since it is demonstrably true that Nature made women weak and men strong, therefore . . . and so on. The Marquis's vision—of which so much has been made in this century—is nothing but a rather simple-minded Manicheism, presented with more passion than logic. Yet in his endless self-justification (un-Natural this: Nature never apologizes, never explains) Sade's tirades often strike the Marlovian note: "It is Nature that I wish to outrage. I should like to spoil her plans, to block her advance, to halt the course of the stars, to throw down the globes that float in space—to destroy everything that serves her, to protect everything that harms her, to cultivate everything that irritates her—in a word to insult all her works." But he stops considerably short of his mark. He not only refused to destroy one of her more diverting creations, himself, but he also opposed capital punishment. Even for a French *philosophe*, Sade is remarkably inconsistent, which is why one prefers his letters to his formal argument. Off duty he is more natural and less Natural. While in the Bastille he described himself as possessing an "extreme tendency in everything to lose control of myself, a disordered imagination in sexual matters such as has never been known in this world, an atheist to the point of fanaticism—in two words there I am,

226

and so once again kill me or take me like that, because I shall never change." Latter-day diabolists have tried to make of his "disordered imagination in sexual matters" a religion and, as religions go, it is no more absurd than that of the crucified tripartite man-god. But though Nature is indeed nonhuman and we are without significance except to ourselves, to make of that same indifferent Nature an ally in behavior which is, simply, harmful to human society is to be singularly vicious.

Yet it is interesting to note that throughout all pornography, one theme recurs: the man or woman who manages to capture another human being for use as an unwilling sexual object. Obviously this is one of the commonest of masturbatory daydreams. Sade's originality was to try, deliberately, to make his fantasies real. But he was no Gilles de Rais. He lacked the organizational sense, and his actual adventures were probably closer to farce than to tragedy, more Charlie Chaplin trying to drown Martha Raye than Ilse Koch castrating her paramours at Buchenwald. Incidentally, it is typical of our period that the makers of the play *Marat/Sade* were much admired for having perversely reduced a splendid comic idea to mere tragedy.

Mr. Girodias's sampler should provide future sociologists with a fair idea of what sex was like at the dawn of the age of science. They will no doubt be as amused as most of us are depressed by the extent to which superstition has perverted human nature (not to mention thwarted Nature). Officially the tribal norm continues. The family is the central unit of society. Man's function is to impregnate woman in order to make children. Any sexual act that does not lead to the making of a child is untribal, which is to say antisocial. But though these assumptions are still held by the mass of human society in the West, the pornographers by what they write (as well as by what they omit to mention) show that in actual fact the old laws are not only broken (as always) but are being questioned in a new way.

Until this generation, even nonreligious enemies of irregular sexuality could sensibly argue that promiscuity was bad

227

because it led to venereal disease and to the making of unwanted babies. In addition, sex was a dirty business since
bodies stank and why should any truly fastidious person want
to compound the filth of his own body's corruption with that
of another? Now science has changed all that. Venereal disease
has been contained. Babies need not be the result of the sexual
act ("I feel so happy and safe now I take the pill"), while
improved bathing facilities together with the American
Mom's relentless circumcision of boys has made the average
human body a temptingly hygienic contraption suitable for all
sorts of experiment. To which the moralists can only respond:
Rome born again! Sexual license and excessive bathing, as
everyone knows, made the Romans effete and unable to stand
up to the stalwart puritan savages from the German forests
whose sacred mission was to destroy a world gone rotten. This
simplistic view of history is a popular one, particularly among
those who do not read history. Yet there *is* a basic point at
issue and one that should be pondered.

Our tribal standards are an uneasy combination of Mosaic
law and the warrior sense of caste that characterized those
savage tribesmen who did indeed engulf the world of cities.
The contempt for people in trade one still finds amongst the
Wasp aristocracy, the sense of honor (furtive but gnawing), the
pride in family, the loyalty to class, and (though covert) the
admiration for the military virtues and physical strength are
all inherited not from our civilized predecessors who lived in
the great cities but from their conquerors, the wandering
tribesmen, who planted no grain, built no cities, conducted no
trade, yet preyed successfully upon those who did these contemptible, unmanly things. Today of course we are all as
mixed in values as in blood, but the unstated assumption that
it is better to be physically strong than wise, violent than
gentle, continent than sensual, landowner or coupon clipper
than shopkeeper, lingers on as a memorial to those marauding
tribes who broke into history at the start of the Bronze Age
and whose values are with us still, as the Gallup Poll attested
recently, when it revealed that the President's war in Vietnam

is most popular in the South, the most "tribal" part of the United States. Yet the city is the glory of our race, and today in the West, though we are all city dwellers, we still accept as the true virtue the code of our wild conquerors, even though our actual lives do not conform to their laws, nor should they, nor should we feel guilty because they don't.

In ten thousand years we have learned how to lengthen human lives but we have found no way to delay human puberty. As a result, between the economics of the city and the taboos of the tribe we have created a monstrous sexual ethic. To mention the most notorious paradox: It is not economically convenient for the adolescent to marry; it is not tribally correct for him to have sex outside of marriage. Solutions to this man-made problem range from insistence upon total chastity to a vague permissiveness which, worriedly, allows some sexuality if those involved are "sincere" and "mature" and "loving." Until this generation, tribal moralists could argue with perfect conviction that there was only one correct sexual equation: man plus woman equals baby. All else was vice. But now that half the world lives with famine—and all the world by the year 2000, if Pope Paul's as yet unborn guests are allowed to attend (in his unhappy phrase) the "banquet of life," the old equation has been changed to read: man plus woman equals baby equals famine. If the human race is to survive, population will have to be reduced drastically, if not by atomic war then by law, an unhappy prospect for civil liberties but better than starving. In any case, it is no longer possible to maintain that those sexual acts which do not create (or simulate the creation of) a child are unnatural; unless, to strike the eschatological note, it is indeed Nature's will that we perish through overpopulation, in which case reliable hands again clutch the keys of Peter.

Fortunately, the pornographers appear to be on the side of survival. They make nothing of virginity deflowered, an important theme for two thousand years; they make nothing of it for the simple reason we make little of it. Straightforward adultery no longer fascinates the pornographer; the scarlet

229

letter has faded. Incest, mysteriously, seldom figures in current pornographies. This is odd. The tribal taboo remains as strong as ever, even though we now know that when members of the same family mate the result is seldom more cretinous or more sickly than its parents. The decline of incest as a marketable theme is probably due to today's inadequate middle-class housing. In large Victorian houses with many rooms and heavy doors, the occupants could be mysterious and exciting to one another in a way that those who live in rackety developments can never hope to be. Not even the lust of a Lord Byron could survive the fact of Levittown.

Homosexuality is now taken entirely for granted by pornographers because we take it for granted. But though there is considerable awareness nowadays of what people actually do, the ancient somewhat ambivalent hostility of the tribe persists; witness *Time* magazine's recent diagnosis of homosexuality as a "pernicious sickness" like influenza or opposing the war in Vietnam. Yet from the beginning, tribal attitudes have been confused on this subject. On the one hand, nothing must be allowed to deflect man the father from his procreative duty. On the other hand, man the warrior is more apt than not to perform homosexual acts. What was undesirable in peace was often a virtue in war, as the Spartans recognized, inventing the buddy system at the expense of the family unit. In general, it would seem that the more warlike the tribe, the more opportunistic the sexual response. "You know where you can find your sex," said that sly chieftain Frederick the Great to his officers, "—in the barracks." Of all the tribes, significantly, the Jews alone were consistently opposed not only to homosexuality but to any acknowledgment of the male as an erotic figure (cf. II Maccabees 4:7–15). But in the great world of pre-Christian cities, it never occurred to anyone that a homosexual act was less "natural" than a heterosexual one. It was simply a matter of taste. From Archilochus to Apuleius, this acceptance of the way people actually are is implicit in what the writers wrote. Suetonius records that of his twelve emperors, eleven went with equal ease from boys to girls and back again without

Suetonius ever finding anything remarkable in their "poly-
morphous perverse" behavior. But all that, as Stanley Kauff-
mann would say, happened in a "different context."

Nevertheless, despite contexts, we are bisexual. Opportunity and habit incline us toward this or that sexual object.
Since additional children are no longer needed, it is impossible
to say that some acts are "right" and others "wrong." Certainly to maintain that a homosexual act in itself is antisocial
or neurotic is dangerous nonsense, of the sort that the astonishing Dr. Edmund Bergler used to purvey when he claimed
that he would "cure" homosexuals, as if this was somehow
desirable, like changing Jewish noses or straightening Negro
hair in order to make it possible for those who have been so
altered to pass more easily through a world of white Christians
with snub noses.

Happily, in a single generation, science has changed
many old assumptions. Economics has changed others. A
woman can now easily support herself, independent of a
man. With the slamming of Nora's door, the family ceased
to be the essential social unit. Also, the newly affluent middle class can now pursue other pleasures. In the film *The
Collector*, a lower-class boy captures an educated girl and
after alternately tormenting and boring her, he says bale-
fully, "If more people had more time and money, there
would be a lot more of this." This got an unintended laugh
in the theater, but he is probably right. Sexual experiment
is becoming more open. A placid Midwestern town was recently appalled to learn that its young married set was systematically swapping wives. In the cities, group sex is popular, particularly among the young. Yet despite the new
freedoms that the pornographers reflect (sadly for them,
since their craft must ultimately wither away), the world
they show, though closer to human reality than that of the
tribalists, reveals a new illness: the powerlessness that most
people feel in an overpopulated and overorganized society.

The sado-masochist books that dominate this year's pornography are not the result of a new enthusiasm for the *vice anglais*

so much as a symptom of helplessness in a society where most of the male's aggressive-creative drive is thwarted. The will to prevail is a powerful one, and if it is not fulfilled in work or in battle, it may find an outlet in sex. The man who wants to act out fantasies of tying up or being tied up is imposing upon his sex life a power drive which became socially undesirable once he got onto that escalator at IBM that will take him by predictable stages to early retirement and the medically prolonged boredom of sunset years. Solution of this problem will not be easy, to say the least.

Meanwhile, effort must be made to bring what we think about sex and what we say about sex and what we do about sex into some kind of realistic relationship. Indirectly, the pornographers do this. They recognize that the only sexual norm is that there is none. Therefore, in a civilized society law should not function at all in the area of sex except to protect people from being "interfered with" against their will.

Unfortunately, even the most enlightened of the American state codes (Illinois) still assumes that since adultery is a tribal sin it must be regarded as a civil crime. It is not, and neither is prostitution, that most useful of human institutions. Traditionally, liberals have opposed prostitution on the ground that no one ought to be forced to sell his body because of poverty. Yet in our Affluency, prostitution continues to flourish for the simple reason that it is needed. If most men and women were forced to rely upon physical charm to attract lovers, their sexual lives would be not only meager but in a youth-worshiping country like America painfully brief. Recognizing this state of affairs, a Swedish psychologist recently proposed state brothels for women as well as for men, in recognition of the sad biological fact that the middle-aged woman is at her sexual peak at a time when she is no longer able to compete successfully with younger women. As for the prostitutes themselves, they practice an art as legitimate as any other, somewhere between that of masseur and psychiatrist. The best are natural healers and, contrary to tribal superstition, they often enjoy their work. It is to the credit of today's pornographer that intentionally or not, he is the one who tells us most about the extraordinary variety of human sexual response. In his way he shows us as we are, rather like those Fun House mirrors which, even as they distort and mock the human figure, never cease to reflect the real thing.

The New York Review of Books, March 31, 1966

THE HOLY FAMILY

From the beginning of the Republic, Americans have enjoyed accusing the first magistrate of kingly ambition. Sometimes seriously but more often derisively, the president is denounced as a would-be king, subverting the Constitution for personal ends. From General Washington to the present incumbent, the wielder of power has usually been regarded with suspicion, a disagreeable but not unhealthy state of affairs for both governor and governed. Few presidents, however, have been accused of wanting to establish family dynasties, if only because most presidents have found it impossible to select a successor of any sort, much less promote a relative. Each of the Adamses and the Harrisons reigned at an interval of not less than a political generation from the other, while the two Roosevelts were close neither in blood nor in politics. But now something new is happening in the Republic, and as the Chinese say, we are living "in interesting times."

In 1960, with the election of the thirty-fifth President, the famous ambition of Joseph P. Kennedy seemed at last fulfilled. He himself had come a long way from obscurity to great wealth and prominence; now his eldest surviving son, according to primogeniture, had gone the full distance and become president. It was a triumph for the patriarch. It was also a splendid moment for at least half the nation. What doubts one may have had about the Kennedys were obscured by the charm and intelligence of John F. Kennedy. He appeared to be beautifully on to himself; he was also on to us; there is even evidence that he was on to the family, too. As a result, there were few intellectuals in 1960 who were not beguiled by the spectacle of a President who seemed always to be standing at a certain remove from himself, watching with amusement his own performance. He was an ironist in a profession where the prize usually goes to the apparent cornball. With such a man as chief of state, all things were possible. He would "get America moving again."

But then mysteriously the thing went wrong. Despite fine rhetoric and wise commentary, despite the glamor of his presence, we did not move, and if historians are correct when they tell us that presidents are "made" in their first eighteen months in office, then one can assume that the Kennedy administration would never have fulfilled our hopes, much less his own. Kennedy was of course ill-fated from the beginning. The Bay of Pigs used up much of his credit in the bank of public opinion, while his attempts at social legislation were resolutely blocked by a more than usually obstructive Congress. In foreign affairs he was overwhelmed by the masterful Khrushchev and not until the Cuban missile crisis did he achieve tactical parity with that sly gambler. His administration's one achievement was the test-ban treaty, an encouraging footnote to the cold war.

Yet today Kennedy dead has infinitely more force than Kennedy living. Though his administration was not a success, he himself has become an exemplar of political excellence. Part of this phenomenon is attributable to the race's need for heroes, even in deflationary times. But mostly the legend is the deliberate creation of the Kennedy family and its clients. Wanting to regain power, it is now necessary to show that once upon a time there was indeed a Camelot beside the Potomac, a golden age forever lost unless a second Kennedy should become the President. And so, to insure the restoration of that lovely time, the past must be transformed, dull facts transcended, and the dead hero extolled in films, through memorials, and in the pages of books.

The most notorious of the books has been William Manchester's *The Death of a President*. Hoping to stop Jim Bishop from writing one of his ghoulish *The Day They Shot* sagas, the Kennedys decided to "hire" Mr. Manchester to write their version of what happened at Dallas. Unfortunately, they have never understood that treason is the natural business of clerks. Mr. Manchester's use of Mrs. Kennedy's taped recollections did not please the family. The famous comedy of errors that ensued not only insured the book's success but also made current certain intimate details which the family preferred for the electorate not to know, such as the President's selection of Mrs. Kennedy's dress on that last day in order, as he put it, "to show up those cheap Texas broads," a remark not calculated to give pleasure to the clients of Neiman-Marcus. Also, the family's irrational dislike of President Johnson came through all too plainly, creating an unexpected amount of sympathy for that least sympathetic of magistrates. Aware of what was at stake, Mrs. Kennedy tried to alter a book which neither she nor her brothers-in-law had read. Not since Mary Todd Lincoln has a president's widow been so fiercely engaged with legend if not history.

But then, legend-making is necessary to the Kennedy future. As a result, most of the recent books about the late president are not so much political in approach as religious. There is the ritual beginning of the book which is the end: the death at Dallas. Then the witness goes back in time to the moment when he first met the Kennedys. He finds them strenuous but fun. Along with riotous good times, there is the constant question: How are we to elect Jack president? This sort of talk was in the open after 1956, but as long ago as 1943, according to *The Pleasure of His Company,* Paul B. Fay, Jr., made a bet that one day Jack would be JFK.

From the beginning the godhead shone for those who had the eyes to see. The witness then gives us his synoptic version of the making of the President. Once again we visit cold Wisconsin and dangerous West Virginia (can a young Catholic war hero defeat a Protestant accused of being a draft dodger in a poor mining state where primary votes are bought and sold?). From triumph to triumph the hero proceeds to the convention at Los Angeles, where the god is recognized. The only shadow upon that perfect day is cast, significantly, by Lyndon B. Johnson. Like Lucifer he challenged the god at the convention, and was struck down only to be raised again as son of morning. The deal to make Johnson Vice-President still causes violent argument among the new theologians. Pierre Salinger in *With Kennedy* quotes JFK as observing glumly, "The whole story will never be known, and it's just as well that it won't be." Then the campaign itself. The great television debates (Quemoy and Matsu) in which Nixon's obvious lack of class, as classy Jack duly noted, did him in—barely. The narrowness of the electoral victory was swiftly erased by the splendor of the inaugural ("It all began in the cold": Arthur M. Schlesinger, Jr., *A Thousand Days*). From this point on, the thousand days unfold in familiar sequence and, though details differ from gospel to gospel, the story already possesses the quality of a passion play: disaster at Cuba One, triumph at Cuba Two; the eloquent speeches; the fine pageantry; and always the crowds and the glory, ending at Dallas.

With Lucifer now rampant upon the heights, the surviving Kennedys are again at work to regain the lost paradise, which means that books must be written not only about the new incarnation of the Kennedy godhead but the old. For it is the dead hero's magic that makes legitimate the family's pretensions. As an Osiris-Adonis-Christ figure, JFK is already the subject of a cult that may persist, through the machinery of publicity, long after all memory of his administration has been absorbed by the golden myth now being created in a thousand books to the single end of maintaining in power our extraordinary holy family.

The most recent batch of books about JFK, though hagiographies, at times cannot help but illuminate the three themes which dominate any telling of the sacred story: money, image-making, family. That is the trinity without which nothing. Mr. Salinger, the late President's press secretary, is necessarily concerned with the second theme, though he touches on the other two. Paul B. Fay, Jr., (a wartime buddy of JFK and Under Secretary of the Navy) is interesting on every count, and since he seems not to know what he is saying, his book is the least calculated and the most lifelike of the ones so far published. Other books at hand are Richard J. Whalen's *The Founding Father* (particularly good on money and family) and Evelyn Lincoln's *My Twelve Years with John F. Kennedy*, which in its simple way tells us a good deal about those who are drawn to the Kennedys.

While on the clerical staff of a Georgia Congressman, Mrs. Lincoln decided in 1952 that she wanted to work for "someone in Congress who seemed to have what it takes to be President"; after a careful canvass, she picked the Representative from the Massachusetts Eleventh District. Like the other witnesses under review, she never says *why* she wants to work for a future president; it is taken for granted that anyone would, an interesting commentary on all the witnesses from Schlesinger (whose *A Thousand Days* is the best political novel since *Coningsby*) to Theodore Sorensen's dour *Kennedy*. Needless to say, in all the books there is not only love and awe for the fallen hero who was, in most cases, the witness's single claim to public attention, but there are also a remarkable number of tributes to the holy family. From Jacqueline (Isis-Aphrodite-Madonna) to Bobby (Ares and perhaps Christ-to-be) the Kennedys appear at the very least as demigods, larger than life. Bobby's hard-working staff seldom complained, as Mr. Salinger put it, "because we all knew that Bob was working just a little harder than we were." For the same reason "we could accept without complaint [JFK's] bristling temper, his cold sarcasm, and his demands for always higher standards of excellence because we knew he was driving himself harder than he was driving us—despite great and persistent physical pain and personal tragedy." Mrs. Lincoln surprisingly finds the late President "humble"—doubtless since the popular wisdom requires all great men to be humble. She refers often to his "deep low voice" [sic], "his proud head held high, his eyes fixed firmly on the goals—sometimes seemingly impossible goals— he set for himself and all those around him." Mr. Schlesinger's moving threnody at the close of *his* gospel makes it plain that we will not see JFK's like again, at least not until the administration of Kennedy II.

Of the lot, only Mr. Fay seems not to be writing a book with an eye to holding office in the next Kennedy administration. He is garrulous and indiscreet (the Kennedys are still displeased with his memoirs even though thousands of words were cut from the manuscript on the narrow theological ground that since certain things he witnessed fail to enhance the image, they must be apocryphal). On the subject of the Kennedys and money, Mr. Fay tells a most revealing story. In December, 1959, the family was assembled at Palm Beach; someone mentioned money, "causing Mr. [Joseph] Kennedy to plunge in, fire blazing from his eyes. 'I don't know what is going to happen to this family when I die,' Mr. Kennedy said. 'There is no one in the entire family, except Joan and Teddy, who is living within their means. No one appears to have the slightest concern for how much they spend.'" The tirade ended with a Kennedy sister running from the room in tears, her extravagance condemned in open family session. Characteristically, Jack deflected the progenitor's wrath with the comment that the only "solution is to have Dad work harder." A story which contradicts, incidentally, Mr. Salinger's pious "Despite his great wealth and his generosity in contributing all of his salaries as Congressman, Senator and President to charities, the President was not a man to waste pennies."

But for all the founding father's grumbling, the children's

attitude toward money—like so much else—is pretty much what he wanted it to be. It is now a familiar part of the sacred story of how Zeus made each of the nine Olympians individually wealthy, creating trust funds which now total some ten million dollars per god or goddess. Also at the disposal of the celestials is the great fortune itself, estimated at a hundred, two hundred, three hundred, or whatever hundred millions of dollars, administered from an office on Park Avenue, to which the Kennedys send their bills, for we are told in *The Founding Father*, "the childhood habit of dependence persisted in adult life. As grown men and women the younger Kennedys still look to their father's staff of accountants to keep track of their expenditures and see to their personal finances." There are, of course, obvious limitations to not understanding the role of money in the lives of the majority. The late President was aware of this limitation and he was forever asking his working friends how much money they made. On occasion, he was at a disadvantage because he did not understand the trader's mentality. He missed the point to Khrushchev at Vienna and took offense at what, after all, was simply the boorishness of the marketplace. His father, an old hand in Hollywood, would have understood better the mogul's bluffing.

It will probably never be known how much money Joe Kennedy has spent for the political promotion of his sons. At the moment, an estimated million dollars a year is being spent on Bobby's behalf, and this sum can be matched year after year until 1972, and longer. Needless to say, the sons are sensitive to the charge that their elections are bought. As JFK said of his 1952 election to the Senate, "People say 'Kennedy bought the election. Kennedy could never have been elected if his father hadn't been a millionaire.' Well, it wasn't the Kennedy name and the Kennedy money that won that election. I beat Lodge because I hustled for three years" (quoted in *The Founding Father*). But of course without the Kennedy name and the Kennedy money, he would not even have been a contender. Not only was a vast amount of money spent for his election in the usual ways, but a great deal was spent in not so usual ways. For instance, according to Richard J. Whalen, right after the pro-Lodge Boston *Post* unexpectedly endorsed Jack Kennedy for the Senate, Joe Kennedy loaned the paper's publisher $500,000.

But the most expensive legitimate item in today's politics is the making of the image. Highly paid technicians are able to determine with alarming accuracy just what sort of characteristics the public desires at any given moment in a national figure, and with adroit handling a personable candidate can be made to seem whatever the Zeitgeist demands. The Kennedys are not of course responsible for applying to politics the techniques of advertising (the two have always gone hand in hand), but of contemporary politicians (the Rockefellers excepted) the Kennedys alone possess the money to maintain one of the most remarkable self-publicizing machines in the history of advertising, a machine which for a time had the resources of the Federal government at its disposal.

It is in describing the activities of a chief press officer at the White House that Mr. Salinger is most interesting. A talented image maker, he was responsible, among other things, for the televised press conferences in which the President was seen at his best, responding to simple questions with careful and often charming answers. That these press conferences were not very informative was hardly the fault of Mr. Salinger or the President. If it is true that the medium is the message and television is the coolest of all media and to be cool is desirable, then the televised thirty-fifth President was positively glacial in his effectiveness. He was a natural for this time and place, largely because of his obsession with the appearance of things. In fact, much of his political timidity was the result of a quite uncanny ability to sense how others would respond to what he said or did, and if he foresaw a negative response, he was apt to avoid action altogether. There were times, however, when his superb sense of occasion led him astray. In the course of a speech to the Cuban refugees in Miami, he was so overwhelmed by the drama of the situation that he practically launched on the spot a second invasion of that beleaguered island. Yet generally he was cool. He enjoyed the game of pleasing others, which is the actor's art.

He was also aware that vanity is perhaps the strongest of human emotions, particularly the closer one comes to the top of the slippery pole. Mrs. Kennedy once told me that the last thing Mrs. Eisenhower had done before leaving the White House was to hang a portrait of herself in the entrance hall. The first thing Mrs. Kennedy had done on moving in was to put the portrait in the basement, on aesthetic, not political grounds. Overhearing this, the President told an usher to restore the painting to its original place. "The Eisenhowers are coming to lunch tomorrow," he explained patiently to his wife, "and that's the first thing she'll look for." Mrs. Lincoln records that before the new Cabinet met, the President and Bobby were about to enter the Cabinet room when the President "said to his brother, 'Why don't you go through the other door?' The President waited until the Attorney General entered the Cabinet room from the hall door, and then he walked into the room from my office."

In its relaxed way Mr. Fay's book illuminates the actual man much better than the other books if only because he was a friend to the President, and not just an employee. He is particularly interesting on the early days when Jack could discuss openly the uses to which he was being put by his father's ambition. Early in 1945 the future President told Mr. Fay how much he envied Fay his postwar life in sunny California while "I'll be back here with Dad trying to parlay a lost PT boat and a bad back into a political advantage. I tell you, Dad is ready right now and can't understand why Johnny boy isn't 'all engines full ahead.' " Yet the exploitation of son by father had begun long before the war. In 1940 a thesis written by Jack at Harvard was published under the title *Why England Slept*, with a foreword by longtime, balding, family friend Henry Luce. The book became a best seller and (Richard J. Whalen tells us) as Joe wrote at the time in a letter to his son, "You would be surprised how a book that really makes the grade with high-class people stands you in good stead for years to come."

Joe was right of course and bookmaking is now an important part of the holy family's home industry. As Mrs. Lincoln
observed, when JFK's collection of political sketches "won the
Pulitzer prize for biography in 1957, the Senator's prominence
as a scholar and statesman grew. As his book continued to be
a best seller, he climbed higher upon public-opinion polls and
moved into a leading position among Presidential possibilities
for 1960." Later Bobby would "write" a book about how he
almost nailed Jimmy Hoffa; and so great was the impact of this
work that many people had the impression that Bobby had
indeed put an end to the career of that turbulent figure.

Most interesting of all the myth-making was the creation of
Jack the war hero. John Hersey first described for *The New
Yorker* how Jack's Navy boat was wrecked after colliding with
a Japanese ship; in the course of a long swim, the young skip-
per saved the life of a crewman, an admirable thing to do.
Later they were all rescued. Since the officer who survived was
Ambassador Kennedy's son, the story was deliberately told
and retold as an example of heroism unequaled in war's history. Through constant repetition the simple facts of the story
merged into a blurred impression that somehow at some point
a unique act of heroism had been committed by Jack Kennedy.
The last telling of the story was a film starring Cliff Robertson
as JFK (the President had wanted Warren Beatty for the part,
but the producer thought Beatty's image was "too mixed up").

So the image was created early: the high-class book that
made the grade; the much-publicized heroism at war; the election to the House of Representatives in 1946. From that point
on, the publicity was constant and though the Congressman's
record of service was unimpressive, he himself was photogenic
and appealing. Then came the Senate, the marriage, the illnesses, the second high-class book, and the rest is history. But
though it was Joe Kennedy who paid the bills and to a certain
extent managed the politics, the recipient of all this attention
was meanwhile developing into a shrewd psychologist. Mr.
Fay quotes a letter written him by the new Senator in 1953.
The tone is jocular (part of the charm of Mr. Fay's book is that

it captures as no one else has the preppish side to JFK's character; he was droll, particularly about himself, in a splendid W. C. Fields way): "I gave everything a good deal of thought. I am getting married this fall. This means the end of a promising political career, as it has been based up to now almost completely on the old sex appeal." After a few more sentences in this vein the groom-to-be comes straight to the point. "Let me know the general reaction to this in the Bay area." He did indeed want to know, like a romantic film star, what effect marriage would have on his career. But then most of his life was governed, as Mrs. Lincoln wrote of the year 1959, "by the public-opinion polls. We were not unlike the people who check their horoscope each day before venturing out." And when they did venture out, it was always to create an illusion. As Mrs. Lincoln remarks in her guileless way: after Senator Kennedy returned to Washington from a four-week tour of Europe, "it was obvious that his stature as a Senator had grown, for he came back as an authority on the current situation in Poland."

It is not to denigrate the late President or the writers of his gospel that neither he nor they ever seemed at all concerned by the bland phoniness of so much of what he did and said. Of course politicians have been pretty much the same since the beginning of history, and part of the game is creating illusion. In fact, the late President himself shortly after Cuba One summed up what might very well have been not only his political philosophy but that of the age in which we live. When asked whether or not the Soviet's placement of missiles in Cuba would have actually shifted the balance of world power, he indicated that he thought not. "But it would have politically changed the balance of power. It would have appeared to, and appearances contribute to reality."

From the beginning, the holy family has tried to make itself appear to be what it thinks people want rather than what the realities of any situation might require. Since Bobby is thought by some to be ruthless, he must therefore be photographed as often as possible with children, smiling and happy and athletic, in every way a boy's ideal man. Politically, he must *seem* to be at odds with the present administration without ever actually taking any important position that President Johnson does not already hold. Bobby's Vietnamese war dance was particularly illustrative of the technique. A step to the Left (let's talk to the Viet Cong), followed by two steps to the Right, simultaneously giving "the beards"—as he calls them—the sense that he is for peace in Vietnam while maintaining his brother's war policy. Characteristically, the world at large believes that if JFK were alive there would be no war in Vietnam. The myth-makers have obscured the fact that it was JFK who began our active participation in the war when, in 1961, he added to the six hundred American observers the first of a gradual buildup of American troops, which reached twenty thousand at the time of his assassination. And there is no evidence that he would not have persisted in that war, for, as he said to a friend shortly before he died, "I have to go all the way with this one." He could not suffer a second Cuba and hope to maintain the appearance of Defender of the Free World at the ballot box in 1964.

The authors of the latest Kennedy books are usually at their most interesting when they write about themselves. They are cautious, of course (except for the jaunty Mr. Fay), and most are thinking ahead to Kennedy II. Yet despite a hope of future preferment, Mr. Salinger's self-portrait is a most curious one. He veers between a coarse unawareness of what it was all about (he never, for instance, expresses an opinion of the war in Vietnam), and a solemn bogusness that is most putting off. Like an after-dinner speaker, he characterizes everyone ("Clark Clifford, the brilliant Washington lawyer"); he pays heavy tribute to his office staff; he praises Rusk and the State Department, remarking that "JFK had more effective liaison with the State Department than any President in history," which would have come as news to the late President. Firmly Mr. Salinger puts Arthur Schlesinger, Jr., in his place, saying that he himself never heard the President express a lack of confidence in Rusk. Mr. Salinger also remarks that though

Schlesinger was "a strong friend" of the President (something Mr. Salinger, incidentally, was not), "JFK occasionally was impatient with their [Schlesinger's memoranda] length and frequency." Mrs. Lincoln also weighs in on the subject of the historian-in-residence. Apparently JFK's "relationship with Schlesinger was never that close. He admired Schlesinger's brilliant mind, his enormous store of information . . . but Schlesinger was never more than an ally and assistant."

It is a tribute to Kennedy's gift for compartmentalizing the people in his life that none knew to what extent he saw the others. Mr. Fay was an after-hours buddy. Mrs. Lincoln was the girl in the office. Mr. Salinger was a technician and not a part of the President's social or private or even, as Mr. Salinger himself admits, political life. Contrasting his role with that of James Hagerty, Mr. Salinger writes, "My only policy duties were in the information field. While Jim had a voice in deciding what the administration would do, I was responsible only for presenting that decision to the public in a way and at a time that would generate the best possible reception." His book is valuable only when he discusses the relations between press and government. And of course when he writes about himself. His 1964 campaign for the Senate is nicely told and it is good to know that he lost because he came out firmly for fair housing on the ground that "morally I had no choice—not after sweating out Birmingham and Oxford with John F. Kennedy." This is splendid but it might have made his present book more interesting had he told us something about that crucial period of sweating out. Although he devotes a chapter to telling how he did not take a fifty-mile hike, he never discusses Birmingham, Oxford, or the black revolution.

All in all, his book is pretty much what one might expect of a PR man. He papers over personalities with the reflexive and usually inaccurate phrase (Eisenhower and Kennedy "had deep respect for each other"; Mrs. Kennedy has "a keen understanding of the problems which beset mankind"). Yet for all his gift at creating images for others, Mr. Salinger seems not to have found his own. Uneasily he plays at being U.S. Senator, fat boy at court, thoughtful emissary to Khrushchev. Lately there has been a report in the press that he is contemplating writing a novel. If he does, Harold Robbins may be in the sort of danger that George Murphy never was. The evidence at hand shows that he has the gift. Describing his divorce from "Nancy, my wife of eight years," Mr. Salinger manages in a few lines to say everything. "An extremely artistic woman, she was determined to live a quieter life in which she could pursue her skills as a ceramicist. And we both knew that I could not be happy unless I was on the move. It was this difference in philosophies, not a lack of respect, that led to our decision to obtain a divorce. But a vacation in Palm Springs, as Frank Sinatra's guest, did much to revive my spirits."

Mr. Fay emerges as very much his own man, and it is apparent that he amused the President at a level which was more that of a playmate escorting the actress Angie Dickinson to the Inaugural than as serious companion to the prince. Unlike the other witnesses, Mr. Fay has no pretensions about himself. He tells how "the President then began showing us the new paintings on the wall. 'Those two are Renoirs and that's a Cézanne,' he told us. Knowing next to nothing about painters or paintings, I asked, 'Who are they?' The President's response was predictable, 'My God, if you ask a question like that, do it in a whisper or wait till we get outside. We're trying to give this administration a semblance of class.' " The President saw the joke; he also saw the image which must at all times be projected. Parenthetically, a majority of the recorded anecdotes about Kennedy involve keeping up appearances; he was compulsively given to emphasizing, often with great charm, the division between how things must be made to seem, as opposed to the way they are. This division is noticeable, even in the censored version of Mr. Manchester's *The Death of a President.* The author records that when Kennedy spoke at Houston's coliseum, Jack Valenti, crouched below the lectern, was able to observe the extraordinary tremor of the President's hands, and the artful way in which he managed to conceal them from the audience. This tension between the serene appearance and that taut reality add to the poignancy of the true legend, so unlike the Parson Weems version Mrs. Kennedy would like the world to accept.

Money, image, family: the three are extraordinarily intertwined. The origin of the Kennedy sense of family is the holy land of Ireland, priest-ridden, superstitious, clannish. While most of the West in the nineteenth century was industrialized and urbanized, Ireland remained a famine-ridden agrarian country, in thrall to politicians, homegrown and British, priest and lay. In 1848, the first Kennedy set up shop in Boston, where the Irish were exploited and patronized by the Wasps; not unnaturally, the Irish grew bitter and vengeful and finally asserted themselves at the ballot box. But the old resentment remained as late as Joe Kennedy's generation and with it flourished a powerful sense that the family is the only unit that could withstand the enemy, as long as each member remained loyal to the others, "regarding life as a joint venture between one generation and the next." In *The Fruitful Bough*, a privately printed cluster of tributes to the Elder Kennedy (collected by Edward M. Kennedy) we are told, in Bobby's words, that to Joe Kennedy "the most important thing . . . was the advancement of his children . . . except for his influence and encouragement, my brother Jack might not have run for the Senate in 1952." (So much for JFK's comment that it was his own "hustling" that got him Lodge's seat.)

The father is of course a far more interesting figure than any of his sons if only because his will to impose himself upon a society which he felt had snubbed him has been in the most extraordinary way fulfilled. He drove his sons to "win, win, win." But never at any point did he pause to ask himself or them just what it was they were supposed to win. He taught them to regard life as a game of Monopoly (a family favorite): you put up as many hotels as you can on Ventnor Avenue and win. Consequently, some of the failure of his son's administration can be ascribed to the family philosophy. All his life Jack Kennedy was driven by his father and then by himself to be first in politics, which meant to be the president. But once that goal had been achieved, he had no future, no place else to go. This absence of any sense of the whole emerged in the famous exchange between him and James Reston, who asked the newly elected President what his philosophy was, what vision did he have of the good life. Mr. Reston got a blank stare for answer. Kennedy apologists are quick to use this exchange as proof of their man's essentially pragmatic nature ("pragmatic" was a favorite word of the era, even though its political meaning is opportunist). As they saw it: give the President a specific problem and he will solve it through intelligence and expertise. A "philosophy" was simply of no use to a man of action. For a time, actual philosophers were charmed by the thought of an intelligent young empiricist fashioning a New Frontier.

Not until the second year of his administration did it become plain that Kennedy was not about to do much of anything. Since his concern was so much with the appearance of things, he was at his worst when confronted with those issues where a moral commitment might have informed his political response not only with passion but with shrewdness. Had he challenged the Congress in the Truman manner on such bills as Medicare and Civil Rights, he might at least have inspired the country, if not the Congress, to follow his lead. But he was reluctant to rock the boat, and it is significant that he often quoted Hotspur on summoning spirits from the deep: any man can summon, but will the spirits come? JFK never found out; he would not take the chance. His excuse in private for his lack of force, particularly in dealing with the Congress, was the narrow electoral victory of 1960. The second term, he declared, would be the one in which all things might be accomplished. With a solid majority behind him, he could work wonders. But knowing his character, it is doubtful that the second term would have been much more useful than the first. After all, he would have been constitutionally a lame duck president, interested in holding the franchise for his brother. The family, finally, was his only commitment and it colored all his deeds and judgment.

In 1960, after listening to him denounce Eleanor Roosevelt

at some length, I asked him why he thought she was so much opposed to his candidacy. The answer was quick: "She hated my father and she can't stand it that his children turned out so much better than hers." I was startled at how little he understood Mrs. Roosevelt, who, to be fair, did not at all understand him, though at the end she was won by his personal charm. Yet it was significant that he could not take seriously any of her political objections to him (e.g., his attitude to McCarthyism); he merely assumed that she, like himself, was essentially concerned with family and, envying the father, would want to thwart the son. He was, finally, very much his father's son even though, as all the witnesses are at pains to remind us, he did not share that magnate's political philosophy—which goes without saying, since anyone who did could not be elected to anything except possibly the Chamber of Commerce. But the Founding Father's confidence in his own wisdom ("I know more about Europe than anybody else in this country," he said in 1940, "because I've been closer to it longer") and the assumption that he alone knew the absolute inside story about everything is a trait inherited by the sons, particularly Bobby, whose principal objection to the "talking liberals" is that they never know what's really going on, as he in his privileged place does but may not tell. The Kennedy children have always observed our world from the heights.

The distinguished jurist Francis Morrissey tells in *The Fruitful Bough* a most revealing story of life upon Olympus. "During the Lodge campaign, the Ambassador told [Jack and me] clearly that the campaign . . . would be the toughest fight he could think of, but there was no question that Lodge would be beaten, and if that should come to pass Jack would be nominated and elected President. . . . In that clear and commanding voice of his he said to Jack, 'I will work out the plans to elect you President. It will not be any more difficult for you to be elected President than it will be to win the Lodge fight . . . you will need to get about twenty key men in the country to get the nomination for it is these men who will control the convention. . . .' "

One of the most fascinating aspects of politician-watching is trying to determine to what extent any politician believes what he says. Most of course never do, regarding public statements as necessary noises to soothe the electorate or deflect the wrath of the passionate, who are forever mucking things up for the man who wants decently and normally to rise. Yet there are cases of politicians who have swayed themselves by their own speeches. Take a man of conservative disposition and force him to give liberal speeches for a few years in order to be elected and he will, often as not, come to believe himself. There is evidence that JFK often spellbound himself. Bobby is something else again. Andrew Kopkind in the *New Republic* once described Bobby's career as a series of "happenings": the McCarthy friend and fellow traveler of one year emerges as an intense New York liberal in another, and between these two happenings there is no thread at all to give a clue as to what the man actually thinks or who he really is. That consistency which liberals so furiously demanded of the hapless Nixon need not apply to any Kennedy.

After all, as the recent gospels point out, JFK himself was slow to become a liberal, to the extent he ever was (in our society no working politician can be radical). As JFK said to James MacGregor Burns, "Some people have their liberalism 'made' by the time they reach their late twenties. I didn't. I was caught in crosscurrents and eddies. It was only later that I got into the stream of things." His comment made liberalism sound rather like something run up by a tailor, a necessary garment which he regrets that he never had time in his youth to be fitted for. Elsewhere (in William Manchester's *Portrait of a President*) he explains those "currents and eddies." Of his somewhat reactionary career in the House of Representatives he said, "I'd just come out of my father's house at the time, and these were the things I knew." It is of course a truism that character is formed in one's father's house. Ideas may change but the attitude toward others does not. A father who teaches his sons that the only thing that matters is to be first, not second, not third, is obviously (should his example be followed) going to be rewarded with energetic sons. Yet it is hardly surprising that to date one cannot determine where the junior Senator from New York stands on such a straightforward issue (morally if not politically) as the American adventure in Vietnam. Differing with the President as to which cities ought to be bombed in the North does not constitute an alternative policy. His sophisticated liberal admirers, however, do not seem in the least distressed by his lack of a position; instead they delight in the *uses* to which he has put the war in Vietnam in order to embarrass the usurper in the White House.

The cold-blooded jauntiness of the Kennedys in politics has a remarkable appeal for those who also want to rise and who find annoying—to the extent they are aware of it at all—the moral sense. Also, the success of the three Kennedy brothers nicely makes hash of the old American belief that by working hard and being good one will deserve (and if fortunate, receive) promotion. A mediocre Representative, an absentee Senator, through wealth and family connections, becomes the president while his youngest brother inherits the Senate seat. Now Bobby is about to become RFK because he is Bobby. It is as if the United States had suddenly reverted to the eighteenth century, when the politics of many states were family affairs. In those days, if one wanted a political career in New York one had best be born a Livingston, a Clinton, or a Schuyler; failing that, one must marry into the family, as Alexander Hamilton did, or go to work for them. In a way, the whole Kennedy episode is a fascinating throwback to an earlier phase of civilization. Because the Irish maintained the ancient village sense of the family longer than most places in the West and to the extent that the sons of Joe Kennedy reflect those values and prejudices, they are an anachronism in an urbanized non-family-minded society. Yet the fact that they are so plainly not of this time makes them fascinating; their family story is a glamorous continuing soap opera whose appeal few can resist, including the liberals, who, though they may suspect that the Kennedys are not with them at heart, believe that the two boys are educable. At this very moment beside the river Charles a thousand Aristotles dream of their young Alexanders, and the coming heady conquest of the earth.

Meanwhile, the source of the holy family's power is the legend of the dead brother, who did not much resemble the hero of the books under review. Yet the myth that JFK was a philosopher-king will continue as long as the Kennedys remain in politics. And much of the power they exert over the national imagination is a direct result of the ghastliness of what happened at Dallas. But though the world's grief and shock were genuine, they were not entirely for JFK himself. The death of a young leader necessarily strikes an atavistic chord. For thousands of years the man-god was sacrificed to ensure with blood the harvest, and there is always an element of ecstasy as well as awe in our collective grief. Also, Jack Kennedy was a television star, more seen by most people than their friends or relatives. His death in public was all the more stunning because he was not an abstraction called The President, but a man the people thought they knew. At the risk of *lèse-divinité*, however, the assassination of President Nixon at, let us say, Cambridge by what at first was thought to be a member of the ADA but later turned out to be a dotty Bircher would have occasioned quite as much national horror, mourning, and even hagiography. But in time the terrible deed would have been forgotten, for there are no Nixon heirs.

Beyond what one thinks of the Kennedys themselves, there remains the large question: What sort of men ought we to be governed by in the coming years? With the high cost of politics and image-making, it is plain that only the very wealthy or those allied with the very wealthy can afford the top prizes. And among the rich, only those who are able to please the people on television are Presidential. With the decline of the religions, the moral sense has become confused, to say the least, and intellectual or political commitments that go beyond the merely expedient are regarded with cheerful contempt not only by the great operators themselves but also by their admirers and, perhaps, by the electorate itself. Also, to be fair, politi-

253

cians working within a system like ours can never be much more than what the system will allow. Hypocrisy and self-deception are the traditional characteristics of the middle class in any place and time, and the United States today is the paradigmatic middle-class society. Therefore we can hardly blame our political gamesmen for being, literally, representative. Any public man has every right to try and trick us, not only for his own good but, if he is honorable, for ours as well. However, if he himself is not aware of what he is doing or to what end he is playing the game, then to entrust him with the first magistracy of what may be the last empire on earth is to endanger us all. One does not necessarily demand of our leaders passion (Hitler supplied the age with quite enough for this century) or reforming zeal (Mao Tse-tung is incomparable), but one does insist that they possess a sense of community larger than simply personal power for its own sake, being first because it's fun. Finally, in an age of supercommunications, one must have a clear sense of the way things are, as opposed to the way they have been made to seem. Since the politics of the Kennedys are so often the work of publicists, it is necessary to keep trying to find out just who they are and what they really mean. If only because should *they* be confused as to the realities of Cuba, say, or Vietnam, then the world's end is at hand.

At one time in the United States, the popular wisdom maintained that there was no better work for a man to do than to set in motion some idea whose time had not yet arrived, even at the risk of becoming as unpopular as those politicians JFK so much admired in print and so little emulated in life. It may well be that it is now impossible for such men to rise to the top in our present system. If so, this is a tragedy. Meanwhile, in their unimaginative fierce way, the Kennedys continue to play successfully the game as they found it. They create illusions and call them facts, and between what they are said to be and what they are falls the shadow of all the useful words not spoken, of all the actual deeds not done. But if it is true that in a rough way nations deserve the leadership they get, then a frivolous and apathetic electorate combined with a vain and greedy intellectual establishment will most certainly restore to power the illusion-making Kennedys. Holy family and bedazzled nation, in their faults at least, are well matched. In any case, the age of the commune in which we have lived since the time of Jackson is drawing to a close and if historical analogies are at all relevant, the rise of the *signori* is about to begin, and we may soon find ourselves enjoying a strange new era in which all our lives and dreams are presided over by smiling, interchangeable, initialed gods.

Esquire, April 1967

THE MANCHESTER BOOK

At any given moment only a handful of people are known to almost everyone in the world. Mr. and Mrs. Richard Burton, the Kennedys . . . and the list is already near its end. There are of course those who enjoy reading about Sir Winston Churchill and General de Gaulle, but their fans are relatively few. Interest in Lyndon Johnson the Man (as opposed to the Warrior) is alarmingly slight; in fact, of the world's chiefs of state, only the enigmatic Mao Tse-tung can be said to intrigue the masses. There is something perversely gratifying in the fact that in an age of intense gossip and global publicity so few people are known to both the alert Malaysian and the average American. Things were different of course in the small world of Europe's Middle Ages. Numerous heroes were much sung about, while everyone was imbued with the Christian ethos. As a result, painters had a subject, scholars had something to argue about, poets had a point of departure. But the idea of Christendom died in Darwin's study, and now perhaps the only thing that we may all be said to hold in common is Bobby and Teddy and Jackie, and the memory of the dead President. Is it enough?

William Manchester thinks so, and his testament, *The Death of a President*, is very much a work of love, even passion. As we learned in the course of his notorious agony last year, the sun set for him when John Kennedy died. Happily, the sun has since risen and Mr. Manchester can now take satisfaction in knowing that he too is part of history, a permanent footnote to an administration which is beginning to look as if it may itself be simply a glamorous footnote to that voluminous text the Age of Johnson. But whether or not Camelot will continue to exert its spell (and perhaps, like Brigadoon, rematerialize), Mr. Manchester has written a book hard to resist reading, despite its inordinate length. The narrative is compelling even though one knows in advance everything that is going to happen. Breakfast in Fort Worth. Flight to Dallas. Governor Connally. The roses. The sun. The friendly crowds. The Governor's wife: "Well, you can't say Dallas doesn't love you, Mr. President." And then one hopes that for once the story will be different—the car swerves, the bullets miss, and the splendid progress continues. But each time, like a recurrent nightmare, the handsome head is shattered. It is probably the only story that everyone in the world knows by heart. Therefore it is, in the truest sense, legend, and like all legends it can bear much repetition and reinterpretation. In classical times, every Greek playgoer knew that sooner or later Electra would recognize Orestes, but the manner of recognition varied significantly from teller to teller.

Mr. Manchester's final telling of the death of Kennedy is most moving; it is also less controversial than one had been led to believe by those who read the original manuscript and found the portrait of President Johnson unflattering. According to the current text, Johnson seems a bit inadequate but hardly villainous. The Kennedys, on the other hand, blaze with light; the author's love is apparent on every page. That love, however, did his writing little service, for the prose of the book is not good—the result, no doubt, of the strain under which the author was compelled to work. Certainly the style shows none of the ease which marked his first book on Kennedy, nor is there any trace of that elegance with which he once portrayed H. L. Mencken. Yet the crowded, overwritten narrative holds. Mr. Manchester is perhaps too haughty in his dismissal of the plot theory, and altogether too confident in analyzing Oswald's character ("In fact, he was going mad"). Nevertheless, if the best the detractors of the book can come up with is a photograph proving that, contrary to what Mr. Manchester has written, a number of Kennedy courtiers did indeed attend the swearing-in of the new President, then it is safe to assume that he has apparently accomplished what he set out to do: describe accurately what happened at Dallas, and immediately after.

Apparently. For there is a certain mystery about the origins of the book. It is known that the Kennedys approached Mr. Manchester and asked him to write the "official" version of the assassination. But in this age of image-making, politicians are never motivated simply. Whatever the moment's purpose, everything must serve it. Certainly nothing must get out of hand, as the Kennedys know better than anyone, for they were stung once before by a writer. Preparing for 1960, they gave Professor James MacGregor Burns a free hand to write what, in effect, was to be a campaign biography of John Kennedy. The result was a work of some candor which still remains the best analysis of the thirty-fifth President's character, but the candor which gave the book its distinction did not at all please its subject or his family. References to Joe Kennedy's exuberant anti-Semitic outbursts combined with a shrewd analysis of John Kennedy's ambivalent attitude toward McCarthy caused irritation. Therefore the next writer must be tractable. The starry-eyed Mr. Manchester seemed made to order: he was willing to swear loyalty; more important, he was willing to sign agreements. With some confidence, Launcelot and Guinevere confided him the task of celebrating the fallen hero.

The comedy began. Right off, there was the matter of President Johnson. Whatever Mr. Manchester's original feelings about Johnson, he could not have spent all those hours communing with members of the exiled court and not get the sense of what a disaster it was for the country to have that vulgar, inept boor in Jack's place. The Kennedys have always been particularly cruel about Johnson, and their personal disdain is reflected and magnified by those around them, particularly their literary apologists, of whom Mr. Manchester was now one. When at last he submitted his work to the family, they proved too great and too sensitve to read it for themselves. Instead friends were chosen to vet the contents of the book. The friends found the anti-Johnson tone dangerous in the political context of the moment. They said so, and Mr. Manchester obediently made changes.

But Mr. Manchester's true ordeal did not begin until Richard Goodwin, a former aide to President Johnson, read the manuscript and found fault. He alarmed Mrs. Kennedy with tales of how what she had said looked in cold print. As a result, she threatened to sue if large cuts were not made. Some were made. Some were not. At last the publishers grew weary: the text could not be further altered. To their amazement, Mrs. Kennedy brought suit against them; meanwhile, in communicating her displeasure to Mr. Manchester, she reminded him that so secure was she in the pantheon of American heroines, no one could hope to cross her and survive—"unless I run off with Eddie Fisher," she added drolly. Needless to say, Mrs. Kennedy had her way, as the world knows.

It is now reasonable to assume that Mr. Manchester is not the same man he was before he got involved with the Kennedys. But though one's sympathy is with him, one must examine the matter from the Kennedy point of view. They are playing a great and dangerous game: they want the presidency of the United States and they will do quite a lot to obtain it. By reflecting accurately their view of Johnson, Mr. Manchester placed in jeopardy their immediate political future. Put simply, they do not want, in 1967, to split fatally the Democratic Party. Unhappily for them, Mr. Manchester's sense of history did not accommodate this necessary fact; nevertheless, since he was, in their eyes, a "hired" writer, he must tell the story their way or not at all. As it turned out, he did pretty much what they wanted him to do. But, in the process of publicly strong-arming Mr. Manchester and the various publishers involved, the Kennedys gave some substance to those "vicious" rumors (so often resorted to by polemicists) that they are ruthless and perhaps not very lovable after all. As a result, Mr. Manchester's contribution to history may prove not to be the writing of this book so much as being the unwitting agent who allowed the innocent millions an unexpected glimpse of a preternaturally ambitious family furiously at work manipulating history in order that they might rise.

It was inevitable that sooner or later popular opinion would go against this remarkable family. In nature there is no raising up without a throwing down. It does not take a particularly astute political observer to detect the public's change of mood toward the Kennedys. Overt ambition has always caused unease in the Republic, while excessive busyness makes for fatigue. Since our electorate is as easily alarmed as it is bored, political ascent has always been hazardous, and the way strewn with discarded idols. Mrs. Kennedy, in particular, is a victim of the public's fickleness; undeserving of their love, she is equally undeserving of their dislike. But then it is a most terrible thing to live out a legend, and one wonders to what extent the Kennedys themselves understand just what was set in motion for them by their father's will that they be great. Theirs is indeed *the* story of our time, and, if it did nothing else, the noisy quarrel with Mr. Manchester made vivid for everyone not only their arrogance but their poignancy. They are unique in our history, and the day they depart the public scene will be a sad one; for not only will we have lost a family as much our own as it is theirs, we shall have also lost one of the first shy hints since Christianity's decline that there may indeed be such a thing as fate, and that tragedy is not merely a literary form of little relevance in the age of common men

but a continuing fact of the human condition, requiring that
the overreacher be struck down and in his fall, we, the chorus,
experience awe, and some pity.

Book Week, April 9, 1967

PARANOID POLITICS

Of the many words with which the mental therapists have enriched our language, "paranoia" is one of the most used if not useful. According to authority, a paranoiac is one who suffers from delusions of persecution or grandeur. Everyone, of course, has paranoid tendencies. In fact, a sizable minority of the people in the world maintain sanity by focusing their fears and sense of outrage upon some vague enemy usually referred to simply as "them." Once the source of distress has been identified as the Jews or the Communists or the Establishment, the moderate paranoiac is then able to function normally—until the magic word is said, as in that famous vaudeville sketch where mention of the town Kokomo makes mad the timid comic, who begins ominously to intone: "Then slowly I turned . . ."

If the poet of the paranoid style is Kafka, one of its best contemporary critics is Professor Richard Hofstadter, whose new book illuminates various aspects of a style which has always flourished in God's country, possibly because the North American continent was meant, literally, to be God's country, a haven for seventeenth-century Protestant fundamentalists who did not understand, as Hölderlin so sweetly put it, what a sin it is "to make the state a school of morals. The state has always been made a hell by man's wanting to make it his heaven." Into this heaven, *they* came: the secular-minded eighteenth-century skeptics who proceeded to organize the United States along freethinking lines. Since then, the paranoid style has been a constant in the affairs of the American Republic. Though it originated with Christian fundamentalists, who could not bear to see their heaven made hell by a national majority which now includes those very elements that caused them to flee the old world in the first place, the style is by no means peculiar to them. Western farmers denouncing Eastern banks, Jews trying to censor the film of *Oliver Twist*, uneasy heterosexuals fearful of a homosexual take-over—all demonstrate that the paranoid style has at one time or another been the preferred manner of nearly every one of the groups that comprise the nation, and in a most engaging essay Professor Hofstadter traces the main line of this illness from the persecution of the Bavarian Illuminati in the eighteenth century to the current obsession with the Communist conspiracy.

It is ironic that a nation which has never experienced a *coup d'état* should be so obsessed with the idea of conspiracy. From the John Birchers who regard General Eisenhower as a crypto-Communist to those liberals who find it thrilling to believe that Lyndon Johnson was responsible for Kennedy's murder, paranoid delusions afflict millions. Knowing this, even the most responsible of politicians finds it difficult not to play upon the collective madness of the electorate.

"*There is a power somewhere so organized, so subtle, so watchful, so interlocked, so complete, so pervasive that they had better not speak above their breath when they speak in condemnation of it.*"

Although this sounds like Joseph McCarthy at his most eloquent, it is actually Woodrow Wilson at his least responsible, warning against "the special interests" (that what he was warning against might indeed exist to some degree is irrelevant; it is the manner in which he exploits the fears of the electorate that gives away the game).

According to Professor Hofstadter, the paranoid style is popular not only with that minority which is prone "to secularize a religiously derived view of the world," but also from time to time with the great majority which has never had any clear sense of national identity. For the American there is no motherland or fatherland to be shared with others of his tribe, for the excellent reason that he has no tribe; all that he holds in common with other United Statesmen is something called "the American way of life," an economic system involving the constant purchase of consumer goods on credit to maintain a high standard of living involving the constant purchase, etc. But though this materialistic, even sybaritic ethos does far less damage in the world than old-fashioned tribalism, it fails to satisfy all sorts of atavistic yearnings. A man might gladly give his life for a totem like the flag or the Cross, but who would give so much as a breath for a washing machine not yet paid for?

As a result, not only are the paranoid stylists of both Left and Right appalled by the soullessness of American society, but a good many nonparanoids are equally concerned by the lack of "national purpose," a phrase whose innocent implication is that a human society is like a factory with a quota to be met. Among the simple, this absence of traditional identity has let some strange obsessions flourish, particularly today when the national majority is made up of third-generation citizens uncertain of just what's expected of them. Not unnaturally, those of a passionate and idealistic nature are driven to displays of one hundred per cent Americanism, ranging from frequent hand-on-heart pledges of allegiance to the country's proto-Op-art flag to the joyous persecution of those suspected of being un-American (the only other society to have such a concept was Nazi Germany).

Analyzing the identity crisis, as the mental therapists would say, Professor Hofstadter makes a distinction between what he terms status politics and interest politics. In times of economic or military distress (that is to say, "normal" times), people vote their economic interests, and new deals are possible. But when the voters are affluent, they feel free to vote not their interests but their prejudices. The election of 1928 was such a time, and in an orgy of anti-Romanism the majority chose Herbert Hoover over Al Smith. Three years ago, when all seemed to be going smoothly for the nation, the Republicans nominated Barry Goldwater, quite aware that not only was he the most radical politician in the country (Supreme Court decisions are not, he declared, "necessarily the law of the land") but also the most consistent morally. Fiercely militant in the holy war against world Communism ("we will never reconcile ourselves to the Communist possession of power of any kind in any part of the world"), he was even more emphatic in his desire to repeal a hundred years of social legislation in order to create a society in which every man has the inalienable right *not* to give a sucker an even break. The fact that by living the "wrong" sort of economic life the United States had become incredibly rich did not disturb him; as a status politician he spoke for virtue, and the millions that heeded him were quite willing (or so they thought) to sacrifice their material prosperity in order to gain spiritual health by obeying the "natural law" of the marketplace.

According to Professor Hofstadter, those going up or down the social scale are the most prone to paranoia. When white Anglo-Saxon Protestants lose status, they often suspect a conspiracy aimed at depriving them of their ancient primacy, while Irish Catholics, moving up, are often disappointed to find that their new riches do not entitle them to more of a say in the governing of the country, and so suspect the Protestant old guard or the Jews of conspiring to deny them dignity. Religious (as well as ethnic) prejudices often decide the way these people vote. Since Americans lack an agreed-upon class system, status tends to originate in race and religion.

The fact that each of Professor Hofstadter's essays was written for an occasion other than the present ought to have inspired him to make some sort of link from piece to piece. Unfortunately, he has not made the effort, even though the paranoid style would have provided a fine common denominator. Nevertheless, he is interesting on such subjects as "Cuba, the Philippines and Manifest Destiny": skillfully, he gives the background to the Spanish-American War, and shows how the paranoid style helped make possible the war, which gave birth to the American empire.

Like most empires, this one was the result of trouble at home. With the settling of California, the frontier shut down and there was no place new to go, a matter of poignant concern to a nomadic and adventurous people. Then came the depression of '93. To those of faint heart, the last best hope of earth appeared to be fading fast. At such times the shrewd politician can usually be counted upon to obscure domestic crises with foreign pageants. Or, as Henry Cabot Lodge confided to a friend, "Should there be a war, we will not hear much of the currency question in the election." Between Lodge's practicality and Theodore Roosevelt's vision of empire ("All the great masterful races have been fighting races. No triumph of peace is quite as great as the supreme triumphs of war!"), history required a war. But who was there to fight? Fortunately, Cuba wanted to be free of Spain; and so the United States, a Goliath posing as David, struck down Spain, a David hardly able to pose at all, and thus was Cuba freed to become a client state, the Philippines conquered and occupied, and westward the course of empire flowed. The Pacific Ocean, at first thought to be the end of the road, proved to be a new frontier whose end is not yet in sight, though it is heartening to know that downtown Hanoi is currently off limits.

The American empire began in a blaze of rhetoric, much of it paranoid. Witness Senator Albert J. Beveridge:

"God has been preparing the English-speaking and Teutonic peoples for a thousand years [to be] master organizers of the world. He has made us adepts in government that we may administer government among savages and senile peoples."

Even thoughtful commentators felt that though "we risk Caesarism, Caesarism is preferable to anarchy." And so, to avoid anarchy (and socialism), the United States chose empire, and contrary to the famous witticism, empires are the deliberate creation of an adroit presence—not absence—of mind. Franklin Roosevelt, in his way, was quite as imperial as his cousin Theodore. Beneath a genuine high-mindedness (puzzling to foreigners who find the American nonparanoid style either hypocritical or unrealistic), American leaders have unconsciously accepted the "English-speaking, Teutonic" role of world conquerors for the world's good. With the result that the Americans are in this age the barbarian horde, as the English were in the last century.

Happily enough, it would also appear that the United States is destined to be the last empire on earth (in the best if not the apocalyptic sense), and there are now stirrings within the camp of the Great Khan at Washington to the effect that new necessities do not always require military force. Barring unexpected catastrophe, the hordes may soon achieve, if not peace, an uneasy stasis which one hopes should endure until the human race begins the infection of other worlds. For more and more do we resemble a proliferating virus, destructive of other organisms, incapable of arresting itself, and so destined—manifestly!—to prevail or vanish furiously in space and time.

New Statesman, January 13, 1967

FRENCH LETTERS: THEORIES OF THE NEW NOVEL

To say that no one now much likes novels is to exaggerate very little. The large public which used to find pleasure in prose fictions prefers movies, television, journalism, and books of "fact." But then, Americans have never been enthusiastic readers. According to Dr. Gallup, only five per cent of our population can be regarded as habitual readers. This five per cent is probably a constant minority from generation to generation, despite the fact that at the end of the nineteenth century there were as many bookstores in the United States as there are today. It is true that novels in paperback often reach a very large audience. But that public is hardly serious, if one is to believe a recent New York *Times* symposium on paperback publishing. Apparently novels sell not according to who wrote them but according to how they are presented, which means that *Boys and Girls Together* will outsell *Pale Fire*, something it did not do in hard cover. Except for a handful of entertainers like the late Ian Fleming, the mass audience knows nothing of authors. They buy titles, and most of those titles are not of novels but of nonfiction: books about the Kennedys, doctors, and vivid murders are preferred to the work of anyone's imagination no matter how agreeably debased.

In this, if nothing else, the large public resembles the clerks, one of whom, Norman Podhoretz, observed nine years ago that "A feeling of dissatisfaction and impatience, irritation and boredom with contemporary serious fiction is very widespread," and he made the point that the magazine article is preferred to the novel because the article is useful, specific, relevant—something that most novels are not. This liking for fact may explain why some of our best-known novelists are read with attention only when they comment on literary or social matters. In the highest intellectual circles, a new novel by James Baldwin or William Gass or Norman Mailer—to name at random three celebrated novelists—is apt to be regarded with a certain embarrassment, hostage to a fortune often too crudely gained, and bearing little relation to its author's distinguished commentaries.

An even odder situation exists in the academy. At a time when the works of living writers are used promiscuously as classroom texts, the students themselves do little voluntary reading. "I hate to read," said a Harvard senior to a New York *Times* reporter, "and I never buy any paperbacks." The undergraduates' dislike of reading novels is partly due to the laborious way in which novels are taught: the slow killing of the work through a close textual analysis. Between the work and the reader comes the explication, and the explicator is prone to regard the object of analysis as being somehow inferior to the analysis itself.

In fact, according to Saul Bellow, "Critics and professors have declared themselves the true heirs and successors of the modern classic authors." And so, in order to maintain their usurped dignity, they are given "to redescribing everything downward, blackening the present age and denying creative scope to their contemporaries." Although Mr. Bellow overstates the case, the fact remains that the novel as currently

269

practiced does not appeal to the intellectuals any more than it does to the large public, and it may well be that the form will become extinct now that we have entered the age which Professor Marshall McLuhan has termed post-Gutenberg. Whether or not the Professor's engaging generalities are true (that linear type, for centuries a shaper of our thought, has been superseded by electronic devices), it is a fact that the generation now in college is the first to be brought up entirely within the tradition of television and differs significantly from its predecessors. Quick to learn through sight and sound, to-day's student often experiences difficulty in reading and writing. Linear type's warm glow, so comforting to Gutenberg man, makes his successors uncomfortably hot. Needless to say, that bright minority which continues the literary culture exists as always, but it is no secret that even they prefer watching movies to reading novels. John Barth ought to interest them more than Antonioni, but he doesn't.

For the serious novelist, however, the loss of the audience should not be disturbing. "I write," declared one of them serenely. "Let the reader learn to read." And contrary to Whitman, great audiences are not necessary for the creation of a high literature. The last fifty years have been a particularly good time for poetry in English, but even that public which can read intelligently knows very little of what has been done. Ideally, the writer needs no audience other than the few who understand. It is immodest and greedy to want more. Unhappily, the novelist, by the very nature of his coarse art, is greedy and immodest; unless he is read by everyone, he cannot delight, instruct, reform, destroy a world he wants, at the least, to be different for his having lived in it. Writers as various as Dickens and Joyce, as George Eliot and Proust, have suffered from this madness. It is the nature of the beast. But now the beast is caged, confined by old forms that have ceased to attract. And so the question is: can those forms be changed, and the beast set free?

Since the Second World War, Alain Robbe-Grillet, Nathalie Sarraute, Michel Butor, Claude Simon, and Robert Pinget, among others, have attempted to change not only the form of the novel but the relationship between book and reader, and though their experiments are taken most seriously on the Continent, they are still too little known and thought about in those countries the late General de Gaulle believed to be largely populated by Anglo-Saxons. Among American commentators, only Susan Sontag in *Against Interpretation, and Other Essays*, published in 1966, has made a sustained effort to understand what the French are doing, and her occasional essays on their work are well worth reading, not only as reflections of an interesting and interested mind but also because she shares with the New Novelists (as they loosely describe themselves) a desire for the novel to become "what it is not in England and America, with rare and unrelated exceptions: a form of art which people with serious and sophisticated [*sic*] taste in the other arts can take seriously." Certainly Miss Sontag finds nothing adventurous or serious in "the work of the American writers most admired today: for example, Saul Bellow, Norman Mailer, James Baldwin, William Styron, Philip Roth, Bernard Malamud." They are "essentially unconcerned with the problems of the novel as an art form. Their main concern is with their 'subjects.' " And because of this, she finds them "essentially unserious and unambitious." By this criterion, to be serious and ambitious in the novel, the writer must create works of prose comparable to those experiments in painting which have brought us to Pop and Op art and in music to the strategic silences of John Cage. Whether or not these experiments succeed or fail is irrelevant. It is enough, if the artist is serious, to attempt new forms; certainly he must not repeat old ones.

The two chief theorists of the New Novel are Alain Robbe-Grillet and Nathalie Sarraute. As novelists, their works do not much resemble one another or, for that matter, conform to each other's strictures. But it is as theorists not as novelists that they shall concern us here. Of the two, Alain Robbe-Grillet has done the most to explain what he thinks the New Novel is and is not, in *Snapshots* and *For a New Novel*, translated by

Richard Howard (1965). To begin with, he believes that any attempt at controlling the world by assigning it a meaning (the accepted task of the traditional novelist) is no longer possible. At best, meaning was

an illusory simplification; and far from becoming clearer and clearer because of it, the world has only, little by little, lost all its life. Since it is chiefly in its presence that the world's reality resides, our task is now to create a literature which takes that presence into account.

He then attacks the idea of psychological "depth" as a myth. From the Comtesse de La Fayette to Gide, the novelist's role was to burrow "deeper and deeper to reach some ever more intimate strata." Since then, however, "something" has been "changing totally, definitively in our relations with the universe." Though he does not define that ominous "something," its principal effect is that "we no longer consider the world as our own, our private property, designed according to our needs and readily domesticated." Consequently:

the novel of characters belongs entirely to the past; it describes a period: and that which marked the apogee of the individual. Perhaps this is not an advance, but it is evident that the present period is rather one of administrative numbers. The world's destiny has ceased, for us, to be identified with the rise or fall of certain men, of certain families.

Nathalie Sarraute is also concerned with the idea of man the administrative number in *Tropisms* and in *The Age of Suspicion*, translated by Maria Jolas (1964). She quotes Claude-Edmonde Magny: "Modern man, overwhelmed by mechanical civilization, is reduced to the triple determinism of hunger, sexuality and social status: Freud, Marx and Pavlov." (Surely in the wrong order.) She, too, rejects the idea of human depth: "The deep uncovered by Proust's analyses had already proved to be nothing but a surface."

Like Robbe-Grillet, she sees the modern novel as an evolution from Dostoevsky-Flaubert to Proust-Kafka; and each agrees (in essays written by her in 1947 and by him in 1958) that one of its principal touchstones is Camus' *The Stranger*, a work which she feels "came at the appointed time," when the old psychological novel was bankrupt because, paradoxically, psychology itself, having gone deeper than ever before, "inspired doubts as to the ultimate value of all methods of research." *Homo absurdus*, therefore, was Noah's dove, the messenger of deliverance. Camus' stranger is shown entirely from the inside, "all sentiment or thought whatsoever appears to have been completely abolished." He has been created without psychology or memory; he exists in a perpetual present. Robbe-Grillet goes even further in his analysis:

It is no exaggeration to claim that it is things quite specifically which ultimately lead this man to crime: the sun, the sea, the brilliant sand, the gleaming knife, the spring among the rocks, the revolver . . . as, of course, among these things, the leading role is taken by Nature.

Only the absolute presence of things can be recorded; certainly the depiction of human character is no longer possible. In fact, Miss Sarraute believes that for both author and reader, character is "the converging point of their mutual distrust," and she makes of Stendhal's "The genius of suspicion has appeared on the scene" a leitmotiv for an age in which "the reader has grown wary of practically everything. The reason being that for some time now he has been learning too many things and he is unable to forget entirely all he had learned." Perhaps the most vivid thing he has learned (or at least it was vivid when she was writing in 1947) is the fact of genocide in the concentration camps:

Beyond these furthermost limits to which Kafka did not follow them but to where he had the superhuman courage to precede them, all feeling disappears, even contempt and hatred; there remains only vast, empty stupefaction, definitive total, don't understand.

To remain at the point where he left off or to attempt to go on from there are equally impossible. Those who live in a world of human beings can only retrace their steps.

The proof that human life can be as perfectly meaningless in the scale of a human society as it is in eternity stunned a generation, and the shock of this knowledge, more than anything else (certainly more than the discoveries of the mental therapists or the new techniques of industrial automation), caused a dislocation of human values which in turn made something like the New Novel inevitable.

Although Nathalie Sarraute and Alain Robbe-Grillet are formidable theorists, neither is entirely free of those rhetorical plangencies the French so often revert to when their best aperçus are about to slip the net of logic. Each is very much a part of that French intellectual tradition so wickedly described in *Tristes Tropiques* by Lévi-Strauss (1964, translated by John Russell):

First you establish the traditional "two views" of the question. You then put forward a common-sensical justification of the one, only to refute it by the other. Finally, you send them both packing by the use of a third interpretation, in which both the others are shown to be equally unsatisfactory. Certain verbal maneuvers enable you, that is, to line up the traditional "antitheses" as complementary aspects of a single reality: form and substance, content and container, appearance and reality, essence and existence, continuity and discontinuity, and so on. Before long the exercise becomes the merest verbalizing, reflection gives place to a kind of superior punning, and the "accomplished philosopher" may be recognized by the ingenuity with which he makes ever-bolder play with assonance, ambiguity, and the use of those words which sound alike and yet bear quite different meanings.

Miss Sarraute is not above this sort of juggling, particularly when she redefines literary categories, maintaining that the traditional novelists are formalists, while the New Novelists, by eschewing old forms, are the true realists because their works, which seek to break away from all that is prescribed, conventional and dead, to turn towards what is free, sincere and alive, will necessarily, sooner or later, become ferments of emancipation and progress.

This fine demagoguery does not obscure the fact that she is obsessed with form in a way that the traditional writer seldom is. It is she, not he, who dreams

of a technique that might succeed in plunging the reader into the stream of those subterranean dreams of which Proust only had time to obtain a rapid aerial view, and concerning which he observed and reproduced nothing but the broad motionless lines. This technique would give the reader the illusion of repeating these actions himself, in a more clearly aware, more orderly, distinct and forceful manner than he can do in life, without their losing that element of indetermination, of opacity and mystery, that one's own actions always have for the one who lives them.

This is perilously close to fine lady-writing (Miss Sarraute is addicted to the triad, particularly of adjectives), but despite all protestations, she is totally absorbed with form; and though she dislikes being called a formalist, she can hardly hope to avoid the label, since she has set herself the superb task of continuing consciously those prose experiments that made the early part of the twentieth century one of the great ages of the novel.

In regard to the modern masters, both Robbe-Grillet and Miss Sarraute remark with a certain wonder that there have been no true heirs to Proust, Joyce, and Kafka; the main line of the realistic novel simply resumed as though they had never existed. Yet, as Robbe-Grillet remarks:

Flaubert wrote the new novel of 1860, Proust the new novel of 1910. The writer must proudly consent to bear his own date, knowing that there are no masterpieces in eternity, but only works in history, and that they have survived only to the degree that they have left the past behind them and heralded the future.

Here, as so often in Robbe-Grillet's theorizing, one is offered a sensible statement, followed by a dubious observation about survival (many conventional, even reactionary works have survived nicely), ending with a look-to-the-dawn-of-a-new-age chord, played fortissimo. Yet the desire to continue the modern tradition is perfectly valid. And even if the New Novelists do not succeed (in science most experiments fail), they are at least "really serious," as Miss Sontag would say.

There is, however, something very odd about a literary movement so radical in its pronouncements yet so traditional in its references. Both Miss Sarraute and Robbe-Grillet continually relate themselves to great predecessors, giving rise to the suspicion that, like Saul Bellow's literary usurpers, they are assuming for themselves the accomplishments of Dostoevsky, Flaubert, Proust, Joyce, and Beckett. In this, at least, they are significantly more modest than their heroes. One cannot imagine the Joyce of *Finnegans Wake* acknowledging a literary debt to anyone or Flaubert admitting—as Robbe-Grillet does—that his work is "merely pursuing a constant evolution of a genre." Curiously enough, the writers whom Robbe-Grillet and Miss Sarraute most resemble wrote books which were described by Arthur Symons for the *Encyclopaedia Britannica* as being

made up of an infinite number of details, set side by side, every detail equally prominent. . . . [the authors] do not search further than "the physical basis of life," and they find everything that can be known of that unknown force written visibly upon the sudden faces of little incidents, little expressive movements. . . . It is their distinction—the finest of their inventions—that, in order to render new sensations, a new vision of things, they invented a new language.

They, of course, are the presently unfashionable brothers Edmond and Jules de Goncourt, whose collaboration ended in 1870.

In attacking the traditional novel, both Robbe-Grillet and Miss Sarraute are on safe ground. Miss Sarraute is particularly effective when she observes that even the least aware of the traditionalists seems "unable to escape a certain feeling of uneasiness as regards dialogue." She remarks upon the self-conscious way in which contemporary writers sprinkle their pages with "he saids" and "she replieds," and she makes gentle fun of Henry Green's hopeful comment that perhaps the novel of the future will be largely composed in dialogue since, as she quotes him, people don't write letters any more: they use the telephone.

But the dialogue novel does not appeal to her, for it brings "the novel dangerously near the domain of the theater, where it is bound to be in a position of inferiority"—on the ground that the nuances of dialogue in the theater are supplied by actors while in the novel the writer himself must provide, somehow, the sub-conversation which is the true meaning. Opposed to the dialogue novel is the one of Proustian analysis. Miss Sarraute finds much fault with this method (no meaning-ful depths left to plumb in the wake of Freud), but concedes that "In spite of the rather serious charges that may be brought against analysis, it is difficult to turn from it today without turning one's back on progress."

"Progress," "*New* Novel," "permanent creation of tomor-row's world," "the discovery of reality will continue only if we abandon outward forms," "general evolution of the genre" ... again and again one is reminded in reading the manifestos of these two explorers that we are living (one might even say that we are trapped) in the age of science. Miss Sarraute par-ticularly delights in using quasi-scientific references. She re-fers to her first collection of pieces as "Tropisms." (According to authority, a tropism is "the turning of an organism, or part of one, in a particular direction in response to some special external stimulus.") She is also addicted to words like "larval" and "magma," and her analogies are often clinical: "Suspicion, which is by way of destroying the character and the entire outmoded mechanism that guaranteed its force, is one of the morbid reactions by which an organism defends itself and seeks another equilibrium. . . ."

Yet she does not like to be called a "laboratory novelist" any more than she likes to be called a formalist. One wonders why. For it is obvious that both she and Robbe-Grillet see themselves in white smocks working out new formulas for a new fiction. Underlying all their theories is the assumption that if scientists can break the atom with an equation, a dedicated writer ought to be able to find a new form in which to redefine the "unchanging human heart," as Bouvard might have said to Pécuchet. Since the old formulas have lost their efficacy, the novel, if it is to survive, must become something new; and so, to create that something new, they believe that writers must resort to calculated invention and bold experiment.

It is an interesting comment on the age that both Miss Sarraute and Robbe-Grillet take for granted that the highest literature has always been made by self-conscious avant-gardists. Although this was certainly true of Flaubert, whose letters show him in the laboratory, agonizing over that double genitive which nearly soured the recipe for *Madame Bovary*, and of Joyce, who spent a third of his life making a language for the night, Dostoevsky, Contrad, and Tolstoi—to name three novelists quite as great—were not much concerned with laboratory experiments. Their interest was in what Miss Sontag calls "the subject"; and though it is true they did not leave the form of the novel as they found it, their art was not the product of calculated experiments with form so much as it was the result of their ability, by virtue of what they were, to transmute the familiar and make it rare. They were men of genius unobsessed by what Goethe once referred to as "an eccentric desire for originality." Or as Saul Bellow puts it: "Genius is always, without strain, avant-garde. Its departure from tradition is not the result of caprice or of policy but of an inner necessity."

Absorbed by his subject, the genius is a natural innovator—a fact which must be maddening to the ordinary writer, who, because he is merely ambitious, is forced to approach literature from the outside, hoping by the study of a masterpiece's form and by an analysis of its content to reconstruct the principle of its composition in order that he may create either simulacra or, if he is furiously ambitious, by rearranging the component parts, something "new." This approach from the outside is of course the natural way of the critic, and it is significant that the New Novelists tend to blur the boundary between critic and novelist. "Critical preoccupation," writes Robbe-Grillet, "far from sterilizing creation, can on the contrary serve it as a driving force."

In the present age the methods of the scientist, who deals only in what can be measured, demonstrated and proved, are central. Consequently, anything as unverifiable as a novel is suspect. Or, as Miss Sarraute quotes Paul Tournier:

> There is nobody left who is willing to admit that he invents. The only thing that matters is the document, which must be precise, dated, proven, authentic. Works of the imagination are banned, because they are invented. . . . The public, in order to believe what it is told, must be convinced that it is not being "taken in." All that counts now is the "true fact."

This may explain why so many contemporary novelists feel they must apologize for effects which seem unduly extravagant or made up ("but that's the way it really happened!"). Nor is it to make a scandal to observe that most "serious" American novels are autobiographies, usually composed to pay off grudges. But then the novelist can hardly be held responsible for the society he reflects. After all, much of the world's reading consists of those weekly news magazines in which actual people are dealt with in fictional terms. It is the spirit of the age to believe that any fact, no matter how suspect, is superior to any imaginative exercise, no matter how true. The result of this attitude has been particularly harrowing in the universities, where English departments now do their best to pretend that they are every bit as fact-minded as the physical scientists (to whom the largest appropriations go). Doggedly, English teachers do research, publish learned findings, make breakthroughs in F. Scott Fitzgerald and, in their search for facts, behave as if no work of literature can be called complete until each character has been satisfactorily identified as someone who actually lived and had a history known to the author. It is no wonder that the ambitious writer is tempted to re-create the novel along what he believes to be scientific lines. With admiration, Miss Sontag quotes William Burroughs:

> I think there's going to be more and more merging of art and science. Scientists are already studying the creative process, and I think that the whole line between art and science will break down and that scientists, I hope, will become more creative and writers more scientific.

Recently in France the matter of science and the novel was much debated. In an essay called *Nouvelle Critique ou Nouvelle Imposture*, Raymond Picard attacked the new critic Roland Barthes, who promptly defended himself on the ground that a concern with form is only natural since structure precedes creation (an insight appropriated from anthropology, a discipline recently become fashionable). Picard then returned to the attack, mocking those writers who pretend to be scientists, pointing out that they

> improperly apply to the literary domain methods which have proved fruitful elsewhere but which here lose their efficiency and rigor. . . . These critical approaches have a scientific air to them, but the resemblance is pure caricature. The new critics use science roughly as someone ignorant of electricity might use electronics. What they're after is its prestige: in other respects they are at opposite poles to the scientific spirit. Their statements generally sound more like oracles than useful hypotheses: categorical, unverifiable, unilluminating.

Picard is perhaps too harsh, but no one can deny that Robbe-Grillet and Nathalie Sarraute often appropriate the language of science without understanding its spirit—for instance, one can verify the law of physics which states that there is no action without reaction, but how to prove the critical assertion that things in themselves are what caused Camus' creature to kill? Yet if to revive a moribund art form writers find it helpful to pretend to be physicists, then one ought not to tease them unduly for donning so solemnly mask and rubber gloves. After all, Count Tolstoi thought he was a philosopher. But whether pseudo-scientists or original thinkers, neither Robbe-Grillet nor Miss Sarraute finds it easy to put theory into practice. As Robbe-Grillet says disarmingly: "It is easier to indicate a new form than to follow it without failure." And he must be said to fail a good deal of the time: is there anything more incantatory than the repetition of the word "*lugubre*" in *Last Year at Marienbad*? Or more visceral than the repetition of the killing of the centipede in *Jealousy*? While Miss Sarraute finds that her later essays are "far removed from the conception and composition of my first book"—which, nevertheless, she includes in the same volume as the essays, with the somewhat puzzling comment that "this first book contains *in nuce* all the raw material that I have continued to develop in my later works."

For Robbe-Grillet, the problem of the novel is—obviously —the problem of man in relation to his environment, a relationship which he believes has changed radically in the last fifty years. In the past, man attempted to personalize the universe. In prose, this is revealed by metaphor: "majestic peaks," "huddled villages," "pitiless sun." "These anthropomorphic analogies are repeated too insistently, too coherently, not to reveal an entire metaphysical system." And he attacks what he holds to be the humanistic view: "On the pretext that man can achieve only a subjective knowledge of the world, humanism decides to elect man the justification of everything." In fact, he believes that humanists will go so far as to maintain that "it is not enough to show man where he is: it must further be proclaimed that man is everywhere." Quite shrewdly he observes: "If I say 'the world is man,' I shall always gain absolution; while if I say things are things, and man is only man, I am immediately charged with a crime against humanity."

It is this desire to remove the falsely human from the nature of things that is at the basis of Robbe-Grillet's theory. He is arguing not so much against what Ruskin called "the pathetic fallacy," as against our race's tendency to console itself by making human what is plainly nonhuman. To those who accuse him of trying to dehumanize the novel, he replies that since any book is written by a man "animated by torments and passion," it cannot help but be human. Nevertheless, "suppose the eyes of this man rest on things without indulgence, insistently: he sees them but he refuses to appropriate them." Finally, "man looks at the world but the world does not look back at him, and so, if he rejects communion, he also rejects tragedy." Inconsistently, he later quotes with admiration Joé Bousquet's "We watch things pass by in order to forget that they are watching us die."

Do those things watch or not? At times Miss Sarraute writes as if she thought they did. Her *Tropisms* are full of things invested with human response ("The crouched houses standing watch all along the gray streets"), but then she is not so strict as Robbe-Grillet in her apprehension of reality. She will accept "those analogies which are limited to the instinctive irresistible nature of the movements . . . produced in us by the presence of others, or by objects from the outside world." For Robbe-Grillet, however, "All analogies are dangerous."

Man's consciousness has now been separated from his environment. He lives in a perpetual present. He possesses memory but it is not chronological. Therefore the best that the writer can hope to do is to impart a precise sense of man's being in the present. To achieve this immediacy, Miss Sarraute favors "some precise dramatic action shown in slow motion"; a world in which "time was no longer the time of real life but of a hugely amplified present." While Robbe-Grillet, in commenting upon his film *Last Year at Marienbad*, declares:

The Universe in which the entire film occurs is, characteristically, in a perpetual present which makes all recourse to memory impossible. This is a world without a past, a world which is self-sufficient at every moment and which obliterates itself as it proceeds.

To him, the film is a ninety-minute fact without antecedents. "The only important 'character' is the spectator. In his mind unfolds the whole story which is precisely imagined by him." The verb "imagine" is of course incorrect, while the adverb means nothing. The spectator is *not* imagining the film; he is watching a creation which was made in a precise historic past by a writer, a director, actors, cameramen, etc. Yet to have the spectator or reader involve himself directly and temporally in the act of creation continues to be Robbe-Grillet's goal. He wants "a present which constantly invents itself" with "the reader's creative assistance," participating "in a creation, to invent in his turn the work—and the world—and thus to learn to invent his own life." This is most ambitious. But the ingredients of the formula keep varying. For instance, in praising Raymond Roussel, Robbe-Grillet admires the author's "*investigation* which destroys, in the writing itself, its own object." Elsewhere: "The work must seem necessary but necessary for nothing; its architecture is without use; its strength is untried." And again: "The genuine writer has nothing to say. He has only a way of speaking. He must create a world but starting from nothing, from the dust. . . ." It would not seem to be possible, on the one hand, to invent a world that would cause the reader to "invent his own life" while, on the other hand, the world in question is being destroyed as it is being created. Perhaps he means for the reader to turn to dust, gradually, page by page: not the worst of solutions.

No doubt there are those who regard the contradictions in Robbe-Grillet's critical writing as the point to them—rather in the way that the boredom of certain plays or the incompetence of certain pictures are, we are assured, their achievement. Yet it is worrisome to be told that a man can create a world from nothing when that is the one thing he cannot begin to do, simply because, no matter how hard he tries, he cannot dispose of himself. Even if what he writes is no more than nouns and adjectives, who and what he is will subconsciously dictate order. Nothing human is random and it is nonsense to say:

Art is based on no truth that exists before it; and one may say that it expresses nothing but itself. It creates its own equilibrium and its own meaning. It stands all by itself . . . or else it falls.

Which reminds us of Professor Herzog's plaintive response to the philosophic proposition that modern man at a given moment fell into the quotidian: so where was he standing before the fall? In any case, how can something unique, in Robbe-Grillet's sense, rise or fall or be anything except itself? As for reflecting "no truth that existed before it," this is not possible. The fact that the author is a man "filled with torments and passion" means that all sorts of "truths" are going to occur in the course of the writing. The act of composing prose is a demonstration not only of human will but of desire to reflect truth—particularly if one's instinct is messianic, and Robbe-Grillet is very much in that tradition. Not only does he want man "to invent his own life" (by reading Robbe-Grillet), but he proposes that today's art is "a way of living in the present world, and of participating in the permanent creation of tomorrow's world." It also seems odd that a theory of the novel which demands total existence in a self-devouring present should be concerned at all with the idea of future time since man exists, demonstrably, only in the present—the future tense is a human conceit, on the order of "majestic peaks." As for the use of the adjective "permanent," one suspects that rhetoric, not thought, forced this unfortunate word from the author's unconscious mind.

The ideal work, according to Robbe-Grillet, is

A text both "dense and irreducible"; so perfect that it does not seem "to have touched," an object so perfect that it would obliterate our tracks. . . . Do we not recognize here the highest ambition of every writer?

Further, the only meaning for the novel is the invention of the world. "In dreams, in memory, as in the sense of sight, our imagination is the organizing force of our life, of *our* world.

Each man, in his turn, must reinvent the things around him."
Yet, referring to things, he writes a few pages later,

They refer to no other world. They are the sign of nothing but
themselves. And the only contact man can make with them is to
imagine them.

But how is one to be loyal to the actual fact of things if they
must be reinvented? Either they are *there* or they are not. In
any case, by filtering them through the imagination (reinven-
tion), true objectivity is lost, as he himself admits in a further
snarling of his argument: "Objectivity in the ordinary sense of
the word—total impersonality of observation—is all too obviously an illusion. But freedom of observation should be possible and yet it is not"—because a "continuous fringe of culture
(psychology, ethics, metaphysics, etc.) is added to things, giving them a less alien aspect." But he believes that "humaniz-
ing" can be kept to a minimum, if we try "to construct a world
both more solid and more immediate. Let it be first of all by
their presence that objects and gestures establish themselves
and let this presence continue to prevail over the subjective."
Consequently, the task of the New Novel is nothing less than
to seek

new forms for the novel . . . forms capable of expressing (or of
creating) new relations between man and the world, to all those who
have determined to invent the novel, in other words, to invent man.
Such writers know that the systematic repetition of the forms of the
past is not only absurd and futile, but that it can even become harmful: blinding us to our real situation in the world today, it keeps us,
ultimately, from constructing the world and man of tomorrow.

With the change of a noun or two, this could easily be the coda
of an address on American foreign policy, delivered by Professor Arthur Schlesinger, Jr., to the ADA.

Like Robbe-Grillet, Nathalie Sarraute regards Camus' *The
Stranger* as a point of departure. She sees the book's immediate

predecessors as "The promising art of the cinema" and "the wholesome simplicity of the new American novel." Incidentally, she is quite amusing when she describes just what the effect of these "wholesome" novels was upon the French during the years immediately after the war:

> By transporting the French reader into a foreign universe in which he had no foothold, [they] lulled his wariness, aroused in him the kind of credulous curiosity that travel books inspire, and gave him a delightful impression of escape into an unknown world.

It is reassuring to learn that these works were not regarded with any great seriousness by the French and that Horace McCoy was not finally the master they once hailed him. Apparently the American novel was simply a vigorous tonic for an old literature gone stale. Miss Sarraute is, however, sincerely admiring of Faulkner's ability to involve the reader in his own world. To her the most necessary thing of all is "to dispossess the reader and entice him, at all costs, into the author's territory. To achieve this the device that consists in referring to the leading characters as 'I' constitutes a means." The use of the first person seems to her to be the emblem of modern art. ("Since Impressionism all pictures have been painted in the first person.") And so, just as photography drove painters away from representing nature (ending such ancient arts as that of the miniaturist and the maker of portrait busts), the cinema "garners and perfects what is left of it by the novel." The novel must now go where the camera may not follow. In this new country the reader has been aided by such modern writers as Proust and Joyce; they have so awakened his sensibilities that he is now able to respond to what is beneath the interior monologue, that "immense profusion of sensations, images, sentiments, memories, impulses, little larval actions that no inner language can convey." For her, emphasis falls upon what she calls the sub-conversation, that which is sensed and not said, the hidden counterpoint to the stated theme (obviously a very difficult thing to suggest, much less write, since "no inner language can convey it").

"Bosquet's universe—ours—is a universe of signs," writes Robbe-Grillet. "Everything in it is a sign; and not the sign of something else, something more perfect, situated out of reach, but a sign of itself, of that reality which asks only to be revealed." This answer to Baudelaire's *The Salon of 1859* is reasonable (although it is anthropomorphic to suggest that reality *asks* to be revealed). Robbe-Grillet is equally reasonable in his desire for things to be shown, as much as possible, as they are.

In the future universe of the novel, gestures and objects will be there before being *something*; and they will still be there afterwards, hard, unalterably, eternally present, mocking their own "meaning," that meaning which vainly tries to reduce them to the role of precarious tools, etc.

One agrees with him that the integrity of the nonhuman world should be honored. But what does he mean (that proscribed verb!) when he says that the objects will be *there*, after meaning has attempted to rape them? Does he mean that they will still exist on the page, in some way inviolate in their thing-ness? If he does, surely he is mistaken. What exists on the page is ink; or, if one wishes to give the ink designs their agreed-upon human meaning, letters have been formed to make words in order to suggest things not present. What is on the page are not real things but their word-shadows. Yet even if the things were there, it is most unlikely that they would be so human as to "mock their own meaning." In an eerie way, Robbe-Grillet's highly rhetorical style has a tendency to destroy his arguments even as he makes them; critically, this technique complements ideally the self-obliterating anecdote.

On the question of how to establish the separateness, the autonomy of things, Robbe-Grillet and Miss Sarraute part company. In contemplating her method, she ceases altogether to be "scientific." Instead she alarmingly intones a hymn to words—all words—for they "possess the qualities needed to seize upon, protect and bring out into the open those subterranean movements that are at once impatient and afraid." (Are those subterranean movements really "impatient and afraid"?) For her, words possess suppleness, freedom, iridescent richness of shading, and by their nature they are protected "from suspicion and from minute examination." (In an age of suspicion, to let words off scot-free is an act of singular trust.) Consequently, once words have entered the other person, they swell, explode, and "by virtue of this game of actions and reactions . . . they constitute a most valuable tool for the novelist." Which, as the French say, goes without saying.

But of course words are not at all what she believes they are. All words lie. Or as Professor Frank Kermode put it in *Literary Fiction and Reality:* "Words, thoughts, patterns of word and thought, are enemies of truth, if you identify that with what may be had by phenomenological reductions." Nevertheless, Miss Sarraute likes to think that subterranean movements (tropisms) can be captured by words, which might explain why her attitude toward things is so much more conventional than that of Robbe-Grillet, who writes:

> Perhaps Kafka's staircases lead *elsewhere*, but they are *there*, and we look at them step by step following the details of the banisters and the risers.

This is untrue. First, we do not look at the staircases; we look at a number of words arranged upon a page by a conscious human intelligence which would like us to consider, among a thousand other things, the fact of those staircases. Since a primary concern of the human mind is cause and effect, the reader is bound to speculate upon why those staircases have been shown him; also, since staircases are usually built to connect one man-made level with another, the mind will naturally speculate as to what those two levels are like. Only a far-gone schizophrenic (or an LSD tripper) would find entirely absorbing the description of a banister.

Perhaps the most naïve aspect of Robbe-Grillet's theory of fiction is his assumption that words can ever describe with absolute precision anything. At no point does he acknowledge that words are simply fiat for real things; by their nature, words are imprecise and layered with meanings—the signs of things, not the things themselves. Therefore, even if Robbe-Grillet's goal of achieving a total reality for the world of things was desirable, it would not be possible to do it with language, since the author (that man full of torments and passions) is bound to betray his attitude to the sequence of signs he offered us; he has an "interest" in the matter, or else he would not write. Certainly if he means to reinvent man, then he will want to find a way of defining man through human (yes, psychological) relations as well as through a catalogue of things observed and gestures coolly noted. Wanting to play God, ambition is bound to dictate the order of words, and so the subjective will prevail just as it does in the traditional novel. To follow Robbe-Grillet's theory to its logical terminus, the only sort of book which might be said to be *not* a collection of signs of absent things but the actual things themselves would be a collection of ink, paper, cardboard, glue, and typeface, to be assembled or not by the reader-spectator. If this be too heavy a joke, then the ambitious writer must devise a new language which might give the appearance of maintaining the autonomy of things, since the words, new-minted, will possess a minimum of associations of a subjective or anthropomorphic sort. No existing language will be of any use to him, unless it be that of the Trobriand Islanders: those happy people have no words for "why" or "because"; for them, things just happen. Needless to say, they do not write novels or speculate on the nature of things.

The philosophic origins of the New Novel can be found (like most things French) in Descartes, whose dualism was the reflection of a split between the subjective and the objective, between the irrational and the rational, between the physical and the metaphysical. In the last century Auguste Comte, accepting this dualism, conceived of a logical empiricism which would emphasize the "purely" objective at the expense of the subjective or metaphysical. An optimist who believed in human progress, Comte saw history as an evolution toward a better society. For him the age of religion and metaphysics ended with the French Revolution. Since that time the human race was living in what he termed "the age of science," and he was confident that the methods of the positive sciences would enrich and transform human life. At last things were coming into their own. But not until the twentieth century did the methods of science entirely overwhelm the arts of the traditional humanists. To the scientific-minded, all things, including human personality, must in time yield their secrets to orderly experiment. Meanwhile, only that which is verifiable is to be taken seriously; emotive meaning must yield to cognitive meaning. Since the opacity of human character has so far defeated all objective attempts at illumination, the New Novelists prefer, as much as possible, to replace the human with objects closely observed and simple gestures noted but not explained.

In many ways, the New Novel appears to be approaching the "pure" state of music. In fact, there are many like Miss Sontag who look forward to "a kind of total structuring" of the novel, analogous to music. This is an old dream of the novelist. Nearly half a century ago, Joyce wrote (in a letter to his brother), "Why should not a modern literature be as unsparing and as direct as song?" Why not indeed? And again, why? The answer to the second "why" is easy enough. In the age of science, the objective is preferred to the subjective. Since human behavior is notoriously irrational and mysterious, it can be demonstrated only in the most impressionistic and unscientific way; it yields few secrets to objective analysis. Mathematics, on the other hand, is rational and verifiable, and music is a form of mathematics. Therefore, if one were to eliminate as much as possible the human from the novel, one might, through "a kind of total structuring," come close to the state of mathematics or music—in short, achieve that perfect irreducible artifact Robbe-Grillet dreams of.

The dates of Miss Sarraute's essays range from 1947 to 1956, those of Robbe-Grillet from 1955 to 1963. To categorize in the

French manner, it might be said that their views are particularly representative of the 50's, a period in which the traditional-minded (among whom they must be counted) still believed it possible to salvage the novel—or anything—by new techniques. With a certain grimness, they experimented. But though some of their books are good (even very good) and some are bad, they did not make a "new" novel, if only because art forms do not evolve—in literature at least—from the top down. Despite Robbe-Grillet's tendency to self-congratulation ("Although these descriptions—motionless arguments or fragments of scene—have acted on the readers in a satisfactory fashion, the judgment many specialists make of them remains pejorative"), there is not much in what he has so far written that will interest anyone except the specialist. It is, however, a convention of the avant-garde that to be in advance of the majority is to be "right." But the New Novelists are not in advance of anyone. Their works derive from what they believe to be a need for experiment and the imposition of certain of the methods of science upon the making of novels. Fair enough. Yet in this they resemble everyone, since to have a liking for the new is to be with the dull majority. In the arts, the obviously experimental is almost never denounced *because* it is new: if anything, our taste-makers tend to be altogether too permissive in the presence of what looks to be an experiment, as anyone who reads New York art criticism knows. There is not much likelihood that Robbe-Grillet will be able to reinvent man as a result of his exercises in prose. Rather he himself is in the process of being reinvented (along with the rest of us) by the new world in which we are living.

At the moment, advance culture scouts are reporting with a certain awe that those men and women who were brought up as television-watchers respond, predictably, to pictures that move and talk but not at all to prose fictions; and though fashion might dictate the presence of an occasional irreducible artifact in a room, no one is about to be reinvented by it. Yet the old avant-garde continues worriedly to putter with form.

Surveying the literary output for 1965, Miss Sontag found it "hard to think of any one book [in English] that exemplifies in a *central* way the possibilities for enlarging and complicating the forms of prose literature." This desire to "enlarge" and "complicate" the novel has an air of madness to it. Why not minimize and simplify? One suspects that out of desperation she is picking verbs at random. But then, like so many at present, she has a taste for the random. Referring to William Burroughs's resolutely random work *The Soft Machine*, she writes: "In the end, the voices come together and sound what is to my mind the most serious, urgent and original voice in American letters to be heard for many years." It is, however, the point to Mr. Burroughs's method that the voices *don't* come together: he is essentially a sport who is (blessedly) not serious, not urgent, and original only in the sense that no other American writer has been so relentlessly ill-humored in his send-up of the serious. He is the Grand Guy Grand of American letters. But whether or not Miss Sontag is right or wrong in her analyses of specific works and general trends, there is something old-fashioned and touching in her assumption (shared with the New Novelists) that if only we all try hard enough in a "really serious" way, we can come up with the better novel. This attitude reflects not so much the spirit of art as it does that of Detroit.

No one today can predict what games post-Gutenberg man will want to play. The only certainty is that his mind will work differently from ours; just as ours works differently from that of pre-Gutenberg man, as Miss Frances Yates demonstrated so dramatically in *The Art of Memory*. Perhaps there will be more Happenings in the future. Perhaps the random will take the place of the calculated. Perhaps the ephemeral will be preferred to the permanent: we stop in time, so why should works of art endure? Also, as the shadow of atomic catastrophe continues to fall across our merry games, the ephemeral will necessarily be valued to the extent it gives pleasure in the present and makes no pretense of having a future life. Since nothing will survive the firewind, the ashes of one thing will be very like those of another, and so what matters excellence?

One interesting result of today's passion for the immediate and the casual has been the decline, in all the arts, of the idea of technical virtuosity as being in any way desirable. The culture (*kitsch* as well as camp) enjoys singers who sing no better than the average listener, actors who do not act yet are, in Andy Warhol's happy term, "super-stars," painters whose effects are too easily achieved, writers whose swift flow of words across the page is not submitted to the rigors of grammar or shaped by conscious thought. There is a general Zen-ish sense of why bother? If a natural fall of pebbles can "say" as much as any shaping of paint on canvas or cutting of stone, why go to the trouble of recording what is there for all to see? In any case, if the world should become, as predicted, a village united by an electronic buzzing, our ideas of what is art will seem as curious to those gregarious villagers as the works of what we used to call the Dark Ages appear to us.

Regardless of what games men in the future will want to play, the matter of fiction seems to be closed. Reading skills—as the educationalists say—continue to decline with each new generation. Novel reading is not a pastime of the young now being educated, nor, for that matter, is it a preoccupation of any but a very few of those who came of age in the last warm years of linear type's hegemony. It is possible that fashion may from time to time bring back a book or produce a book which arouses something like general interest (Miss Sontag darkly suspects that "the nineteenth-century novel has a much better chance for a comeback than verse drama, the sonnet, or landscape painting"). Yet it is literature itself which seems on the verge of obsolescence, and not so much because the new people will prefer watching to reading as because the language in which books are written has become corrupt from misuse.

In fact, George Steiner believes that there is a definite possibility that "The political inhumanity of the twentieth century and certain elements in the technological mass-society which has followed on the erosion of European bourgeois values have done injury to language. . . . " He even goes so far as to suggest that for now at least silence may be a virtue for the writer—when

language simply ceases, and the motion of spirit gives no further outward manifestation of its being. The poet enters into silence. Here the word borders not on radiance or music, but on night.

Although Mr. Steiner does not himself take this romantic position ("I am not saying that writers should stop writing. This would be fatuous"), he does propose silence as a proud alternative for those who have lived at the time of Belsen and of Vietnam, and have witnessed the perversion of so many words by publicists and political clowns. The credibility gap is now an abyss, separating even the most honorable words from their ancient meanings. Fortunately, ways of communication are now changing, and though none of us understands exactly what is happening, language is bound to be affected.

But no matter what happens to language, the novel is not apt to be revived by electronics. The portentous theorizings of the New Novelists are of no more use to us than the self-conscious avant-gardism of those who are forever trying to figure out what the next "really serious" thing will be when it is plain that there is not going to be a next serious thing in the novel. Our lovely vulgar and most human art is at an end, if not the end. Yet that is no reason not to want to practice it, or even to read it. In any case, rather like priests who have forgotten the meaning of the prayers they chant, we shall go on for quite a long time talking of books and writing books, pretending all the while not to notice that the church is empty and the parishioners have gone elsewhere to attend other gods, perhaps in silence or with new words.

Encounter, December 1967

MISS SONTAG'S
NEW NOVEL

The beginning of a novel tends to reveal the author's ambition. The implicit or explicit obeisance he pays to previous works of literature is his way of "classing" himself, thereby showing interest in the matter. But as he proceeds, for better or worse his true voice is bound to be heard, if only because it is not possible to maintain for the length of a novel a voice pitched at a false level. Needless to say, the best and the worst novels are told in much the same tone from beginning to end, but they need not concern us here.

In the early pages of *Death Kit*, Susan Sontag betrays great ambition. Her principal literary sources are Nathalie Sarraute, Robbe-Grillet, Sartre, and Kafka, and she uses these writers in such a way that they must be regarded not so much as influences upon her prose as collaborators in the act of creation. Contemplating Nathalie Sarraute's *Portrait of a Man Unknown*, Sartre made much of Sarraute's "protoplasmic vision" of our interior universe: roll away the stone of the commonplace and we will find running discharges, slobberings, mucus; hesitant, amoeba-like movements. The Sarraute vocabulary is incomparably rich in suggesting the slow centrifugal creeping of these viscous, live solutions. "Like a sort of gluey slaver, their thought filtered into him, sticking to him, lining his insides." This is a fair description of Sarraute's manner, which Miss Sontag has entirely appropriated.

The first few pages of *Death Kit* are rich with Sarrautesque phrases: "inert, fragile, sticky fabric of things," "the soft interconnected tissuelike days," "surfaces of people deformed and bloated and leaden and crammed with vile juices" (but Miss Sarraute would not have written "leaden" because a bloated person does not suggest metal; more to the point, "leaden" is not a soft, visceral word), "his jellied porous boss" (but isn't the particular horror of the true jelly its consistency of texture? a porous jelly is an anomaly). Fortunately, once past the book's opening, Miss Sontag abandons the viscous vision except for a brief reprise in mid-passage when we encounter, in quick succession, "affable gelatinous Jim Allen," "chicken looks like boiled mucus," "oozing prattling woman," "sticky strip of words." But later we are reminded of Miss Sarraute's addiction to words taken from the physical sciences. In "The Age of Suspicion" (an essay admired by Miss Sontag in her own collection of essays *Against Interpretation*), Miss Sarraute wrote that the reader "is immersed and held under the surface until the end, in a substance as anonymous as blood, a magma without name or contours." Enchanted by the word "magma," Miss Sontag describes *her* characters as being "All part of the same magma of sensation, in which pleasure and pain are one." But Miss Sarraute used the word precisely, while Miss Sontag seems not to have looked it up in the dictionary, trusting to her ear to get the meaning right, and failing.

The plot of *Death Kit* is elaborate. Aboard the Privateer (yes), a train from Manhattan to Buffalo, Diddy (a divorced man in his thirties who inhabits a life he does not possess) observes a blind girl and an older woman. He wonders who they are; he also meditates on the other occupants of the compartment (as in Proust). Then the train stalls in a tunnel. The light go out. After what seems a long time, Diddy gets off the train. He makes his way in the dark to the front of the train, where he finds a workman removing a barrier. When the man does not respond to his questions, Diddy grows alarmed. Finally the man does speak: he appears to threaten Diddy, who kills him with a crowbar, a murder which is almost gratuitous, almost Gide. Diddy returns to the compartment to find the older woman asleep. He talks to the blind girl, whose name is Hester (*The Scarlet Letter?*). Then the train starts and he takes Hester to the washroom, where, excited by his murder (Mailer's *An American Dream*), he makes love to her. Later Hester tells him that he did not leave the compartment and so could not have killed the workman. But of course she is blind, while the older woman, her aunt, was asleep and so cannot bear witness. In any case, hallucination has begun, and we are embarked upon another of those novels whose contemporary source is Kafka. Do I wake or dream?

Diddy dreams a very great deal and his dreams are repeated at length. When awake, he attends business meetings of his company, whose trademark is a gilded dome, whose management is conservative, whose business is worldwide, whose prospects are bad . . . too much undercutting from the East (what can Miss Sontag *mean?*). He broods about the "murder" and moons about Hester, who is in a local clinic waiting for an operation to restore her sight. Diddy visits her; he loves her. But he is still obsessed by the murder. In the press he reads that a workman named Angelo Incarnadona (incarnated angel) was killed in the tunnel by the Privateer, which had not, apparently, stalled in the tunnel. Diddy's quest begins. Did he kill the angel? He talks to the widow, who tells him that the body was cremated; he is safe, there can never be an investigation. Meanwhile Hester's operation is a failure. But Diddy has decided to marry her. They return to Manhattan. He quits his job. They withdraw from the world, seldom leaving his apartment. Slowly he begins to fade, grows thinner, vaguer. Finally he (apparently) takes Hester with him to the tunnel in an effort to make her *see* what it was that he did . . . or did he (Diddy)? In the tunnel they find a workman similar to the angel made flesh: again the man is at work removing a barrier. The scene more or less repeats the original, and once again Diddy separates the angel from its fleshly envelope with a crowbar. Then he makes love to Hester on the tunnel floor. But now we cease to see him from the outside. We enter his declining world, we become him as he walks naked through one subterranean room after another, among coffins and corpses heavy with dust, and in this last progress, simply written, Miss Sontag reveals herself as an artist with a most powerful ability to show us what it is she finally, truly sees.

The flash of talent at the book's end makes all the more annoying what precedes it. Miss Sontag is a didactic, naturalistic, Jewish-American writer who wants to be an entirely different sort of writer, not American but high European, not Jewish but ecumenical, not naturalistic in style but allusive, resonant, ambiguous. It is as an heiress to Joyce, Proust, and Kafka that she sees herself; her stand to be taken on foreign rather than on native ground. The tension between what she is and what she would like to be creates odd effects. She presents Diddy as a Gentile. But, to make a small point, middle-class American goyim do not address each other continually by name while, to make a larger point, Diddy's possession of a young brother who is a virtuoso musician seems better suited to a Clifford Odets drama than to one by Sherwood Anderson or William Faulkner. But Miss Sontag is nothing if not contemporary and perhaps she is reflecting the current fashion for Jewish writers to disguise Jewish characters as Gentiles, in much the same way that the homosexualists in our theater are supposed to write elaborate masquerades in which their own pathological relationships are depicted as heterosexual, thus traducing women and marriage. These playwrights have given us all many an anxious moment. Now the Jewish novelists are also indulging in travesty, with equally scandalous results.

As for style, Miss Sontag demonstrates a considerable gift for naturalistic prose, particularly in the later parts of the book when she abandons her sources and strikes out on her own. But she is not helped by the form in which she has cast her work. For no apparent reason, certain passages are indented on the page, while at maddeningly regular but seemingly random intervals she inserts the word "now" in parenthesis. If she intends these (now)s to create a sense of immediacy, of presentness, she fails. Also, though the story is told in the third person, on four occasions she shifts to the first person plural. It is a nice surprise, but one that we don't understand. Also, her well-known difficulties in writing English continue to make things hard for her. She is altogether too free with "sort ofs" and "kind ofs" and "reallys"; she often confuses number, and her ear, oddly enough, is better attuned to the cadences of the lower orders than to those of the educated. In the scenes between Diddy and the dead workman's widow, she writes not unlike Paddy Chayevsky at his best. She is, however, vulgar at moments when she means not to be, and on several occasions she refers to someone as "balding," betraying, if nothing else, her lovely goosey youth: those of us battered by decades of Timestyle refuse to use any word invented by that jocose and malicious publishing enterprise which has done so much to corrupt our Empire's taste, morals, and prose.

In a strange way, Miss Sontag has been undone as a novelist by the very thing that makes her unique and valuable among American writers: her vast reading in what English Departments refer to as comparative literature. As a literary broker, mediating between various contemporary literatures, she is awesome in her will to understand. This acquired culture sets her apart from the majority of American novelists (good and bad) who read almost nothing, if one is to admit as evidence the meager texture of their works and the idleness of their occasional commentaries. When American novelists do read, it is usually within the narrow limits of the American canon, a strange list of minor provincial writers grandiosely inflated into "world classics." Certainly few of our writers know anything of what is now being written in Europe, particularly in France. Yet for all the aridities and pretensions of the French "New Novelists," their work is the most interesting being done anywhere, and not to know what they are up to is not to know what the novel is currently capable of. As an essayist (and of course interpreter!) Miss Sontag has been, more than any other American, a link to European writing today. Not unnaturally, her reading has made her impatient with the unadventurous novels which our country's best-known (and often best) writers produce. She continues to yearn, as she recently wrote, for a novel "which people with serious and sophisticated [sic] taste in the other arts can take seriously," and she believes that such a work might be achieved "by a kind of total structuring" that is "analogous to music." This is all very vague, but at least she is radical in the right way; also her moral seriousness is considerably enhanced by a perfect absence of humor, that most devastating of gifts usually thrust at birth upon the writer in English. Unhindered by a sense of humor, she is able to travel fast in the highest country, unafraid of appearing absurd, and of course invulnerable to irony.

Unfortunately, Miss Sontag's intelligence is still greater than her talent. What she would do, she cannot do—or at least she has not done in *Death Kit*, a work not totally structured, not even kind of. Worse, the literary borrowings entirely obscure her own natural talent while the attitudes she strikes confuse and annoy, reminding one of Gide's weary complaint that there is nothing more unbearable than those writers who assume a tone and manner not their own. In the early part of *Death Kit*, Miss Sontag recklessly uses other writers in much the same way that certain tribes eat parts of their enemies in the hope that, magically, they may thus acquire the virtues and powers of the noble dead. No doubt the tribesmen do gain great psychological strength through their cannibalizing, but in literature only writers of the rank of Goethe and Eliot can feed promiscuously and brazenly upon the works of other men and gain strength. Yet the coda of Miss Sontag's novel suggests that once she has freed herself of literature, she will have the power to make it, and there are not many American writers one can say that of.

Book World, September 10, 1967

GORE VIDAL

In the *Secret Miracle*, Borges remarks of his author-protagonist, "Like every writer, he measured the virtues of other writers by their performances, and asked that they measure him by what he conjectured or planned." This seems to me a sad truth. Even André Gide, when young, used to wonder why it was that strangers could not tell simply by looking into his eyes what a master he would one day be. The artist lives not only with his performances (which he tends to forget), but with his own private view of what he *thinks* he has done, and most important, what he still plans to do. To the writer of a given book, what exists in print is only a small, perhaps misleading, fraction of the great thing to be accomplished; to the critic, however, it is the thing itself entire. Consequently critic and writer are seldom on the same wavelength.

As it must to all American writers who stay the course, and do not have the luck (sometimes good) to die after a first success, I am now confronted with a volume called *Gore Vidal*. It is the work of Ray Lewis White, a young professor at the University of North Carolina. For two years he has written me probing letters (sensibly, he never proposed a meeting), examined my papers at the University of Wisconsin, and immersed himself in what is probably, in plain bulk, the largest *oeuvre* of any contemporary American writer. At all times he has had my sympathy, even awe, as he worked his way through a career that has endured for a quarter century. The result is now at hand, one hundred fifty-seven dense pages, describing and judging ten novels (stopping short of the apocalyptic *Myra Breckinridge*), four plays and seven short stories. Omitted are the politics, most of the essays, the political journalism, the television writing and performing, and the movie hack work. Omitted, too, is the personal element. There are no revelations. Unlike Mary McCarthy, the Subject (as I shall now be known for modesty's sake) does not extend confidences to biographers nor, to Mr. White's credit, were they solicited. He has addressed himself entirely to the work, only bringing in the life as a means to show when and where—if not why —something was written. From this point of view, his book is meticulous and, I would suspect, accurate. Suspect because the Subject has no memory for dates or chronology. As a result, the story of his life unfolds for him like that of a stranger. Even so, the effect is disquieting: what a lot of time the Subject mis-used or simply wasted. And of all that he wrote, how little now seems to him remotely close to what he originally planned and conjectured (but still plans and conjectures!).

Mr. White's detailed plot outlines of the novels and plays will doubtless not encourage many people to read the original works. Worse, in an age of non-readers, those who like to know about writing without actually reading books will be quite satisfied to skim Mr. White's study and feel that their duty to the Subject has been more than discharged since it is well known that in any year there is only One Important Novelist worth reading (there is some evidence that the Subject's year occurred at the end of the 40's). Yet perhaps it is best to be known only in outline: part of the genius of Borges is the lovely way he evades making books by writing reviews of novels that he has not written, demonstrating not only what he might so perfectly have done but inviting our respect for then not doing it.

Mr. White divides the Subject's career as novelist into three parts. The first phase was both precocious and prolific. Between the ages of nineteen and twenty-four (1945-1949), the Subject wrote and published six novels. The first was the war novel *Williwaw*, still regarded by certain romantics as a peak he was never again to scale. Among the other five novels, only *The City and the Pillar*, and perhaps *A Search for the King*, have much interest for anyone today except as paradigms of what was then the national manner: colorless, careful prose, deliberately confined to the surface of things. Then, according to Mr. White, came the second phase and the flowering.

Between 1950 and 1953 the Subject published *The Judgment of Paris*, *Messiah* and the short stories in *A Thirsty Evil*. These works resembled hardly at all the books that had gone before. But unfortunately the Subject was by then so entirely out of fashion that they were ignored. Only gradually did they find an audience. For some years now the paperback edition of *Messiah* has been much read, particularly on the campuses, and now *The Judgment of Paris* ("Vidal's Peacock-like novel-as-dialogue") is being discovered. But the original failure of these books made it necessary for the Subject to earn a living and so from 1954 to 1961, he wrote plays for television, Broadway, films, as well as criticism and political journalism; concluding his head-on encounter with the world by running for Congress in 1960—all in all, an interesting and profitable decade. But looking over Mr. White's neat chronology at the beginning of the book, what a waste it now seems. Yet the Subject was having his life if not art; and Strether would have approved. Then, world exhausted, the Subject resumed an interrupted novel about the apostate emperor Julian, and so became a novelist once more, embarked upon his third (and terminal?) phase.

What does Mr. White make of all this? He is cautious, as well he might be; in many quarters his author is still regarded with profound suspicion. He is adroit at demonstrating the recurring themes from book to book. He makes, however, inadequate use of the essays, relying too heavily upon newspaper interviews—usually garbled—or on taped answers to questions in which the Subject has a tendency to sound like General Eisenhower with a hangover. He also betrays his youth when he tries to reconstruct the literary atmosphere in which the books were published. He places *In a Yellow Wood* (1949) in the company of books by Busch, Heyliger, Burnett and Mayo, who also dealt with the problems of a returned veteran. It may be that these novels were most worthy but they were quite unknown at the time. *Lucifer with a Book, That Winter, Barbary Shore* were the relevant books everyone read. But then no one has yet captured the sense of excitement of the literary scene in the 40's. Between VJ day and the beginning of the Korean war, it looked as if we were going to have a most marvelous time in all the arts; and the novel was very much alive, not yet displaced at the vulgar level by movies, at the highest by film.

These complaints registered, Mr. White has written—how for me to put it?—a most interesting book, astonishingly exact in detail and often shrewd in judgment. The series to which it belongs is aimed at a university audience and Mr. White has kept within the bounds prescribed. Here and there one sees the beginning of something extra-academic, but he shows his tact, as one must in dealing with a living author little prone to autobiography. The inner life will come later—inevitably, since all that is apt to be remembered of any mid-20th century author is his life. Novels command neither interest nor affection but writers do, particularly the colorful ones who have made powerful legends of themselves. I suspect that eventually novels will be read only to provide clues to the author's personality; and once each of his characters has been satisfactorily identified, each of his obsessions duly noted, each key turned in its giving lock, the books may then be put aside for good, leaving us with what most concerns this artless time: the story of the author as monster most sacred, the detritus of his life enriched by our fascinated gaze, the gossip of his day our day's gospel. Of such is the declining kingdom of literature in which Mr. White has staked out with some nicety the wild marches of a border lord.

The New York Times Book Review, September 1, 1968

THE TWENTY-NINTH REPUBLICAN CONVENTION

The dark blue curtains part. As delegates cheer, the nominee walks toward the lectern, arms loose, shoulders somewhat rigid like a man who. . . . No, as Henry James once said in quite a different but no less dramatic context, it cannot be done. What is there to say about Richard M. Nixon that was not said eight years ago? What is there to say that he himself did not say at that memorable "last" press conference in Los Angeles six years ago? For some time he has ceased to figure in the conscious regions of the mind, a permanent resident, one had thought, of that limbo where reside the Stassens and the Deweys and all those other ambitious men whose failures seemed so entirely deserved. But now, thanks to two murders in five years, Richard Nixon is again a presidential candidate. No second acts to American careers? Nonsense. What is lacking are decent codas. At Miami Beach, we were reminded that no politician can ever be written off this side of Arlington.

The week before the convention began, various Republican

leaders met at the Fontainebleau Hotel to write a platform, knowing that no matter what wisdom this document might contain it would be ignored by the candidate. Nevertheless, to the extent issues ever intrude upon the making of Presidents, the platform hearings do give publicity to different points of view, and that is why Ronald Reagan took time from his busy schedule as Governor of California to fly to Miami Beach in order to warn the platform committee of the dangers of crime in the streets. The Governor also made himself available to the flower of the national and international press who sat restively in a windowless low-ceilinged dining room of the Fontaine-bleau from two o'clock to two-thirty to "just a short wait, please, the Governor is on his way," interviewing one another and trying to look alert as the television cameras, for want of a candidate, panned from face to face. At last, His Excellency, as Ivy Baker Priest would say, entered the room, flanked by six secret servicemen. As they spread out on either side of him, they cased us narrowly and I knew that simply by looking into my face they could see the imaginary gun in my pocket.

Ronald Reagan is a well-preserved not young man. Close-to, the painted face is webbed with delicate lines while the dyed hair, eyebrows, and eyelashes contrast oddly with the sagging muscle beneath the as yet unlifted chin, soft earnest of wattle-to-be. The effect, in repose, suggests the work of a skillful embalmer. Animated, the face is quite attractive and at a distance youthful; particularly engaging is the crooked smile full of large porcelain-capped teeth. The eyes are interesting: small, narrow, apparently dark, they glitter in the hot light, alert to every move, for this is enemy country—the liberal Eastern press who are so notoriously immune to that warm and folksy performance which Reagan quite deliberately projects over their heads to some legendary constituency at the far end of the tube, some shining Carverville where good Lewis Stone forever lectures Andy Hardy on the virtues of thrift and the wisdom of the contract system at Metro-Goldwyn-Mayer.

The questions begin. Why don't you announce your candidacy? Are you a candidate? Why do people feel you will take votes away from George Wallace? Having answered these questions a hundred times before, the actor does not pause to consider his responses. He picks up each cue promptly, neatly, increasing the general frustration. Only once does the answer-machine jam. "Do you *want* to be President?" The room goes silent. The smile suddenly looks to have been drawn in clay, fit for baking in a Laguna kiln. Then the candidate finds the right button. He pushes it. We are told what an honor it is for any citizen to be considered for the highest office on earth. . . . We stop listening; he stops listening to himself.

"Governor, even though you're not a candidate, you must know that there is a good deal of support for you. . . ." The questioner's irony is suitably heavy. Reagan's lips purse—according to one biographer this is a sign he is displeased; there was a good deal of lip-pursing during the conference not to mention the days to come. "Well," he speaks through pursed lips, "I'd have to be unconscious not to know what was going on but. . . ." As he continues the performance, his speech interlarded with "my lands" (for some reason Right Wingers invariably talk like Little Orphan Annie), I recalled my last glimpse of him, at the Cow Palace in San Francisco four years ago. The Reagans were seated in a box, listening to Eisenhower. While Mrs. Reagan darted angry looks about the hall (displeased at the press?), the star of Death Valley Days was staring intently at the speaker on the platform. Thus an actor prepares, I thought, and I suspected even then that Reagan would some day find himself up there on the platform: as the age of television progresses, the Reagans will be the rule, not the exception. "Thank you, Governor," said a journalist, and everyone withdrew, leaving Ronald Reagan with his six secret servicemen—one black, a ratio considerably better than that of the convention itself where only two percent could claim Africa as motherland.

Seventy-second Street beach is a gathering place for hustlers of all sexes. With some bewilderment, they watch one of their masters, the Chase Manhattan Bank made flesh—sweating

flesh—display his wounds to the sandy and the dull, a Coriolanus but in reverse, one besotted with the vulgar. In shirt-
sleeves but firmly knotted tie, Nelson Aldrich Rockefeller
stands on a platform crowded with officials and aides (most
seriously crowded by the Governor of Florida, Claude Kirk,
who wears a bright orange sports jacket and a constant smile
for his people, who regard him, the few who know who he is,
with bright loathing). Ordinarily Rockefeller's face is veal-
white, as though no blood courses beneath that thick skin. But
now, responding to the lowering day, he has turned a delicate
conch pink. What is he saying? "Well, let's face it, there's been
some disagreement among the pollsters." The upper class
tough boy accent (most beautifully achieved by Montgomery
Clift in *The Heiress*) proves effective even down here where
consonants are disdained and vowels long. Laughter from the
audience in clothes, bewildered looks from the hustlers in
their bathing suits. "Like, man, who *is* it?"

"But now Harris and Gallup have agreed that I can beat. . . ."
Rockefeller quotes at length from those polls which are the
oracles of our day, no, the very gods who speak to us of things
to come. Over and over again, he says, "Let's face it," a phrase
popular twenty years ago, particularly among girls inclined to
alcoholism ("the Governor drinks an occasional Dubonnet on
the rocks before dinner," where did I read that?). Beside him
stands his handsome wife, holding a large straw hat and looking as if she would like to be somewhere else, no loving Nancy
Reagan or loyal Pat Nixon she. The convention is full of talk
that there has been trouble between them. Apparently. . . .
One of the pleasures of American political life is that, finally,
only personalities matter. Is he a nice man? Is she happy with
him? What else should concern a sovereign people?

Rockefeller puts down the polls, takes off his glasses, and
starts to attack the Administration. "Look at what they're
doing," he says with a fine vehemence. "They're *exhilarating*
the war!" But although Rockefeller now sounds like a peace
candidate, reprising Bobby Kennedy and Eugene McCarthy,
he has always been devoted to the war in Vietnam and to the

principle underlying it: American military intervention wherever "freedom is endangered." Consequently—and consistently—he has never found any defense budget adequate. Two years ago at a dinner in New York, he was more hawk than Johnson as he told us how the Viet Cong were coldbloodedly "shooting little mayors" (the phrase conjured up dead ponies); mournfully, he shook his head, "Why can't they learn to fight fair?" Nevertheless, compared to Nixon and Reagan, Rockefeller is positively Lincolnesque. All of us on 72nd Street Beach liked him, except perhaps the hustlers wanting to score, and we wished him well, knowing that he had absolutely no chance of being nominated.

By adding the third character to tragedy, Sophocles changed the nature of drama. By exalting the chorus and diminishing the actors, television has changed entirely the nature of our continuing history. Watching things as they happen, the viewer is a part of events in a way new to man. And never is he so much a part of the whole as when things do not happen, for, as Andy Warhol so wisely observed, people will always prefer to look at something rather than nothing; between plain wall and flickering commercial, the eyes will have the second. As hearth and fire were once center to the home or lair so now the television set is the center of modern man's being, all points of the room converge upon its presence and the eye watches even as the mind dozes, much as our ancestors narcotized themselves with fire.

At Miami Beach television was everywhere: in the air, on the streets, in hotel lobbies, on the convention floor. "From gavel to gavel" the networks spared us nothing in the way of empty speeches and mindless interviews, but dull and uninformative as the events themselves were, something rather than nothing was being shown and the eye was diverted while the objects photographed (delegates et al.) reveled in the exposure even though it might be no more than a random shot of a nose being picked or a crotch rearranged. No matter: for that instant the one observed existed for all his countrymen. As a

311

result the delegates were docile beyond belief, stepping this way and that as required by men with wired helmets and handmikes which, like magic wands, could confer for an instant total recognition.

The fact that television personalities so notoriously took precedence over the politicians at Miami Beach was noted with sour wonder by journalists who have begun to fear that their rendering of events into lines of linear type may prove to be as irrelevant an exercise as turning contemporary literature into Greek. The fact that in a hotel lobby it was Eric Sevareid not John Tower who collected a crowd was thought to be a sign of the essential light-mindedness of the electorate. Yet Sevareid belongs to the country in a way few politicians ever do. Only Ronald Reagan among the politicians at Miami exerted the same spell, and for the same reason: he is a bona fide star of the Late Show, equally ubiquitous, equally mythic.

Miami Beach is a rich sandbar with a drawbridge, and in no sense part of the main. The televised convention made it even more remote than it is. So locked were we all in what we were doing that Miami's black riots on Wednesday went almost unnoticed. There are those who thought that the Republicans deliberately played down the riots, but that is too Machiavellian. The fact is no one was interested. For those involved in creating that formidable work of television art, the 29th Republican convention, there was only one important task, creating suspense where none was. Everyone pretended that Reagan and Rockefeller could stop Nixon on the first ballot and so persuasive is the medium that by continually acting as if there might be a surprise, all involved came to believe that there would be one.

Even Nixon who should have known better fell victim to the collective delusion. On Tuesday he made his deal with Thurmond: no candidate for Vice-President displeasing to the South. Yet there was never, we now know, any danger of the Southern delegations switching to Reagan, despite the actor's enormous appeal to them. After all, how could they not love a man who had campaigned for a segregationist Southern politician (Charlton Lyons of Louisiana), who had denounced the income tax as "Marxist," and federal aid to education as "a tool of tyranny," and welfare as an "encouragement to divorce and immorality," and who generally sounded as if he wouldn't mind nuking North Vietnam and maybe China, too? He was their man but Nixon was their leader.

By the time the balloting began on Wednesday night, it was all over. There were of course idle pleasures. Everett Dirksen prowling from camera to camera, playing the part of a Senator with outrageous pleasure. Strom Thurmond, High Constable of the South, staring coldly at the delegates with stone catfish face. John Lindsay of New York, slyly separating his elegant persona from any words that he might be called upon to say. The public liked Lindsay but the delegates did not. They regarded him with the same distaste that they regard the city of which he is mayor, that hellhole of niggers and kikes and commies, of dope and vice and smut. . . . So they talk among themselves, until an outsider approaches; then they shift gears swiftly and speak gravely of law and order and how this is a republic not a democracy.

A lady from Vermont read the roll of the States as though each state had somehow grievously offended her. Alabama was plainly a thorn to be plucked, while Alaska was a blot upon the Union. She did achieve a moment of ribald good humor when she asked one state chairman *which* Rockefeller his state was voting for. But long before the Yankee virago had got to Wisconsin it was plain that Nixon was indeed "the one" as the signs had proclaimed, and immediately the Medium began to look in on the hotel suites, to confront the losers, hoping for tears, and reveal the winner, hoping for . . . well, *what* do you hope for with Nixon?

The technician. Once nominated Nixon gravely explained how he had pulled it off. He talked about the logistics of campaigning. He took us backstage. It was a nice background briefing, but nothing more. No plans for the ghettos, no policy for Asia, just political maneuvering. He did assure us that he would select "a candidate for Vice President who does not divide this country." Apparently he would have a free hand because "I won the nomination without paying any price or making any deals." The next day of course he revealed the nature of his deal with the Southerners and the price he must now pay for their support: Spiro Agnew of Maryland. Despite the howls of the party liberals and the total defection of the blacks, Nixon had probably done the wise thing.

Thursday was the big day. Agnew was proposed, opposed, nominated. A lumbering man who looks like a cross between Lyndon Johnson and Juan Perón, his acceptance speech was thin and ungrammatical; not surprisingly, he favored law and order. Adequate on civil rights when he became governor, Agnew behaved boorishly to the black establishment of Baltimore in the wake of riots last spring. This made him acceptable to Thurmond. Even so, all but the most benighted conservatives are somewhat concerned by Agnew's lack of experience. Should Nixon be elected and die, a man with only one year's experience as governor of a backward border state would become Emperor of the West. Though firm with niggers, how would he be on other issues? No one knows, including the candidate himself whose great virtue, in his own eyes, "is that I try to be credible—I want to be believed. That's one of the most priceless assets." So it is. So it is.

Nixon is now on stage, ready to accept for a second time his party's nomination. He is leaner than in the past. In a thickly made-up face, the smile is not unappealing, upper lip slightly hooked over teeth in the Kennedy manner. With his jawline collapsing in a comforting way, the middle-aged Nixon resembles the average voter who, we are told, is a gray-colored forty-seven-year-old. The candidate swings neatly to left, hands raised, two forefingers of each hand making the victory salute. Arms drop. Slide step to right. Arms again extended above head as hands make salute. Then back to center stage and the lectern. The television camera zooms in on the speech:

one can see lines crossed out, words added; the type is large, the speech mercifully short.

Nixon begins. The voice is deep and slightly toneless, without regional accent, like a radio announcer's. We have been told that he wrote his own script. It is possible. Certainly every line was redolent of the man's strange uncharm. He spoke of Eisenhower ("one of the greatest Americans of our time—or of any time") who was watching them from his hospital bed. "His heart is with us!" the candidate exclaimed, reminding us inadvertently that that poor organ was hardly the General's strongest contribution to the moral crusade the times require. No matter, "let's win this one for Ike!" (A rousing echo of *Knute Rockne*, a film in which the youthful Ronald Reagan had been most affecting.) Nixon next paid careful tribute to his Republican competitors, to the platform and, finally, to Spiro Agnew "a statesman of the first rank who will be a great campaigner." He then drew a dark picture of today's America, ending with "did we come all this way for this?" Despite the many hours of literary labor, Nixon's style was seldom felicitous; he was particularly afflicted by "thisness": "This I say is the real voice of America. And in this year 1968 this is. . . ." The real voice of America, needless to say, is Republican; "the forgotten Americans—the nonshouters, the nondemonstrators"; in short, the nonprotesting white Protestants, who must, he enjoined, commit themselves to the truth, "to see it like it is, and to tell it like it is," argot just slightly wrong for now but to Nixon "tell it like it is" must sound positively raunchy, the sort of thing had he been classy Jack Kennedy he might have heard at Vegas, sitting around with the Clan and their back-scratchers.

Solemnly Nixon addressed himself to Vietnam. His administration would "bring to an honorable end the war." How? Well, "after an era of confrontation, the time has come for an era of negotiation." But in case that sounded like dangerous accommodation he quickly reminded us that since the American flag is spit on almost daily around the world, it is now "time we started to act like a great nation." But he did not tell us *how* a great nation should act. Last January, he said that the war will end only when the Communists are convinced that the U.S. "will use its immense power and is not going to back down." In March he said, "There is no alternative to the continuation of the war in Vietnam." It is of course never easy to determine what if anything Nixon means. When it was revealed that his recent support of public housing was not sincere but simply expedient (his secret remarks to a Southern caucus had been taped), no one was surprised. "He just had to say that," murmur his supporters whenever he contradicts himself, and they admire him for it. After all, his form of hypocrisy is deeply American: if you can't be good, be careful. Significantly, he was most loudly applauded when he struck this year's favorite Republican note: *Remember the Pueblo.* "The United States has fallen so low that a fourth rate military power like North Korea [can] hijack a United States naval vessel. . . ." Quite forgotten were his conciliatory words of last spring: "If the captured American Intelligence spy ship violated North Korean waters, the United States has no choice but to admit it."

Nixon next praised the courts but then allowed that some of them have gone "too far in weakening the peace forces as against the criminal forces." Attacks on the judiciary are surefire with Republicans. Witness the old Nixon five years after the Supreme Court's 1954 decision on the integration of schools: "the Administration's position has not been, is not now, and should not be immediate total integration." Like Barry Goldwater he tends to the radical belief that the Supreme Court's decisions "are not, necessarily, the law of the land." Happily, once the present Attorney General is replaced, it will be possible to "open a new front against the filth peddlers and the narcotics peddlers who are corrupting the lives of our children." As for the forty million poor, they can take heart from the example of past generations of Americans who were aided not by government "but because of what people did for themselves." Those small inequities that now exist in the American system can be easily taken care of by "the greatest engine of progress ever developed in the history of man—American private enterprise." The poor man who wants "a piece of the action" (Vegas again) is very apt to get it if the streets are orderly and enough tax cuts are given big business.

If Nixon's reputation as the litmus-paper man of American politics is deserved, his turning mauve instead of pink makes it plain that the affluent majority intend to do nothing at all in regard to the black and the poor and the aged, except repress with force their demonstrations, subscribing finally not so much to the bland hortatory generalities of the platform and the acceptance speech but to the past statements of the real Nixon who has said (1) "If the conviction rate was doubled in this country, it would do more to eliminate crime in the future than a quadrupling of the funds for any governmental war on poverty." (2) "I am opposed to pensions in any form, as it makes loafing more attractive to [sic] working." (3) To tie health care to social security "would set up a great state program which would inevitably head in the direction of herding the ill and elderly into institutions whether they desire this or not." Echo of those Republicans in 1935 who declared that once Social Security was law "you won't have a name any longer, only a number." Most ominous of all, the candidate of the military-industrial complex has no wish to decrease the military budget. Quite the contrary. As recently as last June he was warning us that "the United States has steadily fallen behind the Soviet Union in the levelling of its spending on research and development of advance systems to safeguard the nation." In short, there is no new Nixon, only the old Nixon experimenting with new campaigning techniques in response, as the Stalinists used to say, to new necessities. Nixon concluded his speech on a note of self-love. Most viewers thought it inappropriate: since no one loves him, why should he? To his credit, he sounded slightly embarrassed as he spoke of the boy from Whittier—a mis-fire but worth a try.

Friday. On the plane to New York. John Lindsay remarks, "Awful as it was, he made a vote-getting speech." He is probably right. Nixon has said in the past that no Republican can

COLLECTED ESSAYS 1952–1972

hope to get the black vote, so why try for it? Particularly when the principal danger to Nixon's candidacy is George Wallace, in the North as well as the South. Nixon is also perfectly aware of a little-known statistic: the entire black vote plus the entire vote of whites under twenty-five is slightly less than one-fourth of the total electorate. Since Nixon has no chance of attracting either category, he has, by selecting Agnew, served notice that he is the candidate of that average forty-seven-year-old voter who tends to dislike and fear the young and the black and the liberal; in fact, the more open Nixon is in his disdain of this one-fourth of a nation, the more pleasing he will seem to the remaining three-fourths who want a change, any change, from Johnson-Humphrey as well as some assurance that the dissident forces at work in American life will be contained. The great technician has worked out a winning combination and, barring the (obligatory?) unexpected, it is quite likely that it will pay off and Richard Milhous Nixon will become the 37th President of the United States.

The New York Review of Books, September 12, 1968

MANIFESTO AND
DIALOGUE

Ten percent of the human beings ever born are now alive and breeding like bacteria under optimum conditions. As a result, millions live at famine level. Yet even with the fullest exploitation of the planet's arable land—and a fair system of distribution—it will not be possible to feed the descendants of those now alive. Meanwhile, man-made waste is poisoning rivers and lakes, air and soil; the megalopolis continues to engulf the earth, as unplanned as a melanoma and ultimately as fatal to the host organism. Overcrowding in the cities is producing a collective madness in which irrational violence flourishes because man needs more space in which to *be* than the modern city allows.

But because the West's economy depends upon more and more consumers in need of more and more goods and services, nothing will be done to curb population or to restore in man's favor the ecological balance. Present political and economic institutions are at best incapable of making changes; at worst, they are prime contributors to the spoiling of the planet and the blighting of human life. It could be said that, with almost the best will in the world, we have created a hell and called it The American Way of Life.

To preserve the human race, it is now necessary to reorganize society. To this end, an Authority must be created with the power to control human population, to redistribute food, to purify air, water, soil, to re-pattern the cities. Specifically:

The Authority must have the power to limit births by law. All the usual means of exhortation will be used to convince the citizenry that it is not a good thing to create at random replicas of themselves when the present supply of human beings is already too great a burden for the earth's resources. Put bluntly: to bring into the world an unwanted human being is as antisocial an act as murder. The endlessly delicate problem of who should be allowed to have children might be entirely eliminated by the anonymous matching in laboratories of sperm and ova. If this were done, the raising of children could then be entrusted to those who show some talent for it, on the order of certain of the Israeli kibbutzim.

The Authority must have the power to exploit the food resources of the nation in order to feel not only the 10,000,000 Americans currently at famine level but to use surplus food to assist the feeding of other countries, on condition that they, too, reduce population.

The Authority must have the power to make pure air and water, even though this will mean the banishment of the combustion engine from the automobile, and the placing of many factories underground.

The Authority must have the power to begin the systematic breaking up of cities into smaller units. To avoid a re-creation of the present ghettos, living areas should be limited not only in size but, to avoid that deterioration which is due to poverty, each family entrusted with the raising of children should be given a minimum living allowance.

The Authority may *not* have the power or right to regulate the private lives of citizens.

It is a paradox of the acquisitive society in which we now live that although private morals are regulated by law, the entrepreneur is allowed considerable freedom to use—and abuse—the public in order to make money. The American pursuit of happiness might be less desperate if the situation were reversed.

Since planned (and perhaps anonymous) breeding will eliminate the family as we now know it, those not engaged in bringing up the young would then be free to form whatever alliances they want, of long or short duration, in any mutually consenting arrangement with either sex, on the principle that each man has the right to do as he likes with his own body, including kill it with alcohol, cigarettes, drugs or a bullet. By drawing a line between what is private and of concern only to the individual and what is public and of concern to all, the Authority could begin to realize something of the spirit of this nation's first charter.

Finally, the Authority may not limit free speech in any form, including criticism of itself. In fact, the Authority's affairs should be under constant surveillance by watchful committees as well as by the press, though it might be advisable to deny the employees of the Authority any sort of personal public notice since love of glory has wrecked more human societies than all of history's plagues combined. Unsung managers constantly scrutinized by the wise: that is the ideal, partially achieved in another time (and for quite a different purpose) by the Venetian Republic.

These then are the things which must now be done if the race is to continue. Needless to say, every political and economic interest will oppose the setting up of such an Authority. Worse, those elements which delight in destroying human institutions will be morbidly drawn to a movement as radical as this one. But it cannot be helped. The alternative to a planned society is no society. If we do not act now, we shall perish through sheer numbers, like laboratory rats confined to too small a cage. The human race is plainly nothing in eternity but to us, in time, it is everything and ought not to die.

Dialogue

Each of us contains a Private Self and a Public Self. When the two have not met, their host tends to be an average American, amiable, self-deluding and given to sudden attacks of melancholy whose origin he does not suspect. When the two selves openly disdain each other, the host is apt to be a strong-minded opportunist, equally at home in politics or advertising. When the selves wrangle and neither is for long dominant, the host is more a man of conscience than of action. When the two are in fierce and total conflict, the host is lunatic—or saint.

My own two selves wrangle endlessly. Hedonistic and solipsistic, my Private Self believes the making of literature is the whole self's only proper task. The Public Self, on the other hand, sees world's end plainly and wants to avoid it, sacrificing, if necessary, art and private pleasure in order to be of use. A *Manifesto* has given the two selves a good deal to quarrel about, and in their endless dialogue some of the many questions a *Manifesto* is bound to raise are posed, if not always answered.

Private Self: It is typical of you to state what needs to be done and then not tell us how it should be done—whether it *ought* to be done I'll get to in a moment.

Public Self: And typical of you to dislike any kind of general statement (not to mention political action). One must first draw attention—in the broadest way imaginable—to the nature of the crisis. If the race is not to die of overpopulation, we must. . . .

Private Self: You've made your point. But first, do you really think anyone can change our present course? And, second, why not let the thing die? I find beautiful the vision of an empty planet, made glass by atomic fission, forever circling a cooling sun. . . .

Public Self: And you accuse *me* of rhetoric! I ignore your second question. The thing must not die. As for the first: it is possible to reduce population drastically in one generation. In two generations a viable balance could be arrived at. . . .

Private Self: Could. Yes. But will it come to pass? Remember when we were in Egypt and Hassanein Heikal explained to us that even under Nasser—with all his power—the fellahin could not be persuaded to practice birth control. . . .

Public Self: When persuasion fails, other means will be used.

Private Self: Yes! Force. That Authority of yours gives me the creeps. . . .

Public Self: I don't like it much myself but without it nothing will be done. The Authority must be absolute in certain areas.

Private Self: How does this square with your lofty guarantee of private freedom to everyone?

Public Self: There is only one limit to private freedom: no new citizen can be created without permission.

Private Self: And who will grant permission?

Public Self: Geneticists, biologists, anthropologists, politicians, poets, philosophers . . . in a year one could get some kind of general agreement as to how to proceed. Later, decisions would be made as to which types should be perpetuated and which allowed to die out. . . .

Private Self: I must say, not even the Nazis. . . .

Public Self: None of that! No demagoguery. The Authority's aim is to preserve and strengthen human types through planned breeding. Eugenically, we have had enormous success with everything from cattle to hybrid corn. So why not people? A family in which the members are prone to die of cancer at an early age should probably not be allowed to continue. . . .

Private Self: That means that John Keats would not be reproduced because he had a weak chest which his descendants might inherit, along with his genius. . . .

Public Self: What strains are best worth preserving I'm willing to leave to science . . . with a good deal of overseeing from other disciplines. Anyway, since we descend from common ancestors, no seed can ever die: all men are cousins.

Private Self: Save that for television. Incidentally, it will be decades—if ever—before sperm and ova can be matched outside the human body. . . .

Public Self: One must think in terms of decades as well as of today. In any case, the early stages should be simple. A moratorium on births for a year. Then an inquiry into who would *like* to have children . . . a smaller group than you might think, particularly if the tribe no longer exalts the idea of reproducing oneself. After the last war the Japanese realized that if they were to survive they would have to reduce population. They did so by making it, literally, unfashionable to have large families; overnight they reversed the trend of centuries. It can be done.

Private Self: But only in a disciplined society like Japan. It would be impossible in our country. The United Statesman is conditioned from birth to think only of himself. To think of any larger unit is to fall victim to the international menace of communism.

Public Self: I suspect we shall probably have to write off the generations now alive. They cannot be changed. But the newborn can be instilled with a sense of urgency.

Private Self: Oh, yes. The newborn! How do you plan to bring up the children?

Public Self: At first in the usual way through the family . . . even though the family as we have known it is ending due to the pressures of urban life. Incidentally, contrary to current tribal superstition, the family is not a biological unit. It is an economic one whose deterioration began the day it became possible for women to work and bring up their children without men.

Private Self: With men or without, in the family or in a commune, someone is going to have to look after those few children that you will allow us. Who is that someone?

Public Self: Those best suited.

Private Self: Their parents?

Public Self: Probably not. Very few people are good parents, a fact most are willing to admit—too late.

Private Self: But aren't children psychologically damaged by being brought up communally. . . .

Public Self: Not necessarily. The recent confrontation between a number of American psychiatrists and the products of an Israeli kibbutz was revelatory. The men and women who had been raised communally were alarmingly "healthy."

Private Self: I daresay the end of the family will benefit humanity, but it will destroy the novel. . . .

Public Self: Don't worry. Mythmaking is endemic to our race. Neurosis will simply take new forms.

Private Self: To get back to the Authority. Just who and what is it? And in the United States is it to be achieved through constitutional means?

Public Self: Ideally, the Authority and the Constitutional establishment should exist side by side, each complementing the other. Shabby as our democracy is, I think it a good idea to retain it.

Private Self: But the world is not ideal. President and Congress will not suffer the existence of an Authority over which they have no control.

Public Self: What about the C.I.A., the F.B.I. . . .

Private Self: Flip liberal cant. Congress and President would want control. And once they had it, nothing would be accomplished. Can you imagine those Senators who are in the pay of the oilmen allowing the combustion engine to be superseded?

Public Self: Ultimate power must reside in the Authority.

Private Self: Dictatorship?

Public Self: Yes. But involving only those things that affect the public at large: environment, food, population. . . .

Private Self: Do you really think it possible to order totally the economic and biological life of a country and yet not interfere in the private lives of its citizens?

Public Self: Why not?

Private Self: Because no dictatorship has ever confined itself to the public sector. Sooner or later the dictator. . . .

Public Self: The Authority is not a dictator but a changing

group of men, representing the widest and most divergent interests. . . .

Private Self: Too wide and too divergent and it won't function. . . .

Public Self: All interests will be subordinate to the stated aims of the Authority. Those aims will not be open to dispute.

Private Self: Like "Marxism" in one-party states? I would think that whoever or whatever controls the public life of a society will automatically control the private sector.

Public Self: Obviously there will be a constant tension between public and private necessities. And it is possible that the private will lose. It usually does in authoritarian societies. But then it does not do very well in libertarian ones either. Witness the small-town American's terror of his neighbors' opinion. However, the one novelty I offer is a clear demarcation between public and private. The state may not intrude upon private lives as it does now. And private greed may not intrude upon the public welfare as it does now. And what is "good" and "bad" for the society's welfare will be set down with a minimum of ambiguity.

Private Self: I find your Authority a potential nightmare. The world is already shrinking. Soon there will be no escape from the managers with their Telexes and computers. No border to cross. No place to hide.

Public Self: I am as alarmed as you by a world in which it is altogether too easy for the managers to have their way. And not only through instant communications but through mind-altering drugs and genetic rearrangements of the unborn. . . .

Private Self: Genetic rearrangement! That ought to appeal to you: men bred to be gods, but *whose* gods?

Public Self: Something to brood on. Anyway, I do see the end of the *laissez-faire* society. Quasi-democracies like England and the United States are already moving toward totalitarianism—of Left or Right makes no difference. The result is the same: the control of the individual. Wanting to bolster currency, the British curtail travel and thus limit freedom. Our poor, needless to say, are quite as enslaved as they were when their ancestors built the Pyramids. In fact, they are worse off because technical means now exist for the state to control all its citizens simultaneously. The true nightmare is not the Authority. It is the popular television performer who will subvert the state simply for something to do. . . .

Private Self: That's you. Don't deny it!

Public Self: I confess that if it weren't for you, I might give it a try.

Private Self: I'll bet you would! And we'd both be shot down, probably on *The Tonight Show*.

Public Self: Since an authoritarian society is inevitable, I am for accepting it but only in order to achieve certain goals. Once they are achieved. . . .

Private Self: The Authority will wither away?

Public Self: Something else will take its place. But that is far in the future.

Private Self: Exactly how is the Authority to come into existence?

Public Self: A Party for Human Survival must be formed in the United States, and elsewhere. Naturally—again ideally—it would be best if the Authority were voted into power by a majority. With proper education, through television, it could happen. . . .

Private Self: But if not?

Public Self: Then the Party will seize power and establish the Authority by force.

Private Self: You see yourself as Lenin?

Public Self: With you on my back, I am a natural victim. Anyway, if it does not happen, a *mindless* authority will come into being, one dedicated not to human survival but simply to its own aggrandizement, and we shall perish.

Private Self: What is wrong with that? It is not written in stars that we endure for all eternity. So why not let it end? The way it does for each of us. I have known from birth that when

I die the world ends, too.

Public Self: For us it ends. But there are others.*

Esquire, October 1968

*This sort of dialogue can now be heard in every quarter. Five years ago to discuss these matters was thought eccentric. Progress?

LITERARY GANGSTERS

On a rare visit to the theater in the early sixties (visits have been equally rare in other decades), I opened *Playbill*, a throwaway magazine given me by an usher, and saw my own name; then "Golden Age of Television"; then "Chayefsky." I was startled. A half-dozen years had passed since live television drama ended. Why bring up the subject now? And in *Playbill*? I read on. The tone of the piece was shrill, and the substance altogether too familiar. Apparently the television playwrights had not—oh, God, it's that piece again!—been *good*. The writer did not offer much evidence one way or the other, but then did anyone ever see the three thousand or so plays that were done in those years? Better to dismiss the whole lot as *kitsch*, and refer to me, in particular, as "a culture hero of the 50's." Moss creeping up once-heroic limbs, I looked to see who cared so little for television's twenty-one-inch dramatic Renaissance. Richard Gilman. The name—if not the style—was new to me.

Recently, I spent an evening with several other culture heroes, current and past (wherever we meet, there is the Pantheon), and we got onto the subject of literary gangsters. Since the invention of printing, there has been a need for people to write more or less to order for the press. Some of these professionals have been good, some have been bad, and a sizable minority have been gangsters: hit-and-run journalists, without conscience, forced to live precariously by their wits, and those wits are increasingly strained nowadays because there are fewer places to publish in than there used to be, which means a lot more edgy hoods hanging about the playgrounds of the West Side.

The literary gangster's initial problem is a poignant one: how to be noticed? How to occupy a turf of one's own? Having been for a quarter-century an observer of the scene, with a particular interest in literary crime—to use that well-loved *New York Times Book Review* phrase—I would suggest, right off, that the apprentice criminal write the following on the lid of his typewriter: Today's reader is not interested in analysis but opinion, preferably harsh and unexpected. Some years ago a classic caper began with the statement that although Bernard Shaw was a bad playwright, a few pages of his music criticism were not without value. This caused interest. It was also a splendid heist because no attempt was made to prove a case. An opinion was stated loudly, and contrary evidence was ignored. The young apprentice should also feel free to invent sources and quotations, on the ground that readers of even the most high-minded journals know very little about anything, particularly the past. Needless to say, the more violent and *ad hominem* the style, the more grateful his readers will be. Americans like to be told whom to hate. Finally, the gangster can never go wrong if, while appearing to uphold the highest standards (but never define those standards or say just when it was that the theater, for instance, was "relevant"), he attacks indiscriminately the artists of the day, the popular on the ground that to give pleasure to the many is a sign of corruption and the much-admired on the ground that since all values now

330

held by the society are false (for obvious reasons don't present alternative values), any culture hero must reflect perfectly the folly of those who worship him. It is not wise to praise anyone living; unhappily, every now and then, it may be necessary to *appear* to like something done by a contemporary, in which case select a foreign writer like Borges; he is old, admired abroad, and his works are short enough actually to read. In a few years, he can always be dismissed as a culture hero of the "Silly Sixties." Remember that turnover is now as rapid in literary reputations as it is in women's dresses. So keep moving, and if occasionally you contradict yourself, no one will notice, since no one is keeping score.

Was it ever thus? Yes, since antiquity or at least since newspapers. On February 20, 1767, Voltaire wrote a friend, "The infamous trade of vilifying one's colleagues to earn a little money should be left to cheap journalists. . . . It is those wretches who have made of literature an arena for gladiators."

Gladiators, cheap journalists, gangsters, they are always with us. To the heroes of the forties, John W. Aldridge, Jr., was the first gangster to appear on the scene, and a source of wonder to us all. In 1947 he set himself up as—we thought— a legitimate literary businessman, opening shop with a piece describing the writers of the postwar generation in which he warmly praised John Horne Burns and myself. The praise made us think he was not a hood, his shop a legitimate business not a front. Little did we suspect that Mr. Aldridge was a master literary criminal who wanted to contribute not simply a modest footnote to each of our sagas but a terrible full chapter. To achieve this, he even moved to Connecticut in order to be close to certain of his victims. For several years he covered them with unctuous praise in print as well as in private. Meanwhile, he was thoroughly casing the territory. Then he struck. In a blaze of publicity, Mr. Aldridge bit one by one those very asses he had with such cunning kissed, earning himself an editorial in *Life* magazine congratulating him for having shown up the decadence and immorality of the postwar writers. He has long since faded from the literary scene . . . as have, fortunately, those scars on which we sit.

Other gangsters today? John Simon was lovingly noted. A Yugoslav with a proud if somewhat incoherent Serbian style (or is it Croatian?—in any case, English is his third language),* Mr. Simon has for twenty years slashed his way through literature, theater, cinema. Clanking chains and snapping whips, giggling and hissing, he has ricocheted from one journal to another, and though no place holds him for long, the flow of venom has proved inexhaustible. There is nothing he cannot find to hate. Yet in his way, Mr. Simon is pure; a compulsive rogue criminal, more sadistic Gilles de Rais than neighborhood thug.

Robert Brustein, on the other hand, is not pure; he has ambitions about his station. Mr. Simon knows that he is only an Illyrian gangster and is blessedly free of side; he simply wants to torture and kill in order to be as good an American as Mr. Charles Manson, say, or Lyndon Johnson. But Mr. Brustein wants to matter, to go straight. A failed theater person, he had/has ambitions not only as director but as an actor. The actor side of him explains why one always felt he was playing, in a somewhat hollow way, the part of a stern highbrow critic, and having the field pretty much to himself because true highbrow critics don't deal with theater. His specialty was lamentation, a sort of Broadway Old Testament prophet, wailing for a Jerusalem that never was. Mr. Brustein's ambition has now translated him from literary gangster to academic bureaucrat at Yale but I'm sure he'll be back one of these days. Recidivism is a hundred percent in such cases.

My fellow heroes then mentioned Richard Gilman. A notorious hood, they assured me. But except for my brief glimpse of him in the pages of *Playbill* (like Cosa Nostra, they will infiltrate anything), he was just another face, as it were, on the post-office wall. Now I have read him.

It is difficult to know what to say about *The Confusion of*

---

*Mr. Simon has since instructed us that English is his fifth language.

Realms. Mr. Gilman has collected a number of pieces dealing with the novel and the theater, and he presents them to us for . . . what? Our illumination? Admiration? I have read each piece carefully (something no self-respecting gangster would do) and I took many notes. In some ways I found him worse than I expected—gangsters seldom write so dully; he sounds at times as if he were addressing a not-very-bright class in remedial reading. In other ways, he is better than anticipated: he is not above betraying enthusiasm for a living American writer. Yet at the end of 272 pages I could not make out what he was up to—or, more precisely, just what audience he had in mind. His work is too simple for those who know literature and much too long-winded for those who do not but are sufficiently interested to want to know more.

Mr. Gilman's examination of Norman Mailer (last year's obligatory piece) is typical. He writes thousands of words about Mailer; yet says nothing that the Master has not said better about himself (admittedly it is not easy to deal with Mailer since that sly operative is always there first with the most words), concluding with the emotional argument that although Mailer's novels are not much good, it doesn't really matter because he's *ours*. To which the rude answer is he may be yours, but he's certainly not mine. Mr. Gilman goes even farther off the rails when he finds Mailer's passion for being in history (not to mention the press) harmful to him as an artist. I would say it was the making of him. The idea of the artist as priest is much loved in gangsterland. They believe that worldly commitment is corrupting. Yet what about Goethe, Voltaire, Byron or, to come up to date, Günter Grass (admired by John Simon . . . oh, the dread kiss of the Mafioso!)? But bookchat writers have never been able to understand that there is no correct deportment for the good artist. Some are exhibitionists, some are shy; some are political, some are apolitical. What matters is not a writer's personality or politics or private behavior but his books. This should be obvious, but in an age of slick journalism and swift reputation, it is quite forgotten. More to the point, books are no longer much read, while pieces about writers are. Personality is all that matters —as Mailer has neatly grasped—and the chorus does not yet comprehend.

Mr. Gilman's prose style is . . . well, let him speak for himself: "American critics have rarely possessed any substantial philosophical power or interest (Edmund Wilson accomplished important things without having had any such power or interest at all, but would have been more important, I think, if he had had some) and have shied away from metaphysical areas as from a contagion." This is as bad a sentence as I have ever read and though, admittedly, Mr. Gilman is writing about Miss Susan Sontag, whose style is often not much better, some editor ought to have come to his aid.

Stylistically he—but who cares about language? With each generation American prose grows worse, reflecting confused thinking, poor education, and the incomplete assimilation of immigrant English into the old language (see Henry James's remarks on the subject at Bryn Mawr, 1904). Nevertheless, even in a bad time, a writer's prose does give some idea of the way his mind works. From his prose, I should say that Mr. Gilman's mind is slow and uncertain, more at home with moral exhortation than with analysis. The uncertainty is betrayed by the use of adjectives. He likes them in threes, and even fours, resembling in this many popular lady writers (and at least one good one, Nathalie Sarraute): ". . . documents of the white normative Western consciousness and spirit, which blacks in America today have begun to repudiate in ways that are as yet clumsy, painful and confused." Then, on the same page: " . . . hard, local, intransigent, alien [*The Autobiography of Malcolm X*] remains in some sense unassimilable for those of us who aren't black." He is also unnaturally fond of the word "increment," which he occasionally misuses—or at least I think he does: it is often hard to guess his meaning.

For the most part, Mr. Gilman's subjects are as fashionable as his opinions. He believes that black writing cannot be judged by white standards. Good politics but an intellectual cop-out. This is followed by the usual piece on McLuhan, a solemn meditation on Susan Sontag's theory of the new, which we shall get to in a moment, hesitant praise for William Gass and Donald Barthelme, attacks on Rechy's *City of Night* (why bother?) and Updike, whose mastery of English prose makes Mr. Gilman, predictably, uneasy; and then a good deal about the theater, most of it dated ("the extraordinary public awareness of *Macbird!* as a solid fact, a potent presence"). Excepting Barthelme and Gass, the subjects are familiar, the judgments unsurprising, the uneasy self-importance irritating ("I myself, a 'judge' who passes on writing"—the quotes around the word "judge" are the giveaway). But though Mr. Gilman's theories of art are resolutely secondhand, they are still worth examining for what they have to tell us about—how would he put it?—our life today.

Mr. Gilman has his idols—somewhat. He thinks Miss Sontag "one of the most interesting and valuable critics we possess, a writer from whom it's continually possible to learn, even when you're most dissatisfied with what she's saying, or perhaps especially at those times." Mr. Gilman relies heavily on the "or perhapses" that let him off those critical hooks he has a tendency to get himself hung on as his slow, bumbling sentences unfold like bolts of wet wool. Here are two hooks in one sentence: "We might call her a critic of ideas, except that she has always wished to treat ideas sensuously, aesthetically; or decide that she is a philosopher of cultural forms, except that philosophy for her has always been a drama rather than a method." Reading this, one realizes that Mr. Gilman is a serious literary critic even though he does not actually write criticism; a profound thinker were his mind not shallow.

Throughout *The Confusion of Realms*, Mr. Gilman reminds us that the writers he admires (Gass and Barthelme) are making new things, and the ones he cannot endorse, like Mailer, are simply repeating old forms. But again let us listen to his very own voice: "*The Naked and the Dead* remains at bottom a conventional work of literature. As it shapes itself into a tale, it proceeds along predictable lines, creates no convincingly new style, and offers no new purchase on imaginative reality, noth-

335

ing that can be used by other writers as a model of a way of seeing, or as incontrovertible vision by anyone else." Let us pause (Gilman's "we-ness" is contagious) and try to figure out what he is saying. First, *The Naked and the Dead* is a conventional novel, predictable, no new style, etc. Placed beside Joyce's *Finnegans Wake*, yes, it is an ordinary sort of book, and though one could excuse some of its ordinariness on the ground that most first novels are derivative, let's allow Mr. Gilman the point. Next he tells us that Mailer's novel offers "nothing that can be used by other writers . . . " This is a startling approach to literature. Apparently books are valuable only to the extent that they will help other writers to make newer and newer books to be added as links to some sort of Hegelian chain. Could it be, terrible thought, that Mr. Gilman believes in Progress? If I did not know the reading habits of gangsterdom better, I'd suspect him of having read Comte.

Repeatedly, Mr. Gilman rejects what he thinks of as old forms of theater and the novel on the ground "that the distinction between form and content in art was never valid and that we have not simply come into a new use for content as form but into a condition in which seeming content, 'subject matter,' no longer is needed to serve as pretext and instigation for aesthetic action." "Fiction . . . can no longer be (if ever it wholly was) the expression or [sic?] interruption or simulacrum of life and its values . . ." And finally, ". . . fiction ought not to be an employment of language for ends beyond itself, but language in its own right, mysteriously saturated with reality, perpetually establishing a new synthesis of reality and the imagination, and doing this partly by driving out all language which has accomplished an earlier synthesis." As those interested in theories of the novel will recognize, Mr. Gilman has been reading Robbe-Grillet, or at least he has learned about him through Miss Sontag's high Hollywood or Hollywood High prose. They are great drivers-out of language. But to what end? Everyone agrees that three-act plays imitating real people in a real room are as tedious as realistic novels that deal with quotidian affairs. There is no point in reading a novel which could have been written by Galsworthy or—to be just—a novel which might have been written by Joyce. Nevertheless, as Mr. Gilman himself points out—positively insists—writers do use one another. Literature cannot be born "new" the instant a writer, even a master, starts to write. Writing is a more complicated matter than that and no critic—much less gangster—has yet cracked the code.

Traditionally, what a critic admires defines him, and makes him a critic rather than a gangster. To Mr. Gilman's credit, he does his best to appreciate certain new-seeming writers. Unfortunately, in controlling the Mafioso side to himself he often sounds like an old hood who now serves, somewhat uncomprehendingly, on the board of a bank whose safe he would rather be cracking. Mr. Gilman likes William Gass, and he writes interestingly about Mr. Gass's novel *Omensetter's Luck*—at least his remarks are interesting to one who has not read the novel. He even communicates enthusiasm, up to a point; then the banker feels compelled to give his report to the board. "The novel *is* Gass's prose, his style, which is not committed to something beyond itself" (a paraphrase of Robbe-Grillet, by the way), "not an instrument of the idea . . . he fashions his tale of the mind, which is the tale of his writing a novel." But then, realizing the extent of his endorsement, Mr. Gilman begins to take it back. He confesses to finding the novel faulty because of "its partial organization along narrative lines, its compulsion to tell a 'story' " (those quotes again: doesn't he know what a story is?) "while its whole internal action struggles against the reductions and untruthfulness of story-telling, while its verbal action is struggling to *be* the story." (Note the assumption that storytelling is false, but putting down words —at random?—is the novel's proper "struggle.") "For narrative, which Bernard Shaw long ago called 'the curse of all serious literature' and which every major novelist since Flaubert has either abandoned or used ironically, is precisely that element of fiction which coerces it and degrades it into being a mere alternative to life, *like* life . . ."

None of this is true. Every major novelist since Flaubert has been as much involved with narrative as those who went before; not to mention Flaubert himself as he meticulously maneuvered his Emmas and Homaises logically from place to place. Specialists even assure us that there is a preordained structure to *Finnegans Wake*. As for Lawrence, Conrad, Hardy, Mann, Musil, Proust, none eschewed or treated with irony narrative. One has only to study those extraordinary scenarios Henry James wrote for each of his works to realize just how important narrative is to a master novelist.

Now, if Mr. Gilman were simply to say that we ought not to read bad novels with familiar plots, who would disagree with him? But wanting to be resonant, and radical, and full of certain French critics (at second-hand, I suspect; curiously enough, he seems not to have read Barthes, nor grasped semiology), he writes such inflated nonsense as "What Gass has written is a work of the imagination and the mind whose study is the mind and imagination themselves as they grant us the instruments of knowing, which are at the same time the sources of all our inability to know." It makes one long for the good old days of Bonnie and Clyde, of Simon and Brustein.

"We are bored," Mr. Gilman suddenly announces, "by most plays today . . . bored by Shakespeare, too, and Molière and Greek tragedy (young people have never been so bored by classics), by Shaw and Pirandello and Brecht. Even by Ionesco and Genet." He is probably right (and writers and teachers like Mr. Gilman have certainly helped make art dull for the many) but he never questions the why of this boredom. Instead he gives us his neo-Robbe-Grillet analysis: "As long as we regard [theater] as illusion instead of a form of reality, we will go on being bored with it as we are bored, ultimately, with all illusions." This is fatuous. People live by illusions. Whether it is that college boy who rises at the end of the lecture and declares, not asks, "Don't you think Bob Dylan is the greatest living poet?" or Richard Nixon not wanting to be the first American President to lose a war or the audience of *Easy Rider*, which knows it is not on the road itself but watching actors on a screen create a naturalistic illusion of freedom that corresponds with their own daydreams, we live by illusion in life as in art. Theater is plays. Plays are simulacra of life just as print (to the astonishment of Robbe-Grillet) stands not for its own black inky self but for words which in turn stand for objects and actions. That words and phrases become corrupt with use and misuse is a perennial problem which only high excellence among writers can solve.

Reading *The Confusion of Realms* (with some continence I have refrained from making any play on the title: a gangster would have gone on and on about it), I find myself wondering who reads this sort of writing and what pleasure and revelation they get from it. Is there a public I know nothing of? Quite possibly. After all, I am often away from the United States. For all I know there are students of education who carefully read (with lips moving?) these long confusions. But I doubt it. With the exception of one piece, there is no ease, no joy, no light in Mr. Gilman's writing. Every sentence seems to have been an effort for him to make, as though he knew he had nothing to say but was impelled for career reasons to set down something. Certainly he has no talent at all for our difficult and various language—by no means a deterrent, let me quickly say, to a literary career in America. Yet it must be a terrible strain to have to keep on doing something one does not do easily or well.

As I write, I have been thinking about other careers for Mr. Gilman. English teaching? No. He would be redundant. Political commentary or action seems out; he shows no great interest in such things. Should he be an actor like Mr. Brustein? Manage a team of lady wrestlers? Work with his hands? But I have no way of knowing his true talents. So accepting him for what he would like to be, a writer, I can hold out some hope. I enjoyed his straightforward description of what happened at the Village Gate when two sets of gangsters (the anarchist hoods led by Mr. and Mrs. Beck and the old guard led by Mr. Brustein) had their showdown. Not having to worry about Culture and Meaning, Mr. Gilman has written a genuinely interesting—even witty—report of the evening (all right, he does bring in Artaud and he refers to that profoundly boring play *The Brig* as "remarkable and revivifying" but for him these are small *bêtises*). He has a surprising gift for psychological description, particularly when he records the Livers' doctrine of love (which is really hate). I particularly liked his reference to the Becks as "pushy martyrs."

Quite seriously, I would advise Mr. Gilman to leave respectable gangsterdom to Mr. Brustein. But not go back to his old ways. Leave them to Mr. Simon, who still prowls the criminal night, switch knife at the ready. Instead, I would very much like to see Mr. Gilman write popular journalism; he has a real talent for it. But I fear he will be deceived by the good reviews he has no doubt already arranged for his book, and so persist in error. But should he go straight, we heroes will gladly allow him to attend us, if not at the Pantheon, as a faithful spear-carrier at high Valhalla.

Commentary, March 1970

AN AMERICAN
PRESS LORD

Shortly after Richard Nixon was chosen to bring us together, he announced that he would write each of the many thousands of Americans listed in *Who's Who* a letter requesting guidance. Although everyone would get the same letter, Nixon did want to make one thing very clear: he himself would add a personal postscript complimenting the recipient for his particular contribution to the American imperium. On tender hooks, as the late Alfalfa Bill Murray would say, I waited for my letter. What word of praise would Nixon have for the author of *The Best Man*? The suspense was exquisite. At last the letter arrived. *Office of the President-Elect* (a nostalgic moment as I recalled 1960's joke: the President-Erect) *Richard M. Nixon, Washington, D.C.* was the heading. Under this my name and address; then nothing until the bold signature *Richard Nixon*. Thus did the wittiest administration in American history begin.

Now, a year later, it is plain to almost everyone that Nixon's sense of fun is the most remarkable thing about him, even more appealing than his ability to hear what the silent say (a typical Nixon joke, incidentally, quite lost on ponderous liberals). If he has not yet made America (love it or leave it) one great Laugh-in, the fault's not his but ours, as Max Lerner might put it. He has done his best. From the unveiling on television's prime time of Spiro Agnew (our very own Greek Colonel) to the running commentaries of Martha and John Mitchell (the Allen and Burns of the Nixon Network), he has proved a master entrepreneur as well as source of a thousand jokes, many too subtle for the solemn race history requires him to preside over.

For instance, hardly anyone suspected that something funny was up when Nixon appointed Walter Annenberg as ambassador to England. Yet any student of Nixon mischief ought to have known that he would somehow manage to apple-pie the bed of Harold Wilson's Socialist government, which had sent as ambassador to Washington (in anticipation of a Humphrey administration), one John Freeman, former *New Statesman* editor who had written unkindly of Nixon in 1960. That's just the sort of thing Dick remembers as he surveys those crises which make up his past with an eye to fixing any wagon that ever ran over him: but with sly rather than vindictive wit; with the boffo laugh, not the mean curse.

Before Annenberg was appointed, lovers of Nixon wit were making up lists of possible ambassadors. Dean Acheson? His bland dismissals of postwar England were a high qualification. Claire Boothe Luce? Always good for a wisecrack. H. L. Hunt? This was my choice. A distinguished anti-Commie, he carries his lunch about with him in a used brown paper bag. But then came the news that Walter Annenberg had been inked.

Nothing was known of Annenberg except that he published a couple of bad newspapers in Philadelphia (no great laughing matter) and his father Mo had gone to the clink in the thirties for tax evasion (an event which forced my right-wing Washington family to overcome their anti-Semitism long enough to acknowledge that, Jew or not, Mo was busted because he had the guts to stand up to the anti-Christ FDR). But one prison sentence does not a Nixon joke make. There had to be more to Annenberg than his father's ill luck. Yet a first look at him revealed nothing remarkable (that is to say risible). Very rich. Powerful in Pennsylvania politics. Gave a lot of money to Nixon's campaign (how much is a mystery). Was a friend to Dick in the dark days. All in all, a perfectly unqualified appointee on the order of the late Joe Kennedy. Could it be that Funny Dick had let us down?

Two months later when Annenberg presented his credentials to the Queen of England the world realized that Nixon had done it again. He had, very simply, launched the most brilliant clown since the late Bert Lahr. But as every impresario knows, it is not enough to book a clown into a palace; infinite care must be taken to show the comic at his best. Although Nixon is not known to have initiated the BBC's coverage of Annenberg's meeting with the Queen, I am sure that the CIA had a hand in it. The performances were much too outrageous for the BBC; the comedy too carefully polished.

Annenberg appears at palace and forgets to remove a funny hat; footmen force him to (early Chaplin this); then he is briefed on how to begin the long march to the throne. "We start," he is told sternly, "with our left foot." Starting with the right foot, he approaches the Queen. With that graciousness for which she is insufficiently paid, Britannic Majesty asks if he is living at the embassy. Little does she know she is playing straight to a Nixon joke. Like many Americans who inherit money and evade school, Annenberg has not an easy way with the President's, much less the Queen's, English (Nixon must have auditioned Annenberg a dozen times before he signed him up). At first startled by the difficulty of the question, Annenberg gives a great Bert Lahr *Uhhh*. Then, laboriously, he constructs the following answer (like all great acts, this one improves with each airing): "We're in the embassy residence, subject, of course, to some of the discomfiture as a result of a need for, uh, elements of refurbishing and rehabilitation."

Then a perfectly timed reaction shot of the Queen looking as if a cigar has just exploded in her face. Back in Washington Dick must have been on the floor as he watched her try to maneuver her way out of *that* one.

Untoppable as the premier seg was, Annenberg followed up almost immediately with a speech to the Pilgrims (a group of Americanophile English). In Eddie Mayhoff fashion, he attacked American students as revolutionaries, while praising his friend Ronald Reagan for magisterial restraint. The British were overwhelmed. Nixon had more than paid Wilson back for the appointment of Freeman to Washington, paid him in full with funny money.

But enough of what everyone knows. What is the real Walter Annenberg like? The face behind the successful clown's mask? Like Chaplin, Lahr, Keaton, there must be a heartache, a suppurating wound to go with that comic bow. Just as curiosity seemed never to be satisfied, Mr. Gaeton Fonzi offers us *Annenberg: A Biography of Power*, a book which Morris Ernst believes "should be read by everyone interested in the First Amendment. Very few authors have the temerity to comment on the giants of the mass media." Senior editor of *Philadelphia Magazine*, Mr. Fonzi spent two years raking Philadelphia's muck in order to set in proper context what I take to be the late William Claude Dukinfield's spiritual heir, a true Allegheny carbon in the rough. The result is a devastating account of the misuse of media for private and vindictive ends, as well as a fascinating exposé of the relationship between big money and big politics, a familiar corruption no less disturbing for being, once again, documented.

Mr. Fonzi's study is in two parts. The first is devoted to Mo, founder of the publishing dynasty; the second to Walter's expansion of the business in order to achieve that high respectability his father too had dreamed of but lost when the Feds caught up with him.

Shortly after his release from prison in 1942, Mo died, leaving Walter controlling interest in Triangle Publications, Inc., which owned Philadelphia's *Inquirer* and *Daily News*. Ownership of these two newspapers made Walter, automatically, a power in the land; in fact, they proved to be the making of the ambassador. Once made, he no longer needed them and so they were sold for $55 million, winning Mr. Fonzi's praise: "I believe Walter Annenberg's finest contribution to American journalism was revealed on October 28, 1969. That was the day it was announced he was selling the Philadelphia *Inquirer* and *Daily News* to the John S. Knight Chain."

But Annenberg still owns *TV Guide* (largest weekly circulation of any periodical in the world), *Seventeen*, a dozen radio and television stations, seven cable television companies, and the basis of old Mo's fortune, the *New York Morning Telegraph*. On his own, Walter is the largest stockholder in Penn Central Transportation Co., and an important stockholder in both the Girard Trust Bank and Campbell's Soup Co. Until his translation to what the State Department persists in calling the Court of St. James, he was an active director in these enterprises.

The section on Mo is no doubt of some interest in trying to understand Walter, a task which intrigues Mr. Fonzi as much as it bores me. The Walter Annenbergs are clear as a sheet of cellophane and we need beard no minotaurs in pursuit of hidden rosebuds. He is what he seems. So was Mo, who started the *Morning Telegraph* (a racing sheet), which naturally brought him into close contact with the underworld of gambling or, as Harold Ickes nicely said, "Mo comes from the world and from the lawless tradition commonly associated with Al Capone."

This blast was the result of Mo's attacks on Harold Ickes's master, Christendom's right arm. Originally, as publisher of the Miami *Daily News*, Mo had been a dedicated New Dealer but with the sale of the *News* and the acquisition of the *Inquirer*, he promptly became a dedicated Republican. It was quite simple: wherever he was, he wanted to get in with the gentry. Since the Philadelphia gentry were Republican, Mo became more Republican than the Pews. But in spite of gangster connections, tax evasion on a grand scale, and opportunistic politics, Mo seems to have been, even to Mr. Fonzi, an agreeable monster who—important point in a demos-praising time—mingled genially with his employees. Not so the heir.

Walter dropped out of school as soon as he could; a shy youth who stammered, he "was extremely sensitive about his withered right ear, through which he cannot hear." Nice sentence. Try another preposition; it still sounds funny. Mr. Fonzi's prose style . . . no, not a word about style. Sufficient to say, demos is well served by Mr. Fonzi.

Not taken seriously by his father, Walter idolized him (was it ever otherwise in popular biography?), felt the shame of his imprisonment more than anyone, blamed everything on Roosevelt and the liberal establishment and, not unnaturally, wanted to compensate, to rise to a high place in the national hierarchy. Mr. Fonzi's crude character analysis makes one almost sympathize with Walter. After all, he is a classic American type. At one remove from the European ghetto, the hero makes up his mind to be accepted by the Wasp establishment, which not only looks down on him, his profession, his religion, his manner, but locked up his father. So he gives money to charities (that is the way you get to meet socially important people if you have nothing to recommend you but money). Collects pictures (same motive). And gives money to politicians. Through inspired ignorance, Walter put his money on that onyx-hued horse Richard Nixon; as a result, he got a diplomatic appointment much to his liking (it has been said but not proved that Walter raised several million dollars for Nixon's campaign with the understanding that he be made ambassador to England).

Mr. Fonzi's attempts at psychology are of no great interest. What fascinates, however, is his description of Walter Annenberg's use of the press and television to dominate Philadelphia. It is a remarkably ugly story.

To everyone's surprise, Walter proved a better businessman than his father. In founding *TV Guide*, he outdid all his father's works. But business in itself was always a means to an end: acceptance by the Main Line and a place among the magnates of that empire he so deeply loves and so passionately defends.

To achieve this, he drove his associates hard. Wide-eyed, Mr. Fonzi tells us of heart attacks, breakdowns, betrayals, as though we ought to be outraged at the way Walter used men, drove them beyond their endurance. But this is simplistic: no one is ever driven unless he wants to be. Just as each masochist finds his sadist, so the proto-ulcer is sure to find its emotional trigger.

From a commercial point of view Walter was an excellent publisher. The *Inquirer*'s Sunday edition carried more comic strips than any paper in the country; therefore it sold well. Walter must take credit for the paper's healthy circulation as well as for the eccentricity of its editorial policy and the unreliability of its reporting. Very early on, he began to use his papers and television stations as a means to punish those he disliked and praise those who could advance him socially. Most publishers do this in subtle ways; but Walter was not subtle, and that is the theme to Mr. Fonzi's study . . . the blatant misuse of the power of the press for personal ends.

To begin with, there was a shit list. Certain people could not be mentioned. Usually the politicians on the list were local liberals, and Walter's motives were understandable if dishonorable. But there were all sorts of other people whose names could not be mentioned. From the world of show business, Imogene Coca, Zsa Zsa Gabor, and Dinah Shore all managed somehow to offend Walter. At the height of Dinah Shore's popularity, her program was listed in *TV Guide* without her name. Then, often as not, the ban would be lifted as inscrutably as it had been imposed. Recently the ambassador told an English lady that he was faced with a great problem in public relations. He wanted to invite a dear friend to come and stay at the embassy but because of the unfair way the press had treated her, he didn't dare. The English woman wondered who it could be: Mary McCarthy? Margaret Mead? Madalyn O'Hair? No, said the ambassador, Zsa Zsa Gabor.

Mr. Fonzi makes considerable hay out of the indictment of the *Inquirer*'s top reporter as a blackmailer who belonged to an extortion ring which shook down local businessmen. No doubt a bad business and proof that Walter did not run a tight ship, but he can hardly be blamed for the corruption of an employee in a city where corruption is a way of life. Far worse is the way Walter used the power of his newspapers and television stations to harm others. In 1964 *Holiday* published a piece on Philadelphia, amiably remarking upon Walter's social rise. Overreacting as usual, Walter immediately ordered a story on the imminent collapse of *Holiday*'s publisher, Curtis. Not satisfied with the first story, he had it rewritten, made tougher, and himself wrote the lead. Disliking Ralph Nader, he saw to it that a speech in Philadelphia by the national ombudsman was not mentioned in the *Inquirer*. Thinking that he had been snubbed at a party given by Nubar Gulbenkian, Walter ordered a reporter to write a story "exposing" that jolly oil man. These are examples of capriciousness, idle malice, and relentless triviality. Now for the conflict of interest.

Out of the blue, Walter ordered a story which would "knock the hell out of" one Matthew Fox. The reporter charged with the assignment was puzzled. Why? What was Walter's motive? Fox was a wheeler-dealer, with no Philadelphia interests. But —and the picture came into focus—Fox was deeply involved in California's pay television experiment. Walter opposed pay television not only because it was un-American (as did the networks) but, more specifically, because if Fox's people issued their own listings it would harm *TV Guide*. To the reporter's credit, he wrote a piece so deliberately scurrilous that the *Inquirer*'s lawyers killed it.

Walter's most notorious intervention in politics came in 1966 when Milton Shapp ran for governor of Pennsylvania. Aside from being a Democrat, Shapp had a number of other serious demerits in Walter's eyes. He owned an interest in a cable television firm in direct conflict with Triangle; worse, he had managed to stop Walter from slipping through the city council a motion to grant Triangle exclusive CATV rights for the city. Finally (and the reason Walter gave for the virulence of his opposition), Shapp "made his objection to the merger of the Pennsylvania and New York Central railroads one of the principal campaign issues." This was too much for good Philadelphian Walter. "I had a sympathetic view toward Mr. Shapp long before the campaign," he said, "but then he used the Pennsylvania Railroad as his *schtick* . . . one of the great American corporations . . . chairman of the board . . . personal friend of mine . . ."

It was too much. Consequently the *Inquirer* outdid itself in what a political observer at the time termed "character assassination." Every trick in the book was used, including what is sometimes referred to as *"The Best Man* caper"; hint that the candidate is not right in the head. An *Inquirer* reporter asked Shapp if it was true that he'd sue should the paper print that he'd ever been in a mental home. Having never been in a loony bin, Shapp quite naturally said, yes, he would sue. Next day's headlines: SHAPP DENIES EVER HAVING BEEN IN A MENTAL HOME. After the campaign the general public learned that the largest individual stockholder in the Pennsylvania Railroad was Walter Annenberg.

Mr. Fonzi records with zest a dozen other peculiar uses Walter made of his newspapers and television stations. For instance, he would not allow WFIL-TV to show the ABC documentary "The Political Demise of Richard Nixon" (Walter wasn't so dumb, come to think of it) because a minute or two was devoted to Alger Hiss's view of his nemesis. Then Walter suppressed in his newspapers the national uproar over Hiss's having been allowed to appear on television since Hiss was, in Walter's phrase, "a convicted treasonable spy." Fortunately for Walter, perjurer Hiss did not sue. When Martin Luther King came to town, a reporter was instructed to ask him, "Is it true the ultimate aim of your campaign is interracial marriage?" When a local politician named Musmanno died, Walter (who liked him) wanted to include in the obituary that his death had been hastened by a row with Senator Joseph Clark (whom Walter loathed). And so on and on.

But though it is good to show the corruption of the press under an ambitious, ignorant, and malicious owner, one cannot help wondering what Mr. Fonzi finds so startling. The media in America exist only to serve the financial interests of their owners. That is the way things are and have always been. For sheer breathtaking character assassination the pious Henry Luce did more harm than a dozen crude Walters mucking about in a sad city where, from time to time, nearly everyone is for sale or at least rent (it is sad to note that one of Philadelphia's few admirable politicians, Richardson Dilworth, belonged to a law firm retained by Walter and so he never . . .)

But the pure of heart can take some consolation in the fact that newspapers in America are less and less read. A recent Gallup Poll caused much clucking in the press: apparently 45 percent thought the press biased. How could the good people be so suspicious of the American press, which (because it is American) has to be the world's best, serving the Bill of Rights with lonely fervor? Yet the real surprise was that 37 percent are so stupid as to think that the press is objective. They are the real suckers, and we know what sort of break an earlier Philadelphia clown would have given them.

The case of Walter Annenberg has its touching side. Had he not been born with money he might have found a happy niche for himself as a sales manager in some small firm where his crudeness and lack of civilization would have been a virtue. As it was, an heir to power with a drive for respectability, he had the accidental luck to befriend a future President and so found himself one day facing a mildly contemptuous Senate committee which knew perfectly well (if he did not) that he had no business being an ambassador to anywhere.

Senator Fulbright handled the occasion with many mumbled asides (not all repeated by Mr. Fonzi) to the effect that it really made no difference what the Senate thought of a President's diplomatic appointments, since they were almost always consented to. He did wonder if Walter had given any money to Nixon's campaign. A firm "no" from the ambassador-designate. Later Walter admitted that, well, his wife had. Asked whether or not he had tried to link Musmanno's death with Senator Clark's "persecution," he lied and said "no." He was confirmed.

It is usual for this sort of book to end upon the hortatory note: if only we join together and force the newspapers to be objective, all will again be well. It is to Mr. Fonzi's credit that he tells his sad story simply for its own sake. There is nothing to be done about Walter except defeat the jokester who appointed him and boycott all Triangle publications. The first is possible; the second . . . so what? In any case, as one who loves wit and the appositeness of things, I cannot help but feel Mr. Fonzi is too melodramatic and, finally, unjust. It is altogether right that Walter Annenberg should represent not only the present administration but the nation which elected it. Birds of a feather, as they say; and what birds! Eagles, no less, and like the predatory American eagle, near to extinction as a result of our poisoned environment.

The New York Review of Books, April 9, 1970

MEREDITH

"He did the best things best." Henry James's famous epitaph for George Meredith strikes an ominous note. "He was the finest contriver," wrote E. M. Forster, noun carefully chosen to deflate reluctant superlative. Literary critics tend to regard Meredith's novels much the way music critics responded a few years ago to a singer with a three-octave range; absolutely secure in her highest and lowest notes, she lacked nothing save that middle register in which most music is written. Nevertheless, virtuosity of any kind is so rare in the arts that other artists tend to be fascinated by it. In a letter to Stevenson, James refers to Meredith's "charming *accueil*, his impenetrable shining scales, and the (to me) general mystery of his perversity." Charm and glitter; mystery and perversity.

In the Clark Lectures for 1969 V. S. Pritchett (a critic who can usually be counted on to do the good things well) does his best to come to terms with the Meredithean mystery, and in the process says a number of things about the English novel in general, and its comic tradition in particular.

Mr. Pritchett proposes three literary categories: the masculine, the feminine, and the mythic or fantastic. The masculine line is concerned with the life of the town—that is, "the world" in the eighteenth-century sense. Fielding, Scott, Austen, George Eliot "are robust and hard-headed. They know that in the long run feeling must submit to intelligence." The feminine tradition reverses the field. "The disorderly, talkative, fantasticating tradition" of Sterne in which "the 'I' is not a fixture; it dissolves every minute. . . . Not action but inaction, being washed along by the tide is the principle, astonished that we are a form of life." Among the feminine, Peacock, some of Meredith and Dickens, Firbank, Virginia Woolf, Joyce, with Beckett now busily—no, not busily—contriving game's end.

The fantastic or mythic line reflects a shift in emphasis. Town has been replaced by impersonal city. The Great Crowding has begun. Obsession flourishes, and worldly conversation is replaced by solipsistic monologue. Dickens's characters now "speak as if they were the only persons in the world." People "whose inner life was hanging out, so to speak, on their tongues, outside their persons." Mr. Pritchett's categories are nicely drawn and useful if not strictly applied—as Mrs. Woolf once noted, the best writers are androgynes.

Mr. Pritchett examines in some detail *Harry Richmond, The Ordeal of Richard Feverel* (of all English novelists, Meredith wrote morning best), *The Egoist*, and *Beauchamp's Career* ("His bye-elections are very real"). Education and ordeal are the recurring themes. "Meredith is above all a novelist of youth and growth; for he accepts with pleasure the conceit, the severity, the aggressiveness and self-encumberedness of young men and women, the uncritical impulses and solemn ambitions."

The technique of the novels is theatrical. A series of carefully staged conflicts provide the ordeal through which the hero must pass if he is to arrive at that clarification and sad wisdom which can only be achieved when all pride and self-delusion are burnt away. But it is not the inventions which give the novels their force, it is Meredith himself. He is constantly at stage center, commenting in a first person altogether too singular upon the narrative, upstaging at will his own bright creations. Yet for those of us who are devotees (interest is now declared), Meredith's energy, wit, comedic invention are not only satisfying but like no one else's.

Also, for those who care about such things, Meredith was an innovator whose "originality lies in rejecting realism and parcelling out events among people's minds." While his "dialogue brings in the modern wave. It is brisk, abrupt, allusive and born to its moment. . . ." Finally, he concerns himself with that ever-valid theme, the crippling aspects of egoism and "the death of heart and sense, in those who feed back a false public image into private life." In this, the Tory-Radical Meredith was responding fiercely to those incorrigible self-lovers, the ruling class of his place and time. Only connect? No, only erupt, he seems to say, and in the bright lava flow, if not a cleansing an illumination.

The legend of Meredith's difficult style has been a formidable and now, one suspects, permanent barrier to that dwindling crew of eccentrics who enjoy reading novels. Yet the famous style is no more demanding than Proust's, simpler than Joyce's, less enervating than Beckett's, and if one makes the effort to submit to its strange rhythm, quite addictive in the end. But despite Mr. Pritchett's efforts it is unlikely that Meredith will ever again be much read except by those solemn embalmers, the Specialists in English Lit., for we live at a chiliastic time when even Cyril Connolly has been forced, he tells us, to give up reading Henry James on the grounds that nowadays one can only cope with a single slow exigent master and his is Proust.

Meredith was always odd bird out in Britain's literary aviary. All plumes and hectic color, he is total Cavalier, and so anathema to those Roundheads who form a permanent majority in the literary worlds of both Atlantic East and Atlantic West. The puritan dislike of show, of wit, of uncommon skill continues as relentlessly today as it did in his own time. But (these "buts" are a feeble attempt at selling Meredith) he had a "young pre-adult heart like Dickens"; also unusual among English writers, he not only liked women, he liked them as equals. His comic creations were of such a high order that Mark Twain stole a pair (The Duke and the Dauphin) from *Harry Richmond* in order to enliven *Huckleberry Finn*. As for Meredith's beautifully concentrated elliptical dialogue, it continues to sound in the work of Ivy Compton-Burnett and her imitators while, according to Mr. Pritchett, ". . . the sardonic and reiterated stress on a single essence in his characters" was an influence on D. H. Lawrence. If nothing else, Meredith is a permanent footnote to the great puritan tradition.

"A very honorable disinterested figure in his old age," wrote Henry James, "and very superior to any other here, in his scorn of the beefy British public and all its vulgarities and brutalities." A century later that beefy public is busy writing most of the novels (though still not reading them) and the great good (yes, often silly) places that those two mandarins so powerfully imagined are casualties of lost empire, class shiftings and, above all, that electronic revolution which has found a new way of peopling the popular imagination with alternative worlds. Mr. Pritchett acknowledges as much and notes that Meredith's highly subjective tone is "not so far from the agitated prose of those modern writers who seem to have sensed that the prose of the future will be heard and seen, and perhaps never read."

As prose fiction stutters into silence, it is possible to look back without sadness (three centuries is quite long enough for any literary form) and note that the imperium James and Meredith dreamed of was just that, a territory translated from the quotidian by a rare combination of will and genius. They knew that literature was (let us use the past tense) never a democracy or even a republic. It was a kingdom, and there for a time ruled George Meredith, the tailor's son whose unique art made him what all of Richmond Roy's con-man's cleverness could not, a king.

London *Times*, May 2, 1970

DOC REUBEN

Everything you always wanted to know about sex*
Explained by David Reuben, M.D.
*But were afraid to ask

The title of the current number-one nonfiction best seller is cute as a bug's ear, and we know what Freud thought of those who were cute about sex. ("Very uptight"—Sigmund Freud, M.D.). If a jocose approach to sexual matters is a mask for unease, then David Reuben, M.D. ("currently in private psychiatric practice in San Diego, California"), is in a state of communicable panic and I would be most unwilling to have him privately practice psychiatry on me, even in San Diego, the Vatican of the John Birch Society.

David Reuben, M.D., is a relentlessly cheery, often genuinely funny writer whose essential uncertainty about sex is betrayed by a manner which shifts in a very odd way from night-club comedian to reform rabbi, touching en route almost every base except the scientific. Essentially he is a moralist, expressing the hang-ups of today's middle-aged, middle-class urban American Jews, hang-ups which are not (as I shall attempt to show) necessarily those of the gentile population or, for that matter, of the rising generation of American Jews.

Yes, I am going to talk about class and race-religion, two unmentionables in our free land, and I am going to make a case that Jewish family patterns, sexual taboos, and superstitions are often very different from those of the rest of the population, black, white, and yellow, Roman Catholic, Protestant and Moslem. For gentile readers much of the charm of *Portnoy's Complaint* was its exoticism. And despite those ecumenical reviewers who insist that *everyone's* mother is a Jewish mother, the truth is that Mrs. Portnoy was the result of a specific set of historical circumstances, not applicable to anyone else, including the next generation of American Jews, if we are to believe in her child Alexander's rebellion. Certainly his son (assuming he has not entirely wasted his posterity) will probably resemble next-door neighbor George Apley III rather more than father or grandfather.

I mention Alexander Portnoy because David Reuben, M.D., is his contemporary and they have a good deal in common. But where Portnoy's creator is a highly talented artist often able to view objectively the prejudices and tribal taboos of his mother's ghetto culture, Dr. Reuben is still very much in her thrall. Essentially he is not a man of science but a moderately swinging rabbi who buttresses his prejudices with pious quotations from the Old Testament (a single reference to the New Testament is inaccurate); surprisingly, the only mental therapist he mentions is Freud—in order to set him straight.

But then Dr. Reuben seems not to have been affected at all by the discipline of science. He explodes with snappy generalities ("All children at the time of puberty develop pimples") and opinions ("All prostitutes hate men") and statistics which he seems to have made up ("Seventy to eighty percent of Americans engage in fellatio and cunnilingus"). He makes no attempt to prove anything; he merely states his prejudices and enthusiasms as though they were in some way self-evident. It is possible that his advice to middle-aged, middle-class Jewish heterosexuals is useful, but they make up a very small part of the population he now wants to convert to his notions of "mature" sexuality. Certainly a white Protestant will find much of what he has to say inscrutable, while a black will no doubt regard him as something from outer space (that is to say, suburbia) and yet another good reason for replacing Jerusalem with Mecca.

At two points Dr. Reuben is at odds with Moses. He thinks Onan was quite a guy, and his lonely practice particularly useful in toning up those of our senior citizens whose wheel-chairs will not accommodate two people; and he has a positively Updikean enthusiasm for cunnilingus. Dr. Reuben would like everyone to indulge in this chivalrous practice— except women, of course: Lesbianism is "immature." He is also sufficiently American to believe that more of everything is best. At times he sounds not unlike the late Bruce Barton extolling God as a super-salesman. "Success in the outside world breeds success in the inside world of sex," sermonizes Dr. Reuben. "Conversely, the more potent a man becomes in the bedroom, the more potent he is in business." Is God a super-salesman? You bet!—and get this—*God eats it, too!*

On those rare occasions when Dr. Reuben is not proselytiz-ing, he can be most instructive, particularly when he describes what happens to the body during orgasm (I assume he is cor-rect about the plumbing), and as he lists all the things that take place between the first thought of sex (D. H. Lawrence, appar-ently, was wrong: sex is all in the head) and final emission, the male reader is certain to be impotent for the next twenty-four hours ("You will never again," said Leo Tolstoi wickedly, "step on a crack without thinking of a white bear"). Dr. Reu-ben also has a good plan for eliminating venereal disease by a mass inoculation of the entire population, which he only slightly spoils by suggesting that we use "our gigantic Civil Defense network," which was set up for "just such a mass medical program (in case of bacteriological warfare). This would be a wonderful opportunity for a dry run which might pay off in case of a real war." Well, he does live in San Diego.

Dr. Reuben is also a liberal on abortion, and informative on the subject of contraceptives. He finds something a bit wrong with all the present methods and suspects that the eventual solution will be a morning-after pill for women—as a Jewish patriarch he believes that woman, the lesser vessel, should bear the responsibility. He is also filled with wonderful lore, some of which I hope is true. Want to know the best nonmedical contraceptive? "Coca-Cola. Long a favorite soft drink, it is, coincidentally, the best douche available. A Coke contains carbolic acid which kills the sperm and sugar which explodes the sperm cells . . . The six-ounce bottle is just the right size for one application." Yes, but won't it rot her teeth?

Between mature guys and gals, anything goes (though anal penetration of the gal leaves Doc a bit queasy). Male impotence and female frigidity he recognizes as hazards, but psychiatry, he is quick to point out, will work wonders. He is a remorseless self-advertiser. Every few pages he gives us a commercial with brisk dialogue and characters named Emily who suffer from frigidity until . . . But let's listen in on Emily and her doctor after some months of treatment. Is Emily frigid now? Lordy no! Emily is fucking like a minx. "I'm happy to say, Doctor, this is just a social call. I wanted to tell you how happy I am. I don't know what it's done for other people but psychiatry did what Mother Nature couldn't do—it made a woman out of me!" Music up and out.

Or take the case of Joni, the beautiful airline stewardess who couldn't achieve the big O no matter how hard she (he) tried. After being told that the values she had learned as a girl on a farm in Iowa (Christian puritanism) were not applicable to a flying bunny, she was able in a matter of months to write her doctor "at Christmastime" (when, presumably, all thoughts flow toward the orgasm), "I may have been a stewardess, but I really 'won my wings' in the psychiatrist's office." To one who locates psychiatry somewhere between astrology and phrenology on the scale of human gullibility, the cold-blooded desire to make money by giving one's fellows (at best) obvious advice and (at worst) notions even sillier than the ones that made them suffer smacks of *Schadenfreude*.

Along with testimonials to the efficacy of his art, Dr. Reuben has a good deal to say about many subjects, and since he never attempts to prove anything, his opinions must be taken as just that. Some examples. "Orgasm among nymphomaniacs is as rare as orgasm among prostitutes." To which any liberal arts professor would scribble in the margin, "prove." For Dr. Reuben's instruction, the only bona fide nymphomaniac I ever went to bed with (I had two assistants, let me quickly add; I am no Miller-Mailer man) promptly produced a splendid series of orgasms of the variety known as "skimming." In fact, she enjoyed having orgasms so much that she thought it fun to have sex with a lot of different people, thus betraying her immaturity. Three point two times a week year in and year out with the same mature and loving mate ought to have been quite enough for the saucy shiksa.

Then there is Smiling Jack, who suffers from premature ejaculation. Why? *Because he wants to punish women.* "The smile is characteristic of men with premature ejaculation—they are all profusely apologetic but their regrets have a hollow ring." Fast comer, wipe that smile off your face before you stretch out on Dr. Reuben's couch.

"Blind girls become particularly adept at secret masturbation. They . . ." No. You had better read this section for yourself. At least the author had the courtesy to wait until Helen Keller was dead before rushing into print with the news. Then "The chap who pays to see two ladies perform homosexually also has his problems, as do the father and son who patronize the same hustler." A breath-taking non sequitur, as usual unprovable and also, as usual, an echo of Mosaic law: Thou shalt not look upon thy father's nakedness.

The looniest of Dr. Reuben's folklore is "Food seems to have a mysterious fascination for homosexuals. Many of the world's greatest chefs have been homosexuals." (Who? I'm really curious. Not Brillat-Savarin, not Fanny Farmer.) "Some of the country's best restaurants are run by homosexuals" (Those two at Twenty One?). "Some of the fattest people are homosexuals" (King Farouk? Orson Welles? President Taft?). "The exact reason is complex. . . ." It certainly is, since there is no evidence one way or the other. But if there were, Dr. Reuben had best find himself a friendly shrink because he makes at least eight references in his book to the penis as food, usually "limp as a noodle"; in fact, food is seldom far from the good doctor's mind when he contemplates genitalia—no doubt for a very complex reason (when I met him three years ago in San Diego he was round as a . . . well, butterball; since then, according to the dustjacket photo, he has "matured" and lost weight).

But Reuben the folklorist is nothing compared to Reuben the statistician. "At least seventy-five to eighty-five percent of [prostitutes'] clients want to have their penises sucked." "Ninety-nine percent of johns refuse to wear condoms [with prostitutes]." "Only about one tenth of [aging] females choose celibacy." "Chronic or repeated impotence probably affects about thirty to forty percent of men at any given time." And of course those 70 to 80 percent of men who engage in cunnilingus. Since two can play these games, I shall now open my own private files to the public. Right off, 92 percent of those men who get cancer of the tongue have practiced cunnilingus from once to 3309 times in their lives. Those who practice fellatio, however, are not only better dressed but will take at least one long trip in the coming year. Ninety-six percent of those who practice sixty-nine (for Dr. Reuben's heteros a must) periodically complain of a sense of suffocation. Finally, all major American novelists after forty occasionally have orgasm without a full erection. Further statistics on this poignant condition will be revealed as soon as I have heard from Saul, Vladimir and Mary.

In favor of contraception, abortion, masturbation, oral sex between male and female, Dr. Reuben is up-to-date and a source of comfort to his reformed congregation (though the orthodox must be grimly looking about for some useful anathema to lob his way). On circumcision he is orthodox—nature wanted the glans penis covered but Jehovah knew better (our rabbi quotes from both Genesis and Exodus to support this profitable—for doctors—mutilation); on prostitution he is orthodox but tries not to be; on homosexuality he is Mosaic—it is a bad business strictly for immature freaks. Bisexuality does not exist for reasons he and his mentor the late Dr. Bergler never quite give, though they have a lot of opinions which, in their confident American way, they present as facts.

Parenthetically, the collapse of responsible commentary in the United States is as noticeable in a pseudoscience like psychiatry as it is, say, in literary criticism. No one need *prove* anything; simply state private opinion as public fact, preferably in lurid terms. It is now a national characteristic and part of the general cretinizing effect certain dour biologists (accused, accurately, of elitism) regard as a concomitant of promiscuous breeding and overpopulation.

To his credit, Dr. Reuben realizes the practical uses and pleasures of prostitution, an arrangement necessary to the well-being of many millions of men (and women) since the dawn of money, and he is forced to admit that most of the usual arguments against it are not only hypocritical but inaccurate. Nevertheless, looking up from his well-thumbed Old Testament, he is obliged to remind us that " 'harlots' are mentioned forty-four times in the Bible, 'whores' and 'whore mongers' are featured fifty-three times, and committing 'whoredoms' is mentioned eight times."

He then makes his only allusion to the New Testament. Apparently "[it] began where the Old Testament left off and commenced a religious campaign against prostitution which took on all the attributes of a Crusade. . . ." As J. C.'s numerous readers know, his only reference to prostitution was a proposal that the fallen Mary Magdalene be shown charity. Even St. Paul was not a pornophobe; he was a chiliast who believed the day of judgment was at hand and so thought it wise to keep oneself in a state of ceremonial purity—in other words, no sex of any kind (even mature); but if such continence was unbearable then "it is better to marry than to burn."

It should be noted that in matters of history (excepting always Old Testament studies) and etymology Dr. Reuben is usually wrong. He tells us that the word pornography "comes from two Greek words, *pornos*, meaning dirty, and *graphos*, meaning words." *Graphos* of course means "writing" not "words." *Pornos* does not mean "dirty"; it means "harlot." Though I do not think Dr. Reuben has any Greek, if he did it would be a marvelous tribute to the unconscious mind that he confuses "harlot" with "dirty." He also thinks that homosexual sadists "filled the ranks of Hitler's Gestapo and SS." After the purge of Ernst Roehm and his friends in 1934, only banal heterosexual sadists were recruited by the Gestapo and SS. By 1940 homosexuals were being carted off to concentration camps along with Jews, gypsies, and communists. The text is full of misprints (as if anyone cares), bad grammar, misspellings (on page 142 "syphillitic").

While acknowledging the Old Testament's harsh line on prostitution, our cruise director finds peculiarly contemptible the moralizing of those "ministers and moral educators who couldn't be farther removed from practical knowledge of the subject if they lived on the moon." Although Dr. Reuben is robust in his attacks on Protestant clergymen, neither Roman Catholic priest nor Jewish rabbi is ever noted as a hypocritical enemy of life. Obviously Dr. Reuben knows a militant minority when he sees one. But though he is right in blaming a good deal of what is wrong with our sexual ethos on the Protestant founders, he ought, in all fairness, to note that later arrivals haven't been much help either.

To Dr. Reuben's credit, he puts at rest the myth that prostitutes are wicked people because they spread venereal disease. Of 4700 women arrested for prostitution in New York City (1966), 619 had gonorrhea and only four had syphilis. Not a bad record considering their line of work and the harassment they are subject to. He also reminds us that where prostitution is legal, sex crimes diminish. Finally, "most girls become prostitutes because they like it." But then he can't leave that reasonable opinion alone (those 105 Old Testament cracks about "whores" obviously prey on him). Two paragraphs later we are told that "in prostitution no one's happy." Then Dr. Reuben erupts in a torrent of tribal wisdom worthy of any Baptist divine working out of the Oral Roberts Tabernacle. "All prostitutes have at least one thing in common—they hate men." They are doomed to this sad state unless "some dramatic change like psychiatric treatment intervenes." Unexpectedly "their genitals are usually in better condition than those of the average woman." But unfortunately (for men) "the majority of prostitutes are female homosexuals in their private lives."

This, incidentally, is a beloved post-Freudian myth, quite unproven but perennially exciting to men who want to believe that the women they rent deeply hate them and only go to bed with them because they lack money. It is the ultimate charade in the power fantasy which drives so many men (you are tied up and helpless, my proud beauty), including homosexualists who try, not always vainly, to make that one "totally" heterosexual male either because he needs money or must yield to physical force. To say that all female prostitutes are really Lesbians is to succumb to a pleasant if rather silly daydream.

But then Dr. Reuben the rabbi sooner or later does in Dave the swinger. Harlots must, finally, suffer for their evil ways; therefore few "achieve orgasm even in the privacy of their own bedrooms" (a slightly confusing statement: where do they work? They can't all be represented by Al Fresco), but then how can they be expected to have mature orgasms when the only source of "love for a prostitute is her pimp . . . who provides her with what little emotional warmth he is capable of"? Value judgment. Prove. But then there is no superstition about prostitutes that Dr. Reuben does not offer us as "scientific" fact. Mrs. Portnoy would be proud of Alexander's nice contemporary, particularly when he tells us that the relationship between prostitute and customer is simply "masturbation in a vagina" (a slight contradiction since earlier he told us that 75 to 85 percent of the johns are blown).

Although none of this is provable one way or the other (the nice thing about a pseudoscience like psychiatry is that one can pose any hypothesis upon which to build if not a science a religion), and assuming that a good deal of commercial sex is a kind of joyless masturbation, one is tempted to point out that the same is true of marriage in which, as time passes, the man (and now women are beginning to make the same confession) is constantly forced to rely on inner newsreels in order to make love to a body that no longer excites him yet because of law and tribal custom he must pretend to respond to for thirty or forty or, if Dr. Reuben is counseling him, seventy years of mature sexuality. It is enough to make Malcolm Muggeridge, if not the angels, weep.

In the course of "proving" that a majority of prostitutes are Lesbians and so (naturally) unhappy, Dr. Reuben reveals the bedrock upon which all his superstitions finally rest. "Just as one penis plus one penis equals nothing, one vagina plus another vagina still equals zero." There it is. Dr. Reuben believes in what Roman Catholics term "natural law"—everything is created for a *single* natural purpose. Penis plus vagina equals continuation of the species. Unfortunately the big natural lawyer in the sky slightly confused matters by combining our divine instruments of conception with those of excretion, a source of chagrin and shame to the perennial puritan. Our genitals have always done double duty and cannot be said strictly to have only one sacred function from which all else is deviation, wicked or not, depending on who is doing the moralizing.

Yet from Moses to Freud (despite his discontents) to Dr. Reuben, Judaeo-Christian doctrine has been remarkably unchanging. Man and woman are joined together in a special covenant to bring into the world children; and as it has been since the Bronze Age, so shall it be not only in our Age of Plastic but for all time to come. Those who transgress this law shall be punished, if not with death by stoning then with a mild rash due to neurosis brought on by immature (that is, unholy) attitudes.

365

It is not an overstatement to say that a belief in this ancient covenant has made a hell of Western man's life on earth (try to find a hotel room in which to make love in any American state; a few seedy places exist but by and large the entire society is resolutely determined to keep from carnal knowledge of one another those not joined together by the Jewish/Christian God). Worse, the ancient covenant's injunction to be fruitful and multiply (Dr. Reuben surprisingly omits this text. It is Genesis I:28) has now brought the human race to what may well be a most unpleasant coda as too many people destroy not only the biosphere which supports us but the society which sustains us.

On the subject of homosexuality, Dr. Reuben tries to be a good sport. Yet at heart he is angry with the homosexualist who perversely refuses to enter into a penis-vagina relationship. It would be so easy to straighten him out. If he would only visit "a psychiatrist who knows how to cure homosexuality, he has every chance of becoming a happy, well-adjusted heterosexual." I wonder if Dr. Reuben might be got up on a charge of violating the fair advertising practices act—on the ground that no such psychiatrist exists. It is true that the late Dr. Bergler enjoyed announcing "cures," but since no one knows what a homosexualist is (as opposed to a homosexual act), much less what the psychic life (as opposed to the sex life) of any of his patients was like, his triumphs must be taken on faith.

However, it should be noted that anyone so disturbed by society's condemnation of his natural sexual instinct that he would want to pervert it in order to conform would, no doubt, be a candidate for some kind of "conversion" at the hands of a highly paid quack. Yet to change a man's homosexual instinct is as difficult (if not impossible) as changing a man's heterosexual instinct, and socially rather less desirable since it can hardly be argued, as it used to be—the clincher, in fact, of the natural lawyers—that if everyone practiced homosexuality the race would die out. The fact of course is that not everyone would, at least exclusively, and the race currently needs no more additions.

As a religious rather than a scientific man, Dr. Reuben believes that there is something wicked (he would say sick) about the homosexual act. Therefore those who say they really enjoy it must be lying. He also believes implicitly a set of old queens' tales that any high school boy in Iowa (if not the Bronx) could probably set him straight on. "Most homosexuals at one time or another in their lives act out some aspect of the female role." Aside from his usual inability to define anything (what is a male role? a female role?), he seems to mean that a man who enjoys relations with his own sex is really half a man, a travesty of woman.

This is not the case. The man involved in a homosexual act is engaged in a natural male function; he is performing as a man, and so is his partner. That there are men who think of themselves as women is also a fact, as the visitor to any queer bar will have noticed (those Bette Davis types are with us from Third Avenue to Hong Kong), but they are a tiny minority, not unlike those odd creatures who think of themselves as 100 percent he-men on the order of Lyndon Johnson, another small and infinitely more depressing minority, which of course includes the thirty-sixth President.

Dr. Reuben is also horrified by what he thinks to be the promiscuity of all homosexualists. But then "homosexuals thrive on danger," he tells us, and of course their "primary interest is the penis, not the person." As usual no evidence is given. He takes as fact the prejudices of his race-religion-country, and, most important, as I shall point out, class. Reading him on homosexuality, I was reminded of the lurid anti-Semitic propaganda of the thirties: All Jews love money. All Jews are sensualists with a penchant for gentile virgins. All Jews are involved in a conspiracy to take over the financial and cultural life of whatever country they happen to be living in. Happily, Dr. Reuben is relatively innocent of making this last charge. The Homintern theory, however, is a constant obsession of certain journalists and crops up from time to time not only in the popular press but in the pages of otherwise respectable literary journals. Fag-baiting is the last form of minority baiting practiced at every level of American society.

Dr. Reuben tends to gloss over the social pressures which condition the life of anyone who prefers, occasionally or exclusively, the company of his own sex. Homosexualists seldom settle down to cozy mature domesticity for an excellent reason: society forbids it. Two government workers living together in Washington, D.C., would very soon find themselves unemployed. They would be spied on, denounced secretly, and dismissed. Only a bachelor entirely above suspicion like J. Edgar Hoover can afford to live openly with another man. In any case, homosexual promiscuity differs from heterosexual only in the atmosphere of fear in which the homosexualist must operate. It is a nice joke if a Louisiana judge is caught in a motel with a call girl. It is a major tragedy if a government official with a family is caught in a men's room.

For someone like Dr. Reuben who believes that there is no greater sin than avoidance of "heterosex–penis and vagina," two men who do live together must, somehow, be wretched. "Mercifully for both of them, the life expectancy of their relationship together is brief." Prove? I wrote for the tenth time in the margin. But we are beyond mere empiricism. We are now involved in one of the major superstitions of our place and time and no evidence must be allowed to disturb simple faith.

Dr. Kinsey (dismissed by Dr. Reuben as a mere biologist) did try to find out what is actually going on. Whatever Kinsey's shortcomings as a researcher, he revealed for the first time the way things are. Everyone is potentially bisexual. In actual practice a minority never commits a homosexual act, others experiment with their own sex but settle for heterosexuality, still others swing back and forth to a greater or lesser degree, while another minority never gets around to performing the penis-vagina act. None of this is acceptable to either Dr. Bergler or Dr. Reuben because they *know* that there is no such thing as bisexuality. Therefore Dr. Kinsey's findings must be discredited. To the rabbinical mind, any man who admits to having enjoyed sexual relations with another man must be, sadly, consigned to the ranks of Sodom. That the same man spends the rest of his sex life in penis-vagina land means nothing because, having enjoyed what he ought not to have enjoyed, his relations with women are simply play-acting. Paradoxically, in the interest of making money, the mental therapists are willing to work with any full-time homo-sexualist who has never had a penis-vagina relationship because deep down they know he does not enjoy men no matter what he says. This is the double standard with a vengeance.

Driving through Wyoming, a Jewish friend of mine picked up a young cowhand and had sex with him. Dr. Reuben will be pleased to note that my friend was, as usual, guilt-ridden; so much so that the boy finally turned to his seducer and with a certain wonder said, "You know, you guys from the East do this because you're sick and we do it because we're horny." My friend has never recovered from this insight into that poly-morphic goyisher world best revealed some years ago in Boise, Idaho, where a number of businessmen were discovered frolicking with the local high school boys. Oddly enough (to the innocent), as husbands and fathers, the businessmen were all long-time homesteaders in penis-vagina land. So what were they up to? Bisexuality? No, it does not exist. Evidence dis-missed, just as all accounts of other cultures are also unaccepta-ble. Turks, Greeks, Moslems . . . Well, as one critic likes to say, that is another context (disgusting lot is what he means). I would suggest, however, that a recent book by Brian W. Al-diss, *The Hand-Reared Boy*, be admitted as evidence.

Mr. Aldiss is an English heterosexual—well, he *pretends* to be one, has wife and children—and he tells us in fascinating detail what it was like to go to a second-rate public school just before the Second World War. Admittedly all Americans think all Englishmen are fags, so I daresay this interesting account of a seventeen-year-old who has full sexual relation-ships with other boys as well as a mature penis-vagina relation-ship with a girl will be dismissed on the ground that seventeen is a man for all practical purposes, and so he could not do both wholeheartedly. Yet he did. In this Mr. Aldiss tends to resemble his American counterparts, a world obviously alien to the Dr. Reubens, who cannot accept the following simple fact of so many lives (certainly my own): that it is possible to have a mature sexual relationship with a woman on Monday, and a mature sexual relationship with a man on Tuesday, and perhaps on Wednesday have both together (admittedly you have to be in good condition for this).

Now I am sure that Dr. Reuben would not like for 100-percent heterosexualists to be advised on their behavior by 100-percent homosexualists, so may I, diffidently, suggest that until Dr. Reuben has had a full and mature relationship with a man, he ought not to speak of what he does not know. Finally, realizing that at the deepest level, no rabbi can take this sort of blunt talk from a foreskinned dog (Bernard Malamud's loving phrase), I suggest that he read that grandest of Anti-Rabbis, Paul Goodman. He will learn a lot about the naturalness of bisexuality, and in a Jewish context.

It is ironic (and dismaying) that Dr. Reuben's collection of tribal taboos and reactionary nostrums should be popular just when the entire concept of the family is undergoing a radical revision. Population continues to double at shorter and shorter intervals. Famine is now chronic in half the world. By the 1980's Americans will be short of food, too. If the race is to continue, we must limit human breeding by law. That is the simple fact of our present condition. Once we have acted to regulate population (I am assuming that this will be done: mass suicide is not a characteristic of our race), most people will not have children to raise. Without children, there will be no reason for men and women to enter into lifetime contracts with one another and marriage, as we have known it, will be at an end. Certainly that curious institution is already in a state of advanced decay in America, witness the underlying theme of all the how-to sex books (including Dr. Reuben's): how to stay sexually interested in your mate long after nature has ceased to make either of you attractive to the other.

Needless to say, even if all governments were to act promptly to limit population, marriage would not end at once or (in some forms) ever entirely vanish, but once it ceases to be the central fact of our society, to that extent women will be for the first time in recorded history freed from a particularly debasing relationship in which they are relentlessly conditioned by the Dr. Reubens to be brainless, enticing bunnies whose reward for making a good home in which to raise their husbands' children is a series of wonderful orgasms. The most startling thing about the women's liberation movement is not its ferocity (and ghastly rhetoric) but the fact that it took so long to surface. It is certainly true that women are half-citizens even in the relatively liberated West. From birth they are programmed by the tribalists to serve men, raise children, and be (if they are interested in True Maturity) geishas, as we are told by "J" (a pseudonym for Dr. Reuben? Or for the sly Professor James Moran?) in *The Sensuous Woman*, a volume every bit as fatuous as Dr. Reuben's compendium of tribal taboos. "J" sees woman's job as not only how to get HIM in the sack but how to keep him excited, a job she admits is not easy within marriage since ardor sooner or later flags. Nevertheless, by unexpectedly redoing the bedroom in sexy shades, a new hair style, exotic perfumes, ravishing naughty underwear, an unexpected blow job with a mouth full of cream of wheat, *somehow* a girl who puts her mind to it can keep him coming back for more year after year after year. As far as I know, no one in tribal lore has ever asked the simple question: Why bother? Why not move on?

Finally, it is to be hoped that with the reduction of population by law and the consequent abandoning of the family unit, men and women will be able for the first time to confront one another as equals, no longer resorting to the sick game in which the man thinks the woman means to trap him into a legal arrangement and the woman thinks she is wrong not to want to capture him and sign herself up for a lifetime of dull subservience. In any case, new things are happening as yet undreamed of in the office of David Reuben, M.D. We are coming either to a better understanding of our sexual nature, or to the race's end. Certainly, either is preferable to the way things are.

The New York Review of Books, June 4, 1970

DRUGS

It is possible to stop most drug addiction in the United States within a very short time. Simply make all drugs available and sell them at cost. Label each drug with a precise description of what effect—good and bad—the drug will have on the taker. This will require heroic honesty. Don't say that marijuana is addictive or dangerous when it is neither, as millions of people know—unlike "speed," which kills most unpleasantly, or heroin, which is addictive and difficult to kick.

For the record, I have tried—once—almost every drug and liked none, disproving the popular Fu Manchu theory that a single whiff of opium will enslave the mind. Nevertheless many drugs are bad for certain people to take and they should be told why in a sensible way.

Along with exhortation and warning, it might be good for our citizens to recall (or learn for the first time) that the United States was the creation of men who believed that each man has the right to do what he wants with his own life as long as he does not interfere with his neighbor's pursuit of happiness (that his neighbor's idea of happiness is persecuting others does confuse matters a bit).

This is a startling notion to the current generation of Americans. They reflect a system of public education which has made the Bill of Rights, literally, unacceptable to a majority of high school graduates (see the annual Purdue reports) who now form the "silent majority"—a phrase which that underestimated wit Richard Nixon took from Homer who used it to describe the dead.

Now one can hear the warning rumble begin: if everyone is allowed to take drugs everyone will and the GNP will decrease, the Commies will stop us from making everyone free, and we shall end up a race of Zombies, passively murmuring "groovie" to one another. Alarming thought. Yet it seems most unlikely that any reasonably sane person will become a drug addict if he knows in advance what addiction is going to be like.

Is everyone reasonably sane? No. Some people will always become drug addicts just as some people will always become alcoholics, and it is just too bad. Every man, however, has the power (and should have the legal right) to kill himself if he chooses. But since most men don't, they won't be mainliners either. Nevertheless, forbidding people things they like or think they might enjoy only makes them want those things all the more. This psychological insight is, for some mysterious reason, perennially denied our governors.

It is a lucky thing for the American moralist that our country has always existed in a kind of time-vacuum: we have no public memory of anything that happened before last Tuesday. No one in Washington today recalls what happened during the years alcohol was forbidden to the people by a Congress that thought it had a divine mission to stamp out Demon Rum—launching, in the process, the greatest crime wave in the country's history, causing thousands of deaths from bad alcohol, and creating a general (and persisting) contempt among the citizenry for the laws of the United States.

The same thing is happening today. But the government has learned nothing from past attempts at prohibition, not to mention repression.

Last year when the supply of Mexican marijuana was slightly curtailed by the Feds, the pushers got the kids hooked on heroin and deaths increased dramatically, particularly in New York. Whose fault? Evil men like the Mafiosi? Permissive Dr. Spock? Wild-eyed Dr. Leary? No.

The Government of the United States was responsible for those deaths. The bureaucratic machine has a vested interest in playing cops and robbers. Both the Bureau of Narcotics and the Mafia want strong laws against the sale and use of drugs because if drugs are sold at cost there would be no money in it for anyone.

If there was no money in it for the Mafia, there would be no friendly playground pushers, and addicts would not commit crimes to pay for the next fix. Finally, if there was no money in it, the Bureau of Narcotics would wither away, something they are not about to do without a struggle.

Will anything sensible be done? Of course not. The American people are as devoted to the idea of sin and its punishment as they are to making money—and fighting drugs is nearly as big a business as pushing them. Since the combination of sin and money is irresistible (particularly to the professional politician), the situation will only grow worse.

The New York Times, September 26, 1970

Response to this sensible proposal was not as shrill as I had anticipated. Currently, the Commissioner of Police in New York seems to be moving toward my view.

THE DEATH OF
MISHIMA

A white silky beach just south of Madras. Blue sea full of sharks, blue sky full of clouds like egret plumes. Nearby, half in the water, half on the beach, the gray-violet pyramid of a Hindu temple gradually dissolving as the sea with each century rises. In the foreground, the body of a man, headless, armless, with only one leg whose flesh stops at the knee. Below the knee, a bright beautiful white bone around which a rope has been knotted. The angle of the bone indicates that the man's legs and arms had been tied together behind him. Coolly, I become coroner. Speculate sagely on the length of time the man has been dead. Draw my companions' attention to the fact that there is not a drop of blood left in the body: at first glance we thought it a scarecrow, a bundle of white and gray rags—then saw real muscles laid bare, ropy integuments, the shin bone, and knew someone had been murdered, thrown into the sea alive. But who? And why? Definitely not Chinese, I decide (not only am I at heart a coroner—redundancy—but

I am also a geographer of Strabo's school).

I am interrupted by the arrival of a small Tamil girl resembling the late Fanny Brice. She glares at the corpse. "Not nice, not nice at all!" She shakes her head disapprovingly, hopes we won't get a wrong impression of India. As we do our best to reassure her, we are joined by a friend with a newspaper: Yukio Mishima has committed *seppuku* (the proper word for hara-kiri) in the office of Japan's commanding general, his head was then hacked from his body by an aide. . . . We read the bloody details with wonder. Such is the power of writing (to those addicted to reading) that the actual corpse at our feet became less real than the vivid idea of the bodyless head of Mishima, a man my exact contemporary, whose career in so many ways resembled my own, though not to the degree that certain writers of bookchat in the fifties thought.

Tokyo. Unbeautiful but alive and monstrously, cancerously growing, just as New York City—quite as unbeautiful—is visibly dying, its rot a way of life. That will be Tokyo's future, too, but for the moment the mood is one of boom. Official and mercantile circles are euphoric. Elsewhere, unease.

I meet with a leader of the Left currently giving aid to those GIs who find immoral their country's murder of Asiatics. He is not sanguine about Japan. "We don't know who we are since the war. The break with the old culture has left us adrift. Yet we are still a family."

The first thing the traveler in Japan notices is that the people resemble each other, with obvious variations, much the way members of a family do, and this sense of a common identity was the source of their power in the past: all children of an emperor who was child of the sun. But the sun no longer rises for Japan—earth turns, in fact—and the head of the family putters about collecting marine specimens while his children are bored with their new prosperity, their ugly cities, their half-Western, half-Japanese culture, their small polluted islands.

I ask the usual question: what do the Japanese think of the

Americans? The answer is brisk. "Very little. Not like before. I was just reading an old Osaka newspaper. Fifty years ago a girl writes that her life ambition is to meet a Caucasian, an American, and become his mistress. All very respectable. But now there is a certain . . . disdain for the Americans. Of course Vietnam is part of it." One is soon made aware in Tokyo of the Japanese contempt not only for the American imperium but for its cultural artifacts. Though not a zealous defender of my country, I find goading its Tokyo detractors irresistible, at least in literary matters. After all, for some decades now, Japan's most popular (and deeply admired) writer has been W. Somerset Maugham.

We spoke of Mishima's death and the possibility of a return to militarism. Two things which were regarded as one by the world press. But my informant saw no political motive in Mishima's death. "It was a personal gesture. A dramatic gesture. The sort of thing *he* would do. You know he had a private army. Always marching around in uniform. Quite mad. Certainly he had no serious political connections with the right wing."

Mishima's suicide had a shattering effect on the entire Japanese family. For one thing, he was a famous writer. This meant he was taken a good deal more seriously by the nation (family) than any American writer is ever taken by those warring ethnic clans whose mutual detestation is the essential fact of the American way of life. Imagine Paul Goodman's suicide in General Westmoreland's office as reported by *The New York Times* on page 22. "Paul Goodman, writer, aged 59, shot himself in General Westmoreland's office as a protest to American foreign policy. At first, General Westmoreland could not be reached for comment. Later in the day, an aide said that the General, naturally, regretted Mr. Goodman's action, which was based upon a 'patent misunderstanding of America's role in Asia.' Mr. Goodman was the author of a number of books and articles. One of his books was called *Growing Up Absurd.* He is survived by . . ." An indifferent polity.

But Mishima at forty-five was Japan's apparent master of all letters, superb jack of none. Or in the prose of a Knopf blurb writer,

He began his brilliantly successful career in 1944 by winning a citation from the Emperor as the highest-ranking honor student at graduation from the Peers' School. In 1947 he was graduated from Tokyo Imperial University School of Jurisprudence. Since his first novel was published, in 1948, he has produced a baker's dozen of novels, translations of which have by now appeared in fifteen countries; seventy-four short stories; a travel book; and many articles, including two in English (appearing in *Life* and *Holiday*).

About ten films were made from his novels. *The Sound of Waves* (1956) was filmed twice, and one of Ishikawa's masterpieces, *Enjo*, was based on *The Temple of the Golden Pavillion* (1959). Also available in English are the novels *After the Banquet* (1963) and *The Sailor Who Fell from Grace with the Sea* (1965), and *Five Modern Nō Plays* (1957).

He has acted the title role in a gangster film, and American television audiences have seen him on "The Twentieth Century" and on Edward R. Murrow's "Small World." Despite a relentless work schedule, Mr. Mishima has managed to travel widely in the United States and Europe. His home is in Tokyo, with his wife and two children.

The range, variety, and publicness of the career sound ominously familiar to me. Also each of us might be said by those innocent of literature to have been influenced (as a certain "news" magazine gaily wrote of Mishima) "by Proust and Gide." The fact that Proust and Gide resembled one another not at all (or either of us) is irrelevant to the "news" magazine's familiar purpose—the ever-popular sexual smear job which has so long made atrocious the American scene.

The American press, by and large, played up two aspects of the suicide: Mishima's homosexuality and his last confused harangue to the troops, demanding a return to militarism and ancient virtue. The Japanese reaction was more knowledgeable and various than the American. It was also occasionally dotty. Professor Yozo Horigome of Tokyo University found "a striking resemblance" between Mishima's suicide and the death of Thomas à Beckett, as reported by T. S. Eliot! Apparently the good professor had been working up some notes on Eliot and so absorbed was he in his task that any self-willed death smacked of high jinks at Canterbury Cathedral. Taruho Inagaki thought that by extraverting his narcissism, Mishima could not continue as writer or man. Inagaki also observed, somewhat mysteriously, that since Mishima lacked "nostalgia," his later work tended to be artificial and unsatisfactory.

Professor Taku Yamada of Kanazawa University compared Mishima's suicide to that of an early nineteenth-century rebel against the Shogunate—a virtuous youth who had been influenced (like Mishima) by the fifteenth-century Chinese scholar Wang Yang-ming, who believed that "to know and to act are one and the same." The Japanese, the professor noted, in adapting this philosophy to their own needs, simplified it into a sort of death cult with the caveat "one is not afraid of the death of body, but fears the death of mind." Yamada seems to me to be closest to the mark, if one is to regard as a last will and testament Mishima's curious apologia *Sun and Steel*, published a few months before his death.

The opening sentences set the tone:

Of late, I have come to sense within myself an accumulation of all kinds of things that cannot find adequate expression via an objective artistic form such as the novel. A lyric poet of twenty might manage it, but I am twenty no longer.

Right off, the obsession with age. In an odd way, writers often predict their own futures. I doubt if Mishima was entirely conscious when he wrote *Forbidden Colors* at the age of twenty-five that he was drawing a possible portrait of himself at sixty-five: the famous, arid man of letters Shunsuké (his first collected edition was published at forty-five) "who hated the naked truth. He held firmly to the belief that any part of one's talent . . . which revealed itself spontaneously was a fraud." The old writer amuses himself during his last days by deliberately corrupting a beautiful youth (unhappily, the aesthetic influence of *Dorian Gray* is stronger here than that of *Les Liaisons Dangereuses*) whose initials are—such is the division even at twenty-five in Yukio Mishima—Y. M. The author is both beautiful blank youth and ancient seducer of mind. At the end the youth is left in limbo, heir to Shunsuké who, discreetly, gratefully, kills himself having used Y. M. to cause considerable mischief to others.

Mishima's novels are pervaded with death. In an early work, *Thirst for Love* (1950), a young widow reflects that "it was an occult thing, that sacrificial death she dreamed of, a suicide proffered not so much in mourning for her husband's death as in envy of that death." Later, in *Forbidden Colors*, "Suicide, whether a lofty thing or lowly, is rather a suicide of thought itself; in general, a suicide in which the subject does not think too much does not exist." Not the most elegant of sentences. The translator A. H. Marks usually writes plain American English with only an occasional "trains shrilling" or women "feeling nauseous." Yet from Mr. Marks's prose it is hard to determine whether or not Mishima's writing possesses much distinction in the original. I found Donald Keene's rendering of the dialogue of Mishima's Nō plays unusually eloquent and precise, the work of a different writer, one would say, or is it (heart sinking) simply the distinguished prose of a different translator who has got closer to the original. Unable to read Japanese, I shall never know. Luckily, United Statesmen have no great interest in language, preferring to wrestle with Moral Problems, and so one may entirely ignore the quality of the line (which is all that a writer has of his own) in order to deal with his Ideas, which are of course the property of all, and usually the least interesting thing about him.

Mishima refers to *Sun and Steel* as "confidential criticism." He tells us how he began his life as one besotted with words. And although he does not say so directly, one senses from his career (fame at nineteen, a facility for every kind of writing) that things were perhaps too easy for him. It must have seemed to him (and to his surprisingly unbitter contemporaries) that there was nothing he could not do in the novel, the essay, the drama. Yet only in his reworking of the Nō plays does he appear to transcend competence and make (to a foreign eye) literature. One gets the impression that he was the sort of writer who is reluctant to take the next hard step after the first bravura mastery of a form. But then he was, he tells us, aware from the beginning of "two contradictory tendencies within myself. One was the determination to press ahead loyally with the corrosive function of words, to make that my life's work. The other was the desire to encounter reality in some field where words should play no part."

This is the romantic's traditional and peculiar agony. There is no internal evidence that Mishima read D. H. Lawrence (his rather insistent cultural references consist of hymns in the Winckelmann manner to Greek statuary and the dropping of names like Pater, Beardsley, Poe, Baudelaire, de Sade), but one recognizes a similar tension in Mishima's work. The fascination with the bodies of others (in Mishima's case the young male with a "head like a young bull," "rows of flashing teeth"— sometimes it seems that his ideal is equipped with more than the regulation set of choppers—"wearing sneakers"), and the vain hope of somehow losing oneself in another's identity, fusing two bodies into something new and strange. But though homosexual encounters are in themselves quite as exciting as heterosexual encounters (more so, claim the great pederasts whose testimony echoes down the ages), it is not easy to build a universal philosophy on a kind of coupling that involves no procreative mystery—only momentary delight involving, if one is so minded, the enactment of ritual, the imposition of fantasy, the deliberate act of imagination without which there is no such thing as love or its philosophy, romanticism.

To judge from Mishima's writing, his love ritual was a complex one, and at the core of his madness. He quickly tired of the promiscuity which is so much easier for the homosexualist than for the heterosexualist. More to the point, Mishima could not trick himself into thinking, as Lawrence could, that a total surrender to the dark phallic god was a man's highest goal.

Mishima was too materialistic, too flesh-conscious for that. As for his own life, he married, had two children. But apparently sought pleasure elsewhere. A passage from one of the novels sounds as if taken from life. Mishima describes the bedding of a new husband and wife.

Yuichi's first night had been a model of the effort of desire, an ingenious impersonation that deceived an unexperienced buyer. . . . On the second night the successful impersonation became a faithful impersonation of an impersonation. . . . In the dark room the two of them slowly became four people. The intercourse of the real Yuichi with the boy he had made Yasuko into, and the intercourse of the makeshift Yuichi—imagining he could love a woman—with the real Yasuko had to go forward simultaneously.

One looks forward to the widow Mishima's memoirs.

In *Sun and Steel* Mishima describes the flowering of his own narcissism (a noun always used in a pejorative sense by the physically ill-favored) and his gradual realization that flesh is all. What is the "steel" of the title? Nothing more portentous than weight lifting, though he euphemizes splendidly in the French manner. Working on pecs and lats, Mishima found peace and a new sense of identity. "If the body could achieve perfect, nonindividual harmony, then it would be possible to shut individuality up forever in close confinement." It is easy to make fun of Mishima, particularly when his threnody to steel begins to sound like a brochure for Vic Tanney, but there is no doubt that in an age where there is little use for the male body's thick musculature, the deliberate development of that body is as good a pastime as any, certainly quite as legitimate a religion as Lawrence's blood consciousness, so much admired in certain literary quarters.

To Mishima the body is what one is; and a weak sagging body cannot help but contain a spirit to match. In moments of clarity (if not charity) Mishima is less stern with the soft majority, knows better. Nevertheless, "bulging muscles, a taut stomach and a tough skin, I reasoned, would correspond respectively to an intrepid fighting spirit. . . ."

Why did he want this warrior spirit? Why did he form a private army of dedicated ephebi? He is candid.

Specifically, I cherished a romantic impulse toward death, yet at the same time I required a strictly classical body as its vehicle; a peculiar sense of destiny made me believe that the reason why my romantic impulse toward death remained unfulfilled in reality was the immensely simple fact that I lacked the necessary physical qualifications.

There it is. For ten years he developed his body in order to kill it ritually in the most public way possible.

This is grandstanding of a sort far beyond the capacity of our local product. Telling Bobby Kennedy to go fuck himself at the White House is trivial indeed when compared to the high drama of cutting oneself open with a dagger and then submitting to decapitation before the army's chief of staff.

It should be noted, however, that Japanese classicists were appalled. "So vulgar," one of them told me, wincing at the memory. "*Seppuku* must be performed according to a precise and elegant ritual, *in private*, not" (a shudder) "in a general's office with a dozen witnesses. But then Mishima was entirely Westernized." I think this is true. Certainly he was devoted to French nineteenth-century writing, preferring Huysmans to Flaubert. In fact, his literary taste is profoundly corny, but then what one culture chooses to select from another is always a mysterious business. Gide once spoke to me with admiration of James M. Cain, adding, quite gratuitously, that he could not understand why anyone admired E. M. Forster.

Yet Mishima's passion for physical strength has no counterpart in Western letters. Few of the bourgeois inky men who created Western literature ever believed that the beauty of the sword was:

. . . in its allying death not with pessimism and impotence but with abounding energy, the flower of physical perfection and the will to fight. Nothing could be farther removed from the principle of literature. In literature, death is held in check yet at the same time used as a driving force; strength is devoted to the construction of empty fictions; life is held in reserve, blended to just the right degree with death, treated with preservatives, and lavished on the production of works of art that possess a weird eternal life. Action—one might say —perishes with the blossom. Literature is an imperishable flower. And an imperishable flower, of course, is an artificial flower. Thus to combine action and art is to combine the flower that wilts and the flower that lasts forever . . .

It is often wise (or perhaps compassionate is the better word) to allow an artist if not the last the crucial say on what he meant to make of himself and his life. Yet between what Mishima thought he was doing and what he did there is still confusion. When I arrived in Japan journalists kept asking me what I thought of his death. At first I thought they were simply being polite. I was vague, said I could not begin to understand an affair which seemed to me so entirely Japanese. I spoke solemnly of different cultures, different traditions. Told them that in the West we kill ourselves when we can't go on the way we would like to: a casual matter, really—there is no *seppuku* for us, only the shotgun or the bottle. But now that I have read *Sun and Steel* and a dozen of Mishima's early works, some for the first time, I see that what he did was entirely idiosyncratic. Here then, belatedly, the coroner's report on the headless body in the general's office.

Forty-five is a poignant time for the male, particularly for one who has been acutely conscious of his own body as well as those of others. Worshiping the flesh's health and beauty (American psychiatrists are particularly offended by this kind of obsession) is as valid an aesthetic—even a religion—as any other, though more tragic than most, for in the normal course half a life must be lived within the ruin of what one most esteemed. For Mishima the future of that body he had worked so hard to make worthy of a classic death (or life) was somber. Not all the sun and steel can save the aging athlete.

Yet Mishima wanted a life of the flesh, of action, divorced from words. Some interpreted this to mean that he dreamed of becoming a sort of warlord, restoring to Japan its ancient military virtues. But I think Mishima was after something much simpler: the exhaustion of the flesh in physical exercise, in bouts of love, in such adventures as becoming a private soldier for a few weeks in his middle age or breaking the sound barrier with a military jet.

Certainly Mishima did not have a political mind. He was a Romantic Artist in a very *fin de siècle* French way. But instead of deranging the senses through drugs, Mishima tried to lose his conscious mind (his art) through the use and worship of his own flesh and that of others. Finally, rather than face the slow bitter dissolution of the incarnate self, he chose to die. He could not settle for the common fate, could not echo the healthy dryness of the tenth-century poet (in the *Kokinshū*) who wrote: "If only when one heard/ that old age was coming/ one could bolt the door/ and refuse to meet him!" The Romantic showman chose to die as he had lived, in a blaze of publicity.

Now for some moralizing in the American manner. Mishima's death is explicable. Certainly he has prepared us, and himself, for it. In a most dramatic way the perishable flower is self-plucked. And there are no political overtones. But what of the artificial flowers he left behind? Mishima was a writer who mastered every literary form, up to a point. Reading one of his early novels, I was disturbed by an influence I recognized but could not place right off. The book was brief, precise, somewhat reliant on *coups de théâtre*, rather too easy in what it attempted but elegant and satisfying in a conventional way like . . . like Anatole France, whom I had not read since adolescence. *Le Lys Rouge*, I wrote in the margin. No sooner had I made this note than there appeared in the text the name Anatole France. I think this is the giveaway. Mishima was fatally drawn to what is easy in art.

Technically, Mishima's novels are unadventurous. This is by no means a fault. But it is a commentary on his art that he never made anything entirely his own. He was too quickly satisfied with familiar patterns and by no means the best. Only in his reworking of the Nō plays does Mishima, paradoxically, seem "original," glittering and swift in his effects, like Ibsen at the highest. What one recalls from the novels are simply fleshly obsessions and sadistic reveries: invariably the beloved youth is made to bleed while that sailor who fell from grace with the sea (the nature of this grace is never entirely plain) gets cut to pieces by a group of pubescent males. The conversations about art are sometimes interesting but seldom brilliant (in the American novel there are no conversations about art, a negative virtue, but still a virtue).

There is in Mishima's work, as filtered through his translators, no humor, little wit; there is irony, but of the W. Somerset Maugham variety . . . things are not what they seem, the respectable are secretly vicious. Incidentally, for those who think that Japanese culture is heavy, portentous, bloody, and ritual-minded (in other words, like Japanese samurai films), one should point out that neither of the founders of Japanese prose literature (the Lady Murasaki and Sei-Shōnagon) was too profound for wit. In Sei-Shōnagon's case quite the contrary.

As Japan's most famous and busy writer, Mishima left not a garden but an entire landscape full of artificial flowers. But, Mishima notwithstanding, the artificial flower is quite as perishable as the real. It just makes a bigger mess when you try to recycle it. I suspect that much of his boredom with words* had to do with a temperamental lack of interest in them. The novels show no particular development over the years and little variety. In the later books, the obsessions tend to take over, which is never enough (if it were, the Marquis de Sade

---

*A number of professional Nipponophiles were upset by this passage. Didn't I know that Mishima (in the phrase of one academic lint-head) was "a consummate word-smith," fascinated by language? I did. Boredom with words referred to Mishima's account (on page 382) of the two contradictory tendencies in himself: the life of words versus the life of action. At the end romantic action won out; words failed him—in every sense.

would be as great as the enemies of art claim).

Mishima was a minor artist in the sense that, as Auden tells us, once the minor artist "has reached maturity and found himself he ceases to have a history. The major artist, on the other hand, is always re-finding himself, so that the history of his works recapitulates or mirrors the history of art." Unable or unwilling to change his art, Mishima changed his life through sun, steel, death, and so became a major art-figure in the only way—I fear—our contemporaries are apt to understand: not through the work, but through the life. Mishima can now be ranked with such "great" American novelists as Hemingway (who never wrote a good novel) and Fitzgerald (who wrote only one). So maybe their books weren't so good but they sure had interesting lives, and desperate last days. Academics will enjoy writing about Mishima for a generation or two. And one looks forward to their speculations as to what he might have written had he lived. Another *A la recherche du temps perdu*? or *Les caves du Vatican*? Neither, I fear. My Ouija board has already spelled out what was next on the drawing board: *Of Human Bondage.*

Does any of this matter? I suspect not. After all, literature is no longer of very great interest even to the makers. It may well be that that current phenomenon, the writer who makes his life his art, is the most useful of all. If so, then perhaps Mishima's artificial flowers were never intended to survive the glare of sun and steel or compete with his own fleshly fact, made bloody with an ax. What, after all, has a mask to confess except that it covers a skull? All honor then to a man who lived and died the way he wanted to. I only regret we never met, for friends found him a good companion, a fine drinking partner, and fun to cruise with.

The New York Review of Books, June 17, 1971

WOMEN'S LIBERATION MEETS MILLER-MAILER-MANSON MAN

Every schoolboy has a pretty good idea of what the situation was down at Sodom but what went on in Gomorrah is as mysterious to us as the name Achilles took when he went among women. Or was. Thanks to Eva Figes, author of *Patriarchal Attitudes*, we now know what Gomorrheans are up to. Miss Figes quotes from an eighth-century Palestinian midrash which tries to explain the real reason for the Flood (one of the better jokes in the Old Testament). Apparently passage on the Ark was highly restricted. "Some authorities say that according to God's orders, if the male lorded it over the female of his own kind, both were admitted but not otherwise."

The Founding Father had strong views on the position of woman (under the man) and one of the few mistakes he ever admitted to was the creation of Lilith as a mate for Adam. Using the same dust as his earthly replica . . . but let us hear it in his own words, rabbinically divined in the fifth century.

Adam and Lilith never found peace together; for when he wished to lie with her, she took offense at the recumbent posture he demanded. "Why must I lie beneath you?" she asked. "I also was made from dust, and am therefore your equal." Because Adam tried to compel her obedience by force, Lilith, in a rage, uttered the magic name of God, rose into the air and left him.

The outcast Lilith is still hanging about the *Zeitgeist*, we are told, causing babies to strangle in their sleep, men to have wet dreams, and Kate Millett, Betty Friedan, Germaine Greer, and Eva Figes to write books.

The response to *Sexual Politics, Feminine Mystique*, et al. has been as interesting as anything that has happened in our time, with the possible exception of Richard Nixon's political career. The hatred these girls have inspired is to me convincing proof that their central argument is valid. Men do hate women (or as Germaine Greer puts it: "Women have very little idea of how much men hate them") and dream of torture, murder, flight.

It is no accident that in the United States the phrase "sex and violence" is used as one word to describe acts of equal wickedness, equal fun, equal danger to that law and order our masters would impose upon us. Yet equating sex with violence does change the nature of each (words govern us more than anatomy), and it is quite plain that those who fear what they call permissiveness do so because they know that if sex is truly freed of taboo it will lead to torture and murder because that is what *they* dream of or, as Norman Mailer puts it, "Murder offers us the promise of vast relief. It is never unsexual."

There has been from Henry Miller to Norman Mailer to Charles Manson a logical progression. The Miller-Mailer-Manson man (or M3 for short) has been conditioned to think of women as, at best, breeders of sons; at worst, objects to be poked, humiliated, killed. Needless to say, M3's reaction to Women's Liberation has been one of panic. He believes that if women are allowed parity with men they will treat men the way men have treated women and that, even M3 will agree, has not been very well or, as Cato the Censor observed, if woman be made man's equal she will swiftly become his master.

M3 knows that women are dangerously different from men, and not as intelligent (though they have their competencies: needlework, child-care, detective stories). When a woman does show herself to be superior at, say, engineering, Freud finessed that anomaly by reminding us that since she is a bisexual, like everyone else, her engineering skill simply means that she's got a bit too much of the tomboy in her, as W. C. Fields once remarked to Grady Sutton on a similar occasion.

Women are not going to make it until M3 is reformed, and that is going to take a long time. Meanwhile the current phase of the battle is intense and illuminating. M3 is on the defensive, shouting names; he thinks that to scream "dyke" is enough to make the girls burst into tears, but so far they have played it cool. Some have even admitted to a bit of dyking now and then along with warm mature heterosexual relationships of the deeply meaningful fruitful kind that bring much-needed children into the world ("Good fucks make good babies"—N. Mailer). I love you Marion and I love you too Marvin. The women are responding with a series of books and position papers that range from shrill to literature. In the last category one must place Eva Figes who, of the lot, is the only one whose work can be set beside John Stuart Mill's celebrated review of the subject and not seem shoddy or self-serving.

In effect, the girls are all writing the same book. Each does a quick biological tour of the human body, takes on Moses and St. Paul, congratulates Mill, savages Freud (that mistake about vaginal orgasm has cost him glory), sighs over Marx, roughs up M3 and concludes with pleas for child-care centers, free abortions, equal pay, and—in most cases—an end to marriage. These things seem to be well worth accomplishing. And even M3 is now saying that of course women should be paid the same as men for the same work. On that point alone Women's Lib has already won an important battle because, until recently, M3 was damned if a woman was going to be paid as much as he for the same job.

Figes begins her short, elegant work with an attempt to define masculine and feminine. Is there any real difference between male and female other than sexual gear? Figes admits to the systematic fluctuation of progesterone levels during the woman's menstrual cycle and pregnancy, and these fluctuations make for "moods," which stop with menopause. Yet Figes makes a most telling point when she observes that although there is little or no hormonal difference between girls and boys before puberty, by the age of four or five boys are acting in a very different manner from girls. Since there is no hormonal explanation for this, the answer is plainly one of indoctrination.

What Figes is saying and what anyone who has ever thought with any seriousness about the human estate knows is that we are, or try to be, what our society wants us to be. There is nothing innate in us that can be called masculine or feminine. We have certain common drives involving survival. Yet our drive toward procreation, oddly enough, is not as powerful as our present-day obsession with sex would lead us to believe.

Of all mammals, man is the only one who must be taught how to mate. In open societies this is accomplished through observation but in a veiled, minatory, Puritan society, sex is a dirty secret, the body shameful, and making love a guilty business, often made dreadful through plain ignorance of what to do. Yet the peripheral male and female roles are carefully taught us. A little girl is given a doll instead of a chemistry set. That she might not like dolls, might prefer a chemistry set, will be the start of a nice neurosis for her, a sense of guilt that she is not playing the part society wants her to play. This arbitrary and brutal shaping of men and women has filled the madhouses of the West, particularly today when the kind of society we still prepare children for (man outside at work, woman at home with children) is no longer the only possibility for a restless generation.

Figes quotes Lévi-Strauss. "Men do not act as members of

a group, in accordance with what each feels as an individual; each man feels as a function of the way in which he is permitted or obliged to act. Customs are given as external norms before giving rise to internal sentiments, and these non-sentiment norms determine the sentiments of individuals as well as the circumstances in which they may, or must, be displayed." One sees this in our society's emphasis on what Hemingway called "grace under pressure," or that plain old-fashioned patriotism which so often means nothing more than persuading a man to kill a man he does not know. To get him to do this the society must with its full weight pervert the normal human instinct not to kill a stranger against whom one has no grudge.

This kind of conditioning is necessary for the maintenance of that acquisitive, warrior society to which we belong, a society which now appears to be cracking up in the United States (the dread Consciousness Three emerging?), to the despair of M3, not to mention those financial interests whose profits depend upon the exploitation and conquest of distant lands and markets. Concentrating on social pressures, Figes has written a book concerned with those external norms "which give rise to internal sentiments, with the organization of emotions into sentiments."

For those who like to remind the girls that no woman wrote anything in the same class as *Paradise Lost* or painted anything like the Sistine Chapel or composed *Don Carlos* (in the novel the girls hold their own), Figes observes that women were not expected to do that sort of thing and so did not. It is easy for a talented boy to be a sculptor because there are other males whom he can identify with and learn from. But society does everything to discourage a girl from making the attempt; and so she stifles as best she can whatever secret yearning she might have to shape stone, and gets on with the dishes.

In recent years, however, women have begun to invade (M3's verb) fields traditionally assigned to men. Eventually, M3 will have to face the fact that the arts and sciences are not masculine or feminine activities, but simply human ones. Incidentally, all the girls have a go at one Otto Weininger, a nineteenth-century *philosophe* who at twenty-three wrote a book to prove that women were incapable of genius, then killed himself. The girls tend unkindly to cackle over that.

Figes does the obligatory chapters on Moses and St. Paul, those proud misogynists whose words have caused so much misery down the millennia. The hatred of women that courses through both Old and New Testaments is either lunatic or a mask for something else. What were the Patriarchs so afraid of? Is Robert Graves right after all? Was there really a Great Mother cult the Patriarchs destroyed? Were the attacks on woman political in origin? to discredit the Great Mother and her priestesses? We shall never know.

Perhaps it is simply guilt. People don't like their slaves very much. Women were—and in some cases still are—slaves to men, and attempts to free slaves must be put down. Also, as Figes puts it, "Human beings have always been particularly slow to accept ideas that diminish their own absolute supremacy and importance." For men, "like all people who are privileged by birth and long tradition, the idea of sharing could only mean giving up."

According to Figes, "The rise of capitalism is the root cause of the modern social and economic discrimination against women, which came to a peak in the last century." She remarks upon the degree of equality women enjoyed in Tudor times. From Portia to Rosalind, women existed as people in their own right. But with the simultaneous rise of Puritanism and industry, woman was more and more confined to the home—when she was not exploited in the factories as a cheap source of labor. Also, the Puritan tide (now only beginning to ebb) served to remind man that woman was unclean, sinful, less than he, and the cause of his fall. It was in those years that M3 was born, emigrated to America, killed Indians, enslaved blacks, conned women with sonorous good manners to get them into the wilderness, then tried to dominate them but never quite succeeded: a woman in a covered wagon with a rifle on her lap is going to be a formidable opponent, as the American woman has proved to be, from Daisy Miller to Kate Millett (a name James would have savored, weakly changing "i" to "a").

What does the American woman want? asks M3 plaintively. Doesn't she kill off her husbands with mantis-abandon, inherit the money, become a Mom to Attis-like sons, dominate primary education (most American men are "feminized" in what they would regard as the worst sense of that word by being brought up almost entirely by women and made to conform to American female values which are every bit as twisted as American male values)?

Yet the American woman who seems to have so much is still very much a victim of patriarchal attitudes—after all, she is made to believe that marriage is the most important thing in life, a sentiment peculiarly necessary to a capitalist society in which marriage is still the employer's best means of controlling the employee. The young man with a child and pregnant wife is going to do as he is told. The young man or woman on his own might not be so tractable. Now that organized religion is of little social significance, the great corporations through advertising (remember "Togetherness"?) and hiring policies favor the married, while looking with great suspicion on the bachelor who might be a Commie Weirdo Fag or a Pro-Crypto dyke. As long as marriage (and Betty Friedan's *Feminine Mystique*) are central to our capitalism (and to its depressing Soviet counterpart) neither man nor woman can be regarded as free to be human.

"In a society where men have an overriding interest in the acquisition of wealth, and where women themselves have become a form of property, the link between sexuality and money becomes inextricable." This is grim truth. Most men buy their wives, though neither party would admit to the nature of the transaction, preferring such euphemisms as Marvin is a good provider and Marion is built. Then Marion divorces Marvin and takes him to the cleaners, and he buys with whatever is left a younger model. It is money, not sex, that Puritans want. After all, the English word for "coming" used to be "spending": you spend your seed in the woman's bank and, if the moon is right, nine months later you will get an eight-pound dividend.

Needless to say, if you buy a woman you don't want anyone else using her. To assure your rights, you must uphold all the taboos against any form of sex outside marriage. Figes draws an interesting parallel between our own society and the Mainus, as reported by Margaret Mead.

There was such a close tie between women and property that adultery was always a threat to the economic system. These people devalued sex, were prudish, and tended to equate the sex act with the excretory functions and, perhaps most significant of all, had commercial prostitution which is rare in primitive societies.

Rousseau is briskly dealt with by the girls: his rights of man were just that, for men. He believed women "should reign in the home as a minister reigns in the state, by contriving to be ordered to do what she wants." Darwin? According to Figes, "Darwin was typically a creature of his age in seeing the class and economic struggles as a continuation of the evolutionary one." In this struggle woman was *hors de combat*. "The chief distinction in the intellectual powers of the two sexes is shown by man attaining to a higher eminence, in whatever he takes up, than woman can attain, etc." Schopenhauer found woman "in every respect backward, lacking in reason and true morality . . . a kind of middle step between the child and the man, who is the true human being."

Figes finds a link between anti-feminism and anti-Semitism. It is called Nietzsche. "Man should be trained for war and woman for the recreation of the warrior: all else is folly." Like the effeminate Jews, women subvert the warrior ideal, demanding sympathy for the poor and the weak. Hitler's reaction to this rousing philosophy has not gone unnoticed.

Like her fellow polemicists, Figes is at her most glittering with Freud . . . one almost wrote "poor Freud," as Millett calls him. Apparently Freud's gravest limitation was an inability to question the status quo of the society into which he was born. Politically, he felt that "it is just as impossible to do without control of the mass by a minority as it is to dispense with coercion in the work of civilization. For the masses are lazy and unintelligent."

To Freud, civilization meant a Spartan denial of pleasure in the present in order to enjoy solvency and power in middle age. Unhappily, the main line of Freudian psychoanalysis has served well the status quo by insisting that if one is not happy with one's lot, a better adjustment to society must be made because society is an unalterable fact, not to be trifled with or changed. Now, of course, every assumption about the rights of society as opposed to those of the individual is in question, and Freud's complacency seems almost as odd to us as his wild notion that clitoral excitement was a wicked (immature) thing in a grown woman, and the longer she resisted making the transfer from the tiny pseudo-penis to the heavenly inner space of the vagina (Erik Erikson is not in the girls' good books either) the sicker she would become.

One would like to have been a fly on the wall of that Vienna study as one woman after another tearfully admitted to an itch that would not go away, despite the kindly patriarch's attempts to get to the root of the problem. It is a nice irony that the man who said that anatomy is destiny took no trouble to learn woman's anatomy. He did *know* that the penis was the essential symbol and fact of power and primacy otherwise (and his reasoning was circular) why would girls envy boys' having penises? Why would little boys suffer from fears of castration if they did not instinctively know that the penis is a priceless sign of God the Father, which an envious teeth-lined cunt might want to snap off? Figes's response to Freud's circle is reasonable.

In a society not sexually repressive little boys would be unlikely to develop castration fears; in a society where all the material rewards did not go to those endowed with penises there would be no natural envy of that regalia.

M3's counterattack is only now gathering momentum. So far Figes appears to be unknown to United Statesmen, but Millett has been attacked hereabouts with a ferocity usually reserved for major novelists. She should feel important. The two principal spokesmen for M3 to weigh in so far are Norman Mailer and Irving Howe. Mailer's answer to Millett ("The Prisoner of Sex" in *Harper's*) gave the impression of being longer than her book *Sexual Politics*. Part of this is due to a style which now resembles H. P. Lovecraft rather more than the interesting, modest Mailer of better days. Or as Emma Cockburn (excellent name for a Women's Libber) pointed out, Mailer's thoughts on sex read like three days of menstrual flow.

Mailer begins by reminding the reader who he is. This is cunning and necessary in a country with no past. We learn of marriages, children, prizes (the Nobel is almost at hand), the great novel he will one day write, the rejection of *Time*'s offer to put him on the cover which Millett then gets for, among other things, attacking him. His credits given, he counterattacks, says she writes like a tough faggot, a literary Mafiosa, calls her comrade and commissar. He then makes some excellent points on her disingenuous use of quotations from Miller and Lawrence (she has a tendency to replace those qualifying phrases which make M3 seem human with three dots).

But Mailer's essential argument boils down to the following points. Masturbation is bad and so is contraception because the whole point to sex between man and woman is conception. Well, that's what the Bible says, too. He links homosexuality with evil. The man who gives in to his homosexual drives is consorting with the enemy. Worse, not only does he betray moral weakness by not fighting those drives but he is a coward for not daring to enter into competition with other Alpha males for toothsome females. This is dizzy but at least a new thought. One of the many compliments Mailer has tendered M3 over the years is never having succumbed to whatever homosexual urges M3 might have had. Now, to M2's shock, instead of getting at least a Congressional Medal of Honor for heroism, he sees slowly descending upon his brow an unmistakable dunce cap. All that hanging about boxers, to no good end!

Finally, Mailer's attitude toward woman is pretty much that of any VFW commander in heartland America. He can never understand that a woman is not simply a creature to be used for breeding (his "awe" at the thought of her procreative function is blarney), that she is as human as he is, and that he is dangerous to her since one of his most American dreams was of a man who murdered his wife and then buggered another woman against her will as celebration of the glorious deed.

Miller-Mailer-Manson. Woman, beware. Righteous murder stalks the land, for did not the Lord thy God say, "In sorrow thou shalt bring forth children. And thy desire shall be thy husband. And he shall rule over thee." Which brings us to Figes's remark, "We cannot be iconoclasts, we cannot relinquish the old gods because so much has been sacrificed to them."

Irving Howe's tone is apoplectic. He *knows* what the relations between men and women ought to be and no Millett is going to change his mind or pervert other women if he can do anything about it—which is to write a great deal on the subject in a magazine piece called "The Middle Class Mind of Kate Millett." Astonishingly enough, the phrase "middle class" is used in a pejorative sense, not the most tactful thing to do in a middle-class country. Particularly when one is not only middle class oneself but possessed of a brow that is just this side of high.

Anyway, Howe was aroused enough to address to her a series of *ad hominem* (*ad hysteram?*) insults that are startling even by the vicious and mindless standards of New York book-chat writing. Millett is "squalid," "feckless," "morally shameful," a failed scholar, a female impersonator, and so on. But Howe is never able to take on the essential argument of the girls. Men have enslaved women, made them second-rate citizens, made them hate themselves (this to me is the worst of all . . . I'm a man's woman, says the beauty complacently, I don't like other women; meaning, I don't like myself), and now that woman is beginning to come alive, to see herself as the equal of man, Rabbi Howe is going to strike her down for impertinence, just as the good Christian knows that "it is shameful for women to speak in church."

Howe has always had an agreeable gift for literary demolition and his mind, though hardly of the first quality, is certainly good by American academic standards. But now watch him tie himself in a knot. Millett makes the point, as Figes does, that the Nazis were anti-woman and pro-family. Woman was breeder, man was warrior. Now Irving doesn't want the Nazis to be so "sensible," so much like himself. He writes:

The comedy of all this is that Miss Millett prints, at one point, a footnote quoting from a book by Joseph Folsom. "The Nazis have always wanted to strengthen the family as an instrument of the state. *State interest is always paramount.* Germany does not hesitate to turn a husband against a wife or children against parents when political loyalty is involved." (Emphasis added.) Miss Millett prints this footnote but clearly does not understand it: otherwise she would recognize how completely it undermines her claim that in the totalitarian countries the "sexual counterrevolution" consisted in the reinforcement of the family.

This passage would make a good test question for a class in logic. Find where Howe misses or distorts the point to the Folsom footnote. Point one: the Nazis strengthened the family yet put the state first. All agreed? What does this mean? It means that, on occasion, Nazis would try to turn members of a family against one another *"when political loyalty is involved."* (Emphasis added.) O.K.? Well, class, how many people are politically subversive in any country at any time? Not many, alas; therefore Millett's point still stands that the Nazis celebrated old-time family virtues except in cases of suspected subversion.

Howe's piece is full of this sort of thing and I can only assume that his usually logical mind has been unhinged by all these unnatural girls. Howe ends with a celebration of the values of his immigrant parents in the Depression years. Apparently his mother was no more a drudge than his father (but why in a good society should either be a drudge?), and they were happy in the old-time Mosaic, St. Pauline, Freudian way, and . . . well, this hymn to tribal values was rather better sung by the judge in the movie version of *Little Murders*.

Those who have been treated cruelly will treat others cruelly. This seems to be a fact of our condition. M3 has every reason to be fearful of woman's revenge should she achieve equality. He is also faced with the nightmare (for him) of being used as a sexual object or, worse, being ignored (the menacing cloud in the middle distance is presently no larger than a vibrator). He is fighting back on every front.

Take pornography. Though female nudes have been usually acceptable in our Puritan culture, until recently the male nude was unacceptable to the Patriarchs. After all, the male—any male—is a stand-in for God, and God wears a suit at all times, or at least jockey shorts. Now, thanks to randy Lilith, the male can be shown entirely nude but, say the American censors, never with an erection. The holy of holies, the totem of our race, the symbol of the Patriarchs' victory over the Great Mother must be respected. Also, as psychologists point out, though women are not as prone to stimulus through looking at pictures as men (is this innate or the result of conditioning?), they are more excited by pictures of the male erect than of the male at ease. And excitement of course is bad for them, gives them ideas, makes them insatiable; even the ancient Greeks, though freer in sexual matters than we, took marriage seriously. As a result, only unmarried girls could watch naked young men play because young girls ought to be able to look over a field which married women had better not know about.

Today we are witnessing the breakup of patterns thousands of years old. M3's response is predictable: if man on top of woman has been the pattern for all our known history, it must be right. This of course was the same argument he made when the institution of slavery was challenged. After all, slavery was quite as old an institution as marriage. With the rejection of the idea of ownership of one person by another at the time of our Civil War, Women's Lib truly began. If you could not own a black man, you could not own a woman either. So the war began. Needless to say, the forces of reaction are very much in the saddle (in every sense), and women must fight for their equality in a system which wants to keep them in manageable family groups, buying consumer goods, raising future consumers, until the end of time—or the world's raw resources, which is rather closer at hand.

Curiously enough, not even Figes senses what is behind this new restiveness, this new desire to exist not as male or female but as human. It is very simple: we are breeding ourselves into extinction. We cannot feed the people now alive. In thirty-seven years the world's population will double unless we have the "good luck" to experience on the grandest scale famine, plague, war. To survive we must stop making babies at the current rate, and this can only be accomplished by breaking the ancient stereotypes of man the warrior, woman the breeder. M3's roar is that of our tribal past, quite unsuitable, as the old Stalinists used to say, to new necessities.

Figes feels that a change in the economic system will free women (and men) from unwanted roles. I have another idea. Free the sexes first and the system will have to change. There will be no housewife to be conned into buying things she does not need. But all this is in the future. The present is the battleground, and the next voice you hear will be that of a patriarch, defending his attitudes—on a stack of Bibles.

The New York Review of Books, July 22, 1971

THE FOURTH DIARY
OF ANAÏS NIN

Last year, Anaïs Nin cabled me in Rome: Volume Four of her diaries (1944–47) was to be published. She needed my permission to print what she had written about me. Into the time machine, I thought, as I entered the bar of the Pont Royal in Paris—to find Anaïs, at sixty-seven, as beautiful as ever. "I've been on television all day. West German television, with Jeanne Moreau. In the park." She gave me a hard look. (I had been told that she thought the character of Marietta Donegal in *Two Sisters* was based on her).

"I've marked the pages where you appear. It's very systematic. Edmund Wilson was wonderful about his portrait." Fifteen-love, Vidal's serve. "Now, anything you want cut, I'll take out. But if there is too much to cut, then the whole thing comes out." I was torn. I believe nothing should be suppressed; yet I knew all about Anaïs's "portraits." Once she had copied out in a red notebook everything she had written about me over the years. I kept the notebook for some months, unopened (I had read parts of the diary before); not pleased, she took it back.

Now, drinking tea, I read dutifully the pages that she showed me (not, incidentally, the entire portrait—several fine warts were withheld for the current exhibition). I suggested that she cut a line or two involving a third person. She agreed, obviously relieved that I, too, was intent on being wonderful. Then I was reproached for *Two Sisters.*

"I didn't read it, of course—I don't read that sort of book—but I was told it was a hideous caricature." I explained that neither the character of Marietta Donegal (a racketing, boisterous American lady of letters) nor the Relationship (with Anaïs one feels that the word "relationship" deserves a capital "R" —at least to start with) between her and me in the novel-memoir was at all like ours in life; in fact, rather the reverse. But I did admit that Marietta's "philosophy" ("We must flow deeply from the core of our inner being") was very much like hers and I thought that in an age when mind was under fire and feeling worshiped, a playful travesty was in order. She took that well enough. She was aware that we no longer felt the same way about things. "Anyway, you said—I was told—that I wrote well."

Who then is Anaïs Nin? Born in 1903; daughter of a Spanish composer-pianist; brought up in France; unhappily transplanted to New York as a child, where she began to keep a diary in order to win her absent father's love—a tall order and, consequently, a vast diary running now to many millions of words.

In the early thirties Anaïs returned to France, married a wealthy businessman (not mentioned in her earlier volumes), played at being a poor artist ("Never understood until now— 1945—why I had to make myself poor enough in Paris to go to the pawnshop. It was because all my friends went there, and I wanted to reach the same level of poverty and denial"), met and helped to launch Henry Miller. She also began to write poetic monologues like *House of Incest* and *Winter of Artifice.*

At the start of the war, she came back to New York, with

404

a second wealthy husband who makes—at his request—no appearance in the diaries. Together they created a romantic Bohemian atmosphere in a five-floor walk-up apartment in the Village. Again she played at poverty (I was shocked when she told me one day that I should let her husband pay for dinner because he was not a poor artist, as they had pretended, but a banker). Failing to get her books published commercially, she printed them herself.

One of the books was a volume of short stories, "Under a Glass Bell." Edmund Wilson praised it in *The New Yorker*. She was overnight a celebrity, and the present diary begins.

Right off, we meet her life-force companion of earlier days, Gonzalo. He is working at the press she has financed, and helped him, physically, to set up. "Gonzalo has assumed leadership. He is proud of his place, his machine, his independence. I am very tired, but content. I am proud of my human creation." She is not unlike the Feiffer heroine who wants "a strong man that I can mould." Her persistent fantasy is that she is Joan of Arc forever putting Dauphins on the throne. Unfortunately, whenever Dauphin becomes King, she becomes regicide—that is, when she does not try to seize the throne herself—a normal human power drive, as Women's Lib has taught us, but for a Latin woman of her generation, a source of shame and guilt.

As the months pass, Gonzalo does not keep his word, is destructive, must be sent to Peru—and she worries about how much of herself she gives to others: "Did my faith in Henry [Miller] make him strong enough to go on without me? Does one really create strength in others, or does one merely become that strength?" Each Relationship begins on a high note, and ends with recriminations.

Meanwhile, Edmund Wilson has fallen in love with Anaïs but she prefers the companionship of several young men ("the transparent children") who shield her from the grossness of the harsh, competitive New York world. Incidentally, although she resolutely invades the privacy of others, her own is respected. We never know whom she goes to bed with. But certain emotional patterns do keep recurring and one can work out, up to a point, her Relationships.

It is fun to watch Anaïs as she becomes a figure in the High Bohemia of New York, the world of surrealist emigrés like Breton, of such native ground figures as James Agee, Richard Wright, Maya Deren (another relationship—small "r"— which starts magically and ends with recriminations: Maya made Anaïs look old in her film "Ritual and Ordeal"). Then, 1945, we meet the twenty-year-old author of the novel *Williwaw*, Warrant Officer (still in uniform) Gore Vidal, recently returned from the Aleutians, more recently hired as an editor by E. P. Dutton—where I lasted six months in order to get them to publish Anaïs's *Ladders to Fire* and *Children of the Albatross*. Incidentally, the photograph of me in the book is labeled "Gore Vidal at seventeen." It is actually Gore Vidal at twenty-one, looking glum as a result of a dose of clap picked up the week before in Guatemala City.

Volume Four is most interesting when it deals with Anaïs's career and the way she went about promoting it. She is forever conferring with book publishers, with editors of *Harper's Bazaar* and *Town and Country*, posing for photographs, meeting helpful people, lecturing. At Harvard "I wore a black dress and a shocking pink scarf. I won many people, even some who were openly prejudiced. . . ." She frets about bad reviews, presides eventually over the dissolution of her court of young men. Like everyone else, the children fail her, too.

She strikes a "death blow" at me, ending Phase One of a long, long Relationship. Then, with a friend, she drives across America. This is much the pleasantest part of the journal, for she responds with an uncharacteristic directness and delight to landscape. In Big Sur she meets Miller again, and his new wife. Next she moves on to Acapulco—a fishing village in those days, and there the diary ends.

Over the years defenders of Anaïs Nin—myself included— have maintained that whatever the shortcomings of her books, the diaries, their primal source, would one day establish her as a great sensibility. Now here they are, and I am not so certain. Admittedly, she has left out a great deal. Of the two analysts she was going to (1944–47), only one is mentioned. And at least two Meaningful Relationships are entirely omitted. What she has done is shrewdly excerpt those pages which deal with people well known to readers today. The result is not the whole truth but an interesting *tour d'horizon* of her works and days, loves and hates among the celebrated of lost time, and for me reading her is like a feast of madeleines awash with tea.

The commonest complaint about Anaïs's work is its (her) narcissism. Since I cannot think of any modern writer who is not a narcissist (if you cannot love yourself, you cannot love anyone), it seems to me unfair to accuse her of a fault common to our monkey race. Yet her self-absorption does put people off and I think it has to do with what Wilson calls her "solemn, hieratic style." Not only does she write an inflated, oracular prose, but she is never able to get outside her characters. This would be tolerable if she were able to illuminate their interiors; something she seldom does, and for an odd reason.

There are two kinds of narcissist: objective and subjective. The objective looks into the mirror and sees the lines, sees death upon the brow, and records it. The subjective stares with rapture into the mirror, sees a vision no one else can see and, if he lacks great art, fails entirely to communicate it. At her best, Anaïs Nin can write very beautifully indeed. Suddenly a phrase gleams upon the page: she does notice things, one decides, looking forward to the next line but then the dread flow of adjectives begins and one realizes that she is not seeing but writing. Since she is not a fool, she is aware of her limitations, yet, like the rest of us, she rather treasures them. "What had happened is that I have touched off such a deep level of unconscious life that the women" (in *Ladders to Fire*) "lose their separate and instinctive traits and flow into one another. As if I were writing about the night life of woman and it all became one." Not able to deal with other women, she can only write of herself apostrophized. People exist for her only as pairs of eyes in which to catch her own reflection. No wonder their owners so often disappoint her. They want mirrors, too.

The diaries present a real problem. Anaïs is dealing with actual people. Yet I would not recognize any of them (including myself) had she not carefully labeled each specimen. She is particularly devastating in her portrait of Edmund Wilson. She disliked him almost from the beginning. But since he was the most important critic of the day, even she saw a good deal of him, played at loving friendship. At lunch, "I felt his distress, received his confession. He tells me about his sufferings with Mary McCarthy."

Later Anaïs writes to a young friend, Leonard, assuring him that she prefers his company to that of Wilson "who asserts his opinions, beliefs, and knowledge as the ultimate verity." Then she gives us a fine description of an evening at Wilson's empty house ("Mary took away all the furniture"). But "when he talked about my work, he had more to say about the flaws of 'Winter of Artifice' and little about the achievements." The evening ends with Wilson in the street, crying after her, "Don't desert me! Don't leave me alone!" Like Georges Sand, Anaïs Nin is no gentleman. She meditates on going to bed with him, but decides "if he ever tastes of me, [he] will be eating a substance not good for him, some phosphorescent matter which illuminates the soul and does not answer to lust." The Relationship ends when he offers to teach her how to write, and presents her with a complete set of Jane Austen, the perfect insult. She responds seriously, "I am not an imitator of past styles." This is splendid comedy of the Meredithean sort; made all the finer by the fact that at no point is she aware of having been in the presence of America's best mind. But then Wilson represents all that she hates, history, politics, literature. To her, mind and feeling must be forever at war. Thus has she systematically unbalanced both art and life.

If there is one theme to Volume Four, it is Anaïs's formidable will to power. Yet she is able to write, apropos my own, "For the first time I saw a contrast in our aims. [Gore's] interest is like Miller's, to meet everybody, to win the world." She is even able to record with a straight pen, "Writing in a diary developed several habits: a habit of honesty (because no one imagines the diary will ever be read)." This was written in June 1946, when, at her insistence, I was trying to get Dutton to publish the childhood diary. The diary was always meant to be read, for it was her vindication, her victory over the unloving father.

Anaïs Nin has been, literally, avant-garde. In her contempt for intellect, her mystical belief in Love (the record of human disaster in the journals is not the whole story), in her whole-hearted acceptance of psychoanalysis and astrology, she was a precursor of that generation which now grooves along emotional lines she helped engineer. For them, too, there is no history, no literature, no mind. Feeling is everything and astrology, like man, is heavy. But then mind has never had more than a fragile foothold in the United States, a society where intelligence is always on sufferance, as D. H. Lawrence observed, and subject to the majority's will.

Warning to literary historians. Deal warily with Anaïs's "facts." Small example: at our first meeting, she says, I introduced myself as Lieutenant Vidal. First, I would never have used a military title; second, I was plainly a Warrant Officer, in uniform. When I pointed this out to her in the bar of the Pont Royal, she laughed gaily. "You know, I never get those things right." Nor does she correct them. Best of the lines I was not shown (and the one most apt to give pleasure to the employees at *Time*), "Gore has a prejudice against Negroes." Oh, dear. Well, I was brought up by my grandfather, a Mississippi-born senator. I have since matured. I now have a prejudice against whites.

Finally, I do not really recognize Anaïs—or myself—in these bitter pages. Yet when I think of her and the splendid times we had so many years ago, I find myself smiling, recalling with pleasure her soft voice, her French accent, and the way she always said "yatch" instead of "yacht." That makes up for a lot.

The Los Angeles Times Book Review, September 26, 1971

ELEANOR ROOSEVELT

Nicholas and Alexandra. Now *Eleanor and Franklin.* Who's next for the tandem treatment? *Dick and Pat? J. Edgar and Clyde?* Obviously there is a large public curious as to what goes on in the bedrooms of Winter Palace and White House, not to mention who passed whom in the corridors of power. All in all, this kind of voyeurism is not a bad thing in a country where, like snakes, the people shed their past each year ("Today nobody even remembers there *was* a Depression!" Eleanor Roosevelt exclaimed to me in 1960, shaking her head at the dullness of an audience we had been jointly trying to inspire). But though Americans dislike history, they do like soap operas about the sexual misbehavior and the illnesses—particularly the illnesses—of real people in high places: "Will handsome, ambitious Franklin ever regain the use of his legs? Tune in tomorrow."

The man responsible for the latest peek at our masters, off-duty and on, is Joseph Lash. A journalist by trade, a political activist by inclination, an old friend of Eleanor Roosevelt as luck would have it (hers as well as his), Mr. Lash has written a very long book. Were it shorter, it would have a smaller sale but more readers. Unfortunately, Mr. Lash has not been able to resist the current fashion in popular biography: he puts in everything. The Wastebasket School leaves to the reader the task of arranging the mess the author has collected. Bank balances, invitations to parties, funerals, vastations in the Galerie d'Apollon—all are presented in a cool democratic way. Nothing is more important than anything else. At worst the result is "scholarly" narrative; at best, lively soap opera. No more does prophet laurel flower in the abandoned Delphi of Plutarch, Johnson, Carlyle, Strachey: Ph.D. mills have polluted the sacred waters.

Objections duly noted, I confess that I found *Eleanor and Franklin* completely fascinating. Although Mr. Lash is writing principally about Eleanor Roosevelt, someone I knew and admired, I still think it impossible for anyone to read his narrative without being as moved as I was. After all, Eleanor Roosevelt was a last (*the* last? the *only*?) flower of that thorny Puritan American conscience which was, when it was good, very, very good, and now it's quite gone things are horrid.

A dozen years ago, Mrs. Roosevelt asked me to come see her at Hyde Park. I drove down to Val-Kill cottage from where I lived on the Hudson. With some difficulty, I found the house. The front door was open. I went inside. "Anybody home?" No answer. I opened the nearest door. A bathroom. To my horror, there in front of the toilet bowl, stood Eleanor Roosevelt. She gave a startled squeak. "Oh, *dear!*" Then, resignedly. "Well, now you know *everything*." And she stepped aside, revealing a dozen gladiolas she had been arranging in the toilet bowl. "It does keep them fresh." So began our political and personal acquaintance.

I found her remarkably candid about herself and others. So much so that I occasionally made notes, proud that I alone knew the truth about this or that. Needless to say, just about every "confidence" she bestowed on me appears in Mr. Lash's book and I can testify that he is a remarkably accurate recorder of both her substance and style. In fact, reading him is like having her alive again, hearing that odd, fluting yet precise voice with its careful emphases, its nervous glissade of giggles, the great smile which was calculated not only to avert wrath but warn potential enemies that here was a lioness quite capable of making a meal of anyone.

Then there were those shrewd, gray-blue eyes which stared and stared at you when you were not looking at her. When you did catch her at it, she would blush—even in her seventies the delicate gray skin would grow pink—giggle, and look away. When she was not interested in someone she would ask a polite question; then remove her glasses, which contained a hearing aid, and nod pleasantly—assuming she did not drop into one of her thirty-second catnaps.

The growing up of Eleanor Roosevelt is as interesting to read about as it was, no doubt, hard to have lived through. Born plain. Daughter of an alcoholic father whom she adored. Brought up by a sternly religious maternal grandmother in a house at Tivoli, New York, some thirty miles north of Hyde Park, where her cousin Franklin was also growing up, a fatherless little boy spoiled by his mother, the dread Sara Delano, for forty years the constant never-to-be-slain dragon in Eleanor's life.

Long after the death of Mrs. James (as Sara Delano Roosevelt was known to the Valley), Eleanor would speak of her with a kind of wonder and a slight distention of the knotty veins at her temples. "Only once did I ever *openly* quarrel with Mrs. James. I had come back to Hyde Park to find that she had allowed the children to run wild. Nothing I'd wanted done for them had been done. 'Mama,' I said" (accent on the second syllable, incidentally, in the French fashion), " 'you are *impossible!*' " "And what did she say?" I asked. "Why, nothing." Mrs. Roosevelt looked at me with some surprise. "You see, she was a grande dame. She never noticed *anything* unpleasant. By the next day she'd quite forgotten it. But of course I couldn't. I forgive . . ." One of her favorite lines, which often cropped up in her conversation as well as—now—in the pages of Mr. Lash's book, "but I *never* forget."

But if Mrs. James was to be for Eleanor a life's antagonist, her father was to be the good—if unlikely—angel, a continuing spur to greatness, loved all the better after death. Elliott Roosevelt was charming and talented (many of his letters are remarkably vivid and well-written) and adored by everyone, including his older brother Theodore, the President-to-be. Elliott had everything, as they say; unfortunately, he was an alcoholic. When his drinking finally got out of control, the family sent him south; kept him away from Eleanor and her young brother Hall (himself to be an alcoholic). During these long absences, father and daughter exchanged what were, in effect, love letters, usually full of plans to meet. But when those rare meetings did take place, he was apt to vanish and leave her sitting alone at his club until, hours later, someone remembered she was there and took her home.

Yet in his letters, if not in his life, Elliott was a Puritan moralist—with charm. He wanted his daughter, simply, to be good. It is hard now to imagine what being good is, but to that generation there was not much ambiguity about the word. As Eleanor wrote in 1927, in a plainly autobiographical sketch,

She was an ugly little thing, keenly conscious of her deficiencies, and her father, the only person who really cared for her, was away much of the time; but he never criticized her or blamed her, instead he wrote her letters and stories, telling her how he dreamed of her growing up and what they would do together in the future, but she must be truthful, loyal, brave, well-educated, or the woman he dreamed of would not be there when the wonderful day came for them to fare forth together. The child was full of fears and because of them lying was easy; she had no intellectual stimulus at that time and *yet she made herself as the years went on into a fairly good copy of the picture he painted.*

As it turned out, Eleanor did not fare forth with her father Elliott but with his cousin Franklin, and she was indeed all the things her father had wanted her to be, which made her marriage difficult and her life work great.

In 1894, Elliott died at 313 West 102nd Street, attended by a mistress. The ten-year-old Eleanor continued to live in the somber house at Tivoli, her character forming in a way to suggest that something unusual was at work. The sort of world she was living in could hardly have inspired her to write, as she did at fourteen:

> Those who are ambitious & make a place & a name in the great world for themselves are nearly always despised & laughed at by lesser souls who could not do as well & all they do for the good of men is construed into wrong & yet they do the good and they leave their mark upon the ages & if they had had no ambition would they have ever made a mark?

This was written in the era of Ward McAllister, when the best circles were still intent on gilding the age with bright excess. Eleanor was already unlike others of her class and time.

The turning point—the turning on—of her life occurred at Allenswood, an English school run by the formidable Mlle. Souvestre, a freethinker (doubtless shocking to Eleanor, who remained a believing Christian to the end of her days) and a political liberal. Readers of *Olivia* know the school through the eyes of its author, Dorothy Bussy—a sister of Lytton Strachey. Allenswood was a perfect atmosphere in which to form a character and "furnish a mind." The awkward withdrawn American girl bloomed, even became popular. Some of Eleanor's essays from this period are very good. On literature:

"The greatest men often write very badly and all the better for them. It is not in them that we look for perfect style but in the secondary writers (Horace, La Bruyère)—one must know the masters by heart, adore them, try to think as they do and then leave them forever. For technical instruction there is little of profit to draw from the learned and polished men of genius."

So exactly did Flaubert speak of Balzac (but it is unlikely

that Eleanor could have read that report of dinner Chez Magny). She perfected her French, learned Italian and German, and became civilized, according to the day's best standards.

Nearly eighteen, Eleanor returned to America. It was 1902: a time of great hope for the Republic. Uncle Theodore was the youngest President in history. A reformer (up to a point), he was a bright example of the "right" kind of ambition. But Tivoli was no more cheerful than before. In fact, life there was downright dangerous because of Uncle Vallie, a splendid alcoholic huntsman who enjoyed placing himself at an upstairs window and then, as the family gathered on the lawn, opening fire with a shotgun, forcing them to duck behind trees (in the forties there was a young critic who solemnly assured us that America could never have a proper literature because the country lacked a rich and complex class system!). It is no wonder that Eleanor thought the Volstead Act a fine thing and refused to serve drink at home for many years.

Eleanor came out, as was expected, and suffered from what she considered her ungainly appearance. Yet she was much liked, particularly by her cousin Franklin (known to *their* cousin Alice as "The Feather Duster": "You know, the sort of person you wouldn't ask to dinner, but for afterward"). During this period, Eleanor's social conscience was stirring. She worked at a settlement house where she not only saw how the poor lived but met a generation of women reformers, many of them also active in the suffragette movement. Eleanor was a slow convert to women's rights. But a convert she became. Just as she was able to change her prejudices against Jews and blacks (she was once attacked by the NAACP for referring to the colored, as they were then known, as "darkies").

Franklin began to court her. The letters he wrote her she destroyed—no doubt, a symbolic act when she found him out in adultery. But her letters remain. They are serious (she had been nicknamed "Granny"); they are also ambitious. For a young man who had made up his mind that he would rise to the top of the world she was a perfect mate. It is a sign of

Franklin's genius—if that is the word—that even in his spoiled and callow youth he had sense enough to realize what Eleanor was all about.

The marriage ceremony was fine comedy. The bride and groom were entirely overshadowed by Uncle Ted. Eleanor was amused, Franklin not. Mr. Lash misses—or omits—one important factor in the marriage. For all of Eleanor's virtues (not immediately apparent to the great world which Franklin always rather liked) she was a catch for one excellent reason: she was the President's niece, and not just your average run-of-the-mill President but a unique political phenomenon who had roused the country in a way no other President had since Jackson. I suspect this weighed heavily with Franklin. Certainly when it came time for him to run for office as a Democrat, many Republicans voted for him simply because his name was Roosevelt and he was married to the paladin's niece.

As the world knows, Franklin and Eleanor were a powerful political partnership. But at the personal level, the marriage must never have been happy. For one thing, Eleanor did not like sex, as she confided in later years to her daughter. Franklin obviously did. Then there was his mother. The lives of the young couple were largely managed by Mrs. James, who remained mistress of the house at Hyde Park until she died. It is poignant to read a note from Eleanor to Franklin after the old lady's death in 1941, asking permission to move furniture around—permission generally not granted, for the place was to remain, as long as Franklin lived (and as it is now), the way his mother wanted it—and the most God-awful Victorian taste it is. But surroundings never meant much to any of the family, although Mrs. Roosevelt once told me how "Mr. Truman showed me around the White House, which he'd just redone, and he was so proud of the upstairs which looked to me *exactly* like a Sheraton Hotel!"

Franklin went to the State Senate. Eleanor learned to make speeches—not an easy matter because her voice was high, with a tendency to get out of control. Finally, she went to a voice coach. "You must tell President Kennedy. The exercises did wonders for my voice." A giggle. "Yes, I know, I don't sound *very* good but I was certainly a lot worse before, and Mr. Kennedy does need help because he talks much too fast and too high for the average person to understand him."

I remarked that in the television age it was quite enough to watch the speaker. She was not convinced. One spoke to the people in order to *educate* them. That was what politics was all about, as she was among the last to believe.

It is startling how much is known at the time about the private lives of the great. My grandfather Senator Gore's political career ended in 1936 after a collision with President Roosevelt ("This is the last relief check you'll get if Gore is reelected" was the nice tactic in Oklahoma), but in earlier times they were both in the liberal wing of the Democratic party and when Franklin came to Washington as Assistant Secretary of the Navy under Wilson, he was on friendly terms with the Senator. Washington was a small town then and everyone knew all about everyone else's private life. Not long ago Alice Longworth managed to startle even me by announcing, at a dinner party: "Daisy Harriman told me that every time she was alone with Senator Gore he would pounce on her. I could never understand why he liked her. After all, he was *blind*. But then Daisy always smelled nice."*

Meanwhile, the Gores were keeping track of the Roosevelts. Franklin fell in love with Eleanor's young secretary, Lucy Mercer, and they conducted an intense affair (known to everyone in Washington except Eleanor who discovered the truth in the tried-and-true soap opera way: innocently going through her husband's mail when he was ill). Senator Gore used to say, "What a trial Eleanor must be! She waits up all night in the vestibule until he comes home." I never knew exactly what this meant. Now Mr. Lash tells us "the vestibule story." Angry at her husband's attentions to Lucy at a party,

*My sister responded to this story by reminding Mrs. Longworth of a certain peculiar episode in the Governor's office at Albany between T.R. and a lady. Mrs. Longworth was not amused.

Eleanor went home alone but because Franklin had the keys, she spent much of the night sitting on the stoop.

Later, confronted with proof of Franklin's adultery, Eleanor acted decisively. She would give him a divorce but, she pointed out, she had five children and Lucy would have to bring them up. Lucy, a Catholic, and Franklin, a politician-on-the-make, agreed to cool it. But toward the end of his life they began to see each other again. He died with Lucy in the room at Warm Springs and Eleanor far away. Eleanor knew none of this until the day of her husband's death. From what she later wrote about that day, a certain amount of normal grief seems not to have been present.

When Franklin got polio in 1921, Eleanor came into her own. On his behalf, she joined committees, kept an eye on the political situation, pursued her own good works. When the determined couple finally arrived at the White House, Eleanor became a national figure in her own right. She had her own radio program. She wrote a syndicated column for the newspapers. She gave regular press conferences. At last she was loved, and on the grandest scale. She was also hated. But at fourteen she had anticipated everything ("It is better to be ambitious & do something than to be unambitious & do nothing").

Much of what Mr. Lash writes is new to me (or known and forgotten), particularly Eleanor's sponsorship of Arthurdale, an attempt to create a community in West Virginia where out-of-work miners could each own a house, a bit of land to grow things on, and work for decent wages at a nearby factory. This was a fine dream and a bureaucratic catastrophe. The houses were haphazardly designed, while the factory was not forthcoming (for years any industrialist who wanted to be invited to the White House had only to suggest to Eleanor that he might bring industry to Arthurdale). The right wing of course howled about socialism.

The right wing in America has always believed that those who have money are good people and those who lack it are bad people. At a deeper level, our conservatives are true Darwinians and think that the weak and the poor ought to die off, leaving the spoils to the fit. Certainly a do-gooder is the worst thing anyone can be, a societal pervert who would alter with government subsidy nature's harsh but necessary way with the weak. Eleanor always understood the nature of the enemy: she was a Puritan, too. But since she was Christian and not Manichaean, she felt obliged to work on behalf of those dealt a bad hand at birth. Needless to say, Franklin was quite happy to let her go about her business, increasing his majorities.

"Eleanor has this state trooper she lives with in a cottage near Hyde Park." I never believed that one but, by God, here the trooper is in the pages of Mr. Lash. Sergeant Earl R. Miller was first assigned to the Roosevelts in Albany days. Then he became Eleanor's friend. For many years she mothered him, was nice to his girl friends and wives, all perfectly innocent —to anyone but a Republican. It is a curious fact of American political life that the right wing is enamored of the sexual smear. Eleanor to me: "There are actually people in Hyde Park who knew Franklin all his life and said that he did not have polio but the sort of disease you get from not living the *right* sort of life."

The left wing plays dirty pool, too, but I have no recollection of their having organized whispering campaigns of a sexual nature against Nixon, say, the way the right so often does against liberal figures. Knowing Eleanor's active dislike of sex as a subject and, on the evidence of her daughter, as a fact, I think it most unlikely she ever had an affair with anyone. But she did crave affection, and jealously held on to her friends, helped them, protected them—often unwisely. Mr. Lash describes most poignantly Eleanor's grief when she realized that *her* friend Harry Hopkins had cold-bloodedly shifted his allegiance to Franklin.

Eleanor was also faced with the President's secretary and *de facto* wife Missy Le Hand ("Everybody knows the old man's been living with her for years," said one of the Roosevelt sons to my father who had just joined the subcabinet. My father, an innocent West Pointer, from that moment on regarded the

Roosevelt family arrangements as not unlike those of Ibn Saud). Yet when Missy was dying, it was Eleanor who would ring her up. Franklin simply dropped her. But then Missy was probably not surprised. She once told Fulton Oursler that the President "was really incapable of a personal friendship with anyone."

Mr. Lash writes a good deal about Eleanor's long friendship with two tweedy ladies, Marion Dickerman and Nancy Cook. For years Eleanor shared Val-Kill cottage with them; jointly they ran a furniture factory and the Todhunter School, where Eleanor taught until she went to the White House. The relationship of the three women seems unusually tangled, and Mr. Lash cannot do much with it. Things ended badly with an exchange of letters, filled with uncharacteristic bitterness on Eleanor's side. If only the author of *Olivia* could have had a go at that subject.

In a sense Eleanor had no personal life after the White House years began. She was forever on the go (and did not cease motion during the long widowhood). She suffered many disappointments from friends and family. I remember her amused description of Caroline Kennedy and what a good thing it was that the two Kennedy children would still be very young when they left the White House because, she frowned and shook her head, "It is a terrible place for young people to grow up in, continually flattered and—*used.*"

I was with her the day the news broke that a son had married yet again. While we were talking, he rang her and she smiled and murmured, over and over, "Yes, dear . . . yes, I'm very happy." Then when she hung up, her face set like stone. "You would think that he might have told his mother *first*, before the press." But that was a rare weakness. Her usual line was "people are what they are, you can't change them." Since she had obviously begun life as the sort of Puritan who thought people not only could but must be changed, this later tolerance was doubtless achieved at some cost.

When I was selected as Democratic-Liberal candidate for Congress, Eleanor (I called her Mrs. R) was at first cool to the idea—I had known her slightly all my life (she had liked my father, detested my grandfather). But as the campaign got going and I began to move up in the polls and it suddenly looked as if, wonder of wonders, Dutchess County might go Democratic in a congressional election for the first time in fifty years (since Franklin's senatorial race, in fact), she became more and more excited. She joined me at a number of meetings. She gave a tea at Val-Kill for the women workers in the campaign. Just as the women were leaving, the telephone rang. She spoke a few minutes in a low voice, hung up, said good-by to the last of the ladies, took me aside for some political counsel, was exactly as always except that the tears were streaming down her face. Driving home, I heard on the radio that her favorite granddaughter had just been killed.

In later years, though Eleanor would talk—if asked—about the past, she was not given to strolls down memory lane. In fact, she was contemptuous of old people who lived in the past, particularly those politicians prone to the Ciceronian vice of exaggerating their contribution to history, a category in which she firmly placed that quaint Don Quixote of the cold war, Dean Acheson. She was also indifferent to her own death. "I remember Queen Wilhelmina when she came to visit during the war" (good democrat that she was, nothing royal was alien to Eleanor) "and she would sit under a tree on the lawn and commune with the dead. She would even try to get *me* interested in spiritualism but I always said: Since we're going to be dead such a long time anyway it's rather a waste of time chatting with all of them *before* we get there."

Although a marvelous friend and conscience to the world, she was, I suspect, a somewhat unsatisfactory parent. Descendants and their connections often look rather hard and hurt at the mention of her. For those well-placed by birth to do humanity's work, she had no patience if they were—ultimate sin—unhappy. A woman I know went to discuss with her a disastrous marriage; she came away chilled to the bone. These things were to be borne.

What did Eleanor feel about Franklin? That is an enigma,

and perhaps she herself never sorted it out. He was complex and cold and cruel (so many of her stories of life with him would end, "And then I *fled* from the table in tears!"). He liked telling her the latest "Eleanor stories"; his sense of fun was heavy. A romantic, Mr. Lash thinks she kept right on loving him to the end (a favorite poem of the two was E. B. Browning's "Unless you can swear, 'For life, for death,'/ Oh, fear to call it loving!"). But I wonder. Certainly he hurt her mortally in their private relationship; worse, he often let her down in their public partnership. Yet she respected his cunning even when she deplored his tactics.

I wonder, too, how well she understood him. One day Eleanor told me about something in his will that had surprised her. He wanted one side of his coffin to be left open. "Well, we hadn't seen the will when he was buried and of course it was too late when we did read it. But what *could* he have meant?" I knew and told her: "He wanted, physically, to get back into circulation as quickly as possible, in the rose garden." She looked at me as if this were the maddest thing she had ever heard.

I suspect the best years of Eleanor's life were the widowhood. She was on her own, no longer an adjunct to his career. In this regard, I offer Mr. Lash an anecdote. We were four at table: Mrs. Tracy Dows, Mrs. Roosevelt, her uncle David Gray (our wartime Ambassador to Ireland), and myself. Eleanor began: "When Mr. Joe Kennedy came back from London, during the war . . ." David Gray interrupted her. "Damned coward, Joe Kennedy! Terrified they were going to drop a bomb on him." Eleanor merely grinned and continued. "Anyway he came back to Boston and gave that *unfortunate* interview in which he was . . . well, somewhat *critical* of us."

She gave me her teacher's smile, and an aside. "You see, it's a very funny thing but whatever people say about us we almost always hear. I don't know *how* this happens but it does." David Gray scowled. "Unpleasant fellow, that Joe. Thought he knew everything. Damned coward." I said nothing, since I was trying to persuade Eleanor to support the wicked Joe's son at the Democratic convention; something she could not, finally, bring herself to do.

"Well, *my* Franklin said, 'We better have him down here'—we were at Hyde Park—'and see what he has to say.' So Mr. Kennedy arrived at Rhinecliff on the train and I met him and took him straight to Franklin. Well, ten minutes later one of the aides came and said, 'The President wants to see you right away.' This was unheard of. So I *rushed* into the office and there was Franklin, white as a sheet. He asked Mr. Kennedy to step outside and then he said, and his voice was *shaking*, 'I never want to see that man again as long as I live.'" David Gray nodded: "Wanted us to make a deal with Hitler." But Eleanor was not going to get into that. "Whatever it was, it was *very* bad. Then Franklin said, 'Get him out of here,' and I said, 'But, dear, you've invited him for the weekend, and we've got guests for lunch and the train doesn't leave until two,' and Franklin said, 'Then you drive him around Hyde Park and put him on that train,' and I did and it was the most dreadful four hours of my life!" She laughed. Then, seriously: "I wonder if the *true* story of Joe Kennedy will ever be known."

To read Mr. Lash's book is to relive not only the hopeful period in American life (1933–40) but the brief time of world triumph (1941–45). The book stops, mercifully, with the President's death and the end of Eleanor and Franklin (Mr. Lash is correct to put her name first; of the two she was greater). Also, the end of . . . what? American innocence? Optimism? From 1950 on, our story has been progressively more and more squalid. Nor can one say it is a lack of the good and the great in high places: they are always there when needed. Rather the corruption of empire has etiolated the words themselves. Now we live in a society which none of us much likes, all would like to change, but no one knows how. Most ominous of all, there is now a sense that what has gone wrong for us may be irreversible. The empire will not liquidate itself. The lakes and rivers and seas will not become fresh again. The arms race will not stop. Land ruined by insecticides and fertilizers will not be restored. The smash-up will come.

To read of Eleanor and Franklin is to weep at what we have lost. Gone is the ancient American sense that whatever is wrong with human society can be put right by human action. Eleanor never stopped believing this. A simple faith, no doubt simplistic—but it gave her a stoic serenity. On the funeral train from Georgia to Washington: "I lay in my berth all night with the window shade up, looking out at the countryside he had loved and watching the faces of the people at stations, and even at the crossroads, who came to pay their last tribute all through the night. The only recollection I clearly have is thinking about 'The Lonesome Train,' the musical poem about Lincoln's death. ('A lonesome train on a lonesome track/ Seven coaches painted black/ A slow train, a quiet train/ Carrying Lincoln home again . . .'). I had always liked it so well —and now this was so much like it."

I had other thoughts in 1962 at Hyde Park as I stood alongside the thirty-third, the thirty-fourth, the thirty-fifth, and the thirty-sixth Presidents of the United States, not to mention all the remaining figures of the Roosevelt era who had assembled for her funeral (unlike the golden figures in Proust's last chapter, they all looked if not smaller than life smaller than legend —so many shrunken March of Time dolls soon to be put away). Whether or not one thought of Eleanor Roosevelt as a world ombudsman or as a chronic explainer or as a scourge of the selfish, she was like no one else in her usefulness. As the box containing her went past me, I thought, well, that's that. We're really on our own now.

The New York Review of Books, November 18, 1971

H. HUGHES

Is Howard R. Hughes the most boring American? Admittedly,
the field is large; over two hundred million of us are in competition. Yet on the strength of an old associate's recent
memorial, I am inclined to give Hughes the benefit of the
belief I have long held that the more money an American
accumulates the less interesting he himself becomes. Certainly
there is not much you can do with the fact of someone else's
fortune except stare at all those naughts upon the page. Then,
naughts aside, Hughes the actual man emanates a chloroform
quite his own: the high droning voice, the catatonic manner,
the absence of all humor (a characteristic of the very rich
American, but here quintessential), the lack of interest in the
human, the preoccupation with machinery (yet he is "a lousy
engineer," according to my father, a long-time aviator acquaintance, and "a menace as a flier"), the collecting of beautiful and famous women to no vivid end (although feisty Ava
Gardner did knock him out with an ashtray), and, of course,

the grim eating habits (dinner is always a steak with peas, followed by vanilla ice cream and cookies).

The best thing about Hughes has been his withdrawal from the world—for this, if nothing else, he ought not only to have been honored but encouraged by a grateful nation. Yet even in the shadows of his cloistered motels, the inept tycoon insists on pulling strings, making a mess of TWA, a disaster of RKO, a shambles of vice in Las Vegas, all the while creating the largest unworkable plywood plane in the world at a cost to the taxpayers of twenty-two million dollars. There is something peculiarly inhuman even about his incompetence. At least John D. Rockefeller gave out dimes and drank mother's milk (from other people's mothers, that is). Why then contemplate Howard Hughes? Because he is involved in politics and even a cursory glance at his career is a chilling reminder of the nation's corruption at every level.

In 1925, Noah Dietrich was engaged by the nineteen-year-old Howard Hughes to run the business Hughes had inherited from his father (the manufacturer of a special kind of drill much favored by Texas oil men). The handsome young heir had moved to Hollywood where the girls and the movies were. Aware that he knew nothing about money, Hughes hired Mr. Dietrich, a certified public accountant, to look after his affairs. This profitable association lasted until 1957, when Mr. Dietrich, feeling the shadows lengthen, asked for some stock and a few capital gains to supplement the large salary on which he was forced to pay a large tax. Hughes promptly let him go. If Mr. Dietrich is a bitter man, the book *Howard, the Amazing Mr. Hughes* (by Noah Dietrich and Bob Thomas) does not reveal it. Every page radiates octogenarian serenity—the CPA at Colonus. Nevertheless, despite the sunny manner, Mr. Dietrich and Mr. Thomas, his prose stylist (as such workers are called in *Youngblood Hawke*), have managed to give us a highly detailed and most plausible portrait of what is apparently an honest-to-God American shit.

In Hollywood Hughes produced a number of pictures. Those in which he took no "creative" part sometimes made money (like Milestone's *Two Arabian Knights*); those he himself worked on invariably lost money, including the renowned *Hell's Angels* (the aesthetic value of these works will not be dealt with here). Incidentally, during the first thirty years of his association with Dietrich, Hughes made only one visit to the Hughes Tool Company. As a result, the company was a great success, producing the money Hughes promptly lost on movie-making, on a color process for films, on a new kind of automobile, on the career of Miss Jane Russell (a lifelong search for the perfect set of boobs ended abruptly for Howard in a dentist's office when Nurse Russell suddenly made her appearance carrying a tray of pliers). For an American bore of major standing, Hughes demonstrated, from the beginning, an attractive talent for failure which almost—but not quite—catapults him into the ranks of the human.

"My first objective is to become the world's number one golfer. Second, the top aviator, and third I want to become the world's most famous motion picture producer. Then, I want you to make me the richest man in the world." So spoke the young Faust to Mr. Dietrich, his eager counter-Faust. For a very rich young man the realization of such simple dreams ought to have been an easy matter. Unfortunately, Hughes's golf was not all that good; as a flier, he was the Icarus of an entire generation of aviators; while the movies he produced brought him only publicity. Mr. Dietrich did make him very rich, but not as rich as J. P. Getty.

It would seem, on the evidence of this memoir, that Hughes was never interested in money or movies or airplanes or women. What did absorb him was tinkering with bits of machinery or celluloid. Hour after hour, day after day, he would concentrate totally (and to no ultimate purpose) on a carburetor or the editing of a zoom shot. Detail work was his narcotic. But attempts to relate the details of the work to some larger unit like an automobile or a finished film (or a love affair?) were quite beyond him, as even devotees of *The Outlaw* must admit.

Mr. Dietrich gives us a bit of character analysis, but not

much. This is wise. The point to Hughes is that he is what he seems: a simple, uneducated man, interested in machinery. He apparently never liked anyone very much, man or woman. Suffering from hereditary deafness, he went into retirement because it was difficult for him to hear conversations at parties (he can hear perfectly on an altered telephone and so prefers to conduct his business at long distance). Since his family is not long lived, he has become frightened of the germ and its carrier, people. "Everyone carries germs around with them. I want to live longer than my parents, so I avoid germs." Living alone, with only servants to look after him, he has developed a somewhat solipsistic turn of mind, given to night fears—not only of germs, death, betrayal, but of monsters like the ones he watches so avidly on *The Late Late Show* coming to kidnap him, to eat him up.

The interesting part of Mr. Dietrich's book begins during the war. Over the years, Hughes had managed to offend a number of important generals (Hap Arnold, the army air force's commander, was turned away at the door to the Hughes plant). In the interest of landing war contracts, Hughes decided to corrupt the generals and their masters, the politicians. Why not? All businessmen dealing with the government do—or try to. Hughes hired an amiable man-about-town called Johnny Meyer, who "certainly knew how to please the tired politician or general, and he was lavish with hotel suites, fancy dinners, champagne, and caviar, not to mention $100-per-night beauties. You'd be surprised how many senators, governors and generals partook of his largesse."

I think Mr. Dietrich exaggerates the surprise of those of us born under the dread sign of the unshredded Dita Beard. What we really want to know is not how our masters behave in the sack but what deals they make in the office. "Despite his obviousness Johnny Meyer produced results for the Hughes enterprise." The most important VIP that he snared was Elliott Roosevelt. Parenthetically, when my father became Roosevelt's Director of Air Commerce (1933–1936), young Elliott told him, "Everyone else in the family's got their man in the

Administration. Well, you're going to be mine." Thus from an early age, Elliott showed a great interest in the future of aviation, and worked hard to give America that mastery of the skies she has so long held.

The air force procurement brass was anti-Hughes, particularly General Echols. But air force Brigadier General Roosevelt managed to turn them all around, obtaining for Hughes a contract for one hundred F-11 plywood fighters at $700,000 apiece. Meanwhile, the actress to whom Johnny Meyer had introduced Elliott became his wife—benignly, Hughes paid for both wedding and honeymoon.

Meyer was also working on Major General Bennett Meyers in Materiel, Maintenance, and Distribution. This general had a passion for money unusual even in a military man sworn to defend capitalism. He wanted "to buy government bonds on margin and turn over a quick profit." To accomplish this, Hughes was to lend the general $200,000 "on a short-term, no-interest loan." As it turned out, Hughes's lawyer in Washington aborted the scheme and General Meyers eventually ended up in the clink.

During this period, Hughes was not always himself. Dietrich recalls a telephone conversation in which his employer repeated the same sentence thirty-three times. When this dysfunction was drawn to his attention, Hughes allowed that his doctor was also concerned, and promptly vanished for six months, to return in 1947 ready for his finest hour.

Senator Owen Brewster of Maine, dreaming of the Vice-Presidency as Maine men tend to do during those long hard winters Down East, decided he needed some publicity. What better target than the eccentric young millionaire, flyer, and stud-consort of sinful lascivious Hollywood stars and broads? Forthwith, Brewster summoned Hughes before a Senate committee in order to show the foul ways in which clean-limbed West Pointers, golden Presidential sons, selfless tribunes of the people had been tempted by Johnny Meyer, booze, and women, women, women.

But Senator Brewster had met his match. The inarticulate

Hughes suddenly found his voice. Masterfully, he defended himself, often disingenuously, but then a Congressional committee is not exactly the *Bocca della Verita*. Luckily for Hughes, the senator from Maine was a . . . well, enthusiast for Pan American Airways, even though Pan American made no stops in Maine. Suddenly the alleged corrupter of public virtue turned on Senator Brewster and said, "I specifically charge that during luncheon at the Mayflower Hotel in Washington in the week beginning February 10, 1947, in the suite of Senator Brewster, the senator told me in so many words that if I would agree to merge TWA with Pan Am and go along with this community airline bill, there would be no further hearing in this matter." The career of Senator Brewster was at an end. Not only did he not become Tom Dewey's running mate in 1948, but when he came up for re-election to the Senate in 1952, Hughes gave $60,000 to his opponent. Brewster was defeated.

During the late 1940s and throughout the 1950s, Howard's political contributions ran between $100,000 and $400,000 a year. He financed Los Angeles councilmen and county supervisors, tax assessors, sheriffs, state senators and assemblymen, district attorneys, governors, congressmen and senators, judges—yes, and Vice Presidents and Presidents, too. Besides cash, Howard was liberal in providing airplanes for candidates.

In 1944 a fine comedy took place at the Biltmore Hotel in Los Angeles. Hughes and his lawyer went around to the suite of the candidate for Vice-President, Harry S Truman. Hughes sent the lawyer in to see Truman, with an envelope containing $12,500. Brooding in the outer room, Hughes began to worry that Truman might give the lawyer the credit for the cash. Hughes barged into the politician's presence "and said bluntly, 'I want you to know, Mr. Truman, that is *my* money Mr. McCarthy is giving you.' Truman managed to laugh off Howard's lack of diplomacy. . . ." Ho ho ho all the way to the White House.

For those who are curious as to how large sums of money are got physically into the hands of politicians (barring the direct method favored by a recent mayor of New York who used to accept pillowcases stuffed with cash), Mr. Dietrich is most illuminating. In fact, revelatory.

I asked Trippe [president of Pan Am] how he managed to wield so much influence in Washington—the Pan American lobby was enormously effective, and not only with Senator Brewster. "Well, you know," he confided, "the law says nothing at all about contributions from *foreign* corporations. We have a subsidiary in South America that takes an intense interest in our US elections."

From that moment, Hughes Tool of Canada dispersed three to four hundred thousand dollars a year to American politicians, and it was all legal.

Most notorious of the Hughes loans was to Richard Nixon's brother Don. Apparently Don has two passions: money and food, which he was able to combine in a Whittier, California restaurant starring the Nixonburger. In 1956, shortly after Richard Nixon was reelected Vice-President, he got in touch with Hughes's political lawyer and told him that brother Don needed $205,000. Now Mr. Dietrich was a good Republican who had supported the Eisenhower-Nixon crusade for decency. He was as appalled as Hughes was delighted. "Let 'em have it," said Hughes. After all, $205,000 is not much to buy a Vice-President—particularly when the pro for the quid (yes, wicked partisans do take a sequential view of life) was nothing less than saving Howard Hughes from having to pay taxes.

Prior to the loan, Hughes had been trying to set up a tax-exempt medical foundation with himself as sole trustee. The IRS had twice refused him a tax exemption. Then the loan was made to Donald Nixon, through his mother, the saintly Quaker woman Hannah. As collateral, she put up a lot in Whittier valued at $13,000. Hannah then popped $165,000 into Don's company. No one seems to know what happened to the rest of the loan. A few months later the Howard Hughes

Medical Foundation was exempted from taxes by the IRS.

Alarmed by these shenanigans, Mr. Dietrich went to Washington on his own to talk sense to Richard Nixon. "He was extremely cordial and showed me around his office, pointing out mementos of his visits to foreign lands" (the verisimilitudinous touch which authenticates). "Then we sat down for a serious talk." Mr. Dietrich talked turkey. " 'If this loan becomes public information, it could mean the end of your political career. And I don't believe that it can be kept quiet.' He [Nixon] responded immediately, perhaps having anticipated what I had said. 'Mr. Dietrich,' he said, 'I have to put my relatives ahead of my career.' Nothing further was said about the subject." Not long after, Don's restaurant failed and the Nixonburger was history.

In 1957 Mr. Dietrich ceased to be privy to Howard Hughes's political donations and so his inside narrative is fifteen years out of date. Are bribes still being paid? We do not know. But we do know that Hughes Aircraft is the Pentagon's twelfth largest contractor, and 90 percent of its $750,000,000 annual sales are to the government. This company, incidentally, is the one entirely owned by the tax-exempt Howard Hughes Medical Institute whose great task is to do research around the country on various diseases, with particular emphasis on the heart. As in most successful Hughes enterprises, the living legend has little to do with the company's management.

Political corruption has been with us since the first congress sat at Philadelphia, and there is nothing to be done about it as long as we are what we are. In fact, as election costs mount the corruption will tend to be institutionalized by the small group of legislators and bankers, generals and industrialists who own and govern the United States, Inc. But it does not take great prescience to realize that they are playing a losing game. As the polity becomes more and more conscious of the moral nullity at the center of American life, there will develop not the revolutionary situation dreamed of in certain radical circles but, rather, a deep contempt for the nation and its institutions, an apathy bound to be exploited by clever human engineers. In the name of saving the environment and restoring virtue, they will continue the dismantling of an unloved and unhonored republic. But then republics are social anomalies, as Thomas Jefferson must have suspected when he claimed to see, off there in the distance, no larger than a Federalist's head, the minatory shape of the despot's crown.

The New York Review of Books, April 20, 1972

HOMAGE TO DANIEL SHAYS

To govern is to choose how the revenue raised from taxes is spent. So far so good, or bad. But some people earn more money than others. Should they pay proportionately more money to the government than those who earn less? And if they do pay more money are they entitled to more services than those who pay less or those who pay nothing at all? And should those who pay nothing at all because they have nothing get anything? These matters are of irritable concern to our rulers, and of some poignancy to the rest.

Although the equality of each citizen before the law is the rock upon which the American Constitution rests, economic equality has never been an American ideal. In fact, it is the one unmentionable subject in our politics, as the Senator from South Dakota recently discovered when he came up with a few quasi-egalitarian tax reforms. The furious and enduring terror of communism in America is not entirely the work of those early cold warriors Truman and Acheson. A dislike of economic equality is something deep-grained in the American

Protestant character. After all, given a rich empty continent for vigorous Europeans to exploit (the Indians were simply a disagreeable part of the emptiness, like chiggers), any man of gumption could make himself a good living. With extra hard work, any man could make himself a fortune, proving that he was a better man than the rest. Long before Darwin the American ethos was Darwinian.

The vision of the rich empty continent is still a part of the American unconscious in spite of the Great Crowding and its attendant miseries; and this lingering belief in the heaven any man can make for himself through hard work and clean living is a key to the majority's prevailing and apparently unalterable hatred of the poor, kept out of sight at home, out of mind abroad.

Yet there has been, from the beginning, a significant division in our ruling class. The early Thomas Jefferson had a dream: a society of honest yeomen, engaged in agricultural pursuits, without large cities, heavy industry, banks, military pretensions. The early (and the late) Alexander Hamilton wanted industry, banks, cities, and a military force capable of making itself felt in world politics. It is a nice irony that so many of today's laissez-faire conservatives think that they descend from Hamilton, the proponent of a strong federal government, and that so many liberals believe themselves to be the heirs of the early Jefferson, who wanted little more than a police force and a judiciary. Always practical, Jefferson knew that certain men would rise through their own good efforts while, sadly, others would fall. Government would do no more than observe this Darwinian spectacle benignly, and provide no succor.

In 1800 the Hamiltonian view was rejected by the people and their new President Thomas Jefferson. Four years later, the Hamiltonian view had prevailed and was endorsed by the reelected Jefferson. "We are all Hamiltonians now!" he might have exclaimed had he the grace of the Thirty-Seventh President, whose progress from moth to larva on so many issues gives delight. Between 1800 and 1805 Jefferson had seen to it that an empire *in posse* had become an empire *in esse*. The difference between Jefferson I and Jefferson II is reflected in the two inaugural addresses.

First Inaugural: "a wise and frugal government, which shall restrain men from injuring one another, which shall leave them otherwise free to regulate their own pursuit of industry and improvement, and shall not take from the mouth of labor the bread it has earned. This is the sum of good government. . . ." In other words, no taxes beyond a minimal levy in order to pay for a few judges, a postal service, small executive and legislative bodies.

Second Inaugural: Jefferson II was now discussing the uses to which taxes might be put (once the national debt was paid off, oh Presidential chimera!), "*In time of peace*, to rivers, canals, roads, arts, manufactures, education, and other great objects within each State. *In time of war*—if injustice, *by ourselves*" (those italics, irresistibly, mine) "or others, must sometimes produce war. . . . War will be but a suspension of useful works. . . ." The idea of the rich empty continent best exploited by men unbugged by a central government had now been succeeded by the notion that government ought to pitch in and help with those roads and schools, but of course that's going to take money, so taxes must be raised to pay for these good things which benefit us all equally, don't they?

It is significant that nothing more elevated than greed changed the Dr. Jekyll of Jefferson I into the Mr. Hyde of Jefferson II. Like his less thoughtful countrymen, Jefferson could not resist a deal. Subverting the Constitution he had helped create, Jefferson bought Louisiana from Napoleon, acquiring its citizens without their consent; he then proceeded to govern them as if they had been conquered, all the while secretly—comically—maneuvering, by hook or by crook, to bag the Floridas. The author of the Declaration of Independence was quite able to forget the unalienable rights of anyone whose property he thought should be joined to our empire— a word which crops up frequently and unselfconsciously in his correspondence.

436

In the course of land-grabbing, Jefferson II managed to get himself into hot water with France, England, and Spain simultaneously, a fairly astonishing thing to do considering the state of politics in Napoleonic Europe. But then war is bound to result if you insist on liberating vast tracts of land from colonial nations as well as from home-grown Indians (they were equal to whites, Jefferson thought, in spite of their bad habits, but different from the hopeless black races which had started out white but then, in the unwholesome African climate, contracted a form of leprosy; enlightened optimists like Jefferson's friend the learned Dr. Rush were certain that advanced dermatology would one day restore to these dark peoples their lost prettiness). The result of this finagling was a series of panicky appropriations for the navy and the creation of the American military machine which in the last fiscal year cost us honest yeomen 75.8 billion dollars out of a total of 126 billion dollars paid in personal and corporate income taxes. Forever forgotten was the wisdom of Jefferson I: "Sound principles will not justify our taxing the industry of our fellow citizens to accumulate treasure for wars to happen we know not when, and which might not perhaps happen but from the temptation offered by that treasure."

It is a tribute to the Protestant passion for wanting always to appear to be doing good (particularly when one is robbing the till) that Americans have been constitutionally incapable (*double entendre* intended) of recognizing the truth about themselves or anyone else. Mixing his metaphors, celebrating the empire electric, appealing to the god Demos whose agent he thought himself to be, Jefferson II so clouded over our innate imperialism that we cannot to this day recognize the nature of American society, even as our bombs murder strangers (admittedly leprous) 8,000 miles away. Fortunately, the empire has taken such a shellacking in the last few years that critics (not yet loved) are being listened to at last, and it is now unlikely that even a yeomanry so constantly and deliberately misinformed from kindergarten days to wrap-up time in the Forest Lawn Slumber Room will ever allow another president the fun of destroying someone else's country in the name of Jefferson I self-determination. As the empire falls apart, things may yet come together again in a good—or at least more realistic —way.

To make sense of our situation a simple question must be asked. Why do we allow our governors to take so much of our money and spend it in ways that not only fail to benefit us but do great damage to others as we prosecute undeclared wars— which even our brainwashed majority has come to see are a bad proposition because of the cost of maintaining a vast military machine, not to mention a permanent draft of young men (an Un-American activity if there ever was one) in what is supposed to be peacetime? Whether he knows it or not, the middle-income American is taxed as though he were living in a socialist society. But for the money he gives the government he gets almost nothing back. He does pay for a lot of military hardware, and his congressman will point to all the jobs "defense" (that happy euphemism) contracts bring to his district, as if the same federal money could not create even more jobs doing things that need doing as well as benefiting directly the man who paid the taxes in the first place. Ultimate irony, the middle American still tends to believe that he is living in a Jefferson I society when, in fact, he has been for some decades in a Jefferson II world, allowing an imperial-minded elite to tax him in order to wage a holy war against something called communism.

Fortunately, there are now signs that they don't make suckers like that any more. The taxpayers' revolt has begun. A dislike of all politicians is in the land. Word is out that the rich don't pay as much, proportionately, to maintain their empire as do the middle-income people. Something fishy's going on down in Washington, as the two Georges have been telling folks (that the Georges are a part of what is wrong is not exactly their fault), and the people are responding. They hate socialism and communism and all the things good people are supposed to hate, but they are also beginning to wonder just why they have to give up so much of their income to fight those very same Commies Nixon likes to dine with in Peking and Moscow.

The fact is that our present governors are not very bright, and this may be our salvation. In 1968 they absent-mindedly gave us a president whose schizophrenic behavior and prose style ("This is *not* an invasion of Cambodia") is creepily apparent to even the most woolly-headed yeoman. Now three new books* provide useful information about the small group who own the United States, how our economic and foreign policies are manipulated, how members of Congress are bought, how presidential candidates are selected and financed.

The mold that cast the mind of C. Wright Mills was not broken at his flesh's departure. Another such mind was promptly cast and labeled G. William Domhoff (those first initials and middle names are reminiscent of a generation of three-named Episcopalian clergymen). A Mills disciple, Domhoff has published *Who Rules America?* (1967) and *The Higher Circle* (1970). The subjects of those books are exactly what their titles suggest. Domhoff has now written another illuminating treatise called *Fat Cats and Democrats: The Role of the Big Rich in the Party of the Common Man.*

Domhoff's thesis is straightforward. The country is governed by a small elite which knows pretty much what it is up to and coordinates its various moves in foreign affairs and the economy. Most academics dispute this theory. They tend to be Jefferson I types who believe that the United States is a pluralist society filled with all sorts of dominations and powers constantly balancing and checking one another. To them, anyone who believes that an elite is really running the show is paranoid. But as the late Delmore Schwartz once said with the weary lucidity of his own rich madness, "Paranoids have real

---

* *Fats Cats and Democrats: The Role of the Big Rich in the Party of the Common Man* by G. William Domhoff; *Bella! Ms. Abzug Goes to Washington* by Bella Abzug; *The Washington Pay-off: An Insider's View of Corruption in Government* by Robert Winter-Berger.

enemies, too." Admittedly, it is difficult at first to accept the proposition that the owners of the country also rule it and that the electorate is nothing but a quadrennial chorus whose function is to ratify with hosannahs one or the other of two presidential candidates carefully picked for them by rulers who enjoy pretending that ours is really government of, by, and for the you-know-who. In the same manner, Tiberius always respectfully consulted a Senate to whose irrelevant ranks his heir nicely added a race horse.

Domhoff's style does not command admiration. His manner is disconcertingly gee whiz. He is given to easy liberal epithets like "Godforsaken Mississippi" yet forced to admit that except on the subject of race, the proud folk down there are populist to the core, and populist is the thing to be this year. But if one is not put off by the somewhat slap-dash manner, Domhoff has seen and measured the tip of an iceberg which most of the other passengers on the US *Titanic* have not noticed. He also does his best to figure out what lies beneath the water.

Domhoff's method is to examine those committees and advisory councils, federal and private, that do the actual work of making foreign and economic policy (something like three-quarters of the federal budget has to do with military and foreign aid expenditures—control the spending of that three-quarters and the US is your thing). He then studies the men who serve on these committees. Notes what schools they went to, what banks they work for (most are lawyers or lawyer-bankers), what political contributions they make. He also records the overlapping that goes on, or "linkage" as the American Metternich would say.

In 1968, for instance, 51 of 284 trustees and honorary trustees of the Committee for Economic Development were also members of the Council on Foreign Relations, while 126 were members of the National Council of the Foreign Policy Association. Or as Domhoff puts it,

Policy formation is the province of a bipartisan power elite of corporate rich [Rockefeller, Mellon] and their career hirelings [Nixon,

McNamara] who work through an interlocking and overlapping maze of foundations, universities and institutes, discussion groups, associations and commissions. Political parties are only for finding interesting and genial people [usually ambitious middle-class lawyers] to ratify and implement these policies in such a way that the under classes feel themselves to be, somehow, a part of the governmental process. Politics is not exactly the heart of the action but it is nice work—if you can afford to campaign for it.

If Domhoff's thesis is even partly true (and at least one skeptic is persuaded that it is) much of the malaise one detects among intelligent members of the Senate and House is understandable. It is not so much the removal of power from the Hill to the White House (a resourceful Congress can still break a president if they want, or at least bring him to heel); rather, it is the knowledge or suspicion that the legislative branch reflects not the electorate but the elite who pay for congressional campaigns and are duly paid off with agreeable tax laws and military procurement and foreign aid bills passed at the dark of the moon. There is a constant if gentle tugging of the reins—perhaps Caligula had the right idea about what a proper senator should be. "We don't seem to matter at all," said one East Coast senator to me some years ago. "And I don't know why. We're every bit as bright or brighter than the Borah–La Follette group. But we're just . . . well, nothing." Domhoff agrees and tells us why.

In *Fat Cats and Democrats,* Domhoff describes our rulers. Year in, year out, "About one percent of the population—a socially interacting upper class whose members go to prep schools, attend debutante balls, join exclusive clubs, ride to hounds and travel all over the world for business or pleasure —will continue to own 60 percent to 70 percent of all privately held corporate wealth and receive 24 percent of the national income." Domhoff tends to be a bit wide-eyed about the life style of the nobles but, barring those riders to hounds, he seldom indulges in the sort of solemn generality recently dished up by a sociologist who discovered that most American banking is controlled by the Wasps (true) and that the Wasps at the top of the banking hierarchy have larger and fleshier ears than those farther down (true?).

Domhoff accepts the Ferdinand Lundberg formulation that there is only one political party in the United States and that is the Property Party, whose Republican wing tends to be rigid in maintaining the status quo and not given to any accommodation of the poor and the black. Although the Democratic wing shares most of the basic principles (that is to say, money) of the Republicans, its members are often shrewd enough to know that what is too rigid will shatter under stress. The Democrats have also understood for some time the nature of the American empire. While the Republicans indulge in Jefferson I rhetoric and unrealities, including isolationism, the Democrats have known all along that this is a Jefferson II world. As Dean Acheson put it in 1947, "You must look to foreign markets." As early as 1928 a distinguished member of the Republican wing of the Property Party saw its limitations. After all, Averell Harriman was involved in German zinc mines, Polish iron mines, and Soviet manganese. "I thought Republican isolationism was disastrous." And just before the 1929 crash, he switched.

But essentially the two wings of the Property Party are more alike than not. Witness the bipartisan foreign policy which the elite hammered out twenty-five years ago over the dead bodies of the Republican faithful. The Property Party has known from the beginning how and when to reconcile its two wings in order to survive. After all, according to Domhoff,

The American Constitution was carefully rigged by the noteholders, land speculators, rum runners, and slave holders who were the Founding Fathers, so that it would be next to impossible for upstart dirt farmers and indebted masses to challenge the various forms of private property held by these well read robber barons. Through this Constitution, the overprivileged attempted to rule certain topics out of order for proper political discussion. To bring these topics up in polite company was to invite snide invective, charges of personal instability, or financial ruin.

In other words, don't start a political party in opposition to the Property Party. From Henry Wallace's Progressive Party, so viciously smeared by the liberal ADA, to today's sad attempt to field a People's Party, those who wish to promote economic equality should not be surprised to have their heads handed to them, particularly by a "free" press which refuses to recognize any alternative to the way things are.

Property is power, as those Massachusetts veterans of the revolution discovered when they joined Captain Daniel Shays in his resistance to the landed gentry's replacement of a loose confederation of states with a tax-levying central government. The veterans thought that they had been fighting a war for true independence. They did not want London to be replaced by New York. They did want an abolition of debts and a division of property. Their rebellion was promptly put down. But so shaken was the elite by the experience that their most important (and wealthiest) figure grimly emerged from private life with a letter to Harry Lee. "You talk of employing influence," wrote George Washington, "to appease the present tumults in Massachusetts. I know not where that influence is to be found, or if attainable, that it would be a proper remedy for the disorders. *Influence* is no *government*. Let us have one by which our lives, liberties and properties will be secured or let us know the worst at once." So was born the Property Party and with it the Constitution of the United States. We have known the "best" for nearly 200 years. What would the "worst" have been like?

The rulers of the country are, according to Domhoff, 80 percent to 90 percent Republican. For the most part they are not isolationist. They know that money is to be made overseas either from peace or war, from the garrison state and its attendant machismo charms. Who then supports the Democratic wing? Labor is responsible for 20 percent to 25 percent of the party's financing. Racketeers from 10 percent to 15 percent— obviously certain areas like New York, Chicago, and Las Vegas interest these entrepreneurs more than, say, the Good Government League of Bangor, Maine. Around 15 percent is contributed by the "little man." The rest comes from the fat cats. Who are they? And why do they give money to the wrong wing of the Property Party?

Domhoff rather coldbloodedly divides these perverse investors into two groups. Sentimental liberals—usually from rich families, reacting against Dad's Republicanism, and status seekers among new-money Jews and Catholics with some Texas oilmen thrown in. Yet the margin of action, like that of debate, is deliberately limited by the conservative as well as the reactionary wing of the Property Party. Or as Domhoff puts it, the elite Republicans "must accommodate the reactionaries just enough to keep them from forming an ultra-conservative party, just as it is the task of the wealthy moderate Democrats to assimilate or crush any sanguine liberals who try to stray through the left boundary of the sacred two-party system."

An uneasy alliance of Jewish bankers and Texas oilmen has financed most of the Democratic Party. Yet this Jewish-cowboy axis (Domhoff's phrase), powerful and rich though it is, represents only a small, moderately lunatic fringe to the sturdy fabric of the ruling class. They are the sports who give us Democratic presidential candidates guaranteed to speak of change and different deals while altering nothing. But then how could they change anything and still get the money to buy television spots?

Interestingly enough, Domhoff does not think that the Nixon Southern strategy has a chance of working at the congressional or local level. The South tends to be hawkish and racist—two chords the incumbent Property Party manager knows how to pluck. But the South is not about to support a party which is against federal spending. Nine Rehnquists would not be anywhere near enough to counterbalance the Southward flow of money from Treasury through the conduit of Southern Democratic Congressional leaders who have employed the seniority system to reverse that bad trip at the Appomattox Courthouse. They govern the House in tandem with machine Democrats from the North. Each takes in the other's washing. The Northerners get a few housing bills out of the Southerners, who in turn are granted military bases and agricultural subsidies. Both groups are devoted to keeping the

444

Property Party prosperous and the money where it belongs, in the hands of the elite. Southern Democrats are not about to join with Nixon's true-blue Republicans in turning off federal aid.

At the congressional level, one can see how the elite works even more clearly than at the presidential level, where enthusiasm for attractive candidates often blinds even the sharpest critic (not to mention, very often, the candidate himself) to the charade being enacted by the Property Party. It is in the House and the Senate that the day-by-day dirty work is done, and Bella Abzug gives a splendid account (*Bella!*) of her two years in the House, trying to represent her constituents and her conscience, to the amusement of a genial body of corrupt politicians whose votes are all too often for sale to the highest bidder, usually in the form of cash in white envelopes, if Robert N. Winter-Berger's astonishing book *The Washington Pay-Off* is to be believed. With these two books, one ideological, the other muckraking, the bankruptcy of the House of Representatives has been duly filed.

Bella Abzug was elected from Lower Manhattan to end the war, gain equal rights for women and blacks, and generally be herself, serving the unpropertied. A bright lawyer as well as a formidable self-publicist, she immediately struck the fancy of the press (when they get her full range, she will be dropped —tense?). All in all, Abzug rather likes the floor managers of the Property Party. They are good fun and she always knows where she stands with them. "The men in the Club here are very charming to me," which they can afford to be since "they have all the power." They even "like to be entertained a bit. I don't mean in a ha-ha funny way, but in an interesting way." It is the liberals for whom she has real contempt. They have fallen for "the old crap, the anaesthesia of the liberals: If you want to get along, you've got to go along . . . very little men." They would rather fight one another for such posts as House Majority leader than unite to keep a reactionary from continuing in that job.

For five years (1964 to 1969) Mr. Winter-Berger was a Washington lobbyist, engaged in getting favors done for a wide range of people. Nathan Voloshen was his principle contact.

This extraordinary man had known Representative John W. McCormack since 1945. In 1962, McCormack became Speaker of the House and Voloshen's "public relations" career soared. For use of the Speaker's opulent office in the Capitol, Voloshen paid McCormack $2,500 a month rent, a small amount considering the address. As clients came and went, the Speaker would assure them, "Nat can take care of that for you. Nat's my dear friend and I will do anything I can for him. Any friend of Nat's is a friend of mine." In one form or another, this speech is the ancient Washington formula to indicate that things will be done if you pay the price.

Eventually, Voloshen and company were nabbed by the embarrassingly honest Property Party maverick, US Attorney Robert Morgenthau. Voloshen pleaded guilty. At the trial of one of Voloshen's henchmen,

McCormack pleaded ignorance which, according to the 1925 House Code of Ethics Act, made him innocent. Rather ludicrously, on the stand, McCormack said: "I am not an inquiring fellow." Actually, if ever a man always knew precisely what was going on around him it was John McCormack.

Mr. Winter-Berger also tells us that he was present in the Speaker's office when Lyndon Johnson sailed in and, thinking the Speaker was alone, began a tirade with, "John, that son of a bitch is going to ruin me. If that cocksucker talks, I'm gonna land in jail." Apparently the President did not want his former Senate aide, Bobby Baker, to contest certain charges brought against him. "I will give him a million dollars if he takes the rap," said Johnson.

It is no wonder that most newspapers and magazines have refused to review this book and that many bookstores will not sell it. The fear is not of libel. Something much more elemental is involved. If the corruption and greed of the men the Property Party has placed in the Congress and the White House become common knowledge, the whole rotten business could very well collapse and property itself would be endangered. Had there actually been a two-party system in the

United States, the incoming President would have taken advantage of such an extraordinary scandal in the Democratic ranks. Instead, Nixon moved swiftly to remove Robert Morgenthau from office. If there is one thing Nixon understands, it is dominoes. Or as Mr. Winter-Berger puts it,

At the time, Voloshen said to me: "Mitchell is afraid that if any of the Congressmen are found guilty, the whole public image of the Congress would be destroyed." Voloshen also told me about the proviso which Attorney General Mitchell added to his offer to drop the case against Frenkil [Voloshen's pal]: House Speaker John McCormack would have to resign from Congress. Knowing how much McCormack loved his job and his life in the world of politics, I didn't think such a powerful man would go along. But in fact he did.

Yet the personal enrichment of congressmen and their friends is small potatoes compared to the way the great corporations use the government and its money for their own ends. The recent ITT comedy was just one example—and hardly investigated by the Property Party men in the Senate. The press also plays its supporting role. Mr. Winter-Berger notes that the Bobby Baker scandal became big news with suspicious slowness. "Having been filed in the court records, information about the suit should have been available immediately to any newspaper reporter, but it took the Washington *Post* three days to find out about it and break the story." This was September 12, 1963. *The New York Times* did not think this news fit to print until October 5, and then buried it on page 19. Not until Bobby Baker resigned three days later, did he make the front page of the *Times.*

But then, as Domhoff has remarked, few substantive matters are considered fit for open discussion in our society. Every president is honest because he is our president and we are honest. An occasional congressman may fall from grace because there are always a few rotten apples in every barrel, but the majority are straightshooters. The Congress represents all the interests of the people, at least district by district by district and state by state. *The New York Times* will always call the shots if there is any funny business anywhere. Just as they will always support the best "liberal" candidate (Abzug has a nice horror story about how the *Times* killed a piece on her because it was too favorable). These threadbare myths sustain us. But for how much longer?

After the burning of Newark, the elite wondered, some more reluctantly than others, what might be next for burning if they did not appear to pay off the poor and/or black. To the amazement of the innocent, the Nixon Administration came up with a family income plan for the poor which was favored (fathered?) by the Council for Economic Development. The council then set out to sell the plan to the Right Wing. Predictably, Ronald Reagan was opposed because of a "philosophical antipathy" which he thought reflected the prejudices of his constituency. A number of the council's leaders swiftly materialized in San Francisco and proceeded to instruct the public in the virtues of the plan. They stressed that not only businessmen but *experts* favored it. Even Democrats thought it sound. Gently chiding Reagan, they sold the program to California's media and public in a bipartisan way. The Property Party has no intention of actually putting this plan into effect, of course, but at least they now have something nice to talk about when the poor are restive. The fact that McGovern acts as if he might implement the plan has caused alarm.

Recently (June 18) one of the CED's members, Herbert Stein, now chairman of the President's Council of Economic Advisers, gave us the elite's latest view of McGovern's tax reforms. "All such plans count on the willingness of the non-poor to give money to the poor. There has to be such willingness because the non-poor greatly outnumber the poor and dominate the political process." Elegant sophistry. The not-so-poor do outnumber the poor but if the not-so-poor who are nicked heavily by taxes were to join with the poor they would outnumber the elite by 99 to 1. The politician who can forge that alliance will find himself, at best, the maker of a new society; at worst, in a hole at Arlington.

To maintain its grip on the nation, the Property Party must keep actual issues out of political debate. So far they have succeeded marvelously well. Faced with unemployment, Nixon will oppose abortion. Inflation? Marijuana is a halfway house to something worse. The bombing of North Vietnam? Well, pornographers are using the mailing lists of Cub Scouts. Persuading the people to vote against their own best interests has been the awesome genius of the American political elite from the beginning.

It will be interesting to see what happens to George McGovern. Appealing to the restive young, he came up with a number of tax reforms which threatened to alter the foundation of the Property Party. The result was a terrible squawking from the Alsops and the Restons. We were told that McGovern is the Goldwater of the left (a good joke since Goldwater represented the reactionary country club minority while McGovern would represent the not-so-poor to poor majority), but then any hack journalist knows that his ink-drugged readers will not stand for pot, abortion, amnesty. Now that McGovern is the candidate they have decided that he is, thank God, a pragmatist (i.e. a Property Party opportunist) and so will move where the votes are and where you can bet your sweet ass the Sulzbergers and Schiffs, the Luces and Grahams are.

With each passing day, McGovern will more and more come to resemble a Property Party candidate. This is fair enough, if not good enough. But what happens when he is elected? Then we will know—too late, I fear—to what extent he was simply exploiting the people's deep inchoate hatred of the Property Party in order to become that Party's loyal manager. This would be sad because 1972 could have been the year for a counterparty or for a transformation of the Democratic wing of the Property Party. But barring catastrophe (in the form of home-grown apple-pie fascism), the early response to McGovern (and Wallace, too) is the first indication we have had that there now exists a potential American majority willing to see its best interests served not through the restrictive Constitution of the elite but through the egalitarian vision of Daniel Shays and his road not taken—yet.

The New York Review of Books, August 10, 1972

ABOUT THE AUTHOR

GORE VIDAL was born at West Point in 1925. In 1943 he graduated from the Phillips Exeter Academy and enlisted in the
army. While in the Pacific, at the age of nineteen, he wrote
the much-praised novel *Williwaw*. Among his other novels
are *The City and the Pillar*, *Julian*, *Washington*, *D.C.*, *Myra
Breckinridge* and *Two Sisters*.